Louise Erdrich's *Love Medicine*

A CASEBOOK

CASEBOOKS IN CONTEMPORARY FICTION

General Editor, William L. Andrews

With the continued expansion of the literary canon, multicultural works of modern literary fiction have assumed an increasing importance for students and scholars of American literature. Casebooks in Contemporary Fiction assembles key documents and criticism concerning these works that have so recently become central components of the American literature curriculum. The majority of the casebooks treat fictional works; however, because the line between autobiography and fiction is often blurred in contemporary literature, a small number of casebooks will specialize in autobiographical fiction or even straight autobiography. Each casebook will reprint documents relating to the work's historical context and reception, representative critical essays, an interview with the author, and a selected bibliography. The series will provide, for the first time, an accessible forum in which readers can come to a fuller understanding of these contemporary masterpieces and the unique aspects of the American ethnic, racial, or cultural experiences that they so ably portray.

Toni Morrison's
Beloved: A Casebook
edited by William L. Andrews
and Nettie Y. McKay

Maxine Hong Kingston's
The Woman Warrior : A Casebook
edited by Sau-ling C. Wong

Maya Angelou's
I Know Why the Caged Bird Sings: A Casebook
edited by Joanne M. Braxton

Louise Erdrich's
Love Medicine: A Casebook
edited by Hertha D. Sweet Wong

LOUISE ERDRICH'S
Love Medicine

◆ ◆ ◆

A CASEBOOK

Edited by
Hertha D. Sweet Wong

New York   Oxford

Oxford University Press

2000

Oxford University Press

Oxford   New York
Athens   Auckland   Bangkok   Bogotá   Buenos Aires   Calcutta
Cape Town   Chennai   Dar es Salaam   Delhi   Florence   Hong Kong   Istanbul
Karachi   Kuala Lumpur   Madrid   Melbourne   Mexico City   Mumbai
Nairobi   Paris   São Paulo   Singapore   Taipei   Tokyo   Toronto   Warsaw

and associated companies in
Berlin   Ibadan

Published by Oxford University Press, Inc.
198 Madison Avenue, New York, New York 10016

Library of Congress Cataloging-in-Publication Data
Louise Erdrich's Love medicine: a casebook /
edited by Hertha D. Sweet Wong.
p. cm — (Casebooks in contemporary fiction)
Includes bibliographical references.
ISBN 0-19-512721-8 ; ISBN 0-19-512722-6 (pbk.)
1. Erdrich, Louise. Love medicine.   2. Historical fiction, American—History and criticism.
3. Indians of North America in literature.   4. Racially mixed people in literature.
5. North Dakota—In literature.   6. Ojibwa Indians. I. Wong, Hertha Dawn.
II. Series.
PS3555.R421.625   2000
813. 54—dc21   98-37962

1 3 5 7 9 8 6 4 2

Printed in the United States of America
on acid-free paper

Credits

Peter G. Beidler and Gay Barton, eds., "Chronology of Events in *Love Medicine*," in *A Reader's Guide to the Novels of Louise Erdrich: Geography, Genealogy, Chronology, and Dictionary of Characters*, 9–11 (Columbia: University of Missouri Press, 1999).

Allan Chavkin, ed., "Vision and Revision in Louise Erdrich's *Love Medicine*," in *The Chippewa Landscape of Louise Erdrich*, 84–116 (Tuscaloosa: The University of Alabama Press, 1999).

Louise Erdrich, "Rose Nights, Summer Storms, Lists of Spiders and Literary Mothers," in *The Blue Jay's Dance: A Birth Year*, 142–48 (New York: Harper-Perennial, 1995).

Louise Erdrich, "Where I Ought to Be: A Writer's Sense of Place," *New York Times Book Review*, 28 July 1985, 1, 23–24.

William Gleason, "'Her Laugh an Ace': The Function of Humor in Louise Erdrich's *Love Medicine*," *American Indian Culture and Research Journal* 11.3 (1987): 51–73.

Helen Jaskoski, "From the Time Immemorial: Native American Traditions in Contemporary Short Fiction," in *Since Flannery O'Connor: Essays on the Contemporary American Short Story*, edited by Loren Logsdon and Charles W. Mayer, 54–59 (Macomb: Western Illinois University Press, 1987).

Julie Maristuen-Rodakowski, "The Turtle Mountain Reservation in North Dakota: Its History as Depicted in Louise Erdrich's *Love Medicine* and *The Beet Queen*," *American Indian Culture and Research Journal* 12.3 (1988): 33–48.

Louis Owens, "Erdrich and Dorris's Mixedbloods and Multiple Narratives," in *Other Destinies: Understanding the American Indian Novel,* 192–205 (Norman: University of Oklahoma Press, 1992).

Catherine Rainwater, "Reading between Worlds: Narrativity in the Fiction of Louise Erdrich," *American Literature* 62.3 (1990): 405–22.

James Ruppert, "Celebrating Culture: *Love Medicine,*" in *Mediation in Contemporary Native American Fiction,* 131–50 (Norman: University of Oklahoma Press, 1995).

Kathleen M. Sands, "*Love Medicine*: Voices and Margins," *Studies in American Indian Literatures* 9.1 (Winter 1985): 12–24.

Greg Sarris, "Reading Louise Erdrich: *Love Medicine* as Home Medicine," in *Keeping Slug Woman Alive: A Holistic Approach to American Indian Texts,* 115–45 (Berkeley: University of California Press, 1993).

Robert Silberman, "Opening the Text: *Love Medicine* and the Return of the Native American Woman," in *Narrative Chance: Postmodern Discourse on Native American Indian Literatures,* edited by Gerald Vizenor, 101–20 (Albuquerque: University of New Mexico Press, 1989).

Hertha D. Sweet Wong, "Louise Erdrich's *Love Medicine*: Narrative Communities and the Short Story Cycle," slightly revised version of "Louise Erdrich's *Love Medicine*: Narrative Communities and the Short Story Sequence," in *Modern American Short Story Sequences: Composite Fictions and Fictive Communities,* edited by J. Gerald Kennedy, 170–93 (New York: Cambridge University Press, 1995)

Excerpts of Interviews: "Louise Erdrich and Michael Dorris," in *Winged Words: American Indian Writers Speak,* edited by Laura Coltelli, 41–52 (Lincoln: University of Nebraska Press, 1990); "An Interview with Louise Erdrich and Michael Dorris," by Hertha D. Wong, *North Dakota Quarterly* 55.1 (Winter 1987): 196–218; "Whatever Is Really Yours: An Interview with Louise Erdrich," in *Survival This Way: Interviews with American Indian Poets,* edited by Joseph Bruchac, 73–86 (Tucson: University of Arizona Press, 1987); and "An Interview with Louise Erdrich," in *Conversations with Louise Erdrich and Michael Dorris,* edited by Nancy Feyl Chavkin and Allan Chavkin, 220–53 (Jackson: University Press of Mississippi, 1994).

Contents

Part II. Mixed Identities and Multiple Narratives

Part III. Individual and Cultural Survival: Humor and Homecoming

Part IV. Reading Self/Reading Other

Louise Erdrich's *Love Medicine*

A CASEBOOK

Introduction

SINCE N. SCOTT MOMADAY'S novel *House Made of Dawn* was awarded the Pulitzer Prize for Literature in 1969, fiction by Native North American writers has become increasingly popular with both general readers and academics. The first wave of writers linked with what literary critic Kenneth Lincoln has labeled the Native American Renaissance includes Momaday, Leslie Marmon Silko, Gerald Vizenor, and James Welch. Foremost among writers in what might be considered a second wave is Louise Erdrich. She is a gifted poet and essayist, but she is best known for her fiction and the collaboration with her late husband, Michael Dorris (see bibliography).

A mixed-blood member of the Turtle Mountain Band of the Ojibwa, Louise Erdrich was born in Little Falls, Minnesota, the eldest child of Ralph and Rita (Gourneau) Erdrich.[1] Her German American father and her Ojibwa mother both taught at Wahpeton Indian Boarding School in North Dakota for many years. After attending Wahpeton's primary and secondary schools, Erdrich went to Dartmouth College in 1972 as one of the first group of women to be admitted and as part of an early group of Native Americans to be recruited. She graduated from Dartmouth in 1976 and for two years taught in the Poetry in the Schools Program sponsored by the North Dakota State Arts Council. After earning a Master of Arts degree in writing from Johns Hopkins University in 1979, she edited the Boston Indian Council newspaper, *The Circle*, then returned in 1981 to Dartmouth College as a writer-in-residence in the Native American Studies Program. In October of that year she married Michael Dorris, then chair of the Native American Studies Program, and their now famous collaborative writing began in earnest.

Reviewers, who often focus on the Erdrich-Dorris collaboration, tend to divide into two camps: those who celebrate the fortuitous union of soul mates or those who ridicule the romantic literary-marital collaboration as antithetical to individual creativity. Even so, most mainstream reviewers cannot resist the image of an ideal(ized) marital and literary union, an image that has been supported by book dedications, book jacket photographs, and interviews and heightened to mythic dimensions by establishment critics.[2] In numerous interviews, Erdrich and Dorris have described their collaborative process: one person would come up with the idea, write a draft, and give it to the other for commentary and editing; then the reader would return the piece with suggestions for revisions. This cycle would be repeated many times, even in the midst of a busy family schedule.[3] From characterizations to syntax to word choice, every detail was discussed, argued about, and negotiated, with both reaching agreement before any "finished" work left their hands. As she has noted in many public statements, Erdrich insists that editorial team work is not the same as shared authorship. Clarifying that *The Crown of Columbus* was "the only true collaboration" she and Michael produced, Erdrich explained recently that "*Love Medicine,* though edited generously, was the product of my experience, my solitude, my soul, as were the other books under my name."[4]

Of Erdrich's more than half-dozen novels, the most critically acclaimed is her first, *Love Medicine*. Originally published in 1984 and republished in a new, expanded form in 1993, *Love Medicine* was awarded the National Book Critics Circle Award for the best work of fiction, the Sue Kaufman Prize for best first fiction from the American Academy and Institute of Arts and Letters, and the Virginia McCormick Scully Award for best book of 1984 dealing with Western Indians. In 1985 *Love Medicine* received the *Los Angeles Times* Award for Fiction, the American Book Award from the Before Columbus Foundation, and the Great Lakes Colleges Association Award for best work of fiction. It was received just as enthusiastically by a large international audience.

More than a decade later, *Love Medicine*'s reputation endures. It continues to be read and taught in literature, composition, women's studies, and Native American studies classes at colleges and universities throughout the

United States (and in many other countries as well). *Love Medicine* is both an extraordinary individual work and part of a tetralogy of novels/short story cycles about Ojibwa, mixed-blood, and European American families living on and around a fictional reservation in North Dakota. Collectively, they tell a story of family and community life over several generations. The four novels—*Tracks* (1912–24), *The Beet Queen* (1932–72), *Love Medicine* (1934–84), and *The Bingo Palace* (1981–95)—are linked also by their dominant imagery of the natural elements: water, air, earth, and fire. In all these novels Erdrich displays her deftness in representing and respecting multiple, conflicting voices; her attentiveness to the complex interweaving of Native American and European American histories; and her articulation of a politics of thoughtful engagement.

The first edition of *Love Medicine* (1984) consists of fourteen chapters (the expanded 1993 edition has eighteen), each narrated by a character (or sometimes several characters) in the first person, or occasionally by an omniscient third-person narrator. Although many of the chapters had already been published as short stories, for the novel they were refashioned into a story cycle. Helen Jaskoski describes *Love Medicine*'s structure as a "complex series . . . of tales, interlocking through recurrence of character and event and through variation of point of view."[5] The novel begins in 1981, then jumps backward almost fifty years to 1934 and moves ahead chronologically until it ends in 1984. A variety of characters tell pieces of the story of several generations of Ojibwa and mixed-blood families—the Kashpaws, Lamartines, Lazarres, and Morrisseys. But it is the reader, rather than the unself-conscious narrators, who weaves the disparate, contradictory stories into a vision of community and history and culture.

Love Medicine's dominant themes and figures reflect those found in Native American literatures generally, and many are also relevant, in different registers, to European American literature: the importance of place (represented variously as land, home/land, reservation) to individual, community, and cultural self-definitions; the power of storytelling for individual and cultural survival; the necessity of healing (on individual, social, cultural, historical, and ecological levels); the search for (mixed-blood, cultural) identity; the influence of the past on the present; the breakdown and reformulation of family in the wake of colonization; the centrality of community in the struggle for continuance; and the trickster figure as a trope for the humor, wit, and shapeshifting necessary for indigenous survival, to name a few.

Just as Erdrich's novel both derives and departs from Native North American literature, it draws and differs from European American literature as well. Many critics have noted the influence of William Faulkner (the focus on family sagas, the importance of a specific region, the sense of history haunting the present, the use of multiple voices and achronological narratives, for instance) or post/modernist writers generally. Clearly, Erdrich is also one of many contemporary Native American writers who have returned to (or continued) storytelling as a means of making manifest the many silenced voices of the dispossessed or marginalized, both past and present. This, she says, is the unique task of contemporary Native American writers, who, "[i]n the light of enormous loss, . . . must tell the stories of contemporary survivors while protecting and celebrating the cores of cultures left in the wake of the catastrophe."[6]

A casebook, by definition, is an assemblage of representative materials, a collection of critical case studies, a documentation of what has been said, rather than an introduction to new scholarship; it both presents and produces a history of a work's reception. Although deciding what to include has been a considerable challenge, I have been guided by several principles: to reflect diverse approaches and foci, to make some less accessible essays more widely available, and to include a few select essays and interviews by Louise Erdrich that illuminate readings of *Love Medicine*. I considered also how substantially each essay focused on *Love Medicine*; many wonderful essays have been devoted to Erdrich's novels generally and thus were not included. I used two strategies to maintain the focus on *Love Medicine*. First, I excerpted some discussions of the novel from longer treatments of Erdrich's work (e.g., the excerpts of Jaskoski's and Chavkin's essays and Owens's chapter); second, I made two exceptions in order to include two essays that did not focus exclusively on Erdrich's first novel but that made important points central to it (Maristuen-Rodakowski's discussion of Turtle Mountain Reservation history and Rainwater's consideration of reader response theory). This casebook, then, aims to introduce readers to a variety of critical and theoretical approaches to and readings of *Love Medicine*: historical, New Critical, cultural, genre-based, and reader response, to name a few. The essays have been gathered together from difficult-to-locate (at least for nonspecialists) journal articles, far-flung volumes of essays, and chapters of books in order to provide a concise introduction and overview of critical responses to *Love Medicine*.

Rather than impose my own predetermined critical categories, I derived the divisions of the casebook from the scholarship itself, selecting examples of the dominant themes and questions raised by literary critics. Each of the four parts has a clear focus, yet it is also true that some of the essays might have been moved, just as convincingly, into another category.

Each part concludes with a selection from Erdrich's nonfiction, thus including her "critical" as well as her "literary" voice, both of which tend to be a "storytelling" voice.

Much of the scholarship on Native North American literatures generally has had a tendency to provide historical and cultural contexts for readers unfamiliar with indigenous histories, cultures, and knowledge systems. Often looking to anthropology and history, such scholars attempt to delineate key historical conditions and to (re)construct indigenous cultural and verbal art. Part I of this volume, entitled "Contexts: History, Culture, and Storytelling," reflects such scholarship, providing historical, geographical, and (to some extent) cultural contexts for reading *Love Medicine*. Julie Maristuen-Rodakowski presents a detailed analysis of Turtle Mountain Reservation history, Erdrich's treatment of it in *Love Medicine* and *The Beet Queen*, and Turtle Mountain residents' linguistic practices. Helen Jaskoski highlights numerous Ojibwa narrative traditions in Erdrich's novel, while Kathleen Mullen Sands's very early consideration of *Love Medicine* focuses on Native American storytelling, particularly in the form of "community gossip," as the defining feature of the novel. Concluding this section is Erdrich's essay "Where I Ought to Be: A Writer's Sense of Place"—originally published in the *New York Times Book Review*—an important manifesto about the role of Native American writers, Erdrich's connection to place (community and land), the consequences of being dis/placed, and Ojibwa history.

Part II is entitled "Mixed Identities and Multiple Narratives." Like many Native American writers, Erdrich experiments with indigenous and European, oral and literate forms and focuses on the experience of mixed-blood characters. Louis Owens argues that while Erdrich presents the common figure of the "tortured mixedblood caught between worlds," she focuses on those who endure, those "who confront with humor the pain and confusion of identity" and who hold together their communities. James Ruppert discusses Erdrich's inevitable mediation of Native and non-Native American knowledge systems, which forces each reader to see through another's cultural lenses; the result is the continuance of "a newly appreciated and experienced Native American epistemological reality." Focusing on questions of genre and transcultural adaptations of narrative forms, my own essay reconsiders the novel as a short story cycle (a constellation of short stories) informed by both American modernist techniques (e.g., multiple narrators) and Ojibwa oral narrative forms (e.g., repetition and associational—rather than linear—structure). This section ends with excerpts of interviews in which Erdrich discusses crossings of various sorts—

mixed-blood identity, Roman Catholicism and Native American religious practices, literary collaboration with Michael Dorris, oral and written storytelling, and experiments with genre. Part III, "Individual and Cultural Survival: Humor and Homecoming," highlights two recurring motifs in Native American literature. Countering (mis)readings of *Love Medicine* as painful and "tragic," William Gleason argues that the novel offers instead a vision of redemption that is articulated through humor. He presents a thorough catalog of the types, forms, and techniques of Erdrich's protean humor and illustrates how laughter is a survival technique. Emphasizing the "embattled concept" of "home" and homecoming for a dispossessed people, Robert Silberman illustrates how Erdrich replaces the standard male protagonist with a female who attempts a homecoming. His reading of *Love Medicine* considers the novel in relation to Western literary forms generally and to Native North American literature specifically. He outlines its similarities to Latin American literature as well. Part III concludes with excerpts of two interviews in which Erdrich discusses the roots of her storytelling, the significance of American Indian humor, the strategies of community and cultural continuance, and the geographies of home.

In Part IV, "Reading Self/Reading Other," two essays offer dramatically contrasting reading experiences. Arguing that Erdrich's focus on liminality and marginality is evident in characterization, theme, and structure in *Love Medicine*, *The Beet Queen*, and *Tracks*, Catherine Rainwater concludes that "conflicting cultural codes" (Native American and European American) reproduce an experience of marginality in readers. Greg Sarris, on the other hand, reads across Native borders, writing autobiographically and comparing Lipsha's search for his sense of belonging with Sarris's own search for a Native identity, family, history, and culture. In the final essay, Allan Chavkin compares the 1984 and 1993 editions of *Love Medicine* (the only essay to treat substantively the revised edition) and concludes that in the new edition, Erdrich makes the implied politics of the first edition explicit. In "Rose Nights, Summer Storms, Lists of Spiders and Literary Mothers," excerpted from *The Blue Jay's Dance: A Birth Year* (1995), Erdrich articulates her search for literary foremothers as well as the centrality of mothering in her own life.

Together these essays provide a concise sampling of the critical reception of Louise Erdrich's remarkable first novel. This volume will complement two other volumes on Erdrich's work: *A Reader's Guide to the Novels of Louise Erdrich: Geography, Genealogy, Chronology, and Dictionary of Characters* edited by Peter G. Beidler and Gay Barton (Columbia: University of Missouri Press,

1999) and *The Chippewa Landscape of Louise Erdrich* (Tuscaloosa: The University of Alabama Press, 1999), a collection of new essays on Erdrich's work edited by Allan Chavkin.

I WANT TO THANK THE editor of Casebooks in Contemporary Fiction, William L. Andrews, for the invitation to work on this project and for his unfailing patience throughout the entire process; Oxford University Press editors Susan Chang, Jessica Ryan, and Christopher Kelly for their guidance; the anonymous reviewers of the casebook proposal, for suggesting further essays for inclusion; Tamarind Rossetti-Johnson, my research assistant, for her scrupulous work; my colleague Sau-ling Cynthia Wong, for being a model of professionalism and generosity; Lauren Stuart Muller, for her inspired suggestions about organization and editing; Raoul Granqvist for a thoughtfully rigorous reading; and A. Lavonne Brown Ruoff, for her unfailing wisdom. Finally, I thank all the authors who allowed their works to be reprinted in this casebook.

Notes

1. A word about vocabulary: I want to acknowledge the ongoing, often contentious debates about the most appropriate term to use—Native American, American Indian, Indian, indigenous peoples, First Nation, or precise tribal names. To further complicate the issue, there are also debates about the best name to use for tribal peoples. Erdrich's people, for example, are known variously as Chippewa, Ojibway, Ojibwa, Ojibwe and Anishinaabe, to name a few. Such debates reflect continuing attempts to decolonize the language used to refer to indigenous peoples. In addition, the term *mixed-blood*, generally, is used "neutrally" to mean a person of mixed (usually Native American and European American) descent, though it can be used derogatorily as well. Throughout these essays, you will find no consistency in the use of such terms. My principles of usage are as follows: I use *Native American, Native North American, Native,* and *indigenous peoples* somewhat interchangeably for variety. When referring to Erdrich and her characters, I respect her self-references. For many years, Erdrich used the term Chippewa to refer to herself and her characters, so I followed her lead in my essay (and thus I use Chippewa there). More recently, however, Erdrich has begun to refer to herself and her characters as Ojibwa, the term I use in this introduction.

2. The romantic plot of the Erdrich-Dorris collaboration, constructed by the mainstream press, turned tragic when Michael Dorris took his own life in the spring of 1997.

3. At the time of the writing and debut of *Love Medicine*, Erdrich and Dorris had five children in the house—three who had been adopted by Dorris as a single father and were later adopted by Erdrich as well, and two biological children. A third daughter was born to them later.

4. Louise Erdrich, letter to author, 4 March 1999.

5. Helen Jaskoski, "From the Time Immemorial: Native American Traditions in Contemporary Short Fiction," in *Since Flannery O'Connor: Essays on the Contemporary American Short Story*, edited by Loren Logsdon and Charles W. Mayer (Macomb: Western Illinois University Press, 1987), 59.

6. Louise Erdrich, "Where I Ought to Be: A Writer's Sense of Place," *New York Times Book Review*, 28 July 1985, 23.

PART I

Contexts:
History, Culture, and Storytelling

The Turtle Mountain Reservation in North Dakota

Its History as Depicted in Louise Erdrich's Love Medicine *and* The Beet Queen

JULIE MARISTUEN-RODAKOWSKI

◆　◆　◆

> Now that she was in the city, all the daydreams she'd had were useless. She had not foreseen the blind crowd or the fierce activity of the lights outside the station. And then it seemed to her that she had been sitting in the chair too long. Panic tightened her throat. Without considering, in an almost desperate shuffle, she took her bundle and entered the ladies' room.
>
> —Louise Erdrich, *Love Medicine*

THE PANIC SO VIVIDLY depicted by Louise Erdrich is felt by Albertine Johnson, a fifteen-year-old who is running away from home—not an atypical situation, except that Albertine is a Native American and the home she runs away from is a reservation, one similar to the Turtle Mountain Indian Reservation in north central North Dakota. Albertine sits in a bus depot in Fargo, North Dakota, her destination, her panic partly attributable to the fact that she's never been away from home alone. Through the depiction of the fictitious lives of multiple generations in *Love Medicine* and *The Beet Queen*, Erdrich portrays the movement from an Indian culture to American culture, with the process of assimilation culminating in one individual in particular, Albertine Johnson. These two novels are part of a tetralogy. Of the two novels that are the basis of this article, *Love Medicine* provides more information about this cultural transition, but *The Beet Queen* also provides relevant information, despite the fact that it's not based totally on Native American culture. In these two novels, Erdrich traces the unique Indian history of the Turtle Mountain Reserva-

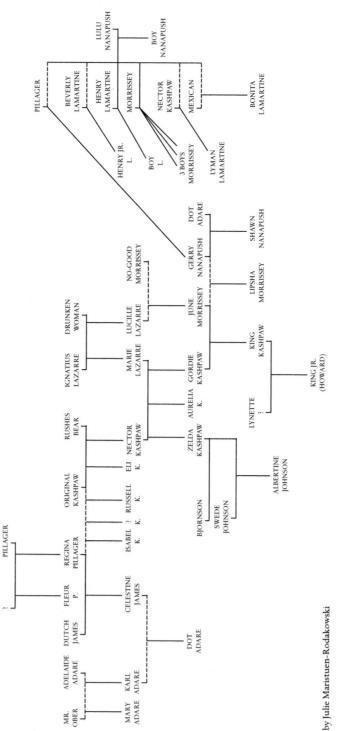

Native American Genealogical Chart for *Love Medicine* & *Beet Queen*.

by Julie Maristuen-Rodakowski

tion in a manner that is both captivating and informational for the reader, providing an enjoyable fictional story that is solidly based in the facts of the Chippewa Indians of the Turtle Mountain Reservation.

The Chippewa Indians originally were an Algonquian-speaking tribe that was driven west by the expanding Iroquois in the Great Lakes area. Many of these Chippewa settled in the Turtle Mountain area, where the reservation itself was established later by an executive order dated 21 December 1882. It is in this area along the Canadian border that Erdrich places the "original Kashpaw" a member of the first generation the author alludes to in her novels.[1] She gives him a name similar to that of a distant relative of her own, Kaishpau Gourneau ("the elevated one"), who was the tribal chairman in 1882.[2] The fictional Kashpaw married a woman named Rushes Bear (*LM*, 17). Just from the names, it seems evident that these two fictional characters are indeed "native" Americans. Their language is most likely Cree (although several synonyms—including Ojibwa and Chippewa—are used academically, in the novel Erdrich uses Cree), an Algonquian language of the Chippewa tribe. These two Native Americans are the great-grandparents of Albertine Johnson, who, four generations later, sits in the bus depot in Fargo after running away from her life on the reservation.

A major historical influence on this Turtle Mountain Chippewa tribe, one that began long before the time of Kashpaw and Rushes Bear and that continues to be felt even today, was the French and English fur traders. These traders, representing either the Hudson Bay Company or the Northwest Fur Company, traveled from Canada to obtain furs from the tribesmen. The Chippewa and the traders maintained considerable friendly contact even though, according to the 1897 journals of two of the earliest traders, Alexander Henry and David Thompson, the voyagers often cheated the Indians out of valuable furs and taught them to use alcohol:

> The Indians totally neglect their ancient customs; and to what can this degeneracy be ascribed but to the intercourse with us, particularly as they are so unfortunate as to have a continual succession of opposition parties [the fur companies] to teach them roguery, and to destroy both minds and bodies with that pernicious article, rum?[3]

The use of alcohol also arises as a problem in these first generations in *Love Medicine*, for Nector Kashpaw (the son of Rushes Bear and the original Kashpaw) describes the family of Marie Lazarre as a "family of horse-thieving drunks" (*LM*, 58). Nector Kashpaw nevertheless marries Marie Lazarre.

The contact between French fur traders and Native Americans, however, extended beyond the economic. The Frenchmen often married Algonquian-speaking women, but whether married or not, they fathered many children. These children, sometimes called *bois brules* because of their dark skin, are labeled half-breeds, mixed-bloods, or Métis (a Canadian term). The Métis appeared as early as the mid-seventeenth century in eastern Canada, and during the time of Erdrich's first fictional generation at Turtle Mountain, the mixed-bloods were quite common. In their centennial history, *North Dakota*, Robert and Winona Wilkins relate that these unions often were encouraged by the fur companies because the liaisons "tended to keep the men contented with their nomadic life in the wilderness as well as to provide new employees for their enterprises." Their influence must have been significant because, according to the centennial history, by the mid-eighteenth century the French fur traders "swarmed" the area.[4] Even now on the reservation, some of the mixed-bloods speak French and celebrate the French holidays (St. Anne's, 92). However, most of these Frenchmen returned to eastern Canada when the fur companies no longer needed their services, leaving their families behind (Wilkins and Wilkins, 31). Marie Lazarre, the grandmother of Albertine, is most likely a "mixed-blood," for Marie says that she doesn't "have that much Indian blood" even though she lives on the reservation (*LM*, 40). Her French name provides another clue to her mixed heritage.

Another allusion to French heritage emerges in this early generation of the novels. The original Kashpaw (married to Rushes Bear) apparently had an affair with a woman named Regina, a common French name. In *The Beet Queen* we learn that this original Kashpaw fathered three children by Regina (Russell Kashpaw, Isabel Kashpaw, and an unnamed Kashpaw), and that Regina later married Dutch James, with whom she had one daughter, Celestine. The older three children, described as Chippewa, were never adopted by James and thus kept the name Kashpaw, but Celestine's surname was James. After Celestine's parents died, she was reared largely by Isabel, her "Chippewa" half-sister: "It was the influence of her big sister that was important to Celestine. She knew the French language, and sometimes Celestine spoke French to lord it over us in school" (*BQ*, 28). Isabel Kashpaw, then, even though described as being Chippewa, speaks French, and her knowledge of this language places her in a higher class than her non-French-speaking friends. We are given no clues as to the origin of the French, but we might assume because of her mother's French name that the mother had considerable association with those French fur traders. According to John Crawford, an expert in the language of this tribe, some of these Native American women did indeed learn French, but some of the Frenchmen also learned the Algonquian language of their mates and of their Indian business associates.[5]

In the fictional second generation, the infiltration of the French continues, as portrayed in two other families in the novels, the Pillagers and the Lamartines. Fleur Pillager, in *The Beet Queen*, carries the young Karl Adare with her as she journeys into a village in the area:

> We began to visit low cabins of mud-mortared logs, inhabited by Chippewa or fiercer-looking French-Indians with stringy black beards and long moustaches. There were board houses, too, with wells, barns, and neat screen doors that whined open when we approached. The women who came out of these doors wore housedresses and had their hair cut, curled, and bound in flimsy nets. They were not like Fleur, but all the same they were Indians and spoke a flowing language to each other. (48)

There is no indication what this "flowing language" is, but any Algonquian language could be described in this way. We might also assume that the women of the village were full-blooded Indians since "they were not like Fleur." Later in the novel, we find that Fleur is Celestine James's aunt. We might presume, then, that Fleur is Regina's sister and that Regina's birth name was Pillager, also a French name, although old man Pillager is described in *Love Medicine* as "a Nanapush man" (244). Nanapush is a family name in the novel (Lulu Nanapush—perhaps he's "her" man) but also is an appellation for a trickster-like cultural hero among the Chippewa.

We learn additional information about Regina and Fleur through a conversation between Celestine and Mary Adare, a brief dialogue in which Celestine begins by naming Fleur as her aunt and ends by disdainfully translating the French that she uses:

> "What aunt?" [Mary asked].
> "Fleur. The one that came down here, you know, when Mama died."
> "What a name. Floor."
> Celestine looked down at me with strained indulgence.
> "Fleur," she said. "It's French for flower." (*BQ*, 177)

The influence from the French is obvious here. It seems evident that both Regina and Fleur Pillager are French-speaking "mixed-bloods," and that their French language heritage has been passed down to Isabel Kashpaw and then to Celestine James, who uses the French language "to lord" over her friends at school (*BQ*, 28).

Another direct reference to the French heritage on the reservation is conveyed through the Lamartines, who also have a French name. Beverly Lamartine, a member of the novels' second generation, has assimilated into the white culture in Minnesota:

> In the Twin Cities there were great relocation opportunities for Indians with a certain amount of natural stick-to-it-iveness and pride. That's how Beverly saw it. He was darker than most, but his parents had always called themselves French or Black Irish and considered those who thought of themselves as Indians quite backward. (*LM*, 77)

This generation of Lamartines is also, then, a generation of "mixed-bloods," although they prefer associating themselves with their European ancestry. The backwardness of the Indians (full-blooded ones, we might assume) did not, however, stop Beverly's brother from marrying one, Lulu Nanapush, a Chippewa, nor did it stop Beverly himself from both having an affair with Lulu and fathering her child.

The earlier generations in the novels represent not only the generations that had considerable contact with the fur traders but also the generations that took part in the land allotment programs designed to assimilate Indian people into the mainstream of Anglo-American society. In the United States the program began with the General Allotment Act of 1887, sometimes referred to as the Dawes Act, the purpose of which was to divide tribally–allotted lands among individual Indians so that these Indians could leave their own culture behind and become "civilized." After the Allotment Act, each head of an Indian household was to receive 160 acres of land, with single members of the tribe receiving various lesser amounts depending upon their age. However, according to Mary Jane Schneider in her book *North Dakota Indians*, the land allotment had the immediate effect of reducing the total number of acres of Indian land by 65 percent.[6] One of the problems was that the Indians who lived on the Turtle Mountain Reservation had to prove their Indian ancestry to receive an allotment from this first treaty—a major difficulty given the considerable French "influence" in the area. Further treaties rectified this situation and mixed-bloods also received land, but another dilemma arose. Since supposedly there was not enough land available on the reservation, several of the Indians received land off the reservation, in places as far away as Montana, although some chose not to move. Albertine Johnson has her own opinions about this program and its effect on her ancestors:

I grew up . . . in an aqua-and-silver trailer, set next to the old house on the land my great-grandparents [the original Kashpaw and Rushes Bear] were allotted when the government decided to turn Indians into farmers.

The policy of allotment was a joke. As I was driving toward the land, looking around, I saw as usual how much of the reservation was sold to whites and lost forever. (*LM*, 11)

Later in the chapter, after she has arrived home, Albertine expands on the program and its effects on her family:

This land had been allotted to Grandpa's mother, old Rushes Bear, who had married the original Kashpaw. When allotments were handed out all of her eighteen children except the youngest—twins, Nector and Eli—had been old enough to register for their own. But because there was no room for them in the North Dakota wheatlands, most were deeded less-desirable parcels far off, in Montana, and had to move there or sell. The older children left, but the twin brothers still lived on opposite ends of Rushes Bear's land. (*LM*, 17)

As this passage shows, the fiction of Louise Erdrich, although not set directly on the Turtle Mountain Reservation, is based solidly on the facts about that area in North Dakota and on its Native American history.

Another massive sociological and linguistic influence on this tribe was the coming of Roman Catholicism in 1817, when residents of the Red River Colony (Winnipeg) wrote to the Bishop of Quebec asking him to send religious leaders to minister to the Indians. In 1818, Bishop Joseph Norbert Provencher blamed contact with the whites for most of the problems of the Indians and the Métis:

I believe that one could say, without fear of making a mistake, that their commerce with the whites, far from bringing them closer to civilization, has kept them from it, because the whites have spoiled the Indians' characters with strong drink, of which the natives are extremely fond, and by their example have taught them debauchery. Most of the *engagés* keep women, by whom they have children, who, like the mothers, are left later to the first comer.[7]

The Catholics felt a moral obligation to "save" the Indians, and they established schools that educated the children and convents that ministered to the needs of the people. Father Belcourt started a school on the reservation in 1885. Others followed, bringing with them several nuns as teachers and building convents for their residences. In Erdrich's novels, the Sacred Heart Convent becomes a "sanctuary" for the fourteen-year-old Marie Lazarre. She feels inferior to the nuns, despite the fact that her French heritage must have been quite similar to theirs. She longs for a time when they will bow down to her:

> So when I went there, I knew the dark fish must rise. Plumes of radiance had soldered on me. No reservation girl had ever prayed so hard. There was no use in trying to ignore me any longer. I was going up there on the hill with the black robe women. They were not any lighter than me. I was going up there to pray as good as they could. Because I don't have that much Indian blood. And they never thought they'd have a girl from this reservation as a saint they'd have to kneel to. But they'd have me. (*LM*, 40)

Marie is staunch in her belief that she is equal to the nuns, even superior, but she soon leaves the convent because of physical abuse from one of the nuns. Marie later hears that the Sacred Heart Convent is a place for nuns who didn't get along anywhere else, and she finds some solace in that. So much for the ministering spirit of the Roman Catholics, if this is true. But another fact, one more important for the historical-linguistic aspects of this study, is that these nuns from eastern Canada spoke French also. The nuns are described by Marie as "mild and sturdy French," and after Marie does not respond to something that was done to her, they remark, "Elle est docile" [She is docile] (*LM*, 51). Later, after an "accident" to her hand, Marie lies on a couch in the Mother Superior's office:

> They looked up. All holy hell burst loose when they saw I'd woke. I still did not understand what was happening. They were watching, talking, but not to me.
> "The marks . . . "
> "She has her hand closed."
> "Je ne peux pas voir." [I can't see.]
> I was not stupid enough to ask what they were talking about. (*LM*, 54)

The nuns are speaking to each other, apparently in a combination of French and English, doing their own form of codeswitching, and despite her partial French heritage, Marie doesn't understand what they say.

The Turtle Mountain tribe of Chippewa Indians, thus, has been influenced by the French, an influence that has affected both the race and language of the tribe, and both these influences are visible in Erdrich's two novels. Normally in this kind of linguistic situation, the higher or "H" language, the language of religion, education, and trade, eventually overtakes the lower or "L" language, the language of the family. But that did not occur with this tribe. Instead, what developed among those who needed to communicate but who did not know one another's language was a mixed language. This mixture is called Michif (an Algonquian pronunciation of the French word Métis), a new language that combines both French and the various Algonquian languages of the tribe, making the polylinguistic nature of the tribe quite unique.

Michif, according to John Crawford, the editor of the *Michif Dictionary*, is appropriately labeled as "'the Cree language of the Turtle Mountain Reservation.' It is also appropriate that it have another label, 'Michif,' because the combination of Cree and French developed under special cultural influences that produced a population neither clearly Indian nor European."[8] The language is a distinct part of the Métis movement; however, "mixed-bloods" from the United States who are closer to Indian than to European heritage are sometimes called "Michif," and this label also has been given to the language of the area. The Michif of the Turtle Mountain tribe is dominated by the French and Cree languages in a syntactic structure that is unique in that the noun phrases are French (including the use of the appropriate French gender), while the verb phrases are Cree. Crawford expands on this situation in the introduction to the *Dictionary*:

> There are many areas in which there is openess [sic] as to the amount of French used, and the patterns of syntactic organization are probably best looked at as Cree but with important influence from French. Nevertheless the overall patterning of the language is anything but haphazard; Michif is a very specific sort of combination of languages. (viii)

Perhaps the added influence of English was another factor in this unusual combination of languages, but perhaps the fact that Michif developed at the community level also was a factor. Crawford believes that "given the prominence of French in education, religion, and commerce, it is likely that Cree had to be the primary element in the French-Cree mixture in the community where it developed, that is at the popular core of that community."[9]

Michif thus developed as the language for communication between the Indians and the French fur traders. Crawford adds that there is evidence that Michif might have developed on this reservation, but it also might have developed elsewhere before the time of the reservation.[10] At any rate, these languages are alluded to in *Love Medicine*, with different generations speaking different languages; the language transformation of the Turtle Mountain Reservation is thereby evident in the novels. The following dialogue appears in *Love Medicine*. The second-generation Uncle Eli, a Faulknerian Uncle Ike, embodies the ancient culture of the Indian heritage, but Gordie, the uncle of Albertine and a member of the third generation, is trying, although seemingly not very seriously, to maintain Michif:

> "Can you gimme a cigarette, Eli?" King asked.
> "When you ask for a cigarette around here," said Gordie, "you don't say can I have a cigarette. You say *ciga swa?*"
> "Them Michifs ask like that," Eli said. "You got to ask a real old Cree like me for the right words."
> "Tell 'em Uncle Eli," Lynette said with a quick burst of drunken enthusiasm. "They got to learn their own heritage! When you go it will all be gone!" (*LM*, 30)

Uncle Eli, the son of the original Kashpaw, is a Cree speaker—apparently the last Cree speaker in their family. He speaks degradingly of the Michif spoken by his nephew Gordie Kashpaw, reflecting a real-life attitude that has been typical on the reservation. The novels indicate that by the third generation, not only some of the language but also much of the Native American culture has changed, creating a redefinition of the "Indianness" of the members of the tribe.

We learn very little in these two novels about the first generations (the subject of *Tracks*), but the later generations are dealt with extensively. Two prominent individuals are Nector Kashpaw, the tribal chairman, and his twin brother Eli Kashpaw, both sons of the original Kashpaw and Rushes Bear. One is the grandfather of Albertine, the other, the uncle. Nector has played a prominent role in the politics of the tribe as tribal chairman, including going to Washington and talking to the governor. Also, he received a formal education, unlike his brother Eli. Their mother, Rushes Bear, recognized the need for schooling, but apparently couldn't bear to lose both her youngest sons to the new culture:

> She [Rushes Bear] had let the government put Nector in school, but hidden Eli, the one she couldn't part with, in the root cellar dug beneath her floor. In that way she gained a son on either side of the line. Nector came home from boarding school knowing white reading and writing, while Eli knew the woods. (*LM*, 17)

Eli was the "last man on the reservation that could snare himself a deer" (*LM*, 27), a "real old-timer" (28) who "could chew pine sap" (70) and could sing songs, "wild unholy songs. Cree songs that made you lonely" (69). He also reared June after "them ignoret bush Crees" found her (64)—June, the girl who many people said was "the child of what the old people called Manitous, invisible ones in the woods" (65). June dies in *Love Medicine*, and even though others of her generation are still living, the Indian heritage is changing. This transformation becomes even more evident in Albertine Johnson, who runs away to Fargo in a section called "The Bridge," in which the bridge indicates the "precarious, linked edges" (*LM*, 135) of the transition from old ways to new ways. She is the one to cross that difficult bridge, and, as mentioned earlier, she feels panic. The Indian and French heritage of the first two generations is changing, and no indication is given that Albertine speaks any language other than English.

The Turtle Mountain tribe has, however, made a concerted effort to maintain some of its linguistic heritage. Chippewa is the most common language of the parents and grandparents of tribal members and continues to be spoken by some, according to John Crawford (*Michif Dictionary,* viii). But Michif, which originally was viewed as a less prestigious language, currently is spoken by more people than is Chippewa, and it is the language the tribe is trying hardest to preserve. When surveying the tribe on its language use, Crawford found several respondents who affirmed that "they, or their parents or grandparents, had made a switch from speaking Ojibwa (or French) to speaking Michif" ("Speaking Michif," 50–51). The general picture on this Indian reservation, he adds, is that "people over about fifty years of age generally know the language [Michif], practically all over sixty-five or seventy learned it as a first language. But the level of use falls off quite rapidly with age, and young persons with familiarity are likely to be those who have spent more time with their grandparents" ("Speaking Michif," 51). Although Erdrich does not give many definite ages in her novels, it seems clear that the relationships between age and linguistic patterns in her novel follow the general pattern outlined by Crawford.

How does Louise Erdrich know so much about this tribe? She is herself a member of the Turtle Mountain tribe, and it is one with which she has familiarity. Her grandparents, the Pat Gourneaus, lived on the reservation and Erdrich visited them often. Even though she doesn't label herself a traditionalist like Eli Kashpaw, she respects the traditions of the tribe, including those of her grandparents:

My grandfather (who was tribal chair of the Turtle Mountain Reservation) was traditional. He spoke the old language, Ojibwa. He was the last person in our family who spoke it from childhood. But it's making a big come-back there. I could never claim to be part of this traditional resurgence, but I support it.[11]

Her parents also were involved with reservation life; both of them taught at the Bureau of Indian Affairs School in Wahpeton, North Dakota. She understands well Indian heritage and writes about it powerfully in her novels. She also understands that her task as a Native American writer is perhaps more onerous than the task of other writers; she says in a *New York Times Book Review* that "in the light of enormous loss, [she] must tell the stories of contemporary survivors while protecting and celebrating the cores of cultures left in the wake of the catastrophe."[12] These contemporary survivors, and Erdrich's celebration of them, are the subjects of the fourth novel in her tetralogy.

Many critics have understood the depth of her sensitivity about this Indian heritage, including James McKenzie, who writes that *Love Medicine* performs the task of "protecting and celebrating the cores of cultures" for the Chippewa and, "thereby, for the American culture as a whole":

> The novel is an act of deep respect for people whose lives are seldom the subject of literary art; it pays homage to the tenacity of a small, minority culture pitted against the Juggernaut of contemporary American life.[13]

The culture of which Erdrich speaks covers several generations, and other reviewers have emphasized the transformation and the difficult process of assimilation into contemporary American life that has occurred among Native Americans over generations. Scott Sanders has written of this assimilation process:

> They are mostly Chippewas, four generations of them, living on a North Dakota reservation or in Minnesota's Twin Cities. In each succeeding generation, their ancestral blood and ways are thinned out by mixture with the ways and blood of whites. If you were drawing a graph of what remains distinctly Indian about them, the curve, as it passes through our time would be heading unmistakably toward zero.[14]

Sanders's curve, applied to Erdrich's novels, would start with the Chippewa Indian heritage of the original Kashpaw and Rushes Bear and would follow through the French and English influences, ending with Albertine Johnson sitting in a bus depot in Fargo, her ancestral heritage "thinned out by mixture with the ways and blood of whites." She is one member of the younger generation who leaves the reservation for the white world, but perhaps her Indian blood is less "thin" than Sanders suggests. She carries with her the Native American culture of her tribe, yet is unsure of her place in that white world, and becomes even more unsure as she listens to her aunt chastising her mother for criticizing a "white girl" in Albertine's presence:

> "How do you think Albertine feels hearing you talk like this when her Dad was white?"
>
> "I feel fine," I said. "I never knew him." I understood what Aurelia meant though—I was light, clearly a breed.
>
> "My girl's an *Indian*," Zelda emphasized. "I raised her an Indian, and that's what she is." (*LM*, 23)

An Indian, yes, but a light-skinned Indian, one whose heritage has passed from full-blooded Chippewa to a mixture of Chippewa, French, and Swedish (her father), through the heritage of an Algonquian language mixed with French, all the way to Michif, then to English. Albertine Johnson is an "Indian," but one whose Indian heritage has gone through a rapid transformation that has redefined the concept of "Indian." And because the transformation has been so rapid, Albertine is unsure of her place in this changing culture. She is human, and she is afraid.

Notes

1. Quotations from Louise Erdrich's works are cited in the text using the following abbreviations: *LM* for *Love Medicine* (New York: Bantam, 1984); *BQ* for *The Beet Queen* (New York: Bantam, 1986).

2. *St. Anne's Centennial* (Belcourt, N.D., 1985), 130, 358. Subsequent references to this work will be identified by page numbers in parentheses in the text.

3. Elliott Coues, *New Light on the Great Northwest: The Manuscript Journals of Alexander Henry and David Thompson, 1799–1814* (New York: Francis P. Harper, 1897), 1:209.

4. Robert P. Wilkins and Winona H. Wilkins, *North Dakota: A History* (New York: Norton, 1977), 31. Subsequent references to this book will be identified by page numbers in parentheses in the text.

5. John Crawford, cited by Mary Jane Schneider, *North Dakota Indians: An Introduction* (Dubuque, Iowa: Kendall/Hunt Publishing, 1986), 43.

6. Ibid., 91.

7. Provencher to Bishop Plessis, cited by Grace Lee Nute, ed., *Documents Relating to Northwest Missions, 1815-1827* (St. Paul: Minnesota Historical Society, 1985), 158.

8. John Crawford, *Michif Dictionary: Turtle Mountain Chippewa Cree* (Winnipeg, Manitoba: Pemmican Publications, Inc., 1983), vii. Subsequent references to this book will be identified by page numbers in parentheses in the text.

9. John Crawford, "Speaking Michif in Four Métis Communities," *Canadian Journal of Native Studies,* 3:50. Subsequent references to this essay will be identified by page numbers in parentheses in the text.

10. John Crawford, personal communication, April 1988.

11. Gail Hand, "Native Daughter: Author Louise Erdrich Comes Home," *Plainswoman* 8:4.

12. Louise Erdrich, "Where I Ought to Be: A Writer's Sense of Place," *New York Times Book Review,* 28 July 1985.

13. James McKenzie, "Lipsha's Good Road Home: The Revival of Chippewa Culture in *Love Medicine," American Indian Culture and Research Journal* 10.3 (1986):56.

14. Scott Sanders, *"Love Medicine," Studies in American Indian Literatures* 9:1 (1985): 8–9.

From the Time Immemorial

Native American Traditions in Contemporary Short Fiction

HELEN JASKOSKI

◆　◆　◆

CONTEMPORARY NATIVE AMERICAN fiction concerns itself with a kind of cultural borderland, where lines between ethnic groups are drawn, denied, defied, and proudly distinguished. Sometimes the lines are territorial, involving geographic boundaries. More often they are psychological, economic, and linguistic—distinguished by separateness and often misunderstanding of custom and worldview.

In discussions of these texts, a generalized set of categories—"Indian" and "white"—emerges, as suggested in the subtitle of Gerald Vizenor's *Wordarrows*: "Indians and Whites in the New Fur Trade." More often, however, the characters' affiliations are specified—for example, Navajo, Laguna, Chippewa, Kiowa, Ute, on the one hand, and Norwegian-American, French-Canadian, Spanish-American, or Mexican, on the other. The subject is complex, and many writers have used innovative and experimental forms to meet the complexity of their subject.[1]

Louise Erdrich's fiction is rich in Chippewa lore and culture. A case in point is the Nanapush family name. Variously spelled as Wenebojo, Nanabush, Nanabozho, the name belongs to the great creator/trickster/ culture hero at the center of Algonquian mythology. Other Chippewa lore is embedded within the gossipy accounts of the ongoing exaltations and tribulations of the Kashpaw, Nanapush, and Lamartine families. Careful reading of Erdrich's stories reveals an intermingling of Chippewa and European motifs and symbols.

A close look at a single story shows Erdrich's use of Chippewa traditions in contrast and parallel with European materials. "Saint Marie," the second story in *Love Medicine*, epitomizes the complex relations between Indians and non-Indians throughout the book. The story's protagonist—tough, intelligent and willful Marie Lazarre—embodies what Paula Gunn Allen describes as "cultural conflict . . . in the psychological and social being" of the individual of mixed heritage.[2] The nuns at the Convent of the Sacred Heart look down on Marie as "Indian," whereas her future husband, Nector Kashpaw, regards her as merely a "skinny white girl" (59) from "a family of horse-thieving drunks" (58).

"Saint Marie" can be read as a ritual tale incorporating both Chippewa and European elements. In the story Erdrich fuses elements of Chippewa Windigo stories with European romance and fairy tale motifs and allusions to Christian practice and iconography. Marie Lazarre's great vision, at the center of her story, is related both to European and to Native American traditions.

The central conflict in "Saint Marie" resembles a legendary joust: a demented nun, Sister Leopolda, sees herself as fighting the devil for control of Marie's soul and insurance of her salvation, while Marie can only regard such control as fatal. The contest is imaged in parodies of chivalric legend: Leopolda hurls her lance at the devil in the schoolroom coat closet and later engages in hand-to-hand fencing with poker and fork. Marie's battle with Sister Leopolda also plays out the larger cultural conflict between European/Christian and Native ways of life, the contradictory aims of Christian colonizers having been to maintain power over colonized peoples while at the same time claiming to elevate them as "brothers in Christ."

In doing battle with Leopolda, Marie actually wars against herself, aiming at the contradictory ends of victory and acceptance. Like the heroines of "Cinderella" and "Hansel and Gretel" and other stories of ritual initiation, Marie Lazarre is searching for a "true" parent. Seeking a better home than her own impoverished family's, she enters the convent as the slave-like protégé of Sister Leopolda, with all the contradictory love/hate motives that belong to her condition of alienation: "I wanted Sister Leopolda's heart. And here was the thing: sometimes I wanted her heart in love and admiration. Sometimes. And sometimes I wanted her heart to roast on a black stick" (45). But, as in the fairy tales, Leopolda turns out to be a wicked stepmother. Like Cinderella, Marie must dress poorly, sleep behind the stove, and eat meager and coarse food. Like the heroine of "Hansel and

Gretel," Marie attempts to thrust her tormentor into the oven. Eventually (but not in this story), she marries a "prince," though that triumph is ambiguous, and she does not, like Gretel, succeed in cremating her tormentor. Instead of the warrior's physical victory, Marie gains the trickster's triumph of cleverness—and, in her special case, moral insight.

Marie Lazarre's ceremony of initiation and maturity also incorporates references to Christian religious traditions. The Christian elements, however, consistently reflect the inversion of putative Christian values in historical relations between Indians and white colonizers.

Sister Leopolda's hooks, first on the long oak window-opening pole and then on the poker, recollect two biblical hooks: the shepherd's crook adopted as a symbol of bishops' guidance and authority, and fishhooks, reminiscent of the New Testament passage in which the apostles are to become "fishers of men" and "catch" souls for heaven. Marie compares herself in her naive faith to a fish that has taken bait, and at the end of the story she squirms like a gaffed fish in her recognition of Sister Leopolda's pathetic hunger for love. Yet in retrospect, Marie has been the one fishing, commenting that "maybe Jesus did not take my bait, but them Sisters tried to cram me right down whole," following this recollection with the pungent comparison of herself to a lure that a walleye has swallowed (41).

The gulping fish is one of many references to food and eating throughout the story (and the whole novel). Further paralleling the comparison of fish bait to the "lure" of faith is Marie's allusion to Indians who had eaten the smallpox-infected hat of a Jesuit; instead of receiving healing power they consumed infection. There are many traditional accounts of the white man's "gift" of smallpox; in some, trade goods are infected, and in one version Smallpox is personified as a missionary himself.[3] In "Saint Marie" the image is a central metaphor for relations between the Christian Sister Leopolda and the powerless children she teaches. In a parody of the sacrament of communion, which to believers imparts life and healing, the Indians swallow disease; Leopolda fasts herself gaunt but is consumed by madness, possessed by the dark power that Marie understands as the Christian's Satan or the Chippewa's Windigo.

While Marie and Leopolda's job in the convent is baking bread—"God's labor" (47) according to Leopolda—Marie does not eat bread in any communion with the nuns; rather, Leopolda feeds the girl first the priest's goat cheese—"that heaven stuff" (47) Marie calls it—and then cold mush. Marie's initiation into the Christian life of the convent also includes a blasphemous "baptism," as Sister Leopolda first pours scalding water over the girl and then rubs her back with salve, parodying the use of anointing oils in several Christian rites. Finally, Marie's eventual triumph also begins with an image of eating, when she envisions Leopolda following her and swallowing the glass she walks through.

In addition to allusions to the sacraments, traditional Christian iconography and pious folklore appear in the story. When Leopolda places her foot on Marie's neck, she is imitating a popular representation of the virgin Mary in which the Madonna is shown standing with her foot on the neck of a serpent representing Satan. Related to this powerful Madonna is the woman clothed with the sun, described in the book of Revelation, an image that Christian art frequently identifies with the Virgin Mary and that resembles Marie's vision of herself as transfigured in gold and diamonds. Finally there is the phenomenon called stigmata, referring to the belief that the bodies of certain holy individuals spontaneously reproduce the wounds of Christ. Marie, seeing that Sister Leopolda has used the appearance of stigmata to escape having to admit that she stabbed the girl's hand, ironically colludes with Leopolda in deceiving the naive nuns and humbling Leopolda.

In finally turning the tables on Leopolda, Marie plays a trickster's part, using her enemy's own weapon against her and accomplishing through apparent acceptance and submission ("swallowing" the stigmata story) the triumph that had eluded direct confrontation and violence. The whole complex of Christian allusions, however, builds to subvert the moral claims of Christianity: the unholy "sacraments," the perversions of images of sanctity and glorification, all tend to underscore the corruption of Sister Leopolda's missionary enterprise.

Less explicit, but essential to the story's significance as a tale of the quest for identity, are the suggestions of traditional Chippewa Windigo stories and allusions to the ritual of "crying for pity." "Windigo story" actually refers to two kinds of stories: traditional tales about the cannibal giant of myth and legend, and reports of real persons afflicted with "Windigo psychosis."[4] In the traditional tales, Windigo is a giant, a skeleton of ice, the embodiment of winter starvation, a cannibal who can devour whole villages. Windigo sickness occurs when this dangerous being takes possession of a human soul, causing an irresistible desire to consume human flesh. Individuals subject to such possession show signs of their vulnerability in greedy gluttony, especially an insatiable appetite for fat and grease. In the legends, the Windigo monster is usually clubbed to death or killed in fighting; the body is often subsequently burned. Cure for the psychosis, however, often involves pouring boiling water or tallow on or into the afflicted one, or even death by fire.

In many stories the Windigo meets defeat at the hands of a child, some-times a little girl. Often, such a hero must become a Windigo herself in order to defeat the monster. Sometimes the monster itself is not killed but returns to natural human life after being relieved of its icy carapace; in the same way, a person afflicted with Windigo psychosis might return to nor-mal after melting or losing the heart of ice. A second, sometimes related complex of Chippewa stories involves one person's using magic or spells to "possess" another; the possessed one, often a younger relative, then defeats the worker of evil.

"Saint Marie" contains several elements of such Windigo and possession stories. Marie apparently recognizes Leopolda's nemesis, Satan, as the Windigo, for she says that the nun "knew as much about him as my grandma, who called him by other names and was not afraid" (42). The earliest known written reference to the Windigo, in the missionary Paul le Jeune's *Relation* (1636), associates Windigo cannibalism with demonic pos-session, and the first reference in English, in James Isham's *Observations and Notes: 1743–1749*, offers the definition "the Devil" for the term *"Whit te co"* (Colombo, 7–9).

Marie describes herself as a potential candidate for intimacy with the Windigo: "Before sleep sometimes he came and whispered conversation in the old language of the bush. I listened. He told me things he never told anyone but Indians. I was privy to both worlds of his knowledge" (43). She has the appetite for fat attributed to the incipient Windigo. "It was the cheese that got to me. When I saw it my stomach hollowed. My tongue dripped. I loved that goat-milk cheese better than anything I'd ever ate. I stared at it. The rich curve in the buttery cloth" (47).

The whole boiling water episode parallels several Windigo tales in which the monster perishes after having boiling water or tallow poured on it, or in which the possessed person is cured by being made to drink boiling tallow. In a number of these tales, moving kettles foreshadow the appear-ance of the Windigo (Barnouw, 120, 122), and in "Saint Marie" the prostrate Marie hears the kettle moving on the stove and takes it as an ill omen. Moreover, the girl's rigid coldness calls to mind the Windigo's heart of ice. Marie recalls herself as clothed in "veils of hate petrified by longing" (42). Leopolda refers several times to the girl's coldness, and before pouring boiling water on her in that depraved baptismal rite, the nun intones, "You're cold. There is a wicked ice forming in your blood," then threatens to "boil [the "evil one"] from your mind if you make a peep . . . by filling up your ear" (49).

But it is the skeletal, starving, spiritually cannibalistic Leopolda who is truly possessed by the Windigo, who tries to possess Marie, and who must be defeated. Leopolda's physical gauntness hints at the anorexia often associated with Windigo sickness (Teicher, 6), just as her spiritual cannibalism manifests itself in her mania for total control of the children she teaches. She has "snared in her black intelligence" (42) the lonely child Marie, first through fear, by locking the irreverent girl in a coat closet, then through a promise of love: "He *wants* you," Leopolda tells the girl. "That's the difference, I give you love" (44). But like the dangerous, domineering uncles, aunts, and strangers in the folk tales, Leopolda offers only sick possession, not the nurturing love the young woman seeks. She must be defeated.

Besides traditional Chippewa tales of the Windigo and of magical possession, "Saint Marie" also alludes to an important ritual complex among many Plains peoples: the youth's ordeal of "crying for pity" from the powers of the spirit world in search of a guiding vision.[5] In Chippewa tradition, both girls and boys alike sought visionary power through fasting and isolated meditation. Boys were encouraged to fast as children in preparation for the great vision quest associated with puberty, and girls sequestered themselves to receive a vision at menarche. Marie Lazarre, "near age fourteen" (40) at the time of the story, has come to the time for her vision quest.

It is characteristic of the irony throughout Erdrich's story that although Sister Leopolda continually fasts, it is Marie who has the vision. Marie's own ordeal of boiling water and piercing fork resembles tests of physical endurance and mutilation practiced by prairie tribes such as the Crow more than it reflects traditional Chippewa practice.[6] Certainly Marie cries out, both in the coat closet and in the kitchen under the scalding water: "God's face. Even that did not disrupt my continued praise. Words came. Words came from nowhere and flooded my mind. Now I could pray much better than any one of them. Than all of them full force" (49).

In the depths of her ordeal Marie undergoes the "loss of self" that precedes the enabling, integrating vision: "I despaired. I felt I had no inside voice, nothing to direct me, no darkness, no Marie" (50). Immediately, she decides to throw out her food—an act of metaphorical fasting—and then receives her magnificent power vision. The vision is a turning point in the story. Afterward, Marie can confront Leopolda with the hard truth that both are engaged with the power of darkness: "'He was always in you,' I said. 'Even more than in me'"(52). And she recognizes for the first time a vulnerability in the nun: "But for the first time I had gotten through some chink she'd left in her darkness. Touched some doubt" (52).

This knowledge of their mutual humanity culminates in Marie's eventual, reluctant understanding of Leopolda's own pathetic need for love, a recognition that destroys the savor of her hard-won, duplicitous triumph. While Marie Lazarre, the stubbornly ambitious, love-starved girl, has been crying for pity from the powers of the universe, Saint Marie, the trickster heroine and emblem of virtue, succumbs to unwilling pity for her tormenter: "I pitied her. Pity twisted in my stomach like that hook-pole was driven through me. I was caught" (56). Here again we catch a sense of those Windigo stories in which, when the ice is chipped away from the monster, "in the center, there was a regular man" (Barnouw, 122); so Marie sees Leopolda "kneeling within the shambles of her love" (56), a "regular human" underneath it all. In her pity for poor old Leopolda, Marie also reaches the "regular human" within the stony defenses of the tough, ambitious little girl.

I have focused in this discussion on "Saint Marie" as an autonomous short story. But the story is more, an integral part of "a novel, a solid, nailed down, compassionate and coherent narrative."[7] The structure of *Love Medicine* is a complex series of such tales, interlocking through recurrence of character and event and through variation of point of view. There is some parallel to those series of episodes that make up the great sequences of traditional Native American myth, and certainly other traditional themes (like motifs from the Nanabozho stories, or the more recent Chippewa adaptations of the Cinderella tale) must be examined to savor the full richness of the work. The nearest parallel in narrative organization, however, is probably the works of William Faulkner. Erdrich shares with Faulkner, above all, a down-to-earth comic vision. Beyond this, *Love Medicine*, like the sagas of the Compsons and the Snopeses, aims at a complex rendering of the intricate and far-reaching minglings and conflicts and interlocking fates among people of differing races and culture groups, all of whom feel a deep sense of their ties to the land and to their history upon it.

Notes

1. Louise Erdrich's work in short fiction, for instance, may be compared with that of Gerald Vizenor and Leslie Marmon Silko: each author uses traditional American Indian material in a unique manner, each plays variations on the short story genre, and each has published a work that, as a single text, is built on the short story form but that, in its final shape, shows more coherence than simply a "collection" of short stories. Erdrich's *Love Medicine*, Vizenor's *Wordarrows*, and Silko's *Storyteller* contain short fiction forms, yet the "short stories" in them can only be understood in the context of each book as an integrated whole.

2. Paula Gunn Allen, *The Sacred Hoop: Recovering the Feminine in American Indian Traditions* (Boston: Beacon, 1986), 81.

3. A discussion of traditional smallpox stories may be found in Helen Jaskoski, "'A Terrible Sickness Among Them': Smallpox and Stories of the Frontier," in *Early Native American Writing: New Critical Essays,* edited by Helen Jaskoski (Cambridge: Cambridge University Press, 1996), 136–157.

4. Material on the Windigo complex comes from the following sources: Victor Barnouw, *Wisconsin Chippewa Myths and Tales and Their Relation to Chippewa Life* (Madison: University of Wisconsin Press, 1977); Sister Bernard Coleman, Ellen Frogner, and Estelle Eich, *Ojibwa Myths and Legends* (Minneapolis: Ross and Haines, 1962); John Robert Colombo, ed., *Windigo: An Anthology of Fact and Fantastic Fiction* (Saskatoon: Western Producer Prairie Books, 1982); Ruth Landes, *The Ojibwa Woman* (New York: Columbia University Press, 1938); Robert E. Ritzenthaler and Pat Ritzenthaler, *The Woodland Indians* (Garden City, N.Y.: Natural History Press, 1970); Morton Teicher, "Windigo Psychosis," in *Proceedings of the 1960 Annual Spring Meeting of the American Ethnological Society,* 1–129, edited by Verne F. Ray (Seattle: American Ethnological Society, 1960); Olivia Vlahos, *New World Beginnings: Indian Cultures in the Americas* (New York: Viking, 1970). Subsequent references to these volumes will be identified in parentheses in the text.

5. Material on the Chippewa vision quest comes from George Copway (Kah-ge-ga-gah-bowh), *Indian Life and Indian History* (Boston: Albert Colby, 1860); Ruth Landes, *Ojibwa Woman*; Christopher Vecsey, *Traditional Ojibwa Religion and Its Historical Changes* (Philadelphia: The American Philosophical Society, 1983).

6. Robert H. Lowie, *Indians of the Plains* (Garden City, N.Y.: The Natural History Press, 1954), 170.

7. Kathleen Sands, *"Love Medicine*: Voices and Margins," *Studies in American Indian Literatures* 9 (1985): 12–24, 12.

Love Medicine

Voices and Margins

KATHLEEN M. SANDS

◆　◆　◆

*L*ove Medicine by Louise Erdrich is a novel of hard edges, multiple voices, disjointed episodes, erratic tone shifts, bleak landscapes, eccentric characters, unresolved antagonisms, incomplete memories. It is a narrative collage that seems to splice random margins of experience into a patchwork structure. Yet ultimately it is a novel, a solid, nailed-down, compassionate, and coherent narrative that uses sophisticated techniques toward traditional ends. It is a novel that focuses on spare essentials, those events and moments of understanding that change the course of life forever.

Like many contemporary novels, *Love Medicine* is metafiction, ironically self-conscious in its mode of telling, concerned as much with exploring the process of storytelling as with the story itself. As marginal and edged, episodic and juxtaposed, as this narrative is, it is not the characters or events of the novel that are dislocated and peripheral. Each is central to an element of the narrative. It is the reader who is placed at a distance, who is the observer on the fringes of the story, forced to shift position, turn, ponder, and finally integrate the story into a coherent whole by recognizing the indestructible connections between the characters and events of the narrative(s). Hence the novel places the reader in a paradoxically dual stance, simultaneously on the fringe of the story yet at the very center of the process—distant and intimate, passive yet very actively involved in the narrative process.

The fact that this is a novel written by an Indian about Indians may not be the reason for Erdrich's particular choice of narrative technique and reader control, but it does provide a point for speculation and perhaps a clue to the novel as not just incidentally Indian but compellingly tribal in character.

We have come to expect certain things from American Indian contemporary fiction. Novels from the Southwest have been overwhelmingly concerned with story, traditional stories reenacted in a ceremonial structure at once timeless and timely. Novels like N. Scott Momaday's *House Made of Dawn* and Leslie Marmon Silko's *Ceremony* are rich in oral tradition and ritual and demand intense involvement of the reader in the texture and event of tribal life and curing processes. James Welch's novels, *Winter in the Blood* and *The Death of Jim Loney*, are less obviously immersed in oral tradition but draw on tribal history, landscape, and psychology to develop stories and characters that are plausible within Northern Plains tribal ways. Gerald Vizenor's *St. Louis Bear-heart* draws on various Plains oral traditions and manipulates them in a satirically comic indictment of a blasted American landscape and culture. In each case, these major American Indian novelists have drawn heavily on the storytelling traditions of their peoples and created new visions of the role of oral tradition in both the events of narrative and narrative process.

In these novels it is the responsibility of both the major characters and the reader to make the story come out right. The authors consciously involve readers in the process of narration, demanding activity that is both intellectual and emotional, remote and intimate. Louise Erdrich's novel works in much the same way, but the materials are different and the storytelling process she draws upon is not the traditional ceremonial process of the reenactment of sacred myth, nor is it strictly the tradition of telling tales on winter nights, though there is some reliance on that process. The source of her storytelling technique is the secular anecdotal narrative process of community gossip, the storytelling sanction toward proper behavior that works so effectively in Indian communities to identify membership in the group and ensure survival of the group's values and its valued individuals. Erdrich's characters are aware of the importance of this tradition in their lives. At one point the lusty Lulu Lamartine matter of factly says, "I always was a hot topic."[1] And the final narrator of the novel, Lipsha Morrissey, searching for the right ingredients for his love potion, comments, "After a while I started to remember things I'd heard gossiped over" (199). Later, on the run from the law with his father, he says, "We talked a good long time about the reservation then. I caught him up on all the little blacklistings and scandals that had happened. He wanted to know everything" (268). Gossip affirms identity, provides information, and binds the absent to the family and the community.

The inclination toward this anecdotal form of storytelling may well derive from the episodic nature of traditional tales, that are elliptical because the audience is already familiar with the characters, their cultural context, and the values they adhere to. The spare, elliptical nature of Erdrich's novel can be loosely related to this narrative process, in which the order of the telling is up to the narrator and the audience members are intimately involved in the fleshing out of the narrative and the supplying of the connections between related stories. The gossip tradition within Indian communities is even more elliptical, relying on each member's knowledge of every individual in the group and the doings of each family (there are no strangers). Moreover, such anecdotal narration is notoriously biased and fragmented, with no individual being privy to the whole story. The same incidents are told and retold, accumulating tidbits of information. There is, after all, no identifiable right version, no right tone, no right interpretation. The very nature of gossip is instability, with each teller limited by his or her own experience and circumstances. It is only from all the episodes, told by many individuals in random order, that the whole may be known—probably not to some community member but, ironically, to some outsider who has been patient enough to listen and frame the episodes into a coherent whole. In forming that integrated whole, the collector has many choices but only a single intention, to present a complete story in a stable form.

Perhaps the novelist in this case, then, is that investigator (of her own imagination and experience) who manipulates the fleeting fragments of gossip into a stable narrative form, the novel, and, because of her artistic distance from the events and characters, supplies the opportunity for irony that the voices in the episodes of the novel are incapable of. Secrets are revealed and the truth emerges from the threads of information. Like the everyday life it emerges from, gossip is not inherently coherent, but the investigator can use both its unreliable substance and its ambiguous form to create a story that preserves the multiplicity of individual voices and the tensions that generate gossip. The novelist can create a sense of the ambiguity of the anecdotal community tradition yet allow the reader to comprehend. Gossip, then, is neither "idle" nor "vicious"; it is a way of revealing secrets and generating action.

So it is with *Love Medicine*. There is no single version of this story, no single tone, no consistent narrative style, no predictable pattern of development, because there is no single narrator who knows all the events and secrets. The dialogue is terse and sharp, as tense as the relationships between the characters. Narrators are introduced abruptly to turn the action, jar the reader's expectations, give words to the characters' tangled lives. This is a novel of voices, the voices of two families whose members interpret and misinterpret, and approve or disapprove (mostly the latter) of one another's activities.

The novel begins with a story that suggests a very conventional linear narrative. June Kashpaw, the erratic and once vivacious beauty of the family, is down and out, heading for the bus that will take her back to her North Dakota reservation. But she is easily seduced by a mud engineer and ends up on a lonely back road on a subfreezing night, wheezing under the drunken weight of her ineffective lover. She walks—not just away, but across the plains into the freezing night and death from exposure. In one chapter she is gone—but the memory of her vitality and the mystery of her death will endure. She is the catalyst for the narrations that follow, stories that trace the intricate and often antagonistic relationships in the two families from which she came. One life—and not a very special life at that, just a life of a woman on the fringes of her tribe and community, a woman living on the margins of society, living on the hard edge of survival and failing, but a woman whose death brings the family together briefly, violently, and generates a multitude of memories and stories that slowly develop into a coherent whole. It is June (and the persistent desire of the family members who survive her to understand her and, consequently, themselves) who allows us to penetrate the chaotic and often contradictory world of the Kashpaw and Lamartine families and to bring a sense of history and order to the story, to bring art out of anecdote and gossip.

The structure of the narrative is not as chaotic and episodic as it first may appear. Time is carefully controlled, with 1981, the year of June's death, the central date in the novel. Subsequent to her death, the family gathers, and even those not present, but central to the narration, are introduced by kinship descriptions. The family genealogies are laid out, and as confusing as they are in that first chapter, they become easy and familiar as the episodes unfold and family secrets are revealed. Chapters 2 through 6 of the novel leap back in time—1934, 1948, 1957, 1980—until the pivotal date, 1981, is reached again at the center of the novel. As one of the characters puts it, "Events loop around and tangle again" (95). From this year, the novel progresses to 1984 and begins to weave together the separate stories into an intricately patterned fabric that ironically, even in the end, no single character fully understands; one secret is never told. This flashback-pivotal-year-progressive chronology, however, is by no means straightforward. Within chapters, time is convoluted by the injection of memory, and each chapter is controlled by the narration of a different character whose voice (style) is markedly different from all the other voices and whose recollection of dialogue complicates the narrative process even further. The system of discourse in the novel is thus dazzlingly complex, demanding very close attention from the reader. But the overlap of characters allows for comprehension. The novel is built layer upon layer. Characters are not lost. Even June, vitally alive at least in memory, stays until the end. In fact, it is she who connects the last voice and the final events of the novel to all the others. It is through June that each character either develops or learns identity within the community, but also, since this is metafiction, in the novel itself.

There is a sort of double-think demanded by Erdrich. The incidents of the novel must be carried in the reader's mind, constantly reshuffled and reinterpreted as new events are revealed and the narrative biases of each character are exposed. Each version, each viewpoint jars things loose just when they seem hammered into place. It's a process that is disconcerting to the reader, keeping a distance between the characters and keeping the reader in emotional upheaval. This tension at times creates an almost intolerable strain on the reader because the gaps in the text demand response and attempted resolution without connected narrative. The characters innocently go about their doing and telling, unaware of other interpretations, isolated from comprehension of the whole, but they are no less agonized, no less troubled, no less comic for their innocence.

The reader must go through a different but parallel discomfort, puzzling right along with them to the end. One character pointedly asks another, "Do you like being the only one that's ignorant?" (243); the question might as easily be asked of the reader, and indirectly it is. At times, the reader is inclined to think June well out of the mixed-up madness of her families, and even wish this narrative might simply be read as a collection of finely honed short stories. But making the story come out right is irresistible, to be in on the whole story is too intriguing to be abandoned. Like the character in the novel, we must respond, "no," to being ignorant. Discovering the truth from the collection of both tragic and comic positions presented in the separate episodes demands that we stick around to bridge the gaps.

There is something funny about gossip, simply because it is unreliable, tends to exaggeration, makes simple judgments, affirms belonging at the very moment of censure. It takes for its topic the events of history, memory, and the contemporary moment and mixes them into a collage of commentary on the group as a whole as well as the individual. Erdrich's novel does exactly that. It takes what might be tragic or solemn in a more conventional mode of telling and makes it comically human (even slapstick), sassy, ironic, and ultimately insightful about those families who live on that hard edge of survival on the reservations of the Northern Plains. It is, of course, the very method of the novel, individuals telling individual stories, that not only creates the multiple effect of the novel but requires a mediator, the reader, to bring the episodes together.

It is exactly the inability of the individual narrators to communicate effectively with one another—their compulsion to tell things to the reader, not to each other—that makes their lives and history so very difficult. At several points in the novel, characters reveal their difficulties in communicating: "My tongue was stuck. I was speechless" (99); "There were other times I couldn't talk at all because my tongue had rusted to the roof of my mouth" (166); "Alternating tongue storms and rock-hard silences was hard on a man" (196). Their very inability to give words to each other except in rage or superficial dialogues masks discomfort, keeps each one of them from giving and receiving the love that would be the medicine to cure their pain or heal their wounds. All but June, and she has the author and the other characters to speak for her, and she is beyond the healing embrace of family love.

In the end, some bridging occurs in the novel; Erdrich even titles the last chapter "Crossing the Water" and an earlier chapter "The Bridge." The water is time: "So much time went by in that flash it surprises me yet. What they call a lot of water under the bridge. Maybe it was rapids, a swirl that carried me so swift that I could not look to either side but had to keep my eyes trained on what was coming" (93). The bridge, of course, is love. But the love in this novel is mixed with pain and failure: "And now I hurt for love" (128); "It's a sad world, though, when you can't get love right even trying it as many times as I have" (218). It demands suffering as well as pleasure: "A love so strong brews the same strength of hate" (222). Surprised at Marie's response to Nector's death, Lipsha explains:

> I saw that tears were in her eyes. And that's when I saw how much grief and love she felt for him. And it gave me a real shock to the system. You see I thought love got easier over the years so it didn't hurt so bad when it hurt, or feel so good when it felt good. I thought it smoothed out and old people hardly noticed it. I thought it curled up and died, I guess. Now I saw it rear up like a whip and lash. (192)

But despite the conflicts and personal tragedies, it is love medicine, a potion that works reconciliation in spite of its unconventional sources, that holds these characters together even as they antagonize and disappoint one another. Love is so powerful that it creates indissoluble ties that even outlast life, and ultimately it allows forgiveness. In the end, in spite of perversions of love, illicit love, and lost love, there is enough love to bring two women together and a lost son home.

Erdrich's characters are lovers in spite of themselves, and the potion that works to sustain that love is language—language spoken by each narrator to the reader, language that leads to the characters' understanding of the fragile nature of life and love. Near the end of the novel, the bumbling "medicine man" discovers the essential truth of life:

> You think a person you know has got through death and illness and being broke and living on commodity rice will get through anything. Then they fold and you see how fragile were the stones that underpinned them. You see how instantly the ground can shift you thought was solid. You see stop signs and the yellow dividing markers of roads you've travelled and all the instructions you had played according to vanish. You see how all the everyday things you counted on was just a dream you had been having by which you run your whole life. (209)

The one thing left that makes life endurable is love. Life is tenuous; love is dangerous, and love potions risky:

> [W]hen she mentions them love medicines, I feel my back prickle at the danger. These love medicines are something of an old Chippewa speciality. No other tribe has got them down so well. But love medicine is not for the layman to handle. You don't just go out and get one without praying for it. Before you get one, even, you should go through one hell of a lot of mental condensation. You got to think it over. Choose the right one. You could really mess up your life grinding up the wrong little thing. (199)

But healing family wounds isn't a matter of chemistry; it's a matter of words. Like an old folk charm spoken to oneself, the stories of love coerce the loved ones. Finally, the novel seduces the reader into affection for these sometimes silly, sometimes sad characters who are only real in the magic of words.

Love Medicine is a powerful novel. It develops hard, clear pictures of Indian people struggling to hold their lives together, hanging on to the edge of the reservation or fighting to make a place for themselves in bleak midwestern cities or devising ingenious ways to make one more break for freedom, but its most remarkable quality is how it manages to give new form to oral tradition. Not the enduring sacred tradition of ritual and myth that we have come to know in contemporary Indian literature, but a secular tradition that is so ordinary, so everyday, so unconscious that it takes an inquirer, an investigator, an artist to recognize its value and adapt its anecdotal structure to the novel. While *Love Medicine* may not have the obvious spiritual power so often found in Indian fiction, its narratives and narrators are potent. They coerce us into participating in their events and emotions and in the exhilarating process of making the story come out right.

As the number of novels by American Indian writers grows, we can begin to see just how varied are the possibilities for Indian fiction, how great the number of storytelling choices available from the various cultures of Indian tribes, how intriguing and unique the stories are within this genre of American fiction. Perhaps the one thread that holds this fabric of literature together is that the best works of American Indian fiction are never passive; they demand that we enter not only into the fictional world but participate actively in the process of storytelling.

Note

1. Louise Erdrich, *Love Medicine* (New York: Holt, 1984), 233. Subsequent references will be identified by parenthetical page numbers in the text.

Where I Ought to Be

A Writer's Sense of Place

LOUISE ERDRICH

✦ ✦ ✦

IN A TRIBAL VIEW OF the world, where one place has been inhabited for generations, the landscape becomes enlivened by a sense of group and family history. Unlike more contemporary writers, a traditional storyteller fixes listeners in an unchanging landscape combined of myth and reality. People and place are inseparable. The Tewa Pueblo, for example, begin their story underground, in complete darkness. When a mole comes to visit, they learn there is another world above and decide to go there. In this new place the light is so intense that they put their hands over their eyes to shield them. Grandmother Spider suggests that they adjust their vision to the light by gradually removing their hands and she points them to Sandia Mountain, the place where they will live. A great deal of wandering, bickering, lessons learned, and even bloodshed occur, but once there, they stay for good.

This is the plot but not the story. For its full meaning, it should be heard in the Tewa language and understood within that culture's worldview. Each place would then have personal and communal connotations. At the telling of it we would be lifetime friends. Our children would be sleeping or playing nearby. Old people would nod when parts were told the right way. It would be a new story and an old story, a personal story and a collective story, to each of us listening.

What then of those authors nonindigenous to this land? In renaming and historicizing our landscapes, towns, and neighborhoods, writers from Hawthorne to Cather to Faulkner have attempted to weld themselves and their readers closer to the New World. As Alfred Kazin notes in "On Native Grounds," "the greatest single fact about our American writing" is "our writers' absorption in every last detail of this American world, together with their deep and subtle alienation from it." Perhaps this alienation is the result of one difficult fact about Western culture—its mutability. Unlike the Tewa and other Native American groups who inhabited a place until it became deeply and particularly known in each detail, Western culture is based on progressive movement. Nothing, not even the land, can be counted on to stay the same. And for the writers I've mentioned, and others, it is therefore as if, in the very act of naming and describing what they love, they lose it.

Faulkner's story "The Bear" is set in "that doomed wilderness whose edges were being constantly and punily gnawed at by men with plows and axes who feared it because it was wilderness." That shrinking area is haunted by a spirit, the bear, which is "shaggy, tremendous, red-eyed, not malevolent but just big, too big for the dogs which tried to bay it, for the horses which tried to ride it down, for the men and the bullets they fired into it; too big for the very country which was its constricting scope."

To Europeans the American continent was so vast that only a hundred years ago it seemed that nothing and no one could ever truly affect it. Yet William Faulkner wrote nostalgically of a wilderness that had already vanished. What is invented and lamented is the bigness and vastness that was lost piecemeal to agriculture. The great bear, which is the brooding and immense spirit of the land, had all but disappeared from settled areas before Faulkner was born and exists today largely by virtue of human efforts on his behalf. The wilderness that once claimed us is now named and consumed by us. Carefully designated scraps of it are kept increasingly less pristine to remind us of what was.

Just as Faulkner laments the passing of the Southern forests into farmland, so Willa Cather's novels about Nebraska homesteaders are elegies to vanishing virtues, which she links with an unmechanized and pastoral version of agriculture. That view has given way ever since as developments in chemical fertilizers, hybrid seed, animal steroids, and farm equipment become part of a more technological treatment of the land.

Douglas Unger's recent novel, *Leaving the Land*, tells of the rise and fall of a small town in South Dakota that bases its economy on large-scale turkey farming. When prices fall and the farmers can't afford to ship their stock, they slaughter the turkeys themselves, pile them in a trench and burn them. Mr. Unger writes of the unlikely, apocalyptic scene, "The prairie filled with thick smoke whirling up day after day, rolling, tumbling, dark scarves of smoke blown for an instant to the shapes of godheads, vague monuments, black smoke tornadoes that scarred the summer skies with waste and violence."

Instead of viewing a stable world, as in pre-invasion Native American cultures, instead of establishing a historical background for the landscape, American writers seem bound into the process of chronicling change and forecasting destruction, of recording a world before that world's very physical being shifts. As we know, neighborhoods are leveled in a day, the Army Corps of Engineers may change the course of a river. In the ultimate kitsch gesture of a culture's desperation to engrave itself upon an alien landscape, a limestone mountain may be blasted into likenesses of important men.

Our suburbs and suburban life may be more sustaining and representative monuments than Mount Rushmore. There is a boring grandeur to the acres on acres of uniform cul-de-sacs and wide treeless streets, each green yard adorned with a swimming pool that sparkles like a blue opal. The large malls are awe-inspiring Xanadus of artificial opulence. Although created as escapes, as places halfway between country and city life, but without the isolation of the one or the crime of the other, suburbs and the small-town way of life that they imitate are often, in our literature, places to escape from. One departs either back to the evil thrills, pace, and pollution of the city, or to the country, where life is supposedly more deeply felt, where the people are supposedly more genuine, where place is idiosyncratic and not uniform.

Writers such as John Cheever and Joy Williams admirably show that suburbs can be as strange as the next place in fiction. Any completely imagined description, from neighborhood to small town, creates a locus that the reader mentally inhabits. I don't know whether Fingerbone, the town in Marilynne Robinson's novel, *Housekeeping*, exists in fact, but it does for me because of this passage, in which the narrator describes the town's losses in the aftermath of a flood:

> Fingerbone was never an impressive town. It was chastened by an outsized landscape and extravagant weather, and chastened again by an awareness that the whole of human history had occurred elsewhere. That flood flattened scores of headstones. More disturbing, the graves sank when the water receded, so that they looked a little like hollow

sides or empty bellies. And then the library was flooded to a depth of three shelves, creating vast gaps in the Dewey decimal system. The losses in hooked and braided rugs and needlepoint footstools will never be reckoned.

Of course not every writer feels compelled to make specific his or her setting. Samuel Beckett, Alain Robbe-Grillet, Nathalie Sarraute, and Donald Barthelme are among those whose fiction could take place anywhere, or nowhere. Besides, in our society mobility is characteristic of our experience. Most of us don't grow up in a single community anymore, and even if we do we usually leave it. How many of us live around the corner from parents, grandparents, even brothers and sisters? How many of us come to know a place intimately over generations? How many places even exist that long? We are part of a societal ebb and flow, a people washing in and out of suburbs and cities. We move with unparalleled ease, assisted by Mayflower Van Lines and superhighways. We are nomadic, both by choice, relocating in surroundings that please us, and more often by necessity. Like hunter-gatherers, we must go where we will be fed, where the jobs are listed.

But if for many readers and writers place is not all-important, there still remains the problem of identity and reference. An author needs his or her characters to have something in common with the reader. If not the land, which changes, if not a shared sense of place, what is it then that currently provides a cultural identity? What is it that writers may call on now for communal references in the way that a Tewa could mention Sandia Mountain?

Whether we like it or not, we are bound together by that which may be cheapest and ugliest in our culture, but which may also have an austere and resonant beauty in its economy of meaning. We are united by mass culture to the brand names of objects, to symbols like the golden arches, to stories of folk heroes like Ted Turner and Colonel Sanders, to entrepreneurs of comforts that cater to our mobility, like Conrad Hilton and Leona Helmsley. These symbols and heroes may annoy us, or comfort us, but when we encounter them in literature, at the very least, they give us context.

Brand names and objects in fiction connote economic status, upbringing, aspirations, even regional background. It is one thing for a character to order an imported Heineken, another for that person to order a Schlitz. There is a difference in what we perceive in that character's class and sensibility. It means a third thing for that person to order a Hamm's beer, a brew said to be made of Minnesota's sky-blue waters and which is not widely available outside the Middle West. Very few North Dakotans drive Volvos even though quite a few North Dakotans are of Swedish descent. The Trans-Am is not the car of choice for most professors of English in Eastern colleges.

In Bobbie Ann Mason's short stories, characters drink bourbon and Coke out of coffee cups, while the people in Robb Forman Dew's novels use pitchers for milk instead of pouring it from cartons, and transfer jam from jars to crystal dishes. Raymond Carver's characters drink Teachers, nameless gin, or cheap pink champagne. Few of Eudora Welty's characters imbibe that sort of thing, while some of William Kennedy's characters would be happy to get it.

Though generalized, these examples show the intricacies of our cultural shorthand. And if it seems trivial or vulgar to cling to and even celebrate the stuff that inundates us, consider America without football, television, or the home computer, a prospect that would only be possible in the event of some vast and terrible catastrophe.

We live with the threat of nuclear obliteration, and perhaps this is a subliminal reason that as writers we catalogue streets, describe landmarks, create even our most imaginary landscapes as thoroughly as we can. No matter how monotonous our suburbs, no matter how noxious our un-zoned Miracle Miles and shopping centers, every inch would seem infinitely precious were it to disappear.

In her essay, "Place in Fiction," Eudora Welty speculates that the loss of place might also mean the loss of our ability to respond humanly to anything. She writes: "It is only too easy to conceive that a bomb that could destroy all traces of places as we know them, in life and through books, could also destroy all feelings as we know them, so irretrievably and so happily are recognition, memory, history, valor, love, all the instincts of poetry and praise, worship and endeavor, bound up in place."

I don't know whether this is true. I hope that it is not, and that humanity springs from us and not only from our surroundings. I hope that even in the unimaginable absence of all familiar place, something of our better human qualities would survive.

But the danger that they wouldn't, we wouldn't, that nothing else would either, is real and present. Leonard Lutwack urges, in his book *The Role of Place in Literature*, that this very fear should inform the work of contemporary writers and act as a tool to further the preservation of the earth. "An increased sensitivity to place seems to be required," he says, "a sensitivity inspired by aesthetic as well as ecological values, imaginative as well as functional needs. . . . Literature must now be seen in terms of the contemporary concern for survival."

In our worst nightmares, all of us have conceived what the world might be like *afterward* and have feared that even our most extreme versions of a devastated planet are not extreme enough. Consider, then, that to American Indians it is as if the unthinkable has already happened, and relatively recently. Many Native American cultures were annihilated more thoroughly than even a nuclear disaster might destroy ours, and others live on with the fallout of that destruction, effects as persistent as radiation—poverty, fetal alcohol syndrome, chronic despair.

Through diseases such as measles and smalllpox, and through a systematic policy of cultural extermination, the population of Native North Americans shrank from an estimated 15 million in the mid-fifteenth century to just over 200,000 by 1910. That is proportionately as if the population of the United States were to decrease from its present level to the population of Cleveland. Entire pre-Columbian cities were wiped out, whole linguistic and ethnic groups decimated. Since these Old World diseases penetrated to the very heart of the continent even faster than the earliest foreign observers, the full magnificence and variety of Native American cultures were never chronicled, perceived, or known by Europeans.

Contemporary Native American writers have therefore a task quite different from that of other writers I've mentioned. In the light of enormous loss, they must tell the stories of contemporary survivors while protecting and celebrating the cores of cultures left in the wake of the catastrophe.

And in this, there always remains the land. The approximate 3 percent of the United States that is still held by Native American nations is cherished in each detail, still informed with old understandings, still known and used, in some cases, changelessly.

All of this brings me, at last, to describe what a sense of place means from my own perspective. I grew up in a small North Dakota town, on land that once belonged to the Wahpeton-Sisseton Sioux but had long since been leased out and sold to non-Indian farmers. Our family of nine lived on the very edge of town in a house that belonged to the Government and was rented to employees of the Bureau of Indian Affairs boarding school, where both my parents worked, and where my grandfather, a Turtle Mountain Chippewa named Pat Gourneau, had been educated. The campus consisted of an immense central playground, classrooms, two dormitories, and numerous outbuildings. All of these places were made of a kind of crumbly dark red local brick. When cracked, smashed, or chipped back to clay this brick gave off a peculiar, dry, choking dust that I can almost still taste.

On its northern and western sides, the campus ran, with no interference from trees or fence lines, into fields of corn, wheat, soybeans, or flax. I could walk for miles and still find nothing but fields, more fields, and the same perfectly straight dirt township road. I often see this edge of town—the sky and its towering and shifting formations of clouds, that beautifully lighted emptiness—when I am writing. But I've never been able to describe it as well as Isak Dinesen, even though she was not writing of the American Great Plains but about the high country of Kenya.

"Looking back," she says in her reminiscence, *Out of Africa*, "you are struck by your feeling of having lived for a time up in the air. The sky was rarely more than pale blue or violet, with a profusion of mighty, weightless, everchanging clouds towering up and sailing on it, but it has a blue vigour in it, and at a short distance it painted the ranges of hills and woods a fresh deep blue. In the middle of the day the air was alive over the land, like a flame burning; it scintillated, waved and shone like running water, mirrored and doubled all objects. . . . Up in this high air you breathed easily, drawing in a vital assurance and lightness of heart. In the highlands you woke up in the morning and thought: Here I am, where I ought to be."

Here I am, where I ought to be.

A writer must have a place where he or she feels this, a place to love and be irritated with. One must experience the local blights, hear the proverbs, endure the radio commercials. Through the close study of a place, its people and character, its crops, products, paranoias, dialects, and failures, we come closer to our own reality. It is difficult to impose a story and a plot on a place. But truly knowing a place provides the link between details and meaning. Location, whether it is to abandon it or draw it sharply, is where we start.

IN OUR OWN BEGINNINGS, we are formed out of the body's interior landscape. For a short while, our mothers' bodies are the boundaries and personal geography which are all that we know of the world. Once we emerge we have no natural limit, no assurance, no grandmotherly guidance like the Tewa, for technology allows us to reach even beyond the layers of air that blanket earth. We can escape gravity itself, and every semblance of geography, by moving into sheer space, and yet we cannot abandon our need for reference, identity, or our pull to landscapes that mirror our most intense feelings.

The Macondo of Gabriel García Márquez, Faulkner's Yoknapatawpha County, the island house of Jean Rhys in *Wide Sargasso Sea* are as real to me as any place I've actually been. And although fiction alone may lack the power to head us off the course of destruction, it affects us as individuals and can spur us to treat the earth, in which we abide and which harbors us, as we would treat our own mothers and fathers. For, once we no longer live beneath our mother's heart, it is the earth with which we form the same dependent relationship, relying completely on its cycles and elements, helpless without its protective embrace.

PART II

*Mixed Identities and
Multiple Narratives*

Erdrich and Dorris's Mixed-bloods and Multiple Narratives

LOUIS OWENS

◆　◆　◆

DESPITE THE IMPORTANCE OF N. Scott Momaday's Pulitzer Prize for *House Made of Dawn* in 1969, no American Indian author has achieved such immediate and enormous success as Louise Erdrich with her first novel, *Love Medicine*. A best-seller, *Love Medicine* not only outsold any previous novel by an Indian author, but it also gathered an impressive array of critical awards, including the National Book Critics Circle Award for Fiction in 1984, the American Academy and Institute of Arts and Letters award for best first novel, the Virginia McCormack Scully Prize for best book of 1984 dealing with Indians or Chicanos, the American Book Award from the Before Columbus Foundation, and the *L.A. Times* award for best novel of the year.

Why such astounding success for an author writing about a subject—Indians—in which Americans had previously shown only a passing interest (and that predominantly in the romantic vein mined by non-Indian authors)? The answer to such a question delves into the heart of Louise Erdrich's achievement with *Love Medicine* as well as her very popular second and third novels, *The Beet Queen* (1986) and *Tracks* (1988). And to examine Erdrich's fiction closely is also to explore that of her husband/agent/collaborator, Michael Dorris, whose first novel, *A Yellow Raft in Blue Water* (1987), has also been received with enthusiasm by readers and critics.[1]

Like almost every other Indian novelist, Louise Erdrich is a mixed-blood. A member of the Turtle Mountain Chippewa band, Erdrich is of German, French, and Chippewa descent. She was born in Minnesota and grew up in Wahpeton, North Dakota, where her parents taught in the Wahpeton Indian School. In her novels, Erdrich draws upon both her mother's Chippewa heritage and her experiences as the daughter of a Euramerican growing up in middle America. Both the wild reservation bushland and the weathered edge of the North Dakota prairie permeate her novels, stamping their character upon Indian and non-Indian alike. "When you're in the plains and you're in this enormous space," Erdrich has stated, "there's something about the frailty of life and relationships that always haunts me."[2]

In her published novels—which together form a quartet—Erdrich weaves genealogies and fates as characters appear and reappear in successive, interconnected stories. This web of identities and relationships arises from the land itself, that element that has always been at the core of Native Americans' knowledge of who they are and where they come from. Central to Native American storytelling, as Momaday has shown so splendidly, is the construction of a reality that begins, always, with the land. In Erdrich's fiction, those characters who have lost a close relationship with the earth—and specifically with that particular geography that informs a tribal identity—are the ones who are lost. They are the Ishmaels of the Indian world, waiting like June Kashpaw to be brought home. Imagining her role as a storyteller, Erdrich has explained: "In a tribal view of the world, where one place has been inhabited for generations, the landscape becomes enlivened by a sense of group and family history. Unlike most contemporary writers, a traditional storyteller fixes listeners in an unchanging landscape combined of myth and reality. People and place are inseparable." In laying out her fictional terrain, a coherently populated geography often compared to that of William Faulkner, Erdrich tells stories of survival, as she has also explained: "Contemporary Native American writers have therefore a task quite different from that of other writers. . . . In the light of enormous loss, they must tell the stories of contemporary survivors while protecting and celebrating the cores of cultures left in the wake of the catastrophe [cultural annihilation]. And in this, there always remains the land."[3] Perhaps it is, in part, Erdrich's positive emphasis upon survival that has endeared her to the reading public. Though the frailty of lives and relationships and the sense of loss for Indian people rides always close to the surface of her stories, Erdrich's emphasis in all her novels is upon those who survive in a difficult world.

Like every other Native American novelist, Erdrich writes of the inevitable search for identity. "There's a quest for one's own background in a
lot of this work," she has explained. "One of the characteristics of being
a mixed-blood is searching. You look back and say, 'Who am I from?' You
must question. You must make certain choices. You're able to. And it's a
blessing and it's a curse. All of our searches involve trying to discover
where we are from." She has commented upon her own identity as a
writer conscious of both her Indian heritage and her somewhat insecure
place in the American mainstream: "When you live in the mainstream and
you know that you're not quite, not really there, you listen for a voice to
direct you. I think, besides that, you also are a member of another nation.
It gives you a strange feeling this dual citizenship. . . . It's kind of incom-
prehensible that there's the ability to take in non-Indian culture and be
comfortable in both worlds."[4]

The seemingly doomed Indian or tortured mixed-blood caught between worlds surfaces in Erdrich's fiction, but such characters tend to disappear behind those other, foregrounded characters who hang on in spite
of it all, who confront with humor the pain and confusion of identity and,
like a storyteller, weave a fabric of meaning and significance out of the
remnants.

Love Medicine is an episodic story of three inextricably tangled generations of
Chippewa and mixed-blood families: the Kashpaws, Morrisseys, Lamartines, and Lazarres. In fourteen chapters, seven narrators weave their many
stories into a single cloth that becomes, very gradually, a coherent fabric of
community—a recovered center. Along the way, Erdrich's masterful use
of discontinuous and multiple narrative underscores, formally, the displacement and deracination that dominate her narrators' tales while at the
same time forcing upon the reader his or her own sense of radical displacement and marginality. Ultimately, however, the fragmentated narratives
and prismatic perspectives of the novel emphasize not the individual anguish of an Abel, Jim Loney, Cecelia Capture, Chal Windzer, Archilde
Leon, or most other protagonists of Native American novels, but the
greater anguish of lost communal/tribal identity and the heroic efforts of a
fragmented community to hold on to what is left.

Love Medicine begins with an illumination of liminality—a conflation of
Christian religion and Native American mythology, of linear/incremental
time and cyclic/accretive time—on the "morning before Easter Sunday."
Like the traditional trickster narrative, the story opens with the protago-

nist, June Kashpaw, on the move: "June Kashpaw was walking down the clogged main street of oil boomtown Williston, North Dakota, killing time before the noon bus arrived that would take her home."⁵ Soon, the character around whom this novel will cohere is dead, and it is ironic that June is attempting to "kill" time—to break the entropic grip of linear, Western time—while it is precisely this time that is killing June, the historical time that has eroded a Chippewa sense of identity just as it has overseen the loss of the Chippewa's traditional homeland. Rather than return from her desperate life to the reservation, June walks deliberately into a blizzard and accepts her death. Like Tayo's mother and Helen Jean in Leslie Marmon Silko's *Ceremony*, June is one of those women who have washed up in the no-woman's-land of prostitution on the parasitic edge of the reservation, displaced and alone. When she decides to go with one of the roustabouts from a bar rather than return home, she thinks, "The bus ticket would stay good, maybe forever. They weren't expecting her up home on the reservation" (3). With a bus ticket that will never expire, and no expectations, June—like trickster—assumes the role of a permanent traveler, infinitely dislocated with no family/community/tribe to expect her return. Her fragmentation is emphasized when Erdrich writes: "And then she knew that if she lay there any longer she would crack wide open, not in one place but in many pieces" (5). As with virtually every other aspect of June, this fear of cracking into "many pieces" represents a kind of dialogic, a hybridized utterance that can be read in two ways. In a Euramerican context it underscores June's alienation, approaching schizophrenia, her loss of a centered identity. Fragmentation in Native American mythology is not necessarily a bad thing, however. For the traditional culture hero, the necessary annihilation of the self that prefigures healing and wholeness and a return to the tribal community often takes the form of physical fragmentation, bodily as well as psychic deconstruction.

With no family to draw her home, June deliberately chooses death, for as Albertine Johnson tells us in the novel's second chapter, "June grew up on the plains. Even drunk she'd have known a storm was coming" (9). Raised by her great-uncle Eli, the one character in the novel who never loses touch with either earth or identity, June knows where, if not who, she is: "Even when it started to snow she did not lose her sense of direction" (6). And Erdrich ends the first chapter with the words, "The snow fell deeper that Easter than it had in forty years, but June walked over it like water and came home" (6). She comes home to an "unchanging landscape . . . of myth and reality," the feminine Christ-figure resurrected as trickster, the fragmented culture hero made whole within memory and story, returning through the annual cycle of Easter/spring—death/resurrection—to her Indian community as mythic catalyst.

Erdrich begins *Love Medicine* with a subtle displacement of time and an invocation of peripatetic trickster, "going along." Just as the traditional trickster's role is not only to upset and challenge us but also to remind us—obversely—of who we are and where we belong, June will figure throughout the novel as a touchstone for the other characters. Just as the tribal community in *Ceremony* desperately wants Tayo's lost mother to come home, the response of characters throughout *Love Medicine* to June's loss will underscore each character's sense of identity within the tribal community and, concomitantly, each character's potential for survival. And just as trickster transcends both time and space as well as all other definitions, June does indeed "kill time" as she moves freely, after death, in the thoughts and stories of the other characters. Jay Cox has noted June's resemblance to trickster, suggesting perceptively that June is the "chaotic everything" to all the characters in *Love Medicine* and that "June's death in the first chapter does little to impede her spirit from going along throughout the novel."[6] When, at the end of the novel, Lipsha Morrissey crosses the water to "bring her home," we know that Lipsha has finally arrived at a coherent sense of his place within the community (including the land itself) from which identity springs. And at the novel's end another trickster will be on the move as Gerry Nanapush heads across the "medicine line" into the depths of Canada, telling Lipsha, "I won't ever really have what you'd call a home" (268). Lipsha, son of the two powerful characters with whom the novel opens and closes—June Kashpaw and Gerry Nanapush—ends the novel on a note of profound resolution of identity.

By the time June walks away from the car toward her death, it is very likely after midnight and therefore officially Easter Sunday, the day the "snow fell deeper . . . than it had in forty years." By invoking Easter, Erdrich brings into the novel the myth of the crucifixion and resurrection, an analogy ironically underscored when she writes that June's ejection (with her pants pulled halfway up) from the warm car into the cold "was a shock like being born" (5). By associating June with both Christ and trickster, Erdrich underscores the twin elements that will make whole the fragmented lives of the novel: the commitment beyond the self that lies both at the heart of the Christian myth and, very crucially, at the center of the American Indian tribal community where individualism and egotism are shunned and "we" takes precedence over the "I" celebrated in the Euramerican tradition, and, just as important, a refusal to acquiesce to static definitions of identity. When she writes of the snow that "June walked over it like water and came home," Erdrich merges an image of Christ with the primary element that will figure prominently throughout the book: water. Erdrich has said, "In *Love Medicine* the main image is the recurrent image of the water—transformation (walking over snow or water) and a sort of transcendence. . . . The river is always this boundary. There's a water monster who's mentioned in *Love Medicine*. It's not a real plot device in *Love Medicine*. It become more so in *Tracks*. . . . We really think of each book [of the quartet] as being tied to one of the four elements." In the same interview, Erdrich and Dorris point out that the central elemental image in *The Beet Queen* is air, while in *Tracks* it is earth and in *The Bingo Palace,* fire.[7] As in *House Made of Dawn*, this beginning is also the novel's ending, a circularity familiar to Native American storytelling, and it underscores the important place of water imagery in Chippewa storytelling, an importance understandable for a people whose traditional homeland was once the region of the Great Lakes.

Our first encounter with a family in the novel comes through Albertine in the second chapter.[8] After describing her relationship with her mother as "patient abuse," Albertine arrives home simply to be ignored at first by both mother and aunt. Albertine is one-half Swedish, the daughter of a white father who abandoned his wife and child at Albertine's birth, an Anglo outcast "doomed to wander" (the quintessential Euramerican condition of eternal migration). Albertine's mother is Zelda, one of the daughters of Nector Kashpaw and Marie Lazarre. Marie, a mixed-blood who insists, "I don't have that much Indian blood," is from a family considered white trash by their Indian neighbors. Albertine, who thinks of herself as "light, clearly a breed," is approximately one-quarter Chippewa, but she identifies herself as Indian, complaining bitterly about allotment and following Henry Lamartine down the street just because he looks Indian.

Though Albertine has run away in the past and has apparently flirted with the kind of disastrous life that killed June, she is the character in the novel who, among those of her generation, is most secure in her identity, a certainty provided, ironically, by her mother, who says defiantly, "I raised her an Indian, and that's what she is" (23). Zelda, married for the second time to a Scandinavian husband and living in a trailer on the edge of the reservation, is the one who has the strength and certainty to retrieve her father, Nector, from the clutches of Lulu Lamartine and the one capable of providing her daughter with a sense of self lacking in many of the novel's characters. Albertine's strength comes from this unshakable knowledge of who she is and from her awareness that the past is a formative part of the present. Albertine emphasizes the power of the past—through stories—to inform the present when she says of June: "She told me things you'd only tell another woman, full grown, and I had adored her wildly for these adult confidences. . . . I had adored her into telling me everything she needed to tell, and it was true, I hadn't understood the words at the time. But she hadn't counted on my memory. Those words stayed with me" (15–16). The past permeates the present, coexisting through cyclical temporality within the spatial reality of the Native American world, staying with us, telling us in a single breath where we have been, where we are, and where we are going. As nearly every Native American author has sought to demonstrate, the loss of the past means a loss of self, a loss of order and meaning in the present moment, and an inability to contemplate a future that is part of that moment. Storytelling serves to prevent that loss; it bears, as Michel Foucault has said, "the duty of providing immortality."[9]

It is Albertine who understands the motivation of her great-grandmother, old Rushes Bear, in keeping Eli at home while allowing Nector to be educated at the government school. "In that way," Albertine explains, "she gained a son on either side of the line" (17). And it is Albertine who points out that Eli, who "knew the woods," had stayed mentally sharp while Nector's "mind had left us, gone wary and wild" (17). When Albertine, always seeking stories of the past, asks Nector to "tell me about things that happened before my time," the old man just shakes his head, "remembering dates with no events to go with them, names without faces, things that happened out of place and time" (18). Schooled by the government to be a bureaucrat, Nector has been molded into chairman of his tribe by his ambitious wife, Marie, but he retains only the meaningless ciphers of dates and names that have neither bearing nor mooring in Albertine's world. He has become a victim of mechanical, entropic, historic time, while his brother has remained alert to the reality of his more traditional life on the other side of the time line. Finally, it is Albertine who puts June's (as usual, contradictory) accomplishment into perspective for us when she intones: "Her defeat. Her reckless victory. Her sons" (35). June's sons are King and Lipsha, one recognized and damned, the other abandoned and saved.

Lipsha is June's reckless victory, just as her legitimate son, King, epitomizes her defeat and the defeat of all the failed characters in the novel. Throughout most of the novel Lipsha does not know who his parents are; he lacks an identity and even believes of his mother that she "would have drowned me" (37). When Albertine comes close to telling him the secret of his mother, Lipsha refuses to hear, saying, "Albertine, you don't know

what you're talking about." He goes on to declare, "As for my mother
. . . even if she came back right now, this minute, and got down on her
knees and said, 'Son, I am sorry for what I done to you,' I would not relent
on her" (36). Ultimately, Lipsha *will* relent on her; like Tayo in *Ceremony*, he
will forgive his mother for abandoning him; and by bringing her home, he
will come home to a knowledge of who he is. When Albertine asks, "What
about your father? . . . Do you wish you knew him?" Lipsha replies, "I
wouldn't mind" (37). At the end of the novel Lipsha will meet his father,
Gerry Nanapush, and he will realize that his own healing "touch" has de-
scended most powerfully from Old Man Pillager, the shaman who is the
trickster's father and who will figure prominently in *Tracks*.

Gerry Nanapush, described by Lipsha as a "famous politicking hero,
dangerous armed criminal, judo expert, escape artist, charismatic member
of the American Indian Movement, and smoker of many pipes of kinnikinnick in the most radical groups" (248), is the most unmistakable trickster
of the novel, bearing the traditional name of the Chippewa trickster, *nanapush* or *nanabozhu*. Impossible to contain, a shape shifter capable of impossible
physical feats, when he arrives at King's apartment to confront the stoolie
who has informed on him, Nanapush speaks the classic trickster line: "'I
want to play,' said Gerry very clearly and slowly, as if to a person who
spoke a different language. 'I came to play'" (262). Gerry Nanapush is
"mainly in the penitentiary for breaking out of it" ("breaking out" is, of
course, trickster's *modus vivendi*), and, according to Lulu, "In and out of
prison, yet inspiring Indian people, that was his life. Like myself he could
not hold his wildness in" (227). Nanapush is a culture hero and shaman/
trickster. At the same time, Nanapush, who, according to Albertine "shot
and killed a state trooper" on the Pine Ridge Reservation (170), bears a
strong resemblance to American Indian activist Leonard Peltier, impris-
oned for the alleged murder of two FBI agents at Pine Ridge. In an interview, Erdrich described her response when she attended Peltier's trial:
"When the jury came back with that guilty verdict, I stood up and
screamed. It was a real dislocation growing up thinking there was justice,
and then seeing this process and knowing they were wrong in delivering
that verdict" (Tompkins 15).

Like so many other characters in fiction by Indian writers, Lipsha's
quest is for a sense of self and authenticity. Lulu Lamartine, his grandmother (whom Lipsha describes as "the jabwa witch") and a female trickster, finally forces him to listen to the story of his parentage. About his
mother, June, Lulu says, "She watched you from a distance, and hoped you
would forgive her some day" (244). About his father, Lulu says, "There

ain't a prison that can hold the son of Old Man Pillager, a Nanapush man. You should be proud that you're one" (244). Finally, Lulu sees directly to the heart of Lipsha's strangeness, saying, "Well I never thought you was odd. . . . Just troubled. You never knew who you were. That's one reason why I told you. I thought it was a knowledge that could make or break you" (244–45). Upon learning of his heritage, Lipsha muses: "I could not help but dwell upon the subject of myself . . . Lipsha Morrissey who was now on the verge of knowing who he was" (244). Seeking his father, Lipsha declares, "I had to get down to the bottom of my heritage" (248), and once he sits down to play cards with his father, Lipsha says, "I dealt myself a perfect family. A royal flush" (264). Lipsha has learned to mark the cards from his grandmother, Lulu Lamartine, and Gerry recognizes the feel of trickery on the deck: "Those crimps were like a signature—his mother's" (260). And, as the patterns of his heritage and identity become clear, Lipsha deals, saying, "I dealt the patterns out with perfect ease, keeping strict to Lulu's form" (263).

Finally, when he learns that Lipsha is on the run from the military police, Gerry works his magic, beginning with an affirmation of his son's identity: "'You're a Nanapush man,' he said. . . . 'We all have this odd thing with our hearts.'" Nanapush reaches out a hand and touches his son's shoulder, and Lipsha says, "There was a moment when the car and road stood still, and then I felt it. I felt my own heart give this little burping skip" (271). With a "heart problem," Lipsha will fail his physical and be exempted from the military, and to his father's relief he will not have to become a fugitive. The "odd thing" about Nanapush hearts is, of course, their ability to care deeply for others, individuals and Indians as a whole. This is the "love medicine" of the novel, as Lipsha comes to realize after Nector's blackly comic death, when Lipsha tells Marie, "Love medicine ain't what brings him back to you, Grandma. . . . He loved you over time and distance, but he went off so quick he never got the chance to tell you how he loves you. . . . It's true feeling, not magic" (214).

In the figure of Nector, tribal chairman and patriarch of the Kashpaws, who are "respected as the last hereditary leaders" of the tribe (89), Erdrich introduces the clichéd view of the "vanishing American." Nector has been in a Hollywood movie. "Because of my height," he says ironically, "I got hired on for the biggest Indian part" (89). The biggest Indian part, however, isn't much: "'Clutch your chest. Fall off that horse,' they directed. That was it. Death was the extent of Indian acting in the movie theater" (90). Nector escapes from cinema death to the wheat fields of Kansas, where he is paid to pose for a painter. "Disrobe," the artist says, and Nector, stalling for time, replies, "What robe?" The painting that results is entitled *Plunge of the Brave* and shows a naked Nector leaping to his death in a raging river. Nector, who possesses perhaps the most subtly ironic sense of humor in the novel, concludes: "Remember Custer's saying? The only good Indian is a dead Indian? Well from my dealings with whites I would add to that quote: 'The only interesting Indian is dead, or dying by falling backwards off a horse'" (91). Nector says finally, "When I saw that the greater world was only interested in my doom, I went home on the back of a boxcar. . . . I remembered that picture, and I knew that Nector Kashpaw would fool the pitiful rich woman that painted him and survive the raging water. I'd hold my breath when I hit and let the current pull me toward the surface, around jagged rocks. I wouldn't fight it, and in that way I'd get to shore" (91). Nector recognizes the epic and tragic role white America has reserved for the Indian, a role in which, as Bakhtin pointed out, the hero must perish.[10] For Indians who go to the movies or read novels, it would indeed appear that the greater world is interested only in their doom, and Nector articulates the direction of Indian characters in nearly all novels by Indian authors when he says, "I went home." Going home to reservation, family, tribe, or simply an Indian identity is the way Native Americans create "another destiny or another plot."

Nector also articulates here the strategy he will follow throughout the course of his life: he goes consistently with the current, never fighting very strongly if at all. Thus he ends up married to Marie Lazarre because she simply takes him, forcing him to abandon at least temporarily his true love, Lulu Lamartine. Thus he allows Marie to manipulate him into the tribal chairmanship and a somewhat stable and respectable life. And thus he is swept, late in the novel, into Lulu's passionate current for a brief time before being towed to anchorage at home by his determined daughter, Zelda. "Call me Ishmael," Nector says, taking the line from *Moby-Dick*, the only book he has read. "For he survived the great white monster," Nector explains, "like I got out of the rich lady's picture. He let the water bounce his coffin to the top. In my life so far I'd gone easy and come out on top, like him. But the river wasn't done with me yet" (91–92).

What Nector fails to understand about Ishmael is that Melville's narrator survives for two primary reasons. The first is that he alone is able to see both good and evil—he is the "balanced man" aboard the cursed Calvinist ship named for the Pequots, a tribe slaughtered by the colonists in the name of a monomaniacal Calvinist vision. And the coffin that bounces Ishmael to the surface of the sea belongs to Queequeg, the Native to whom Ishmael is bound by a shared bed and pipe. Ishmael floats atop the symbol

of Queequeg's doom as Melville's novel ends. If Nector is Ishmael the survivor, it is at the expense of his Indian self. And it is clear in the novel that
Nector, though he is an effective bureaucratic leader for the tribe, has lost
a great deal. When he signs the letter evicting Lulu from her home, he assumes no responsibility for the act, saying, "As tribal chairman, I was presented with a typed letter I should sign that would formally give notice
that Lulu was kicked off the land" (104). Lulu is being evicted so that a factory making "plastic war clubs" and other false Indian "dreamstuff" (in
Lulu's words) can be built. Lulu's perspective is the Indian one: "If we're
going to measure land, let's measure it right. Every foot and inch you're
standing on, even if it's on the top of the highest skyscraper, belongs to the
Indians. That's the real truth of the matter" (221).

When he comes to the agonizing decision to leave Marie for Lulu, Nector says, "It seems as though, all my life up to now, I have not had to make
a decision. I just did what came along. . . . But now it is one or the
other, and my mind can't stretch far enough to understand this" (106). In
coming to a decision, Nector has attempted to confront the monsters in
his life for the first time when he takes off his clothes and dives into the
lake: "I swam until I felt a clean tug in my soul. . . . I gave her [Lulu] up
and dived down to the bottom of the lake where it was cold, dark, still, like
the pit bottom of a grave. Perhaps I should have stayed there and never
fought. . . . But I didn't. The water bounced me up" (103). In diving
deep into the lake, Nector has dared the water monster, Missepeshu, who,
according to Lipsha, "lives over in Lake Turcot" (194). And as a Chippewa
he has assumed even greater risk, for as Lulu explains, "drowning was the
worst death for a Chippewa to experience. By all accounts, the drowned
weren't allowed into the next life but forced to wander forever, broken
shoed, cold, sore, and ragged. There was no place for the drowned in
heaven or anywhere on earth" (234).

In spite of his official position with the tribe, and despite the fact that he
is, as Lipsha points out, a kind of Indian monument unto himself, Nector
is, like the Ishmael with whom he identifies, one of the novel's cultural
outcasts. Nector wanders mentally between Indian and white worlds,
eventually retreating to a second childhood where responsibility will never
be forced upon him. In contrast, Eli, who has lived closer to the traditional
Chippewa ways, knows precisely who and where he is to the end. In Eli the
past is alive, and King's white wife, Lynette, perceives this when she shrieks,
"Tell 'em Uncle Eli. . . . They've got to learn their own heritage! When
you go it will all be gone!" (30). It is Eli who shows Nector's progeny "how
to carve, how to listen for the proper bird-call, how to whistle on their

own fingers like a flute," and it is Eli who remembers how to hunt in the old ways.

In *Love Medicine*, the searing pain of Indian lives found in such novels as *House Made of Dawn, Ceremony, Winter in the Blood, The Death of Jim Loney, Sundown, The Surrounded, The Jailing of Cecelia Capture*, and others is not as immediately evident. Lives and loves fail in *Love Medicine*, but not with the whetted edge found in fiction by most other Indian authors. Deracination is the crucible in which identities are both dissolved and formed, but the suffering is kept at a distance through the constantly shifting narrative and surface complexity of the text. Caught up in the tangled lives of mixed-bloods who have the foolishness, cruelty, and courage to love whom they will and abandon what they must, the reader experiences the human comedy of these generations. But the non-Indian reader is not made to feel acutely, as he or she is in other Indian novels, a sense of responsibility for the conditions portrayed. Unlike many other works by Native Americans, Erdrich's first novel does not make the white reader squirm with guilt, and this fact may well have contributed significantly to the book's popularity with mainstream American readers. However, to say that Erdrich does not foreground the oppression and genocide that characterize white relations with Indians over the centuries is not to say that *Love Medicine* ignores that aspect of Indian consciousness. Formally, the novel's fragmented narrative underscores the fragmentation of the Indian community and of the identity that begins with community and place; and the fragmentation of this community, the rootlessness that results in an accumulation of often mundane tragedies among the assorted characters, subtly underscores the enormity of what has been lost.

In addition to this subtle fabric of alienation, deracination, and despair that forms the backdrop for the often darkly comic drama in this novel, Erdrich provides brief glimpses of more pointed Indian resentment. Even Lipsha, troubled by a tangled identity but also perhaps the most compassionate character in the novel, can be very bitter, musing upon "the old time Indians who was swept away in the outright germ warfare and dirty-dog killing of the white," and admitting, "Oh yes, I'm bitter as an old cutworm just thinking of how they done to us and doing still" (195). Albertine, heading home, declares, "The policy of allotment was a joke. As I was driving toward the land, looking around, I saw as usual how much of the reservation was sold to whites and lost forever" (11).

The Catholic Church itself comes in for a severe scourging in the form of Sister Leopolda, the mad nun who tortures Marie Lazarre and struggles with Satan. Leopolda, as we discover in *Tracks*, is the mother who abandoned and never acknowledged Marie, the Indian who denied her Indianness, the demented murderer of her daughter's father, and the Christian who never relinquished her belief in Missepeshu, the lake monster of Matchimanito. Though Father Damien in *Tracks* will redeem the church considerably, in Leopolda we are confronted with evidence as damning as that D'Arcy McNickle presents in *The Surrounded*. About this thread in *Tracks*, the "prequel" to *Love Medicine*, Erdrich has said, "There are two major Catholic figures in *Tracks*, Pauline [Leopolda] and Father Damien. Pauline took over the book. She's every aspect of Catholicism taken to extremes. . . . There's no question that the church on reservations has become more tolerant, and that there have been many committed priests who fought for Indian rights. But the church has an outrageous view on women—damaging and deadly."[11]

Erdrich does not ignore the racism and brutality of Euramerica's dealings with Indian people, but for the first time in a novel by a Native American author, she makes the universality of Indian lives and tragedies easily accessible to non-Indian readers. Kashpaws and Morrisseys and Lazarres and Lamartines are people readers can identify with much more easily and closely than they can with an Archilde, Abel, or Tayo. These tangled lives are not so radically different from the common catastrophes of mainstream Americans, certainly no more so than those dreamed up by a Faulkner or Fitzgerald. And yet no reader can come away from *Love Medicine* without recognizing the essential Indianness of Erdrich's cast and concerns.

Notes

1. Despite the obvious stylistic differences between *A Yellow Raft in Blue Water* and Louise Erdrich's novels, both Erdrich and Dorris insist that each of their novels has been to some extent a collaboration. In a 1989 conversation with me, Michael Dorris said simply, "We've worked very closely together on each of the novels," and in a published interview, he explained: "The process of everything that goes out, from book reviews to magazine articles to novels, is a give and take" (Sharon White and Glenda Burnside, "On Native Ground: An Interview with Louise Erdrich and Michael Dorris," *Bloomsbury Review* 8 [1988]: 17).

2. J. H. Tompkins, "Louise Erdrich: Looking for the Ties That Bind," *Calendar Magazine*, October 1986, 15. Subsequent references to this will be identified by parenthetical page numbers in the text.

3. Louise Erdrich, "Where I Ought to Be: A Writer's Sense of Place," *New York Times Book Review*, 28 July 1985, 1, 23.

4. Joseph Bruchac, ed., *Survival This Way: Interviews with American Indian Poets* (Tucson: University of Arizona Press, 1987), 77, 79, 83.

5. Louise Erdrich, *Love Medicine* (New York: Holt, 1984), 1. Subsequent references to the novel will be identified by parenthetical page numbers in the text.

6. Jay Cox, "Dangerous Definitions: Female Tricksters in Contemporary Native American Literature," *Wicazo Sa Review* 5, no. 2 (1989): 19.

7. Hertha D. Wong, "An Interview with Louise Erdrich and Michael Dorris," *North Dakota Quarterly* 55 (1987): 210.

8. Although it is tempting to see in Albertine a version of the author, Michael Dorris has declared, "There's the assumption that because this character has some education, she must be Louise. And it's certainly not" (Wong, "Interview," 206).

9. It should be noted, of course, that Foucault says at the same time that the "authored" work "now possesses the right to kill, to be its author's murderer" (Michel Foucault, "What Is an Author?" in Robert Con Davis and Ronald Schleifer, eds., *Contemporary Literary Criticism: Literary and Cultural Studies* (New York: Longman, 1989). 264.

10. Mikhail M. Bakhtin, *The Dialogic Imagination,* translated by Caryl Emerson and Michael Holquist, edited by Michael Holquist (Austin: University of Texas Press, 1981), 7.

11. Laurie Alberts, "Novel Traces Shattering of Indian Traditions," *Albuquerque Journal*, 23 October 1988, G-8.

Celebrating Culture

Love Medicine

JAMES RUPPERT

◆ ◆ ◆

> Contemporary Native American Writers have
> therefore a task quite different from that of other
> writers I've mentioned. In light of enormous loss,
> they must tell the stories of contemporary sur-
> vivors while protecting and celebrating the cores of
> cultures left in the wake of catastrophe.
> —Louise Erdrich, "Where I Ought to Be"

Love Medicine is a dazzling, personal, intense novel of survivors, who struggle to define their own identities and fates in a world of mystery and human frailty. In her writing, Louise Erdrich attempts both to protect and celebrate this world. To effectively assume the roles of protector and celebrant, Erdrich must mediate between two conceptual frameworks, non-Native and Native, in order to avoid future catastrophes. She endeavors to manipulate each audience so that it will experience the novel through the paths of understanding unique to each culture, thus assuring protection and continuance of a newly appreciated and experienced Native American epistemological reality.

Celebrating and protecting the stories of survivors of cross-cultural catastrophe can imply the creation of characters formed by competing senses of identity. Many people have commented that cultural concepts of identity appear to differ in Native American and non-Native cultures. For example, Kenneth Lincoln refers to Native Americans' "alternative senses of family, kinship, communal property, lineage, language, history, geography, even space-time conceptions."[1] For both Native and non-Native implied readers, the stories Erdrich tells address, clarify, and define the various ways that identity exists in both cultural frameworks. As she layers these identities in the text, they become visible through the merging of epistemological codes that are used to signify psychological, social, communal, and mythic senses of identity. The mediational actions of the author serve to protect and celebrate culture by a continuing re-creation of the multiple facets of identity through multiple narratives allowing negotiation to replace simple concepts of identity in either system.

Mediation, as the generative organizational principle, often downplays mechanically plotted novel structures while encouraging multiple narratives. In this process the voices and ideas of a variety of culturally linked positions, a variety of identities, compete for the reader's ear and thus his or her allegiance. They also engage both Native and non-Native discourse fields. This "struggle going on within discourse," as Mikhail Bakhtin calls it, characterizes many mediational texts whose nature is essentially dialogic. For Erdrich, plot is far less important than the voices of her characters. She posits the tribal language against the half-breed language and the contemporary American language, evoking discourse fields only to realign their original speaker positions. Bakhtin, in his discussion of narrative discourse, offers an insight useful to understanding the relationship of plot to language in Erdrich's work. He writes of plot serving to "represent speaking persons and their ideological worlds." In the process of reading a novel, the reader is compelled by dialogics (and doubly so, by mediation) to come "to know one's own language" and "one's own belief system in someone else's system." This process, as I have noted before, is referred to by Bakhtin as "ideological translation."[2]

Love Medicine is a successful mediational novel because the plot organizes the different social languages and ideologies in such a way as to allow the reader into a new way of seeing and speaking about the world, thus promoting ideological translation. Erdrich conceives of this new perspective for the implied reader as a dynamic one whereby he or she can adopt a variety of perspectives from the Native and non-Native cultural spectrum. *Love Medicine* then becomes for the reader what Bakhtin envisions: "the experience of a discourse, a world view, and an ideologically based act" (365). Erdrich's goals include nothing less than ideological and epistemological transposition, since the implied non-Native reader is exposed to Native values and the implied Native reader is shown that new perspectives and new languages can sustain cores of culture.

To understand Erdrich's mediational positioning, we can consider the discourses embedded in the text. She attempts to present an oral discourse in a written format. Erdrich's first-person narrators talk directly to both implied readers as if they were chatting around a kitchen table. They speculate, remember, complain, come to conclusions, and describe their actions; indeed, almost all the information, the meaning, the significance of the novel is developed through this homage to the most personal and least codified type of oral communication. Private, personal narratives, the most informal of all oral communication, carry the feel of gossip and confession. Scott Sanders has likened reading *Love Medicine* to "being drawn into a boisterous family reunion in a crowded kitchen."[3] Oral tradition in this book defines the nature of all knowledge; for characters like Lipsha, what they hear defines who they are.

Each character's personal narration competes with another's, and whatever significance is developed, is created by the constant interplay of events and their interpretation. Kay Sands suggests the importance of these personal oral narratives when she writes, "The source of her [Erdrich's] storytelling technique is the secular anecdotal narrative process of community gossip, the storytelling sanction toward proper behavior that works so effectively in Indian communities to identify membership in the group and insure survival of group values and its valued individuals. . . . Gossip affirms identity, provides information, and binds the absent to the family and the community."[4]

Yet Erdrich's effort is structured by a set of highly Western novelistic conventions that have contemporary parallels in experimental novels, semiotic poetry, and cinema verité. Catherine Rainwater suggests that Erdrich's novels engage the familiar discourse of "Western family saga" only to redirect it.[5] Erdrich never seems to be totally content with letting the characters speak solely for themselves. The author makes her presence known both through the voice of a third-person omniscient narrator and in her use of highly structured images that resonate symbolically through each section, especially those that close each section. Robert Silberman posits that Native writers, and especially Erdrich, in their attempts to move writing toward storytelling, have been developing "conventions of the oral," conventions every bit as necessary for generation of the text as the conventions of realism or naturalism.[6] He identifies the use of a dramatic present tense and the occasional address to the reader with the second-person pronoun "you." But an examination of oral tradition would quickly add many more elements to the list. Erdrich's constant switching from past to present tense, her shifts from omniscient to first-person narration, her episodic structure, her use of dialect, and her use of foreshadowing and flashbacks provide an evocative rendition of a traditional storyteller's art.

However, it is also clear that what we have is a novel, a Western structure, whose task it is to re-create something of a Native oral tradition. Erdrich uses a Western field of discourse to arrive at a Native perspective and illuminates the conventions, significations, assumptions, and strengths of both as she does so. In adopting oral features for her novel, her goal is not to be a traditional storyteller, nor is it merely to add a sense of immediacy to her novel. Rather, her primary purpose is to position both audiences to accept an oral discourse whose codes she can mediate. Through this mediation, she shows both audiences how to value contemporary Native ways of meaning and thereby contemporary Native cultures—the ultimate sources of value in the novel.

Humorous examples of the oral style of Erdrich's mediation in *Love Medicine* are found in Lipsha Morrissey's malapropisms. Lipsha, who has taken some college classes, alternates, as Albertine tells us, between using "words I had to ask him the meaning of" and not making "the simplest sense."[7] Lipsha's malapropisms, such as when he refers to "mental condensation" (199) when he means concentration, or when he says he was in a "laundry" (192) when he means quandary, reveal his lack of familiarity with a vocabulary that is learned from reading rather than from conversation.[8] Yet Lipsha can also turn around and use the vocabulary of conversation to create an illuminating metaphor. At a moment when death surrounds him, Lipsha likens his revelations about himself and the world to a video game: "You play those games never knowing what you see. When I fell into the dream alongside both of them [Grandpa and Grandma Kashpaw] I saw that the dominions I had defended myself from anciently was but delusions of the screen. Blips of light. And I was scot-free now, whistling through space" (210). His mediational style of expression reveals Erdrich's concern with embedding every level of epistemological double-code and with engaging a number of discourse fields at once. Lipsha enters traditional religious discourse and, at the same time, employs contemporary Indian humor and the discourse of pop culture.[9]

If one considers the larger goals of this mediational process, much of the richness of the text emerges. Central to a Chippewa worldview, and that of much of Native America, is a sense of the reciprocal nature of the relationships between human beings and the spiritual powers that activate the world. A person's actions in the natural world have spiritual repercussions. For instance, an Eskimo elder, worried about the actions of his people and the response of the spirit world, once said, "No bears have come because there is no ice, and there is no ice because there is no wind, and there is no wind because we have offended the powers."[10] The reciprocal relationship between human beings and nature, and between human beings and the spirit world, is also portrayed in *Love Medicine*. In the novel, the survival of individuals is the function of a reciprocal relationship that they establish with the spiritual powers of the universe. The touch that Lipsha loses and regains, or Gordie's relationship with June, are examples of negotiations for survival with the universe in which they participate. Erdrich seems to be assuming the complete interpenetration of the tangible and intangible worlds. Much Native American thought assumes that mental and physical phenomena are inseparable, and that thought and speech can deeply influence a natural world in which no circumstance is accidental or free from personalized intent. As Paula Gunn Allen writes:

> It is reasonable that all literary forms should be interrelated, given the basic idea of the unity and relatedness of all the phenomena of life. Separation of parts into this or that category is not agreeable to American Indians, and the attempt to separate essentially unified phenomena results in distortion. . . .
>
> The purpose of a ceremony is to integrate: to fuse the individual with his or her fellows, the community of people with that of the other kingdoms, and this larger communal group with the worlds beyond this one.[11]

With their emphasis on ceremony, Native Americans unify the various levels of meaning that Western non-Natives tend to separate. This unity of experience is what Joseph Epes Brown refers to as "a polysynthetic metaphysic of nature."[12] Erdrich merges this Native sense of multiple levels of meaning for each physical act with a powerful belief in the mystery of events. What begins on a physical level may start to take on a larger significance, but Erdrich leaves the connections mysterious. These mysterious connections show both the characters and the implied readers the paths to sacred processes of the universe. For example, Nector takes Marie on a path during what appears to be a moment of heedless lust, but both are caught up in an event that defines their lives. They give themselves over to a mysterious force that shapes their spirits. Only years later do they understand something of that mystery. Understanding slowly builds in the novel as people tell us more of their stories. Events, which in Western thought would have only physical significance, take on spiritual, mythic, cultural, personal, and religious significance. As Rainwater notes, Erdrich's novels "confront the problems of origination of knowledge" (413). In them, the implied non-Native reader is coaxed "to abandon fixed notions about what kinds of experience are 'important.'" (416). New possibilities are now credible. Reciprocity between the various levels of existence ties the meaning together and helps Erdrich express a Chippewa worldview that appreciates a dynamic process of signification, or as Allen so strikingly puts it, a worldview that sees the "self as a moving event within a moving universe," a universe where "everything moves in dynamic equilibrium" (247) By encoding this alternate way of creating meaning, Erdrich challenges the implied non-Native reader.

On the other hand, Erdrich has an alternative goal: to present a complementary vision of individual will and history that is more psychologically based than communally oriented. The effects of Nector's actions on those around him, the exploration of Marie in terms of her relationship to the nun, Sister Leopolda, and King's vision of his life all suggest a psychological dimension that uses dominant-culture conceptual categories. Moreover, the novel clearly displays a sociological agenda, as illustrated by its treatment of such themes as changes in family structure and the influences on the reservation of the dominant society, especially its Christian segment. The implied Native reader is encouraged to perceive levels of text such as these in terms of Western analysis.

This use of both cognitive systems to illuminate each other supports Bakhtin's understanding of the novel's task: a "coming to know one's own belief system in someone else's system." As Hayden White has pointed out, this is a self-reflexive act, one wherein the reader's personal involvement is demanded in the process of reading and misreading the text.[13] In creating meaning, both implied readers will reevaluate their own system and each other's. This process is integral to Erdrich's goals as a "citizen of two nations."[14] Sands observes: "There is a sort of double-think demanded by Erdrich. The incidents must be carried in the reader's mind, constantly reshuffled and reinterpreted as new events are revealed and the narrative biases of each character are exposed" (18). Rainwater sees the text as maneuvering the reader into a position "between worlds," which frustrates one's expectations of Western narrativity: "This frustration amounts to a textually induced or encoded experience of marginality as the foremost component of the reader's response" (406). From this position, the reader will be required to "consider perceptual frameworks as the important structural principles in both textual and nontextual realms" (412). Ultimately the reader's new perceptual position allows him or her to consider the possibility that "the world takes on the shapes of the stories we tell" (422).[15] Both Rainwater and Sands emphasize the deep level restructuring required of the implied non-Native reader.

One example of how these two perceptual frameworks merge in the text lies in the portrayal of Henry Lamartine. According to a Western set of epistemological codes, he is clearly a prototype of the displaced soldier returning home; the reader can easily respond to his situation with the commonplace insight that the experience of combat often destroys the soldier's sense of reality, making it difficult if not impossible for him to reintegrate himself back into society. We know this by looking at the chronological series of events in Henry's life, drawing a set of inferences based on causal reasoning. When he dies, we are not surprised because we have drawn a straight line from the shattering experience early in his life to his inevitable death. We have seen many stories like this; the ending is a convention of stories of returned veterans. However, Henry's story seems more socially complex when both implied readers also consider that his war was the Vietnam War, with all its political controversy and high number of minority participants. With these non-Native social and psychological codes giving meaning to the events of Henry's life, the implied non-Native reader has an easy-to-read, satisfying text, complete with closure. When Lyman drives the red convertible into the river after Henry has drowned, the psychological orientation of the implied non-Native reader encourages the conclusions that Henry committed suicide and that Lyman wished to make the suicide look like an accident in order to save his brother's reputation.

However, a Native perspective leads to a different interpretation of events. Henry's inability to resume normal life at home and his subsequent death can be seen as resulting from the fact that his actions are out of harmony with the Chippewa sense of war, death, honor, and right thinking. As a draftee, Henry has no choice in his actions. He does not go off to war with a vision that will give him power, nor does he dance the warrior's dance. He has not participated in any ritual actions that will let the souls of his dead enemies rest.[16] In the one wartime action of Henry's that we learn about, he is ordered to interrogate a dying woman who claims the bond of relationship with him. His implication in the death of a relative puts him in conflict with Chippewa cultural values. He is not prepared ritually for his departure for war, he breaks the bonds of kinship, and, because his mother is afraid to take him to the old medicine man, he is not purified of the spirits of dead enemies when he returns. At the end of the chapter entitled "The Red Convertible," Henry's renewal of interest in his brother and in the wild dance seems to undercut the possibility of psychologically motivated suicide. His one comment as he stands in the water—"My boots are filling up"—does not have the purposeful ring of someone who is committing suicide. Perhaps his drowning, which is performed in an unpurified state, can be understood as a response to Henry's improper behavior by the spiritual forces of the world around us—the water spirits' revenge.[17] As the balance is set right again, Lyman's driving of the car into the river represents the custom of burying the dead person's private possessions along with him.

Each of these two perspectives on the meaning of the character Henry has a certain level of completeness, yet the novel's richness is revealed when each story, each narrative viewpoint, is seen in contrast to the other. Since each perspective creates a coherent and meaningful story, implied readers are given a chance to experience complementary meaning structures. Yet their differences encourage a self-reflexive examination of familiar patterns of thought as the legitimacy of other forms becomes clear.

The psychological interpretation underlies and enriches the cultural one. As Michael Dorris has remarked, he and Erdrich are always concerned with giving "the readers a choice" between a "mystical reason" and "a more psychological explanation" ("Conversation"). Both stories' realities present valid worldviews and can stand alone to explain the meaning of the actions, yet each level of the text forces us to question exactly what we, as readers, believe. Can both be right? Can one be right and the other wrong? It seems clear that each reveals the strengths and weaknesses of the other code. An understanding of one level enhances our understanding of the other.

The use of one cultural code to illuminate the other is best shown in Erdrich's treatment of ghosts in *Love Medicine*. Although ghosts are a very real part of the Chippewa worldview, they are not believed to be often troubling to the living if dealt with properly. Ruth Landes observes that death still was a time of great danger, when careful action was required of the people: "The passage from life was considered tricky, beset with personified evils intent on murdering the wandering soul."[18] But the proper instructions and recommendations delivered over a grave would assure the soul's passage to the village of shadows. Conventional Western thought does not consider ghosts as real. Although we allow them entrance into our world through literature, especially children's tales, ghosts are generally considered to be a storytelling convention with no substance. So when Gordie sees June's ghost, a reader whose orientations are Western will not see the encounter as real but will instead see it as a delusion brought on by alcohol and grief. That in his drunken frenzy Gordie should hit a deer and mistake it for June has no meaning other than as a revelation of his psychological state of mind; it does not seem surprising that at the end of the encounter with Sister Mary Martin, he should end up running mad in the woods. However, in the traditional Chippewa worldview, the spirit world is the source of special insight and power. Human and non-human beings can be transformed to assume a variety of appearances. A. Irving Hallowell, in discussing Ojibwa worldview, notes: "Both living and dead human beings may assume the form of animals. So far as appearance is concerned, there is no hard and fast line that can be drawn between animal form and human form because metamorphosis is possible."[19]

According to traditional Chippewa custom, a dead wife's returning to visit the husband who abused her would not be surprising, especially if she has not been buried in the appropriate manner. At the time of her death, June was unable to complete her journey home. Her ghostly visit to Gordie completes her return but also allows her wandering spirit to find the path to the spirit world. She visits Gordie because he has called her name and thus violated one of the most important prohibitions designed to keep the spirits of the dead on the trail to the spirit world. It is understandable that June would use a deer to aid her visit, as the spirits of animals are much closer to the world of the spirit than humans are, and the cultural perception of the deer as a willing prey adds ironic resonance. When Gordie clubs the deer with the tire iron, it is an action reminiscent of the times he hit his wife when she was alive. Therefore his confession to the nun that he has killed June carries a ring of ironic truth and becomes more than the baseless ravings of a crazed drunk; he provides for implied Native readers insight into how actions can take place on an other-than-human plane. Indeed, Victor Barnouw, in his discussion of Chippewa oral narratives, observes the importance of "the notion that visible forms are deceptive and that human and animal forms are interchangeable."[20] Such a Chippewa epistemological position clearly informs many of the events in the text.

The return of Nector Kashpaw's ghost also expresses the text's mediational positioning. The suddenness of Nector's death deprives him of the chance to say good-bye to the two women he loves. Lipsha and Marie observe that when ghosts return they have a "certain uneasy reason to come back" (212). He visits Lulu, Lipsha, and Marie until he is persuaded to go back to the spirit world by Lipsha, who has accidentally killed him. Nector's visit cannot be explained away, as in Gordie's case, as a drunken hallucination. Psychologically, we can explain the presence of the ghost as being a figment of the women's imagination under the stress of grief. However, even by Western epistemological standards, three independent visits observed by three independent observers come dangerously close to constituting corroborated reality. However, the reality they tend to corroborate is one in which Western tradition places no credence. Yet in Chippewa religious thought, the concept of a return to life is central. Barnouw notes that this concept is "implicit in the Midewiwin ceremony, in which members shoot one another with their medicine hides but come back to life again" (252). Lipsha comments on the puzzling interaction of the human and spirit worlds: "Whether or not he had been there is not the point. She had *seen* him, and that meant anyone else could see him, too. Not only that but, as is usually the case with these here ghosts, he had a certain uneasy reason to come back. And of course Grandma Kashpaw had scanned it out" (212).

Lipsha's comments convey both readers' attitudes toward the reality of ghosts and thus validate each worldview and epistemological framework. On the one hand, he seems to say that it might not matter if the ghost were real, since it was real to Grandma in her altered psychological state. On the other hand, Lipsha also says that if she saw him, others could see him—a statement that attributes to the ghost an objective reality. When he refers to the ghost's motivation in coming back, he shows that his own belief in the existence of the spirit world and of ghosts is undisturbed. There is no question that the ghost was there, because his spirit is still around; the problem is not that he cannot, but rather that he *can* be seen and that he refuses to let go of this world. The ghost needs to be instructed as to what to do, and Lipsha's admonition to Nector's ghost to return to the company of the spirits parallels recorded Midewiwin orations to the dead.

The thrust of such mediational discourse is to take a Western issue of nontruth—or nonreality—and treat it with the assumptions of Chippewa reality while layering psychological motivation and Native custom. Each code is used and illuminates the other. The end result of Erdrich's technique is that both implied readers are forced to look at the multiple meanings of an event. And both implied readers must hold all these versions of reality together in some meaningful mediational structure. As Sands points out: "It is, of course, the very method of the novel, individuals telling individual stories, that not only creates the multiple effect of the novel but requires a mediator, the reader, to bring the episodes together" (20). These implied readers must follow the text so as to mediate between stories, cultural codes, definitions of identity, and versions of reality.

Clearly, the two sets of cultural codes produce a doubling of narrative textures as distinct as the two implied readers Erdrich tries to reach. Each implied reader is satisfied in many ways, but primarily by the developing sense of identity as the implied readers animate the emerging characters. The contemporary survivors that Erdrich depicts are people for whom navigating change and defining identity are vitally important ways to protect and celebrate individual and cultural values. Since both audiences experience the variety of culturally framed definitions of identity, part of the ideological translation of which Bakhtin wrote is accomplished. Both implied readers must actively work to read the narratives in a unified manner, never completely sure they are reading it right or reading it completely. This active, self-reflexive role of the implied readers in Erdrich's mediation is required when they begin to understand the multiple narratives through which she achieves ideological translation. Sands observes: "The novel places the reader simultaneously on the fringe of the story yet at the very center of the process—distant and intimate, passive yet very actively involved in the narrative process" (12). An implied reader can feel distant from one story reality while intimate with another, appreciating an identity for a character while experiencing a new sense of identity in a different narrative for that same character. Rainwater explains that while Erdrich's texts suggest traditional Western definitions of identity, they "are also traversed by a conflicting code which has to do with American Indian concepts of individuation that are not based on psychological essence or individual psychology" (421).[21]

Returning to Henry Lamartine for a moment will clarify the functioning of multiple narrative in *Love Medicine*. How does a reader define Henry's identity? Surely his identity can be defined sociologically when he is seen as a shell-shocked veteran unable to adjust to the world back home, but as I have suggested, he can also be seen as a warrior haunted by the ghosts of his dead enemies that he cannot expel ritualistically. Through this latter perspective, Henry is given a communal role, an identity based on his relation to the community and family as a young warrior and dutiful son. Each sense of identity satisfies its appropriate audience, but also, because both implied readers hold at once two senses of identity, the text validates both perspectives. Even more central to the novel are the stories that define Nector's identity. Nector comes from a family that is "respected as the last hereditary leaders of this tribe" (89). His communal identity is set from the beginning, and much of his life is an attempt to live up to that identity, to understand it and grow into it. The Kashpaw sense of worth and the Chippewa tradition constitute the essence of how Nector sees himself. Socially, he is the tribal chairman. Whereas the dominant culture would assume that this status places him as the leader of his tribe, tribal custom does not give him that role unless he can live up to the traditional function of the leader. Nector's psychological sense of identity as someone with no control over events, however, undermines this Western social definition as leader in much the same way his communal role as a Kashpaw supports it. He is both a communal leader and a follower because, as he says, "Chippewa politics was thorns in my jeans" (102).

Psychologically, Nector sees himself as floating down a river that has calm spots, rapids, and unexpected branchings. His sense of himself is that of a person being carried along by events as he struggles to maintain control of them. Nector's retreat to apparent senility becomes a way in which he can finally completely define himself in the midst of the river flow of emotions and the demands of politics. Lulu recognizes the essential psychological truth of who he is when she says, "People said Nector Kashpaw had changed, but the truth was he'd just become more like himself than ever" (230). Various layers of Nector's identity created by the narrative are embedded in the text and held simultaneously in dialogic interaction by both implied readers.

Marie Lazarre has an identity defined by the community as one of those "dirty Lazarres." Despite her attempts to re-create this identity, the community has defined her role and position in its complex structure. This communal identity is contrasted with her psychological identity as molder of Nector, as defeater of Sister Leopolda, as woman defined by her household. These two senses of identity complement each other. Though she contends to herself, "I was solid class" (113), the sociological level remains mostly latent. As wife of the tribal chairman, her social position should be one of leadership, but her communal identity as "a dirty Lazarre" deprives her of this status. As a wife who is left at home during an ongoing extramarital relationship, her sense of a sociological identity is also undercut. While as a woman who takes in lost children, she performs a social function that helps her clarify her sense of self on the psychological and communal level, she is unable to allow this to help her develop a clearly defined social identity.

Lulu Lamartine plays the communal role of the libertine. As a woman with eight boys and one girl who are fathered by a variety of husbands, she is hated by the wives in the community and loved by their husbands. Though a disrupter of families, her own family is vitally important to her. Her identity as libertine is in contrast to her psychological identity as consummate lover of beauty. After a grisly look at death in her early childhood, she comes to define herself as someone "in love with the whole world and all that lived in its rainy arms" (216). What is viewed from the communal realm as irresponsible action is, for Lulu, an honest attempt to drink in beauty and let it fill her up, if only for a moment. Each sense of identity enriches the reader's understanding of the other and encourages the audiences to clarify their codes.

Whereas, in the other characters discussed, Erdrich has developed something of the psychological, social, and communal stories, in her portrayal of Gerry Nanapush she displays all four levels of narrative identity. On a sociological level, he is the convict-Indian turned political hero. As a member of the American Indian movement, he is seen and sees himself as a social symbol to both the non-Native and the Native worlds, but one who believes in justice, not laws. On a psychological level, he is presented as a loving husband and father; as such, Gerry is motivated by personal passions. His communal identity hinges on his relationships as son of Old Man Pillager and Lulu Lamartine, lover of June Morrissey, and father to Lipsha Morrissey. As warrior against the social institutions of modern America, Gerry presents the community with an image through which it can project itself as successful and yet evasive, the image of an unwilling warrior who is not destroyed by the spirit of dead enemies, however all-pervasive and overpowering they may be. Yet on a more timeless plane, his actions recall the daring and rebellion of the trickster Nanabosho of Chippewa oral tradition. His magical escapes enhance Chippewa cultural identity while they add to his own idea of himself. Gerry consciously takes on a mythic role and becomes a living embodiment of the trickster.

Lipsha's character is the most obvious expression of the four kinds of narrative identity. Sociologically, he is the outcast orphan with no clear parentage. He cares for the aged Nector and Marie out of gratitude but also out of lethargy. His role as orphan and care provider involves a series of social relations that define him but against which he struggles. Psychologically, his desire is to find for himself a place in the family that coincides with the unique individual he senses that he is. He sees himself as needing to stay innocent and simple, but he also wants to know about his roots and his background. As Lulu says, "Well, I never thought you was odd. . . . Just troubled. You never knew who you were" (244–45).

Communally, Lipsha is a healer, grandson of the powerful old shaman, Old Man Pillager. Although his "touch" has been commonly acknowledged on the reservation, his identity as a member of the tribe, with clear family ties and a useful function in the community, has not been acknowledged. After he learns of his true parentage, he confusedly tries to join the army and become a warrior like his father, Gerry Nanapush. However, it is not on the battlefields of the U.S. Army that he will fight, but on the battlefields of culture and community. By the end of the novel, he learns that he is defined by his family and communal position: "Now as you know, as I have told you, I am sometimes blessed with the talent to touch the sick and heal their individual problems without ever knowing what they are. I have some powers which, now that I think of it, was likely come down from Old Man Pillager. And then there is the newfound fact of insight I inherited from Lulu, as well as the familiar teachings of Grandma Kashpaw on visioning what comes to pass within a lump of tinfoil" (248). With his new realizations comes a new understanding of communal identity.

Ultimately, however, Lipsha emerges as the son of trickster Gerry. His mythic identity is linked to the tradition of the powerful trickster/transformer whose job it is to create the form of the world, to modify its contours in keeping with the Earthmaker's plans. Lipsha's medicine trick with the turkey hearts, in keeping with the nature of a trickster's actions, proves to be an event that backfires on him. But this is an event that also is in keeping with the Earthmaker's plan for all beings. Kenneth Lincoln identifies a Western mythic analogue for Lipsha: "His is the ancient story of the orphan adopted and finally reclaimed by true royalty (June and Gerry as queen and king tricksters). In a comic way, Lipsha figures as the 'divine child' of ancient myth" (230). By engaging both Native and non-Native mythic discourse, Erdrich directs the reader's attention to the importance of mythic identity, a decidedly Native epistemological perspective.

Finally, by driving Gerry to freedom, Lipsha concludes a mythic narrative that will live forever in Chippewa imagination. At the bridge, Lipsha physically delivers the trickster Gerry Nanapush to Canada, but this act also takes on communal significance when it is remembered that for many Midewiwin initiates the land of the dead is also called Nehnehbush's land and that the passage from the physical world to the spirit world is made over a bridge.[22] After Lipsha delivers Gerry to the world of myth, he takes June's wandering soul in hand and prepares to lead her, as he did Nector, to her proper resting place. These actions show us that his identity will be both defined communally as something akin to a Midewiwin official, a healer, and mythically as a new reincarnation of Nehnehbush.

Lipsha concludes that "belonging is a matter of deciding to" (255). This existential realization unifies who he is on the psychological, sociological, communal, and mythic levels; Lipsha thus becomes a complete human being—an experienced adult, a loving son, a healer, and a trickster/transformer. He feels all the threads of identity intertwining and forming a pattern: "In that night I felt expansion, as if the world was branching out in shoots and growing faster than the eye could see. I felt smallness, how the earth divided into bits and kept dividing. I felt stars. I felt them roosting on my shoulders with his hands" (271). Feeling Nanapush's touch still on his shoulder, Lipsha is transformed in a moment of splendid mythic vision. Because he is a new complete human, he thinks of June Morrissey and is strong enough to bring her home, to help her, to help all of the characters in the novel, and to help himself complete a journey started long ago.

By guiding the reader into experiencing this cosmic unifying vision, Erdrich achieves the ultimate goal of most contemporary Native American literature. As the text embeds the multiple narrative, it compels the implied readers into the same perspective that Lipsha experiences, a perspective from which an individual's perception is expanded and multiple connections are revealed. Lipsha and the other characters of *Love Medicine* embrace the mystery of the world, where knowledge, meaning, truth, and signification already exist in a nontangible realm—one that Whorf calls "manifesting."[23] The characters of *Love Medicine* perceive the world as constantly in the process of becoming what it always was; they see meaning in their lives and the world revealing itself, manifesting what has always been there, much in the same way that meaning in Lipsha's life involves the process of letting the forces at work in the world manifest themselves. In *Love Medicine*, Erdrich succeeds in opening the epistemological perspective of the implied non-Native reader to create a more Native American appreciation of meaning and knowledge, one that values the manifesting over the manifested. Implied Native readers, in turn, are positioned to value Western perspectives on meaning.

Erdrich's achievement is to shift the paradigm of both implied readers' thoughts, to recharge implied Native readers and inspire implied non-Native readers with an appreciation of Native American epistemology and worldview. As the text opens its mysteries to these readers, perception expands beyond the boundaries of the text, overcoming otherness, and the universe reveals itself as timeless and mythic.

Notes

1. Kenneth Lincoln, *Indi'n Humor: Bicultural Play in Native America* (New York: Oxford University Press, 1993), 216. Subsequent references to this book will be identified by parenthetical page numbers in the text.

2. Mikhail M. Bakhtin, *The Dialogic Imagination*, translated by Caryl Emerson and Michael Holquist, edited by Michael Holquist (Austin: University of Texas Press, 1981), 365. Subsequent references to this book will be identified by parenthetical page numbers in the text.

3. Scott Sanders, "Review of *Love Medicine*," *Studies in American Indian Literatures* 9.1 (Winter 1985): 7.

4. Kathleen Sands, "*Love Medicine*: Voices and Margins," *Studies in American Indian Literatures* 9.1 (Winter 1985): 14. Subsequent references to this essay will be identified by parenthetical page numbers in the text.

5. Catherine Rainwater, "Reading between Worlds: Narrativity in the Fiction

of Louise Erdrich," *American Literature* 62.3 (1990): 418. Subsequent references to this essay will be identified by parenthetical page numbers in the text.

6. Robert Silberman, "Opening the Text: *Love Medicine* and the Return of the Native American Woman," in *Narrative Chance: Postmodern Discourse on Native American Indian Literatures*, edited by Gerald Vizenor (Albuquerque: University of New Mexico Press, 1989), 118.

7. Louise Erdrich, *Love Medicine* (1984 New York: Bantam Books, 1987), 36. Subsequent references to the novel will be identified by parenthetical page numbers in the text.

8. See Kenneth Lincoln for a discussion of humor built on oral sources (*Indi'n Humor*, 20–53).

9. In *Indi'n Humor*, Lincoln quotes Erdrich as saying that Indian readers appreciate much of the humor of her book that non-Indian readers miss (239).

10. Quoted in Alfonso Ortiz, "American Indian Philosophy," in *Indian Voices: the First Convocation of American Indian Scholars* (San Francisco: Indian Historian Press, 1970), 18.

11. Paula Gunn Allen, *The Sacred Hoop: Recovering the Feminine in American Indian Traditions* (Boston: Beacon Press, 1986), 62. Subsequent references to this book will be identified by parenthetical page numbers in the text.

12. Joseph Epes Brown, "The Roots of Renewal," in *Seeing with a Native Eye: Essays on Native American Religion* edited by Walter H. Capps (New York: Harper and Row, 1976), 30. Brown is in particular discussing Native American attitudes toward place, but as he develops his idea, he acknowledges multiple spirits as well as the existence of a universal principle. Consequently, he is forced to define this multiple experiencing of levels of reality. He also discusses the idea of the unity of all being and things.

13. Hayden White, *The Tropics of Discourse: Essays in Cultural Criticism* (Baltimore: Johns Hopkins University Press, 1978), 4.

14. Erdrich may have had an interesting exposure to this "double think." In a television interview with Bill Moyers, Erdrich remembers that her "grandfather was the last person in our family who spoke Ojibwa." His mixture of cultures and epistemologies influenced her, because he "really had a sense of what it was like to grow up before so many changes. . . . He was very Catholic" but prayed in Chippewa. "When I'd be with him, I'd question everything. I felt an entirely different way about religion." Erdrich knew that he used "the very old beliefs that he had to make sense of things." When asked if these beliefs still influenced her, she hesitates, acknowledging that they are part of her but so "subterranean, that probably it comes out mainly in the writing. . . . I'm not sure." ("A Conversation with Louise Erdrich and Michael Dorris," *A World of Ideas with Bill Moyers* PBS. WNET, New York: 1990. Subsequent references to this videotaped interview will be identified in the text.)

15. In her otherwise valuable article, Rainwater does not consider the re-

sponses of a Native reader, nor acknowledge that the existence of such an audience might influence not only the text but also the nature of the marginalization required of the reader. For her, the final position of the disempowered reader is one of equating story and reality. However, this is not a "between worlds" position that resists "any interpretative urge which is founded on epistemological or theological certainty" (413). Rather, the point that she misses is that it is a more Native epistemological position; it protects the core of culture.

16. In various works Ruth Landes discusses the necessity of vision, religious preparation, and continual discussion of spiritual purpose for a successful war party. Landes also notes that some Ojibwa contend that the souls of warriors who had been scalped or beheaded were prone to wander the land between the human world and the ghost village. Other writers have commented that the souls of those who have drowned must also wander forever.

17. For information on water spirits, see both Annette Van Dyke, "Questions of the Spirit: Bloodlines in Louise Erdrich's Chippewa Landscape," *Studies in American Indian Literatures* 4.1 (1992): 15–27 and Christopher Vecsey, *Traditional Ojibwa Religion and Its Historical Changes* (Philadelphia: The American Philosophical Society, 1983).

18. Ruth Landes, *Ojibway Religion and the Midewiwin* (Madison: University of Wisconsin Press, 1968), 87–88. Subsequent references to this book will be identified by parenthetical page numbers in the text.

19. A. Irving Hallowell, "Ojibway Ontology, Behavior, and World View," *Culture in History: Essays in Honor of Paul Radin* edited by Stanley Diamond (New York: Columbia University Press, 1960), 38.

20. Victor Barnouw, *Wisconsin Chippewa Myths and Tales and Their Relation to Chippewa Life* (Madison: University of Wisconsin Press, 1977), 247. Barnouw also notes the "curious equation between hunting and courting" in Chippewa language and social custom (248). Subsequent references to this book will be identified by parenthetical page numbers in the text.

21. I agree with Rainwater here, but not with her view that the code of identity is based on natural elements. Claims Rainwater, "Especially in *Love Medicine*, characters are formed through various syntagmatic series of references to natural elements such as air, earth, fire, and water" (421). This seems to me as tantamount to equating Native American concepts of identity with ancient Greek philosophy. Closer to my point is Jeanne Smith's insight that "in *Love Medicine*, characters build identity on transpersonal connections to community, to landscape, and to myth" ("Transpersonal Selfhood: The Boundaries of Identity in Louise Erdrich's *Love Medicine*," *Studies in American Indian Literatures* 3.4 [1991]: 13), though Keith Basso, Robin Riddington, and others have also shown that identity connections to landscape are created in the context of community and myth.

22. The name of the trickster varies in much of Chippewa literature. Landes records it as Nehnehbush (193–99).

23. Benjamin Lee Whorf, "An American Indian Model of the Universe," in *Teachings from the American Earth: Indian Religion and Philosophy* edited by Dennis and Barbara Tedlock (New York: Liveright, 1975), 121–29.

Louise Erdrich's *Love Medicine*

Narrative Communities and the Short Story Cycle

HERTHA D. SWEET WONG

◆ ◆ ◆

LOUISE ERDRICH'S *Love Medicine* (1984)[1] is most often classified as a novel. In fact, if we have any doubts about its genre, the title page informs us: "*Love Medicine*: A Novel by Louise Erdrich." When asked what they thought about the fact that some reviewers of the "novel" insisted on labeling it a "collection of short stories," Erdrich and her husband-collaborator Michael Dorris were not particularly interested in the topic. "It's a novel in that it all moves toward some sort of resolution," explained Erdrich. "It has a large vision that no one of the stories approaches," added Dorris.[2] In addition, even though half of the fourteen chapters of the first edition had been published previously as short stories in literary journals or popular magazines, Erdrich and Dorris insisted that they had adapted these individual stories significantly in order to create, extend, or enhance thematic, structural, and other literary connections.[3] Erdrich, who describes herself as "a person who thought in terms of stories and poems and short-things," credits Dorris's influence for how the "book became a novel."[4] "By the time readers get half-way through the book," noted Dorris, "it should be clear to them that this is not an unrelated, or even a related, set of short stories, but parts of a larger scheme" (Wong, 212). Length, an expansive vision, and some sense of unity seem to inform their notion of what constitutes a novel.

It was surprising, then, to find little difference between the chapters of

Love Medicine and the short stories published earlier. At least two of the seven published short stories, "Love Medicine" (which becomes the "Flesh and Blood" chapter in *Love Medicine*) and "Lulu's Boys," were essentially the same as they appeared in the novel, except no narrators or dates were announced as they are at the beginning of each chapter in the collection. In fact, added to two of the story titles, very likely by an editor, was the descriptive label "a short story." Similarly, "Saint Marie" had only minor syntactic and word changes, but everything else was the same. In "Scales," the editing was more extensive, but still not substantial. In addition to minor alterations in word choice, phrasing, and punctuation, Dot's five-month pregnancy became a six-month pregnancy, and her baby boy was transformed into a baby girl. Although the gender switch is dramatic, it does nothing to unify the narratives in *Love Medicine*. Why, then, does Dorris say that at first they were "a series of stories," but in "the last several drafts we went back and tied them together" (Coltelli, 43)? The distinction between a collection of short stories and a novel remains somewhat elusive.

Certainly novels appeal to a larger market and generate greater prestige than short stories or poems. Perhaps the Erdrich-Dorris revisions refer simply to a Jamesian type of reenvisioning. Placing the short stories between the covers of a book encourages the reader to note their juxtaposition, association, and overall relation to one another. But what narrative theorists, particularly those focusing on the difficult-to-define "short story," have been postulating about *collections* of short stories complicates definitive notions of the genre and provides another vocabulary for this discussion. *Love Medicine* is neither a novel, if by novel we insist on a continuous and unified narrative, nor a collection of unrelated short stories. Nor is it a "short story composite," a "short story compound," or even an "integrated short story collection," since these definitions emphasize the autonomy of each story within a collection more than the particular dynamism created by their organization and juxtaposition.[5] The series of narratives in *Love Medicine* may very well be, though, what Forrest Ingram refers to as a "short story cycle" or what Robert Luscher calls "the short story sequence."

A short story cycle, explains Ingram, is "a set of short stories linked to each other in such a way as to maintain balance between the individuality of each of the stories and the necessities of the larger unit." In addition, the reader's experience of each story is modified by the experience of all the others. Ingram proposes a narrative spectrum with the "collection of unconnected stories" on one end, the novel on the other end, and the short story cycle balanced between them. Outlining the parameters of the short story cycle itself, Ingram delineates three basic types: a *composed* cycle (the most tightly structured), a series of linked stories "conceived as a whole from the time" of the "first story"; an *arranged* cycle (the most loosely structured), stories "brought together to illuminate or comment upon one another by juxtaposition and association"; and a *completed* cycle, stories formed into a set by adding, revising, and rearranging them.[6] Within Ingram's tripartite categories (problematically organized according to the process of composition, as Gerald Kennedy notes), *Love Medicine* most closely resembles a completed cycle because Erdrich and Dorris neither planned the whole narrative network from the first story nor simply assembled and arranged a collection of stories, but added new stories and at least slightly revised earlier ones.

Whereas Ingram's framework highlights *Love Medicine*'s construction, Luscher's notion of "the short story sequence" may more fully delineate its structure, both the form constructed by the writer and that structure experienced (or co-created) by the reader. According to Luscher, the short story sequence is "a volume of stories, collected and organized by their author, in which the reader successively realizes underlying patterns of coherence by continual modifications of his [or her] perceptions of pattern and theme" (148–49). Thus the reader becomes aware of "a network of associations that binds the stories together and lends them cumulative thematic impact" (148–49). Although it seems that similar claims can be made for chapters in a novel (and the reader's sequential experience of reading them), the distinction is that, unlike the chapters in a novel, each narrative unit can stand on its own. Its meaning is modified and enriched, however, in proximity to other stories.

But how can a short story sequence accommodate Native American narratives, which are often associated with a communal narrator and a nonlinear sense of time? The notion of a sequence assumes or imposes linearity on the inherent nonlinearity of multivoiced, achronological narrative. With no singular point of view or authoritative narrative voice to unify a collection of short stories, without a straightforward chronology to connect the narrative action over time, a sequence may not reflect the structure of many Native American short story clusters as precisely as it charts the experience of reading the collection, one story following another. The image of a web or a constellation of short stories might more accurately reflect the cyclical and recursive nature of stories that are informed by both modernist literary strategies (for instance, multiple narrative voices) and oral traditions (such as a storyteller's use of repetition, recurrent development, and associational structure).[7]

In numerous Native American oral traditions, the spider's web is a common image to convey the interconnectedness of all aspects of life. Just as one individual filament cannot be touched without sending vibrations throughout the entire network, one story, although it can be read in isolation from the others, cannot be fully comprehended without considering its connection to the whole. Such an interrelationship is fundamental to oral traditions, in which a storyteller and an audience create a community, a "web of responsibility," as Henry Glassie calls it.[8] Many scholars have lamented (or at least noted) the loss of the intimacy of direct human contact when stories moved from storyteller to text, from voice to print, from cycle to sequence, from interactive to isolated experience. But many Native American writers have been engaged in a counter movement, re-creating the spoken word in written form, suggesting (even rekindling) a relationship between writer/teller and reader/listener, and restoring voice to their histories and communities. In particular, Erdrich's story cycles chronicle the centrality of one's relationships, tenuous though they may be, with one's land, community, and family, and the power of these relationships, enlivened by memory and imagination and shaped into narrative, to resist colonial domination and cultural loss and to (re)construct personal identity and communal history on one's own terms.

The novel, in its construction of a multivocal unity from various modes of discourse, may be the fundamental expression of the pluralism embedded in language, as Mikhail Bakhtin suggests, but Native American oral traditions have long reflected such inherent polyvocality. Paula Gunn Allen has noted that many Native American traditional literatures have "the tendency to distribute value evenly among various elements," reflecting an "egalitarian," rather than a hierarchical, organization of society and literature. In such a narrative structure, "no single element is foregrounded" (*Sacred Hoop,* 240–41). This organization is particularly notable in *Love Medicine,* whose multiple narrators confound conventional Western expectations of an autonomous protagonist, a dominant narrative voice, and a consistently chronological linear narrative. In some indigenous oral traditions, "the presence in narratives of regularly occurring elements that are structured in definable, regularly occurring ways, employed to culturally defined ends and effects," is what determines a work's category.[9] That is, variable but measured repetition of narrative features (in a specific cultural context), not chronology, character development, or a narrative voice (for a general reader), is what may sometimes shape a story type. But if we insist, for instance, on isolating a protagonist in *Love Medicine,* it would most likely be the community itself. For many Native American writers, such a collective protagonist does not reflect fragmentation, alienation, or deterioration of an individual voice, as is often suggested by modernist and postmodernist explanations, but the traditional importance of the communal over the individual, the polyphonous over the monovocal.

Although nineteenth-century American and British novelists often experimented with multiple plots, they rarely expanded point of view, tending instead to unify the narrative action from a single narrative voice. With modernism, often associated with the disintegration of communities and the consequent alienation and fragmentation of individuals, writers fractured multiple plots into multiple narrative voices as well. Such a breakdown, exacerbated for many indigenous people by colonialism, is reflected in some early Native American novels as well, but more in theme than in form. Closer to the detailed description of realism and the narrative fatalism of naturalism than to the innovation of modernism, D'Arcy McNickle's (Cree/Salish) 1936 novel, *The Surrounded*, incorporated oral storytelling into the Western narrative model of conflict-crisis-resolution (in this case, resolution equaled surrender and destruction).

But particularly since the 1960s, Native American writers have emphasized the possibility of reconciliation along with a degree of formal experimentation (most often by combining and juxtaposing Native American and European American verbal art forms). Whereas McNickle used a standard Western singular, omniscient third-person narrator to tell the story of Archilde's alienation, contemporary Native writers often use multiple points of view. But ironically, despite a history of colonialism, Native use of multiple narrators often has little to do with alienation and loss and much more to do with the coherent multiplicity of community. What is experienced as loss of control, a breakdown of unified consciousness, an indeterminacy of language, by many non-Native Americans is a natural reflection of the interplay of difference for many Native people. After five hundred years of adaptive survival, Native writers know how to entertain difference without labeling it "Other." The task, as Erdrich describes it, is to "tell the stories of the contemporary survivors while protecting and celebrating the cores of cultures left in the wake of the catastrophe."[10]

Narrative Communities and Intratextuality

Although each of the short stories in *Love Medicine* is inextricably interrelated to a network of other stories beyond its covers, the sequence of stories within the book has its own coherence, just as each story has its own integrity. Helen Jaskoski best describes *Love Medicine's* structure as a "complex series of . . . tales, interlocking through recurrence of character and event and through variation of point of view."[11] The first edition of *Love Medicine* consists of fourteen stories (actually fifteen, if you count June's story in the first section of Chapter 1 as a separate short story, that is, as a story that can stand on its own), each narrated by a character in the first person (or, in some cases, several characters) or, less frequently, by a third-person omniscient narrator. A brief overview of the structure will help to clarify the following discussion. In general, the work is organized as the juxtaposed stories of eight narrators: Albertine Johnson, Marie (Lazarre) Kashpaw, Nector Kashpaw, Lulu Lamartine, Lipsha Morrissey, Lyman Lamartine, Howard Kashpaw, and a third-person narrator.[12] No new narrators were added to the 1993 edition unless we consider Lulu Nanapush (the young Lulu who becomes Lulu Lamartine) as a new voice. But her voice parallels that of the young Marie Lazarre (who becomes Marie Kashpaw), highlighting the proliferation of subject positions (in this case, identities at different stages) as well as voices. (See the outline at the end of this essay for an overview of narrative voices in *Love Medicine*.) Throughout the work, these narrators and their unique voices, perspectives, and uses of language convey surprising revelations about other characters as well as themselves. Their stories, like their lives, are intimately interrelated.

Certainly *Love Medicine* was not designed for the short stories to be read randomly (although with a few exceptions that would be possible). There is clearly an intended narrative sequence, not organized chronologically so much as associationally, even though the book begins in 1981 and ends in 1984. After the first chapter, the action shifts back to 1934 and from there moves progressively forward to 1984. Macroscopic unifying aspects of *Love Medicine* include a common setting (the flat, expansive farm and woodlands of North Dakota) and a set of narrators (Albertine, Marie, Nector, Lipsha, Lulu, Lyman, and Howard Kashpaw). On the microscopic or intratextual level, there are numerous connective devices, such as the repetition of the same event narrated from various perspectives, to consider as well. Patterned after spoken as well as written narrative voices, the characters tell and retell family and community stories from their particular points of view and in their own unique idioms, reflecting the polyphony of individual, family, and community voices and the subjectivity of personal and communal history.

Often, stories are embedded within stories. Family and community narratives are told and retold from different perspectives throughout the book, so that the reader is forced to integrate, interpret, and reinterpret the narrative(s). For instance, Marie's story of how she met Nector on her way down the hill from the convent is juxtaposed to Nector's version of that event in the next section. Similarly, an anecdote about one of June's childhood escapades (when the children almost hang her) is recounted several times from varying perspectives. Marie, who balances on her "stool like an oracle on her tripod" in preparation for telling the story, begins: "There was the time someone tried to hang their little cousin."[13] When Zelda and Aurelia jump into the storytelling, the story dimensions shift and sway as they are pulled now from three narrative voices. A fourth is added when the mixed-blood Albertine urges them to move the story ahead: "Then [June] got madder yet . . ." she prompts (20). Of course, none of these interpretive retellings is exactly the same, and according to Albertine, who narrates the entire storytelling session (providing a fifth perspective that organizes the others), the story of June's hanging was at one time "only a family story," but it becomes, after her death, "the private trigger of special guilts" (19). Later, in her own words, Marie, June's adoptive mother, tells the story of saving June from hanging, of punishing June for her insolence, and of learning of June's sadness, a deep, untouchable "hurt place" that was "with her all the time like a broke rib that stabbed when she breathed" (68). Often such narratives are told in isolation, each person nurturing his or her own private interpretation of events. Finally, it is only the reader who hears all the stories and can attempt to link them to a larger significance.

In addition to the incremental repetition of personal and community stories from various points of view, several repeated images—water, for example—create a structural connectivity. The recurrent imagery of water appears most often in the form of rivers (or lakes) and is associated with a series of oppositions: water can join or separate, cleanse or kill, save or erode. Flood imagery is used to describe Nector's sexual union and emotional release during his affair with Lulu. "I was full of sinkholes, shot with rapids," Nector remembers. "Climbing in her bedroom window, I rose. I was a flood that strained bridges" (100). But water also obstructs. After the violent sexual encounter between Albertine and the troubled army veteran Henry Junior, the third-person narrator describes the gulf separating them. From Henry's perspective, it seems "as if she had crossed a deep river and disappeared" (141). The flood of exuberant passion transforms into the river of separation.

As well as uniting or separating, rivers can cleanse or kill. Nector seeks to purify himself of his adulterous affair with Lulu by diving naked into the cold, deep lake, hoping to feel "a clean tug in [his] soul" before he returns home to his wife, Marie (103). But while Nector achieves at least a temporary purification by immersing himself in water, Henry Junior gains a permanent watery relief from his haunted life. Jumping into the flood-swollen river, Henry Junior announces calmly, "My boots are filling," before he goes under. Alone on the shore, his brother, Lyman, senses "only the water, the sound of it going and running and going and running and running" (154).

Similarly, rivers can save or erode. When Nector poses for the rich white woman who paints a picture of him jumping naked off a cliff, "down into a rocky river," he imagines fooling her, letting the current pull him safely to shore (91). But later, just as water erodes rock, time erodes Nector. "Time was rushing around me like water around a big, wet rock," Nector explains. "The only difference is, I was not so durable as stones. Very quickly I would be smoothed away" (94). Such an erosion of self is shared by Marie. When she thinks of "small stones" on "the bottom of the lake, rolled aimless by the waves," she sees "no kindness in how the waves are grinding them smaller and smaller until they finally disappear" (73).

Although not necessarily related to each other, two associated aspects of water imagery appear in the form of fishing and bridges, which, like rivers, serve either to unite or divide. Lipsha's voice is "a steady bridge over a deep black space of sickness" (35); heart-damaged Henry Junior builds a danger-ous and impassable "bridge of knives" (135), trying to impress Albertine with his bar tricks. Henry lacks a bridge back to a healthy life and ends up committing suicide, while Lipsha drives across the bridge to return home.

Whereas bridges are structures built to help us pass from one place or state to another, fishing is a process of acquiring, pulling something back to ourselves. As an old and senile man, Nector fishes for thoughts in the depths of Lake Turcot, while the would-be martyr, Sister Leopolda, fishes for souls, hooking children together like a stringer of fish.[14] Water and its associated imagery, both negative and positive, dominate the book, provid-ing a network of images and references that link character and action.

Although less persistent than water imagery, images of edges and boundaries recur also. Erdrich has described her own perspective as one she remembers developing as a child, lingering unnoticed on the outskirts of a group of grown-ups, hanging on the fringe of conversation. Similarly, Al-bertine remembers that, unlike other grown-ups, Aunt June never kept her on the "edge of conversation"; Albertine's mother's house is on "the very edge of the reservation"; and many of the characters are on the edges of so-ciety. Many characters are marginalized not only in white towns, but some-times even in their own community. Being a perpetual onlooker (in both Native and non-Native communities) is often the situation of a mixed-blood Indian; and, says Erdrich, it is "the condition of a writer" as well (Wong, 211). Such multiple marginality is reflected structurally in the proliferation and juxtaposition of individual voices (voices often not speaking or listening to each other) positioned between the covers of *Love Medicine*.

A final connective element is the variable repetition of humor—in this case, humor with a decided edge to it. As William Gleason has stated, "The humor in *Love Medicine* is protean. Laughter leaks from phrase, gesture, incident, situation, and narrative comment" and takes the form of "farce, slapstick, and outright joke-telling" as well as sarcasm, tricksterism, and verbal shenanigans.[15] Some of the humor is *verbal*, often based on malapropisms, such as Lipsha's account of God's deafness: the God who "used to raineth bread from clouds, smite the Philippines, sling fire down on red-light districts where people got stabbed. He even appeared in person once in a while" (194). Some is *literary*, like Nector's description of the "famous misunderstanding" about *Moby-Dick*. When he explains to his mother that the book was the story of the great white whale, she thinks hard for a while and asks, "What they got to wail about, those whites?" (91).

But almost all of the humor is *political*, indirectly (like the first two examples) or directly, like Nector's description of the rich white woman who wanted him to pose for her painting, *The Plunge of the Brave*. "Remember Custer's saying?" Nector asks. "'The only good Indian is a dead Indian'? Well, from my dealings with whites I would add to that quote: 'The only interesting Indian is dead or dying by falling backwards off a horse'" (91). Similarly, after a bar fight with a particularly offensive racist, the trickster-ish Chippewa[16] "outlaw" Gerry Nanapush learns: "There is nothing more vengeful and determined in this world than a cowboy with sore balls. . . . He also found out that white people are good witnesses to have on your side, because they have names, addresses, social security numbers, and work phones. But they are terrible witnesses to have against you, almost as bad as having Indians witness for you" (162). Social criticism may be more palatable when it is delivered through humor. But perhaps, more important, humor can be a survival strategy or even an act of resistance. Laughing at oppression, "survival humor," as Erdrich calls it (Coltelli, 46), is recognizing and reformulating it on your own terms.

Even though such elements as a common setting, a set of narrators, juxtaposition of perspectives, recurring themes and images, and repeated humor provide an overall interconnectedness, most of the short stories can also function individually. At this point, one brief example will suffice. In the first section of Chapter 1, a third-person narrator tells about June Kashpaw's life in the "oil boomtown Williston, North Dakota," where she looks perpetually for the man who "could be different" this time (3). Here Erdrich introduces the water (in this case, snow) imagery, male-female relationships, Native American-European American interactions, the North Dakota landscape, and the impulse to return home to one's family and community. By the end of the section, "the snow fell deeper that Easter than it had in forty years, but June walked over it like water and came home" (6). The sense of closure (a concept so crucial to the short story) seems evident here. June's story ends, albeit somewhat ambiguously, with her death. Death is the ultimate closure (at least from the perspective of an earthbound body), yet June's death is used as the beginning of the entire series of stories.

The conclusion of this brief story opens the sequence of narratives to come. June's untimely death provides the occasion for the gathering of all the characters, her relatives. In fact, even though June dies on page 6, she is the common link among the highly individual characters throughout. All of the characters (with the exception of the child Howard Kashpaw) remember June and define themselves, in some degree, according to their relationship to her. June is Gordie's ex-wife, Marie's unofficially adopted daughter, Albertine's aunt, King and Lipsha's mother, and Gerry's ex-lover. Even though she never narrates a word, June (or at least her memory) is a palpable absence and the most dominant character in the entire work. Just as readers interpret and reinterpret the linked stories, the characters construct and reconstruct June. The beginning also suggests the end. The final story concludes with Lipsha, who, like his mother before him, travels across the water to return home.[17]

In fact, the structure of *Love Medicine* (in its original form) is somewhat chiasmic, the first and last stories thematically mirroring each other, the second and thirteenth echoing each other, and so on. Specifically, the first and final stories focus on homecomings, one failed, one successful. Stories two and thirteen both address Marie's spiritual condition: her early desire to be a martyred saint contrasted with her truly saintly behavior in forgiving and helping to heal her life-long rival, Lulu. The third and twelfth stories deal with Nector and Marie's relationship: its beginning when they meet on the hillside and its end as Nector chokes on Lipsha's love medicine, meant to restore Nector's love for his wife. Stories four and eleven focus on memories of June: Marie muses about taking in June and Gordie hallucinates about June's return. The fifth and tenth stories share the vaguest connection, but both focus on Lulu's boys. The first introduces them and the latter develops the character of one son, Gerry. Stories six and nine mirror each other more clearly as Nector poses for the painting *The Plunge of the Brave* in one and Henry Junior literally plunges to his death in the other. Finally, the seventh and eighth stories seem linked by an explosive combination of love and violence. In the first, Marie returns to the convent to see the crazed, would-be saint, Leopolda, and in the second, Albertine leaves home for the big city.

In the expanded 1993 edition, the roughly chiasmic structure breaks down. While the first and eighteenth, second and seventeenth, third and sixteenth, fourth and fifteenth, and ninth and tenth stories appear to have clear links, the sixth and thirteenth, seventh and twelfth, and eighth and eleventh do not. The first and final chapters remain the same as those in the 1984 edition; both focus on homecoming. The second and penultimate stories both present characters seeking a "better" life by adapting to colonial impositions, in particular, Catholicism and capitalism. Whereas Marie seeks sainthood by joining a convent, fifty years later Lyman Lamartine seeks wealth by planning to build a gambling casino on Indian land. The third and sixteenth stories are connected tenuously through the central figure of Nector. In the third story, Nector meets Marie (the woman he will marry), and the sixteenth concludes with a scene in which Lyman (Nector's son with Lulu) dances with Marie (Nector's wife) and, in the process, both (re)connect to the now-deceased Nector. Stories four and fifteen both turn on the difficult relationship between Lulu and Marie. In the former, the young Lulu loses Nector to Marie, and in the latter, after a lifetime of rivalry, Marie assists Lulu. On the surface, stories five and fourteen address Marie's mothering (and to a lesser extent, her own need to be mothered). In the fifth story, Marie tries to form a relationship with her adoptive daughter, June (and, in the second section, gives birth with the help of her mother-in-law), and in the fourteenth, Marie attempts to save her birth son, Gordie, from alcoholism. Finally, stories nine and ten focus on running away. Albertine runs away to a new life in Fargo, and Henry Junior runs away from a painful life by committing suicide. There is also a development from Henry Junior's debilitating war trauma to his self-destruction in the two narratives. As noted above, though, there seem to be few explicit connections between the other paired chapters. Mirrors turn into multiple refractions.

Overall, Erdrich's additions serve several purposes: to more fully develop certain characters (we hear more from Lyman Lamartine, for instance); to introduce new characters (like Rushes Bear, who was merely mentioned in the first edition); to fill in parts of the characters' personal histories (such as learning about Lulu as a young woman returning from boarding school); to bring some of the characters up to the present of the book (for example, the elderly Lulu's political activism and Lyman's plans for Indian-owned gambling are emphasized); to include more overt reservation politics as well as social commentary about the ongoing effects of more than two hundred years of colonial rule (e.g., jobs—or the lack of them—on the reservation, Indian gambling, alcoholism, poverty, pressures to "sell out," and Native political activism generally); and to cross-reference characters and incidents between and among *Love Medicine, The Beet Queen, Tracks,* and *The Bingo Palace* (for example, adding the young Lulu's voice provides a clear link to her story in *Tracks*). All of these help the reader understand more about the relationships in *Love Medicine,* but, more important, they help make clearer and more coherent connections to the tetralogy of narrative sequences overall. In the 1993 edition, the fact that these stories are "parts of a larger scheme" (Wong, 212) is made even more explicit.

Narrative Constellations and Intertextuality

What I am particularly interested in here is not so much to insist that *Love Medicine* is a short story cycle rather than a novel, but to consider how it fits into a network of stories—what we might call, using Kennedy's image, "a constellation of narratives," both Native American and European American, family and community, oral and written.[18] Just as many of the short stories within the narrative network of *Love Medicine* shape and reshape themselves in relation to each other, the work as a whole is part of a larger constellation of stories. "Intertextuality for Indians," claims Paula Gunn Allen, "is use of tradition" (Allen, *Spider,* 17), but these days tradition comes in a variety of packages. Erdrich retells family, community, and mythical narratives, continuing traditions of oral storytelling. Family stories are particularly important, since traditionally, for the Chippewa, family was seen as "the basic political and economic unit . . . and the primary source of personal identity."[19] "Sitting around listening to our family tell stories," Erdrich has explained, "has been a more important influence on our work than literary influences in some ways. These you absorb as a child when your senses are the most open, when your mind is forming" (Wong, 204). Erdrich's grandmother, grandfather, father, and mother all told stories. But Erdrich has taken special care to note also that "some of [her] father's stories are just indelible" (Wong, 204). Both Chippewa and German American family narratives, then, have influenced the book.

Even more important than family stories are community narratives, natural extensions of Chippewa familial and clan identity and of identity shaped by a small-town community. In fact, Kathleen M. Sands suggests aptly that the root of Erdrich's "storytelling technique is the secular anecdotal narrative process of community gossip."[20] For Erdrich and Dorris, community—with its attendant sense of place (geographical, cultural, and social) and personal identity—are irrevocably linked. "We both grew up in small communities where you were who you were in relation to the community," explained Erdrich. "You knew that whatever you did there were really ripples from it" (Wong, 204–5). Growing up, Erdrich's community included Turtle Mountain Reservation (which she visited) as well as the small town of Wahpeton, North Dakota. She is not re-creating a "traditional" Chippewa community in writing as much as she is describing the vexed boundaries between the reservation and white towns. In fact, claims James Stripes, she is "inscribing revisionist histories of the cultural borderlands."[21] It is no accident that family histories, fragmented by the effects of colonialism, are continually retold by community tellers who attempt to reweave the familial, communal, and cultural narratives into a coherent pattern in the present. No one story is more important than any other; but each narrative has special significance for a specific context and listener (both within and outside of the book) and a unique meaning in its proximity to other stories. Each story, like each individual, although complete in itself is reconnected to the whole through remembering and telling.

As well as family and community stories, Erdrich has incorporated some traditional mythical and contemporary Chippewa (and, to a certain extent, pan-Indian) narratives, characters, and images into her fiction. Nanabozho (variant spellings include Nanabush, Wenebojo, Nanabozho, and Manabozho), the mythical Chippewa trickster who serves as a creator and culture hero, is one of the most dominant. The family name Nanapush echoes the trickster's, just as the 250-pound Gerry Nanapush's antics in outwitting the police recall the trickster's mythical and hyperbolic escapades.[22] Another mythical figure is Missepeshu, the Chippewa water monster who is responsible for pulling attractive young girls to the bottom of the lake.

Just as vital as Erdrich's adaptations of Chippewa myth is her use of contemporary Native American and mixed-blood history, particularly evident in her stories about the tricksterlike Chippewa political activist Nanapush, who spends half his life incarcerated for resisting European American law (which he distinguishes from justice). Nanapush's life, modeled after American Indian Movement (AIM) members, recalls the political activism of the 1970s. Because Erdrich moves "toward the historical novel and the family saga," as Robert Silberman notes, "she is able to touch upon economic and political matters" effectively.[23] Throughout the stories, there are references to political, historical, and legal policies (e.g., the General Allotment Act and the inequity of the U.S. legal system in general) that still shape Native peoples' lives. Similarly, Gordie's alcoholism is an all-too-familiar story in some Indian communities. In "Crown of Thorns," Erdrich deftly links Gordie's spiritual death by (fire)water to Chippewa tradition as the story ends with Gordie "crying like a drowned person, howling in the open fields" (188).

Beyond Chippewa history and oral traditions, Erdrich has been influenced by the Western literary tradition. Although the "entire literary canon" has been an influence, the impact of William Faulkner, whom Erdrich has referred to as that "wonderful storyteller" (Wong, 203), is dramatic and obvious. Like Faulkner's *Go Down, Moses*, for instance, *Love Medicine* emphasizes a collection of characters, often family or extended family members, and their interrelations in a specific community in a particular regional setting. Like Faulkner, Erdrich examines the effects of race, miscegenation, the haunting power of the past, and the ironic intersections of the comic and tragic. Like Faulkner, Erdrich uses multiple narrators who tell their own stories, many of which overlap, confirm, contradict, or extend the others. Although each short story is autonomous, each acquires a new significance in relation to the others. Similarly, like Faulkner's *As I Lay Dying*, *Love Medicine* begins with the death of a central female character, which initiates the actions and memories of the characters and, to a great degree, unifies the narrative sequence.

While Erdrich's fiction may seem like a direct descendant of William Faulkner's, it also arises from a literate tradition of Native American fiction. Both Pauline Johnson (Canadian Mohawk) and Zitkala-Sa (the Sioux writer also known as Gertrude Simmons Bonnin), for instance, wrote short fiction in which they grappled with the Indian issues of their day. Although *Cogewea, the Half-Blood* (1927) by Mourning Dove (Christine Quintasket), a member of the Colville Confederated Tribes of Washington State, was until recently considered "the first novel written by an American Indian woman," it may really be, as Paula Gunn Allen points out, "a long story composed of a number of short stories" (Allen, *Spider*, 17).[24] The reasons for Mourning Dove's short-story format are clear. With little education or money, she had to support herself and her family by working long hours as a migrant laborer or housekeeper. "After backbreaking days in the orchards and fields," explains Jay Miller, the editor of her autobiography, "she would write for most of the night in a tent or cabin."[25] Little education and scant leisure time, combined with a cultural familiarity with cycles or series of short narratives (rather than novels), contributed to the production of short stories by this early twentieth-century Native American writer.

Like Mourning Dove, Leslie Marmon Silko (Laguna Pueblo) has struggled with acquiring the "large expanses of time and peace" necessary for writing long fiction.[26] Like Erdrich, she has written novels, but in *Storyteller* she has also combined short narratives from multiple points of view into a story cycle or narrative sequence. But because, unlike *Love Medicine, Storyteller* has not been presented as a novel, the reader feels freer to select a narrative trail through the text, reading a poem here or a story there.[27]

Far from being unusual, then, Erdrich's short-story cycle arises from both Native American and European American literary and oral traditions. Her work reflects the activity of many twentieth-century writers who emphasize multiple narrators, re-create oral narratives for the written page and for an expanded readership, and create and maintain community through literary discourse. Women writers of color, in particular, seem to have returned to local roots—family, community, and ethnicity—as sources of personal identity, political change, and creative expression. Telling one's story or the story of one's people as an act of self-definition and cultural continuance is a strong collective impulse. Jay Clayton has noted that the current emphasis on the theme of storytelling in fiction is "related to the emphasis in a postmodern society on local political struggles," rather than to a new conservatism. Storytelling can be "empowering" because it creates community and because stories are all we have to counter the "grand metanarratives" of history.[28]

But although the sequence of short stories in *Love Medicine* is connected to the network of oral and literate narrative traditions noted above, it is also part of another series of stories. In fact, this short story cluster is one component, manifold though it may be, of a series of narrative sequences. Erdrich and Dorris planned a tetralogy of short story cycles, the predominant imagery of each focusing on a different natural element: *Love Medicine* (water), *The Beet Queen* (air), *Tracks* (earth), and *The Bingo Palace* (fire). Together these works tell the multivoiced story of several generations of Chippewa, mixed-blood, and European American relations in North Dakota. *Love Medicine* (1984 and 1993) tells the story of Chippewa and mixed-blood families on and near a reservation in North Dakota. Polyphonous community voices narrate the events of fifty years, 1934–84. An assortment of narrators in *The Beet Queen* (1986) tells a somewhat parallel series of personal stories from 1932 to 1972 but focuses on European American and mixed-blood Indian characters in the small town of Argus, North Dakota. In *Tracks* (1988) only two individuals, Nanapush and Pauline, narrate the history of Chippewa and mixed-blood families from 1912 to 1924. *The Bingo Palace* (1994) begins and ends with a literal communal narrator (the speaker—"we"—is the community itself); in between, an anonymous third-person narrator and Lipsha (in the first-person) narrate contemporary events on the fictional reservation. Deciding to write four works was no accident. Four, according to Erdrich, "the number of completion in

Ojibway mythology" (Wong, 211), is a sacred number associated with the four cardinal directions, the four elements, and the four seasons. Erdrich's narrative quartet is like a literary medicine wheel in which the personal, family, community, and mythical narratives are figured in precise relation to one another.

Participatory Narrative: Readers and *Love Medicine*

Because the life of the story outside the text, the story the reader brings to the text—what Susan Garland Mann refers to as "trans-story dynamics"— is important, and because "stories become meaningful only within particular acts of reading," a brief consideration of reader responses to *Love Medicine* is in order.[29] Certainly there is no monolithic readership. Some reviewers and students have seen the characters overall as poverty-stricken, alcohol-addicted Indians who are "durable," but desperate and ultimately "doomed." However, this is a simplistic recapitulation of nineteenth-century stereotypes of the noble but doomed Indian—a figure to be pitied or condemned, rather than understood. What is often overlooked is the role of humor, love, and endurance, precisely what Erdrich portrays, as aspects of daily life and as modes of resistance to colonial conditions. Others have relished Erdrich's humor and have seen the characters as complex and resilient humans (who cope with problems all too common in some Indian communities). Still others have raised difficult questions about "authenticity" and appropriation.[30]

Catherine Rainwater has contributed an interesting analysis of reader responses to Erdrich's fiction. Noting "Erdrich's concern with liminality and marginality," Rainwater suggests that Erdrich's texts "frustrate narrativity," which "amounts to a textually induced or encoded experience of marginality" in the reader. Although this leads to a temporary disempowerment because the reader must "cease to apply the conventional expectations associated with ordinary narrativity," it results finally in a new kind of power, a new vision.[31] Rainwater aptly distinguishes the bicultural filaments from which Erdrich spins her narratives. But although this model makes perfect sense and may be true for many (or even most) readers, it is based on two potentially problematic assumptions: that readers are non-Indians or, at the very least, not marginal themselves; and that Western conventions amount to "ordinary narrativity."[32] What happens to a mixed-blood or Native reader? Does a reader who is comfortable with oral traditions, achronology, and extended kinship networks also experience such marginality? Is there always a degree of slippage between a text and its interpreter? Is it possible for a reader to be biliterate or multiliterate, that is, to negotiate linguistic or cultural code switching with facility? Although it is impossible to imagine a model of narrativity that encompasses the infinite diversity of individual readers, these are particularly important and vexed questions to consider as we move to an increasingly pluralistic American literature.

Erdrich's work challenges Western-trained readers, but Western expectations of narrativity are actively confounded by writers like Leslie Marmon Silko, N. Scott Momaday, Maxine Hong Kingston, Amy Tan, Sandra Cisneros, Ana Castillo, and many others. Like Erdrich, they present a variety of voices from (multi)ethnic communities in interlaced cycles/sequences of short stories. Amy Tan writes a series of linked short stories about four sets of mothers and daughters, told from different points of view, emphasizing family and community, and spanning two cultures and generations. The short story collections of Sandra Cisneros offer diverse Chicana voices of Chicago and Texas, highlighting the influences of class, gender, and ethnicity. Ana Castillo playfully invites readers to select and vary the sequence of her epistolary short story sequence, *The Mixquiahuala Letters.* "Dear Reader," she writes in a prefatory note, "It is the author's duty to alert the reader that this is not a book to be read in the usual sequence. All letters are numbered to aid in following any one of the author's proposed options." Although she offers three options—*for the conformist, for the cynic,* and *for the quixotic*—she concludes: "For the reader committed to nothing but short fiction, all the letters read as separate entities. Good luck whichever journey you choose!"[33] Like Erdrich, all of these writers construct stories that create community and challenge readers to broaden their understanding of both narrative and community.

These contemporary short-story networks are important means to promote each generation's education, to enhance personal and community renewal, to assist cultural continuity, in short, to ensure survival. Narrative theorists have long noted the reflexive dynamism of storytelling. We tell and retell stories, our own and others'. Today, more overtly than ever, Native American writers raise questions about self-representation, about who controls the production and transmission of meaning. Many are actively wresting control of community stories and histories from anthropologists and academics. The contemporary impulse to remember and retell, not the continuous, unified narrative of the dominant history, but the discontinuous narratives of individual survivors, is part of what motivates writers like Erdrich. In her short-story cycles, she narrates (and in so doing, constructs) not ethnographic artifacts, but living narratives derived from family and community. The "stories of the contemporary survivors" (Erdrich, "Where," 23), the network of individual stories recycled and reshaped, may, in fact, turn out to be an ongoing short-story cycle, reconfigured perpetually by the writers and their readers, the tellers and their listeners.

Outline of Narrators in *Love Medicine*

(Chapters added in the 1993 edition are unnumbered; the narrator added to Chapter 4 of the 1993 edition is italicized.)

Chapter	Narrator	Year
1. "The World's Greatest Fisherman"	1. 3d pers.—June Kashpaw 2. 1st pers.—Albertine Johnson 3. 3d pers.—anonymous 4. 1st pers.—Albertine Johnson	1981
2. "Saint Marie"	1st pers.—Marie Lazarre	1934
3. "Wild Geese"	1st pers.—Nector Kashpaw	1934
"The Island"	1st pers.—Lulu Nanapush	n.d.
4. "The Beads"	1. 1st pers.—Marie (Lazarre) Kashpaw 2. *1st pers.—Marie (Lazarre) Kashpaw*	1948
5. "Lulu's Boys"	3d pers.—Lulu (Nanapush) Lamartine	1957
6. "The Plunge of the Brave"	1st pers.—Nector Kashpaw	1957
7. "Flesh and Blood"	1st pers.—Marie (Lazarre) Kashpaw	1957
8. "A Bridge"	3d pers.—Albertine Johnson	1973
9. "The Red Convertible"	1st pers.—Lyman Lamartine	1974
10. "Scales"	1st pers.—Albertine Johnson	1980
11. "Crown of Thorns"	3d pers.—Gordie Kashpaw	1981
12. "Love Medicine"	1st pers.—Lipsha Morrissey	1982
"Resurrection"	3d pers.—Marie (Lazarre) Kashpaw, Gordie Kashpaw, Marie (Lazarre) Kashpaw	1982
13. "The Good Tears"	1. 1st pers.—Lulu Lamartine 2. 1st pers.—Lulu Lamartine	1983
"The Tomahawk Factory"	1st pers.—Lyman Lamartine	1983
"Lyman's Luck"	3d pers.—Lyman Lamartine	1983
14. "Crossing the Water"	1. 3d pers.—Howard Kashpaw 2. 1st pers.—Lipsha Morrissey 3. 1st pers.—Lipsha Morrissey 4. 1st pers.—Lipsha Morrissey	1984

Notes

1. The first edition of *Love Medicine* is the focus of this essay. The new and expanded edition of *Love Medicine* (1993) came out too late to consider fully here, but it does not significantly change my reading of the work. Although there are eighteen chapters in the 1993 edition, they function in the same ways as the fourteen chapters of the 1984 edition.

2. Hertha D. Wong, "An Interview with Louise Erdrich and Michael Dorris," *North Dakota Quarterly* 55.1 (1987): 212. Subsequent references to this interview will be identified by parenthetical page numbers in the text.

3. The seven chapters of the 1984 edition of *Love Medicine* published as short stories include "Crown of Thorns," "Flesh and Blood," "Lulu's Boys," "The Red Convertible," "Saint Marie," "Scales," and "The World's Greatest Fisherman." I examined "Flesh and Blood," published as "Love Medicine" in *Ms. Magazine* 13.5 (1984): 74–84, 150; "Lulu's Boys," published in *Kenyon Review* 6.3 (1984): 1–10; "Saint Marie," published in *Atlantic Monthly* 253.3 (1984): 78–84; and "Scales," published in *North American Review*, 267.1 (1982): 22–27.

4. Laura Coltelli, ed., *Winged Words: American Indian Writers Speak* (Lincoln: University of Nebraska Press, 1990), 49; Subsequent references to this interview will be identified by parenthetical page numbers in the text.

5. For a fuller discussion of Raymond Joel Silverman, Joseph W. Reed Jr., Pleasant Reed and Timothy C. Alderman, who introduced these terms, see Robert M. Luscher, "The Short Story Sequence: An Open Book," in *Short Story Theory at a Crossroads*, edited by Susan Lohafer and JoEllyn Clarey (Baton Rouge: Louisiana State University Press, 1989); Susan Garland Mann, *The Short Story Cycle: A Genre Companion and Reference Guide* (New York: Greenwood Press, 1989); and J. Gerald Kennedy, "Towards a Poetics of the Short Story Cycle," *Journal of the Short Story in English* 11 (1988): 9–25. Subsequent references to these works will be identified by parenthetical page numbers in the text.

6. Forrest L. Ingram, *Representative Short Story Cycles of the Twentieth Century: Studies in a Literary Genre* (The Hague: Mouton, 1971), 13–15, 17–18.

7. Paula Gunn Allen has written extensively about the significance of web imagery in Native American literature (see *The Sacred Hoop: Recovering the Feminine in American Indian Traditions* [Boston: Beacon, 1986]). Subsequent references to this book will be identified by parenthetical page numbers in the text. The idea of a constellation of short stories was suggested by J. Gerald Kennedy ("Towards a Poetics").

8. Henry Glassie, *Passing the Time in Ballymenone* (Philadelphia: University of Pennsylvania Press, 1982), xiii.

9. Paula Gunn Allen, Introduction to *Spider Woman's Granddaughters: Traditional Tales and Contemporary Writing*, edited by Paula Gunn Allen (Boston: Beacon, 1989), 5. Sub-

sequent references to this book will be identified by parenthetical page numbers in the text.

10. Louise Erdrich, "Where I Ought to Be: A Writer's Sense of Place," *New York Times Book Review*, 28 July 1985, 23. Subsequent references to this essay will be identified by parenthetical page numbers in the text.

11. Helen Jaskoski, "From the Time Immemorial: Native American Traditions in Contemporary Short Fiction," in *Since Flannery O'Connor: Essays on the American Short Story*, edited by Loren Logsdon and Charles W. Mayer (Macomb: Western Illinois University Press, 1987), 59.

12. Albertine Johnson narrates sections 2–4 of Chapters 1 and 10; Marie Lazarre (who becomes Marie Kashpaw) narrates Chapters 2, 4, and 7; Marie's husband, Nector Kashpaw, narrates Chapters 3 and 6. Lulu Lamartine (Nector's lover) and her son, Lyman, narrate one chapter each—Chapters 13 and 9, respectively. Howard Kashpaw narrates only the first section of the final chapter. Lipsha Morrissey narrates Chapter 12 and the final three sections of Chapter 14. Finally, a third-person narrator tells the story of June's death in the first section of Chapter 1, explains Lulu's behavior in Chapter 5, describes Albertine's experiences as a fifteen-year-old runaway in Chapter 8, and details Gordie's breakdown in Chapter 11. Four new chapters, or stories, are added in the expanded 1993 edition. The first, positioned between Chapters 3 and 4 of the 1984 edition, is narrated in the first person by Lulu Nanapush (who becomes Lulu Lamartine); the second, placed between Chapters 12 and 13, is narrated in the third person from alternating points of view: Marie (Lazarre) Kashpaw, Gordie Kashpaw, and Marie (Lazarre) Kashpaw. The final two new stories, both narrated by Lyman Lamartine (one in the first person, the second in third person) are placed together between Chapters 13 and 14. In addition, a second section (narrated in the first person by Marie Kashpaw) has been added to "The Beads."

13. Louise Erdrich, *Love Medicine* (New York: Holt, Rinehart, & Winston, 1984), 19. Subsequent references to the novel refer to this edition and will be identified parenthetically by page numbers in the text.

14. Leopolda's attempts to hook children for God grotesquely echo, as Jaskoski has noted, "the New Testament passage in which the apostles are to become 'fishers of men' and 'catch' souls for heaven" as well as the colonial imposition of Christianity on Native people ("From the Time Immemorial," 55).

15. William Gleason, "'Her Laugh an Ace': The Function of Humor in Louise Erdrich's *Love Medicine*," *American Indian Culture and Research Journal* 11.3 (1987): 51–52.

16. In order to be consistent with Erdrich's usage, I will use the term Chippewa, rather than Anishinaabe or Ojibwa(y), throughout this essay.

17. For a discussion of how, in Native American fiction, the characters are always trying to go home, see William Bevis, "Native American Novels: Homing In,"

in *Recovering the Word: Essays in Native American Literature*, edited by Brian Swann and Arnold Krupat (Berkeley: University of California Press, 1987), 580–620.

18. To avoid oversimplification, it is important to keep in mind that each of these communities of stories—family, community, Native American, European American—sometimes collapses into the others because they are not discrete categories and each has both an oral and a literate component.

19. Gerald Vizenor, *The Everlasting Sky: New Voices from the People Named the Chippewa* (New York: Crowell-Collier Press, 1972), ix.

20. Kathleen M. Sands, "*Love Medicine:* Voices and Margins," *Studies in American Indian Literatures* 9.1 (1985): 14.

21. James D. Stripes, "The Problem(s) of (Anishinaabe) History in the Fiction of Louise Erdrich: Voices and Contexts," *Wicazo Sa Review* 7.2 (1991): 26.

22. For a detailed consideration of how Erdrich retells trickster tales and "fuses Chippewa Windigo stories with European romance and fairy-tale motifs and allusions to Christian practice and iconography" (55), see Helen Jaskoski, "From the Time Immemorial" in *Since Flannery O'Connor*.

23. Robert Silberman, "Opening the Text: *Love Medicine* and the Return of the Native American Woman," in *Narrative Chance: Postmodern Discourse on Native American Indian Literatures*, edited by Gerald Vizenor (Albuquerque: University of New Mexico Press, 1989), 113.

24. For an astute discussion of *Cogewea* as the first novel by a Native American woman, see A. LaVonne Brown Ruoff, *American Indian Literatures: An Introduction, Bibliographic Review, and Selected Bibliography* (New York: Modern Language Association, 1990), 70. The collection of short narratives in *Cogewea* includes traditional oral narratives from the Colville, personal narratives adapted from Mourning Dove's life, and popular narratives from the dime-novel Western. All of these narratives were shaped and edited by Lucullus Virgil McWhorter, Mourning Dove's literary advocate, and published as a novel.

25. Jay Miller, Introduction to *Mourning Dove: A Salishan Autobiography* (Lincoln: University of Nebraska Press, 1990), xi.

26. Anne Wright, ed., *The Delicacy and Strength of Lace: Letters between Leslie Marmon Silko and James Wright* (St. Paul, Minn.: Graywolf Press, 1986), 91.

27. In many ways, Silko's *Storyteller* is more radical in its structure than *Love Medicine*. The narrative voices are manifold, arising from the mythical long ago, the historical past, and the present. Figures from Keres myth speak in their own voices, recalled and imagined, of course, by Silko, and through the contemporary narratives. The stories take on the forms of letters, poems, autobiographical accounts, myths, photographic images, and short stories.

28. Jay Clayton, "The Narrative Turn in Recent Minority Fiction," *American Literary History* 2.3 (1990): 378–79, 383.

29. Susan Garland Mann, *The Short Story Cycle: A Genre Companion and Reference Guide* (New York: Greenwood Press, 1989); Ian Reid, "Destabilizing Frames for Story," in *Short Story Theory at a Crossroads*, edited by Susan Lohafer and JoEllyn Clarey (Baton Rouge: Louisiana State University Press, 1989), 299. See also Wolfgang Iser, *The Act of Reading* (Baltimore: Johns Hopkins University Press, 1978).

30. For a discussion of students at Turtle Mountain Reservation who feared that, if not read with care, *Love Medicine* would "confirm ugly, dangerous stereotypes" of the "drunken Indian," see James McKenzie, "Lipsha's Good Road Home: The Revival of Chippewa Culture in *Love Medicine*," *American Indian Culture and Research Journal* 10.3 (1986): 53. Another controversy involves questions of appropriation. Were stories of community members on or near Turtle Mountain Reservation reshaped, but not enough to ensure anonymity? Who is entitled to tell or write such stories? As the works of many contemporary indigenous writers attest, these are not rhetorical questions. But they are difficult questions to answer, particularly when many publishers and readers want each Native American writer to be a "representative" Indian (often based on non-Indian notions of what is "authentically" or "suitably" Indian). Certainly, the label "Native American literature" is too general to delineate precisely the varieties of Native languages, cultures, communities, and individuals.

31. Catherine Rainwater, "Reading between Worlds: Narrativity in the Fiction of Louise Erdrich," *American Literature* 62.3 (1990): 406, 422.

32. This model is particularly suitable for applying to what often happens in introductory Native American literature classes, in which many students, having little or no knowledge of Native cultures and contexts, feel temporarily lost or marginalized.

33. Ana Castillo, *The Mixquiahuala Letters* (Binghamton, N.Y.: Bilingual Press/Editorial Bilingue, 1986).

Interviews with Louise Erdrich
and Michael Dorris

◆ ◆ ◆

Louise Erdrich, Michael Dorris, and Hertha D. Wong
from *North Dakota Quarterly* (1987)

Hertha Wong: Do you consider yourselves Native American writers? What do you think of such labels?

Louise Erdrich: I think of any label as being both true and a product of a kind of chauvinistic society because obviously white male writers are not labeled "white male writers." However, I suppose that they're useful in some ways. I could as well be "woman writer" or whatever label one wants to use. But I really don't like labels. While it is certainly true that a good part of my background, and Michael's background, and a lot of the themes are Native American, I prefer to simply be a writer. Although I like to be known as having been from the Turtle Mountain Chippewa and from North Dakota. It's nice to have that known and to be proud of it for people back home. . . .

Wong: Collaboration is an idea that makes many writers who emphasize individual creativity uneasy. You two work together. Would you describe your collaborative process?

Erdrich: It's not very mysterious.

Dorris: We'll start talking about something a long time in advance of it—the germ of a plot, or a story that has occurred to us, or an observation that we've seen. . . . After we talk, one of us, whoever thought of it probably, will write a draft. It might be a paragraph; it might be ten pages; it might be something in between. We then share that draft with the other person. Shortly thereafter they will sit down with a pencil and make comments about what works and what doesn't work, what needs expanding and what might be overwritten. Then they give that draft with their suggestions back to the person who wrote it who has the option of taking or leaving them, but almost always taking them. Then that person does a new draft, gives it back to the other, and goes through the process again. This exchange takes place five or six times. The final say clearly rests with the person who wrote the piece initially, but we virtually reach consensus on all words before they go out, on a word-by-word basis. There is not a thing that has gone out from either one of us that has not been through at least six rewrites, *major* rewrites. . . .

Wong: You have mentioned that William Faulkner, Toni Morrison, and Barbara Pym have all influenced your writing. Would you say a little about what, in particular, they contribute to your work? . . .

Erdrich: As for William Faulkner, I guess I can't really pin down what his influence is. I think one absorbs him through the skin. He is just such a wonderful storyteller. He is so much of an *American* writer. I have read him over and over. I really like the other writers you mentioned as well. Everybody that you read is a literary influence. I had a literary education so the entire literary canon is a background. I'm very fond of John Donne.

Wong: Besides a literary tradition, what about an oral tradition? Have family stories influenced your work?

Erdrich: Sitting around listening to our family tell stories has been a more important influence on our work than literary influences in some ways. These you absorb as a child when your senses are the most open, when your mind is forming. That really happened, I know, in our family and [to Michael] certainly with yours. . . .

Wong: [In *Love Medicine,* t]he reader gets the sense of *hearing* bits and pieces of gossip. We don't have an omniscient narrator to tell us how it *really* is. There is no one with authority that imposes some kind of order and stasis on a character or a character's life.

Erdrich: No, I really agree with that. We both grew up in small communities where you were who you were in relation to the community. You knew that whatever you did there were really ripples from it. I don't think you can grow up like that and ignore it once you start writing. . . .

Wong: We've been talking about "A Writer's Sense of Place." I'm wondering about the whole notion of living in New Hampshire and writing about North Dakota.

Erdrich: I wonder about that, too. I feel a lot of affection for New Hampshire. It's just lovely as a place, but I don't have the history there, the connections with a particular culture, the family connections, the feelings for the history that one gets over time living in a certain place. I'm so attached to our home, in particular, that I really love being there, but I certainly miss North Dakota and this area [Minnesota] a lot. Those are the two places I've really *been*. . . .

Sometimes I think that the sheer nostalgia sends me back emotionally in a stronger way. . . .

Wong: Louise, you've described your perspective as one you remember as a child—lingering unnoticed on the outskirts of a group of grown-ups, hanging on the fringe of conversation. . . . In *Love Medicine*, Albertine remembers that Aunt June never kept her on the "edge of conversation"; the Kashpaws' house is on "the very edge of the reservation"; many of the characters are on the edges of society. How does this point of view inform your writing?

Erdrich: In a way it's the condition of a writer. You're not always the most *popular* person, the center of attention, everybody looking to you for the answers. I always felt like I was more the one who listened in on everything else. . . .

Dorris: . . . In a way, it's kind of a mixed-blood condition as well.

Louise Erdrich, Nancy Feyl Chavkin, and Allan Chavkin from *Conversations with Louise Erdrich and Michael Dorris* (1994)

Chavkin: Perhaps because of your interrelated stories and interweaving divergent points of view, you have been compared to Faulkner. Is that comparison useful? Has your reading of Faulkner's work influenced your own work?

Erdrich: Faulkner is probably an influence on any writer, but yes, I do love his work and I read it over and over, especially *The Hamlet* and *Absalom, Absalom!* Is the comparison useful? I guess it depends on what sort of use you might make of it. I don't think it is a comparison that deepens the experience of the writing; however, it probably points toward an interesting academic question—that is, how white Southerners and Native American writers might partake of a similar (contained, defeated, proud, undefeated) sense of history, and of place. Strange bedfellows.

Chavkin: Do you think there is any truth in the theory that serious writing is prompted by unhappiness or a sense of loss?

Erdrich: There is probably some truth to that. Unfortunately I've noticed as I grow older that most of us increase our understanding through experiencing personal sorrows and setbacks. Slowly, perhaps, my children are teaching me what it is to experience deep joy. They do it so effortlessly, and there is such wisdom in their direct embrace of joy, that I at least understand from being with them that I know very little of what it means to concentrate and be at peace with the world. I don't know how exactly we lose this talent. I'm trying to get it back. . . .

Chavkin: Can you give us some examples of how ideas for some of your stories come to you?

Erdrich: Getting a first line is immensely satisfying. The first line of "Scales" is written on the back of a Travelhost napkin. The first line of "Saint Marie" came to me in the bathtub where I was sulking after Michael told me that the *n*th draft of the story wasn't quite right. My grandmother once got irritated with a yapping dog and excused herself to "go pound the dog." It became a line in a story. She didn't end up pounding the dog, by the way. She loved animals. My father told me about his first ride in a barnstormer's airplane. My sisters and brothers and aunts and uncles like to talk. Stories came from just about anywhere, unpredictably, and I try to stay open. Try to leave the door open.

Chavkin: One of the things we like so much about your writing is the feeling of unpredictability, that anything is possible—it's a feeling one often has when reading "magical realism." Joyce Carol Oates calls you a "magical realist." Do you see yourself as one? Do you think that's a useful term to describe your work?

Erdrich: That must have been a while ago, and it was very good of her, a great compliment, but I think now that the rage to imitate Márquez has declined. Probably your word unpredictable is more accurate. It is certainly the reaction I'd like. The thing is, the events people pick out as magical don't seem unreal to me. Unusual, yes, but I was raised believing in miracles and hearing of true events that may seem unbelievable. I think the term is one applied to writers from cultures more closely aligned to religious oddities and the natural and strange world. . . .

Chavkin: Is it possible to collaborate closely with another writer and to still maintain an individual imagination?

Erdrich: The heart of our collaboration is a commitment to one another's separateness. I certainly respect the solitude and silence it takes for Michael's work, and he does the same for me. The idea of linking brains or even working in the same space—I find that impossible. As would anyone. An imagination is composed of all the signs and wonders of childhood, as well as the range of trivialities and possibilities that come with age. In a collaboration such as *The Crown of Columbus* we shared in one book the creations of our own selves, but the source itself, that is a well closed except to the free wondering of an individual mind. In each of the books we've written separately, it is that source, naturally, that dictates the substance of the work. However, there is no putting aside the sheer volume of sweaty maneuvering it takes to shape books, and we have done so much of that between ourselves that I find it impossible to ever thank Michael enough for his passionate commitment.

Chavkin: One of the qualities we especially like about your work is a sympathy, a real compassion, for your characters—a quality one finds so often in Chekhov's short stories but often lacking in many contemporary writers, where there's a cold-heartedness disguised as ironic detachment. Is that sympathy something you consciously attempt to inject into your work?

Erdrich: I'm glad you find it there, and no, I'm not conscious of putting it in the work. I don't think that compassion is a quality that can be injected or added as an afterthought. Either it is there, or it is not, and certainly the reader brings hidden shades of the sympathy into existence during the act of reading. . . .

Chavkin: In an article published in *American Literature* in September 1990, Catherine Rainwater argues that you include in your work structural features that "frustrate narrativity" in order to produce in the reader an "experience of marginality." What do you think of this argument?

Erdrich: I think it is true, although of course I don't do it with an object directly in mind. I am on the edge, have always been on the edge, flourish on the edge, and I don't think I belong anywhere else.

Chavkin: In your work is a Native American's knowledge of Roman Catholic beliefs and Native American religious beliefs an advantage, or is he/she torn between two systems of belief?

Erdrich: Torn, I believe, honestly torn. Religion is a deep force, and a people magnetize around the core of a belief system. It is very difficult for one individual to remain loyal to both, although my own grandfather managed the trick quite well, by not fully participating in either traditional or Roman Catholic church, and also by refusing to see distinctions between the embodiments of spirit. He prayed in the woods, he prayed in the mission, to him it was all connected, and all politics.

Chavkin: In his essay, "Opening the Text: *Love Medicine* and the Return of the Native American Woman," published in *Narrative Chance* edited by Gerald Vizenor (Albuquerque: University of New Mexico Press, 1989), Robert Silberman suggests that in Native American literature the book is accepted as a necessary evil—the story and storytelling are the ideals. How important is the oral tradition in your work?

Erdrich: It is the reason so many stories are written in the first person—I hear the story told. At the same time I believe in and deeply cherish books and believe the library is a magical and sacred storehouse. A refuge. I'm a poorly educated person in some ways. Not even Dartmouth could catch me up in having missed an intellectual life in high school. The town library was my teacher every bit as much as sitting in the kitchen or out under the trees swapping stories or listening to older relatives. So the two are not incompatible to me. I love the voice and I love the texture of writing, the feel of the words on the page, the construction. . . .

Chavkin: [Leslie Marmon] Silko suggests you are ambivalent about your Native American origins. How would you respond to this charge?

Erdrich: Of course, I'm ambivalent, I'm human. There are times I wish that I were one thing or the other, but I am a mixed-blood. *Psychically doomed*, another mixed-blood friend once joked. The truth is my background is such a rich mixed bag I'd be crazy to want to be anything else. Nor would Silko, probably, or any Native writer who understands that through the difficulty of embracing our own contradictions we gain sympathy for the range of ordinary failures and marvels.

PART III

Individual and Cultural Survival:
Humor and Homecoming

"Her Laugh an Ace"

The Function of Humor in Louise Erdrich's Love Medicine

WILLIAM GLEASON

◆　◆　◆

> We have one priceless universal trait, we Americans. That trait is our humor. What a pity it is that it is not more prevalent in our art.
>
> —William Faulkner

MANY EARLY REVIEWERS OF Louise Erdrich's *Love Medicine* treat the novel as though it were at heart a tragic account of pain. They see Erdrich as merely a recorder of contemporary Indian suffering, as an evoker of her characters' "conflicting feelings of pride and shame, guilt and rage—the disorderly intimacies of their lives on the reservation and their longings to escape." These critics classify *Love Medicine* as "a tribal chronicle of defeat," a "unique evocation of a culture in severe social ruin," and an "appalling account of . . . impoverished, feckless lives far gone in alcoholism and promiscuity." Each of these descriptions betrays a fundamental misunderstanding of the novel; any reckoning of *Love Medicine* as an ultimately tragic text begs contradiction.[1]

To be sure, the book contains much that is painful. Its unifying vision, however, is one of redemption—accomplished through an expert and caring use of humor. Erdrich's characters by novel's end are not far gone, but close to home; she evokes a culture not in severe ruin, but about to rise; she chronicles not defeat, but survival. Love, assisted by humor, triumphs over pain.

The humor in *Love Medicine* is protean. Laughter leaks from phrase, gesture, incident, situation, and narrative comment equally. Much of what is funny seems subtly so, but farce, slapstick, and outright joke telling by no means remain absent. In many ways, humor mirrors hurt in this novel, broad or sharp. After King and Lynette wheel up to Aurelia's house with King Junior bundled in the front seat and Grandma and Grandpa Kashpaw stuffed into the tiny back, for example, we quickly understand that Grandpa's perceptive powers have precipitously diminished. He does not realize that the car has stopped, does not notice things that happen right in front of him, and does not recognize his own house or granddaughter:

> Lynette rolled out the door, shedding cloth and pins, packing the bare-bottomed child on her hip, and I couldn't tell what had happened.
>
> Grandpa hadn't noticed, whatever it was. He turned to the open door and stared at his house.
>
> "This reminds me of something," he said.
>
> "Well, it should. It's your house!" Mama barreled out the door, grabbed both of his hands, and pulled him out of the little backseat.
>
> "You have your granddaughter here, Daddy!" Zelda shrieked carefully into Grandpa's face. "Zelda's daughter. She came all the way up here to visit from school."
>
> "Zelda . . . born September fourteenth, nineteen forty-one . . ."
>
> "No, Daddy. This here is my daughter, Albertine. Your grand-daughter."
>
> I took his hand.[2]

"Shrieked carefully" here is delightful, as is the deadpan understatement of "This reminds me of something." Indeed, much humor threatens to slip by unnoticed. King buys a "big pink gravestone" for his mother's plot before purchasing his blue Firebird with the insurance money (21). And Dot's hair must be ferociously comic. Albertine mentions that "by the cold months it had grown out in thick quills—brown at the shank, orange at the tip. The orange dye job had not suited her coloring" (159). Gerry Nanapush is a "six-foot plus, two-hundred-and-fifty pound Indian" who nevertheless tries to hide behind a "yellow tennis player's visor" in a dimly lit bar (160, 156). When Gerry later escapes from the local cops by squeezing through a hospital window and jumping three stories onto the hood of a police car, he is sufficiently emboldened to "pop a wheelie" on his motorcycle before disappearing (169).

Words play games in this novel, too. Albertine's nursing student textbook is "spread out to the section on 'Patient Abuse'" (7). We are not quite sure how funny this is intended to be; narratively, we have just found out that June is dead. But by the time we reach Nector's ("Grandpa" in the first chapter) recounting of his pose for *Plunge of the Brave*, we know that words—

especially when they lead to Indian-white confusions—can be very play-ful. "Disrobe," commands the "snaggletoothed" painter with "a little black pancake on her head" (90). Nector "pretended not to understand her. 'What robe?' [he] asked" (90). Another "famous misunderstanding" occurs when Nector tells Rushes Bear about *Moby-Dick*:

> "You're always reading that book," my mother said once. "What's in it?"
> "The story of the great white whale."
> She could not believe it. After a while, she said, "What do they got to wail about, those whites?" (91)

Lipsha's word perversions entertain. For example, regarding malpractice suits: "I heard of those suits. I used to think it was a color clothing quack doctors had to wear so you could tell them from the good ones" (203). When Marie ("Grandma" in the first chapter) tells the children at Nector's funeral that "she had been stepping out onto the road of death," Lipsha asks if "there [were] any stop signs or dividing markers on that road" (210). And when he relates the story of the "little blue tweety bird" that flew up Lulu's dress and got lost (never, apparently, to come out alive), he chris-tens it a "paraclete" (201).

Much humor is slyly sexual. When Beverly Lamartine recalls the strip poker game that he, his brother Henry, and Lulu once played, Lulu tells him something he never knew: "It was after I won your shorts with my pair of deuces and Henry's with my eights, and you were naked, that I de-cided which one to marry" (82). And moments later: "'Some men react in that situation and some don't,' she told him. 'It was reaction I looked for, if you know what I mean'" (83). After Nector and Marie couple on the slope between the convent and the town (we are never quite sure who seduces whom), she sneers, "I've had better" (61). Dot and Gerry beget little Shawn "in a visiting room at the state prison. Dot had straddled Gerry's lap in a corner the closed-circuit TV did not quite scan. Through a hole ripped in her pantyhose and a hole ripped in Gerry's jeans they somehow managed to join and, miraculously, to conceive" (160).

Two other forms of humor deserve attention: slapstick and sarcasm. Examples of the former cavort throughout the novel, though often in contexts that are not entirely humorous. Lipsha's moment of revelation concerning his father, for instance, is triggered—without comment—by an empty bottle of rotgut flipped over someone's shoulder that hits him "smack between the eyes" (247). When Marie is a young girl at the convent and decides to treat Sister Leopolda to an ovenlike taste of hell, things backfire comically: "She bent forward with her fork held out. I kicked her with all my might. She flew in. But the outstretched poker hit the back wall first, so she rebounded. The oven was not so deep as I had thought" (53). In the midst of Lulu and Nector's laundry tryst, washers and dryers shaking and moaning in the background, Lulu's poodlelike wig jumps off her head and spoils the moment. "Not only that," Lipsha tells us, "but her wig was almost with a life of its own. Grandpa's eyes were bugging at the change already, and swear to God if the thing didn't rear up and pop him in the face like it was going to start something" (197). Lipsha terms Lulu (now bald, but somehow elegant) an "alien queen" (197). Had he told her to her face it might be insulting; here it is merely quick (and slick) description, to modify Clifford Geertz for a moment.

Sharp barbs, however, do fly through *Love Medicine*, and they can be crudely amusing. For example, Zelda, rather pointedly to Lynette, concerning Albertine: "'She's not married yet,' said Zelda, dangling a bright plastic bundle of keys down to the baby. 'She thinks she'll wait for her baby until *after* she's married'" (23; italics Zelda's). Or Marie to Leopolda, post-oven fiasco: "'Bitch of Jesus Christ!' I shouted. 'Kneel and beg! Lick the floor!'" (53). And Marie, teasing the neighborhood gossip-cows with their own bad lives: "How's your son? Too bad he crossed the border. I heard he had to go. Are you taking in his newborn?" (70).

Mary Douglas suggests that humor always contains an element of aggression, that jokes subvert, and therefore comedy attacks control.[3] Though she is critical of Henri Bergson's theory of laughter for failing to account for certain types of humor, she would likely agree with him that some humor is "above all, a corrective. Being intended to humiliate, it must make a painful impression on the person against whom it is directed."[4] But surely vengeance and intimidation are not at the root of all humor in *Love Medicine*.

To consider other explanations for what I have been offering as funny in the novel, let us turn first to Johan Huizinga. In *Homo Ludens*, Huizinga argues that play structures inform nearly all human activity, including law, religion, philosophy, and art. "Play," he explains, "is a voluntary activity or occupation executed within certain fixed limits of time and place, according to rules freely accepted but absolutely binding, having its aim in itself and accompanied by a feeling of tension, joy and the consciousness that it is 'different' from 'ordinary life.'"[5] When Beverly creates a fantasy world in which Lulu's boy Henry Junior becomes his son, he is engaged in almost pure play. Though he has never seen Henry Junior in person, Beverly believes he is, biologically, his son (having slept with Lulu, his brother's widow, a week after Henry Sr.'s death). He uses a single prop—

the boy's photograph, willingly supplied each year by Lulu—to weave a persuasive daydream that doubles as a shrewd marketing pitch. Beverly convinces working-class parents around Minneapolis to buy enrichment workbooks for their kids by telling tales of Henry Junior's self-initiated success. In fact, "with every picture Beverly grew more familiar with his son and more inspired in the invention of tales he embroidered, day after day, on front porches that were to him the innocent stages for his routine" (78).

The fabled Henry Junior succeeds as student, athlete, and social climber, clearing "the hurdles of class and intellect with an ease astonishing to Beverly" (78). Unfortunately, Henry Junior becomes too real, and the boundary between fantasy and reality blurs perceptibly in Beverly's mind. When he drives back to the reservation to claim the boy, he is at first unable to pick him out from among Lulu's shuffling octet. Each child "was Henry Junior in a different daydream, at a different age" (80).

When play becomes too "real," confusion intrudes. June's mock hanging—at best darkly comic—is nearly the novel's most tragic scene. June, Gordie, Aurelia, and Zelda are out "playing in the woods," when Zelda runs shrieking back to Marie: "'It's June,' she gasped. 'Mama, they're hanging June out in the woods!'" (67). When Marie arrives at the place on a dead run, she "saw Gordie was standing there with one end of the rope that was looped high around a branch. The other end was tied in a loose loop around June's neck" (67). They protest that they were only *playing*, but Marie refuses to believe their "lies." Until June speaks up:

> "You ruined it." Her eyes blinked at me, dry, as she choked it out. "I stole their horse. So I was supposed to be hanged."
>
> I gaped at her.
>
> "Child," I said, "you don't know how to play. It's a game, but if they hang you they would hang you for real."
>
> She put her head down. I could almost have sworn she knew what was real and what was not real, and that I'd still ruined it. (67–68)

The tension dissipates a moment later when June mutters "damn old bitch" under her breath and Marie summarily packs her mouth with soap flakes (68).

Henry Junior as an adult is a character for whom nonplay displaces the ludic. When we first see him as a boy, he is engaged in mock play, learning to "cradle, aim, and squeeze-fire" a .22, with a jug as his target (85). Later we discover he has been to Vietnam, where, after nine months of jungle combat, he is captured by the North Vietnamese Army. And although Huizinga cogently argues that a rooted element of play is *agon*, or competitive struggle, and that war therefore can still be a game, he admits that "modern warfare has, on the face of it, lost all contact with play" (210). It certainly has for Henry Junior, an American Indian with "almost Asian-looking eyes" sent to the Orient to kill Asians (83). In "A Bridge," Henry is bitter, violent, jumpy. He relives confused Vietnam scenarios in the real world of Fargo. Albertine, with her runaway's bundle, looks to him like a Vietnamese refugee—or is she a terrorist?—carrying a loosely wrapped package of possessions or, potentially, explosives. Henry still wears his "dull green army jacket" (132). In the hotel where he and Albertine rent a room for the night, he takes a "violent dislike" to the "lazy motherfucker" clerk: "'I could off this fat shit,' he told himself" (136). When he sees Albertine crouching over her belongings in the bathroom, he imagines her as the hemorrhaging village woman he was once supposed to interrogate. And he has told Albertine, apparently, about the war: "He said those men took trophies. Skin pressed in the pages of a book" (135). War as contest here has gone perversely evil. "When the combat has an ethical value," Huizinga points out, "it ceases to be play" (210). No longer capable of restful sleep, let alone meaningful play, Henry explodes, shrieking, when Albertine touches him the next morning. Inside of a year he will commit suicide.

King Kashpaw's own "Vietnam" experience is comically chiastic to Henry's. "He's no vet," Lipsha assures us in the first chapter (36). But King seems to think he is: "Like I was telling you, I was in the Marines. You can't run from them bastards, man. They'll get you every time. I was in Nam" (253). King's daydream is, in fact, quite elaborate, in spite of Lipsha's skepticism:

"*BINH,*" he popped his lips. "*BINH, BINH.*"
   That was the sound of incoming fire exploding next to his head.
   "Apple, Apple?"
   "What Banana?"
   "Over here, Apple!"
   That was what he and his buddy, who King said was a Kentucky Boy, used to call each other, in code.
   "How come you didn't just use names?" I asked between gulps. "What difference?"
   "The enemy." He glared at me. He was getting into the fantasy.
   "They're a small people." He put his hand out at Howard's height. "Hard to see." (253–54)

"There is yet another use of the word 'play,'" Huizinga suggests, "which is just as widespread and just as fundamental as the equation of play with serious strife, namely, in relation to the erotic" (43). Sexual play frisks through this novel, but the edges between eroticism and war frequently blur. During June's roadside encounter with slick-vested Andy, "she let him wrestle with her clothing," and then ends up with the crown of her head "wedged . . . against the driver's door" (4–5). King and Lynette, after a drunken evening in which he nearly drowns her in the kitchen sink, instinctively modulate from rage to sex: "They got into the car soon after that. Doors slammed. But they traveled just a few yards and then stopped. The horn blared softly. I suppose they knocked against it in passion" (39). Roaring car heaters, moreover, accompany the "auto" eroticisms of both June and her son. When Lulu and Beverly make love after Henry Sr.'s funeral, we sense the agonistic component for both parties:

> Then passion overtook them. She hung onto him like they were riding the tossing ground, her teeth grinding in his ear. . . . Afterward they lay together, breathing the dark in and out. He had wept the one other time in his life besides post combat, and after a while he came into her again, tasting his own miraculous continuance. (87)

Henry Junior and Albertine's lovemaking is nearly brutal; after ejaculating "helplessly, pressed against her, before he was even hard"—excited by Albertine's fear, we are told—Henry pins her face down on the bed and takes her harshly from behind (140–41). Sex can become ritualized, as when Nector follows the same routine with Lulu—meat to dogs, in through window, wash hands, make love, leave before dawn: a veritable "clockwork precision of timing"—for five years (101). Or passion can turn into the repressed rage of latent lesbianism, as with Leopolda, whose vicious scalding of Marie as an example of Satan's "hellish embrace" is followed by "slow, wide circles" of ointment rubbed into Marie's naked back (49, 51).

Sigmund Freud believes that all love objects serve as "mother-surrogates," and he argues for a model of humor as a release or free discharge of emotional energy.[6] Jokes can occasion freedom from anxiety, or simply from the burden of being grown up. Many Indian societies feature comic figures whose roles work precisely in this way: the Western Pueblo *kachinas*, for example, or the *heyokas* of the Lakota. The reversing humor of the latter is especially prevalent in *Love Medicine*. According to John (Fire) Lame Deer, a *heyoka* "is an upside-down, backward-forward, yes-and-no man, a con-trary-wise." "A *heyoka* does strange things," acknowledges Lame Deer. "He says 'yes' when he means 'no.' He rides his horse backward. He wears his moccasins or boots the wrong way. When he's coming, he's really going."[7] Lyman Lamartine tries to renew his brother Henry's interest in their red convertible by taking a hammer to its underside and making it "look just as beat up as [he] could" (149). Howard Kashpaw (King Junior) curiously inverts proper cereal-making sequence, pouring the milk into the bowl first, then the cereal. "'He does it all backwards,' observed King" (252). Lipsha even sees Howard as a sort of sacred clown: "Howard didn't say nothing. He carried the bowl and the box of cereal very carefully in to the television. It was like he was going to make a religious offering" (252).

Lipsha, who later prepares himself a backward bowl of cereal, is in his own way a holy fool. He is a modern pinball medicine man, who believes he has "the touch" (190). "I know the tricks of mind and body inside out without ever having trained for it," he asserts. "It's a thing you got to be born with. I got secrets in my hands that nobody ever knew to ask" (189–90). In the Lakota system, a man need merely dream of lightning, "the thunderbirds," to become a *heyoka*. Lipsha doesn't exactly do this, but early in the novel he does lie out under the night sky with Albertine, watching the Northern Lights: "At times the whole sky was ringed in shooting points and puckers of light gathering and falling, pulsing, fading, rhythmical as breathing" (34).

But he's not especially diligent about his medicine, particularly in acquiring the two goose hearts for Marie's love charm. (Lipsha is probably better at Space Invaders than at ritual healing.) And the medicine he does provide—two frozen turkey hearts—misfires horribly, killing Nector in a ludicrously sad choking scene. When Marie tells Lipsha that Nector had come back to her after death, Lipsha says his "head felt screwed on backwards" (212). Even some of Lipsha's diction recalls Lame Deer's earthy phrasings, as in "I don't got the cold hard potatoes it takes to understand everything" (195).

Nector himself is another candidate for *heyoka* status, although more as someone affected by contraries than in the strictly magical sense. He is a man trapped by opposites, caught between the conflicting worlds of Marie and Lulu. Sitting hand in hand with Marie, after their co-seduction on the hill, he narrates his internal contradiction: "I don't want her, but I want her, and I cannot let go" (62). He feels the same toward Lulu after deciding to leave her forever: "No sooner had I given her up than I wanted Lulu back" (104). He is a marvelously inappropriate churchgoer, who turns the normally hushed tone of the Catholic sanctuary into an evangelical shouting contest. "He shrieked to heaven," Lipsha says, "and he pleaded like a movie actor and he pounded his chest like Tarzan in the Lord I Am Not Worthies. I thought he might hurt himself" (194). He even converts the Virgin's name to his wife's: "HAIL MARIE FULL OF GRACE" (194). And in true *heyoka* fashion, on the topic of his "second childhood," he tells Lipsha, "I been chosen for it. I couldn't say no" (190).

Another pan-Indian character who pops up in the novel is the untiring trickster. Paul Radin terms Trickster the oldest of all figures in American Indian mythologies, perhaps in all mythologies.[8] He (or she) is typically depicted as wandering, hungry, highly sexed, ageless, and animal-named. Many characters in *Love Medicine* act tricksterian; the men in particular roam, eat, and love their way through the book. King warms up the topic by relating a little trickster-style tale. First he claims that he once "shot a fox sleeping" through "that little black hole underneath [his] tail"—with a bow and arrow, no less (29). Then: "But I heard of this guy once who put his arrow through a fox then left it thrash around in the bush until he thought it was dead. He went in there after it. You know what he found? That fox had chewed the arrow off either side of its body and it was gone" (30). Though the details Lyman offers from the summer trip he and Henry make to the Northwest are scanty, they suggest a typical trickster journey. Henry and Lyman simply wander, stopping to eat and sleep, or, say, pick up a girl from Chicken, Alaska. And drive her home. When it gets cold, they leave. Marie is moderately mischievous when she tries to drop-kick Leopolda into the oven, and more so when she switches Nector's farewell note from the salt can to the sugar jar. Nector fantasizes playing trickster after he poses for *Plunge of the Brave*, imagining himself surviving the jump and being washed to safety. He also revels in the way that loving Lulu lets him assume different forms: "I could twist like a rope. I could disappear beneath the surface. I could run to a halt and Lulu would have been there every moment" (100).

Lulu herself is a critical nexus for trickster behavior. She sleeps with Old Man Pillager (trickster is also known as "Old Man,"[9] and "Pillager" is as good a tag as any for his scavenging ways), and their union spawns Gerry Nanapush, a paradigmatic modern trickster figure. Lulu's no prankish slouch herself; in her "secret wildness" she dallies with men for the sheer exhilarating pleasure of it (218). When Beverly visits her, he is bewildered by her magical homemaker's touch, noting her pin-neat rooms and particularly her preparation of dinner: "She seemed to fill pots with food by pointing at them and take things from the oven that she'd never put in. The table jumped to set itself. The pop foamed into glasses, and the milk sighed to the lip" (86).

But Gerry *is* Trickster, literally. Alan R. Velie records that "the Chippewa Trickster is called Wenebojo, Manabozho, or Nanabush, depending on how authors recorded the Anishinabe word."[10] This Trickster (as is true for most tribes) is able to alter his shape as he wishes, and, says Gerald Vizenor, "wanders in mythic time and transformational space." He is, Vizenor explains, a "teacher and healer in various personalities," but he is also capable of "violence, deceptions, and cruelties: the realities of human imperfections."[11] The first time we meet the adult Gerry, he performs a miraculous escape: though spotted by Officer Lovchik in the confines of a "cramped and littered bar. . . . Gerry was over the backside of the booth and out the door before Lovchik got close enough to make a positive identification" (155–56). But even as a boy, we are told, Gerry had Lulu's ways in him:

> He laughed at everything, or seemed barely to be keeping amusement in. His eyes were black, sly, snapping with sparks. He led the rest in play without a hint of effort, just like Lulu, whose gestures worked as subtle magnets. He was a big boy, a born leader, light on his feet and powerful. His mind seemed quick. It would not surprise Bev to hear, after many years passed on, that this Gerry grew up to be both a natural criminal and a hero whose face appeared on the six-o'clock news. (84–85)

Early in his career as natural criminal, Gerry gets arrested, breaks out of prison, gets re-arrested, and so on. "He broke out time after time," Albertine tells us, "and was caught each time he did it, regular as clockwork" (160). He seems to escape primarily because he can, so skilled are his metamorphic abilities, and the escape-recapture cycle becomes ritualized trickster play. "He boasted that no steel or concrete shitbarn could hold a Chippewa, and he had eellike properties in spite of his enormous size. Greased with lard once, he squirmed into a six-foot-thick prison wall and vanished" (160). He shows up at Dot and Albertine's weigh shack without a sound and "cat-quick for all his mass" (165). Then he and Dot, "by mysterious means, slipped their bodies into Dot's compact car" (166). While the two reunited behemoths are absent, Albertine daydreams an indulgent trickster scene, combining food, animals, and sex:

> I pictured them in Dot's long tan trailer house, both hungry. Heads swaying, clasped hands swinging between them like hooked trunks,

they moved through the kitchen feeding casually from boxes and bags on the counters, like ponderous animals alone in a forest. When they had fed, they moved on to the bedroom and settled themselves upon Dot's king-size and sateen-quilted spread. They rubbed together, locked and unlocked their parts. (167)

At the end of the novel, supposedly up to 320 pounds, Gerry noiselessly (except to Lipsha, who senses him) scrabbles his way up the skylight shaft into King and Lynette's grubby Twin Cities kitchen. By then teaming with Lipsha to defeat King in a quick card game ("five-card punk," Gerry says), Gerry unwittingly re-enacts a classic Chippewa trickster story. For, according to legend, Manabozho/Nanabush journeys until he meets his principal enemy, "the great gambler," whom he defeats, saving his own life and the spirit of the woodland tribes from "the land of darkness" (Vizenor, 4–6). Is it any surprise that a Road Runner cartoon has been playing in the apartment? Or that Lipsha roots for "old Wiley Coyote?" (251). Gerry then vanishes without a trace when the police barge in. As Lipsha drives off in his newly won car, he gets to "waxing eloquent" about Gerry as trickster:

I knew my dad would get away. He could fly. He could strip and flee and change into shapes of swift release. Owls and bees, two-toned Ramblers, buzzards, cottontails, and motes of dust. These forms was interchangeable with his. He was the clouds scudding over the moon, the wings of ducks banging in the slough. (266)

Gerry can take on animal forms, but animals that ludicrously enact human activity—such as the poker-playing bulldogs pictured in King's garish velvet wall-hanging—seem to me a particularly "white" touch in the novel. To be sure, red and white paths do cross, at times with humorous results. Zelda, whose rule is "never marry a Swedish," has undone herself by marrying two (14). The Morrissey who fathers June and brings her to Marie when his wife dies is a white-trash "whining no-good" (63). Dot delights in telling the fooled Lovchik that "no one's been through all night," and then asks him in mock seriousness what he thinks of "Ketchup Face" as a name for her child (156). "Making sense of other people is never easy," Keith Basso opens *Portraits of "The Whiteman,"* "and making sense of how other people make sense can be very difficult indeed."[12] Thus Nector pretends not to understand the painter's instructions to disrobe, and is about to help *her* undress when she starts "to demonstrate by clawing at her buttons" (90). Nector, updating Custer's opinion of the value of Indians to accommodate modern cinema, declaims, "The only interesting Indian is dead, or dying by falling backwards off a horse" (91).

Gerry has a particularly hard time making sense of the United States judicial system, getting convicted in a case he thought "would blow over if it ever reached court. But there is nothing more vengeful and determined in this world than a cowboy with sore balls, and Gerry soon found this out. He also found out that white people are good witnesses to have on your side, because they have names, addresses, social security numbers, and work phones. But they are terrible witnesses to have against you, almost as bad as having Indians witness for you" (162). Lyman, having smashed up the red convertible, acidly recalls the joke about what reservation roads and government promises have in common—holes. And Lulu, perhaps echoing Vine Deloria's suggestion that what Indians really need from whites is a "cultural leave-us-alone agreement," refuses to let the United States census taker in her door: "I say that every time they counted us they knew the precise number to get rid of" (221).[13]

Armed, then, with some notions of what gives humor its torque in *Love Medicine*, key questions remain: Why is Erdrich writing a humorous book? How does laughter relate to what the novel tries to accomplish? To formulate answers, we need first to contextualize the novel's aims. "I don't know what purpose I had in mind," says Erdrich herself in a 1985 interview, "except to write as honestly as possible, and to resolve things for a few characters. I wanted to tell a story, so if I told it, that's done."[14] But in a subsequent article on a writer's "sense of place" for the *New York Times Book Review*, she elaborates the duty of her fellow Indian authors: "Contemporary Native American writers have . . . a task quite different from that of other writers I've mentioned. In the light of enormous loss, they must tell stories of contemporary survivors while protecting and celebrating the cores of cultures left in the wake of the catastrophe."[15]

Love Medicine is a redemptive, regenerative, celebratory text that begins with characters separated by time and space and family relationships and gradually pulls some of them home. The novel opens off the reservation with June, "walking down the clogged main street of oil boomtown Williston, North Dakota, killing time before the noon bus arrived that would take her home" (1). June is "aged hard" but feeling fragile; she is liable to "fall apart at the slightest touch" (1, 4). But she pulls herself back together and by the end of the first section, as snow falls, she "walked over it like water and came home" (6). What part of her comes home, though, is problematic, because she dies on the way in a sudden storm. Apparently her spirit endures, for the image of June the survivor returning home—in spite of death—pervades the book. Right up, in fact, to the closing scene, in which Lipsha, June's son, discovers "there was nothing to do but cross the water, and bring her home" (272).

A passel of interrelated stories brings the reader home in the novel. Five not-so-distinct clans (Nanapush, Lamartine, Lazarre, Morrissey, Kashpaw) vie for narrative dominance until coalescing—literally as well as figuratively—in Lipsha. *Love Medicine* spans fifty years and four generations, played out by a sometimes bewildering array of characters; but the themes of survival, endurance, redemption, and regeneration prevail. June, we discover, was a quintessential survivor: as a child alone in the bush, she sucked pine sap to stay alive. Marie survives Leopolda's scalding and vengeful stabbing and is even transformed, briefly, into a saint. She later survives Nector's attempt to throw her over for Lulu, redeeming him with her love: "I did for Nector Kashpaw what I learned from the nun. I put my hand through what scared him. I held it out there for him. And when he took it with all the strength of his arms, I pulled him in" (129).

But this enduring is a difficult business. The weight of adversity, of heartache, of sorrow threaten to crush hope flat, or at least wear it down by degrees. Marie sees an analogy in the action of waves when she touches June's beads:

> It's a rare time when I do this. I touch them, and every time I do I think of small stones. At the bottom of the lake, rolled aimless by the waves, I think of them polished. To many people it would be a kindness. But I see no kindness in how the waves are grinding them smaller and smaller until they finally disappear. (73)

And Lipsha, when he believes Marie has herself crumpled under the pressure of Nector's death, expresses the same idea in similar terms: "You think a person you know has got through death and illness and being broke and living on commodity rice will get through anything. Then they fold and you see how fragile were the stones that underpinned them. You see how instantly the ground can shift you thought was solid" (209).

A legacy of devastation menaces *Love Medicine*'s characters, and some succumb. Henry Junior, for example, epitomizes those Indians Paula Gunn Allen describes in *The Sacred Hoop* as victims of alienation: "These are the most likely to be suicidal, inarticulate, almost paralyzed in their inability to direct their energies toward resolving what seems to them an insoluble conflict." Allen identifies the principal literary symbol of this lack of power as "tonguelessness"; Henry, we recall, approximates this when he silently bites through his lip while watching television. And yet, Allen says, Indians do survive:

We survive war and conquest; we survive colonization, acculturation, assimilation; we survive beating, rape, starvation, mutilation, sterilization, abandonment, neglect, death of our children, our loved ones, destruction of our land, our homes, our past, and our future. We survive, and we do more than just survive. We bond, we care, we fight, we teach, we nurse, we bear, we feed, we earn, we laugh, we love, we hang in there, no matter what.[16]

Laughter is not merely a by-product of survival, it is a critical force behind it. Northrop Frye, pointing out humor's regenerative effect, notes that "something gets born at the end of comedy." Freud approaches the subject differently, describing humor as a defense mechanism and suggesting that we use it to "withdraw the energy from the ready held pain release, and through discharge change the same into pleasure." Julia Kristeva argues that "laughing is a way of placing or displacing abjection." Yet each of these theories buttresses Tim Giago's simple observations at the end of a column on Indian humor in the *Lakota Times*: "It has been said that humor pulled the Jewish and Black people through the hard times. It is said they could not have survived without it. Well, the moral of this column is, if you want to see some real survivors, just sit in on an Indian joke session. There's nothing in this world that can top it!"[17]

How *does* humor promote endurance? The explanation seems twinned to humor's binate nature. Laughter can wound, or it can bond. One power destroys, the other builds up. Faced with five hundred years of physical, cultural, and spiritual genocide, Indians seek to steal power from their aggressors through inversion: by turning hatred to humor, the weakness of suffering is transformed into the strength of laughter. This *a*-versive power, according to Allen, is not only infinitely renewable but discoverable in the natural world:

For however painful and futile our struggle becomes, we have but to look outside at the birds, the deer, and the seasons to understand that change does not mean destruction, that life, however painful and even elusive it is at times, contains much joy and hilarity, pleasure and beauty for those who live within its requirements of grace. (*Sacred Hoop,* 163)

What Allen finds interesting about the use of humor in American Indian poetry (and I believe her comments apply to fiction as well) "is its integrating effect: it makes tolerable what is otherwise unthinkable; it allows a sort of breathing space in which an entire race can take stock of itself and its future" (*Sacred Hoop*, 159).

In *Love Medicine*, certain scenes yield dramatic instances of such "breathing space." Consider those that hover precipitously between comedy and tragedy. Erdrich graphically prefigures these moments during Gordie's telling of the Norwegian joke. An absurd variant on a standard joke pattern, it relates the stupidity of the Norwegian who, during the French Revolution, explains to his executioners how to repair their guillotine. But each section of the joke is interrupted by King's screams at Lynette outside. The evening is already tainted with a certain sad ugliness—King has earlier announced, "You'd eat shit," to Lynette (29)—but now it teeters toward violence. Each time King screams, Gordie pauses. After the second round of "Fuckin' bitch!" Albertine wonders whether they should stop the joke and go out (32). But Gordie continues to the joke's end, and only then do he, Albertine, and Lipsha investigate.

Comedy and tragedy each have their say, but only the development of the novel will uncover a victor. The gallows humor is nearly played for keeps during June's lynching (although chronologically it precedes the Norwegian joke). As Gordie and Aurelia hang June, the child, in apparent earnest, says, "You got to tighten it . . . before you hoist me up" (67). Though we as readers know that June survives, the situation is still potentially horrible. By the end of the scene, however, comedy supplants tragedy.

This is not always the case. Before Henry Junior drowns himself, he and Lyman oscillate between laughter and anger. They fight when Henry rips the arm off Lyman's "class act" jacket; then, punch-drunk, they dissolve into hysterics (152). The brothers drain a cooler of beers, but Henry's mood turns again. Lyman tries to bring him around with more humor:

> "You're crazy too," I say, to jolly him up. "Crazy Lamartine boys!"
>
> He looks as though he will take this wrong at first. His face twists, then clears, and he jumps up on his feet. "That's right!" he says. "Crazier 'n hell. Crazy Indians!"
>
> I think it's the old Henry again. He throws off his jacket and starts swinging his legs out from under the knees like a fancy dancer. He's down doing something between a grouse dance and a bunny hop, no kind of dance I ever saw before, but neither has anyone else on all this green growing earth. He's wild. He wants to pitch whoopee! He's up and at me and all over. All this time I'm laughing so hard, so hard my belly is getting tied up in a knot. (153)

As Lyman experiences the pleasure (and pain) of intense laughter, Henry decides to jump in the water to "cool me off!" (154). Lyman soon realizes that his brother is being taken away, without apparent resistance, by the current. Henry's last words, spoken in a normal voice across half a river under a darkening sky, devastate: "'My boots are filling,' he says" (154). And then he's gone.

Humor doesn't help Henry endure, at least not long enough. It does, however, help Marie and Lipsha after Nector dies at the end of his tragi-comic choking scene. (The novel's other choker is Henry, who *laughs* like "a man choking" when he comes back from Vietnam [148].) Nector gags when Marie slugs his back to get him to eat the love medicine. Lipsha narrates this esophagal misfire as pure stand-up comedy: "You ever sit down at a restaurant table and up above you there is a list of instructions what to do if something slides down the wrong pipe? It sure makes you chew slow, that's for damn sure" (207). Even as his restorative powers fail, Lipsha jests with death: "Time was flashing back and forth like a pinball machine. Lights blinked and balls hopped and rubber bands chirped, until suddenly I realized the last ball had gone down the drain and there was nothing" (208). But when Marie stumbles, Lipsha's heart and mind short-circuit: he thinks she's going to die, too. She does not, and his humor reconnects.

At Nector's funeral, the family also reconnects, leading Lipsha to a re-demptive understanding of tragedy: "Once you greet death," he says, "you wear your life like a garment from the mission bundle sale ever after—lightly because you realize you never paid nothing for it, cherishing because you know you won't ever come by such a bargain again" (213–14). As the chapter closes, Lipsha is digging dandelions—and reconnects power-fully with the ground: "I felt [the sun] flow down my arms, out my fingers, arrowing through the ends of the fork into the earth" (215). Each dande-lion is "a globe of frail seeds that's indestructible" (215). But what else is laughter? Or life? In Chippewa mythology a dandelion is a reminder of something lost. When a chief named Shawandasse waited too long to court a lovely girl, she became a spirit maiden, whose dissipating halo turned into the seeds of this "yellow-crowned flower."[18] Thus Lipsha sees his new perspective on life confirmed in the "secret lesson" of a dandelion, which to others is merely a weedy nuisance (215).

Other images in the novel are similarly double-acting. Water and its cognate, the color blue, both share humor's ability to cut two ways. Blue can be a positive color (a "blue day" is a good day for the Chippewa, and blue is the North Dakota Indian color for the moon, thunder, water, and the west), or it can be negative (the "blues").[19] Both, like humor, are curi-ously connected with displacement. Objects viewed through "blue" water become distorted, while Julia Kristeva points out that blue may have a perceptual "noncentered or decentering effect."[20] Water, furthermore (which Erdrich calls *Love Medicine*'s "main image"), can cleanse or drown. Water claims a few victims in this novel, notably June (in the form of snow) and Henry Junior, and attempts to grab a few more, including Gordie (in the form of alcohol) and Nector (in both "Plunge of the Brave" and "Flesh and Blood"). But for Erdrich water is ultimately a symbol of "transformation (walking over snow or water)" and "transcendence," because it allows life to go on.[21] Allen notes that "the most important theme in Native American novels is . . . transformation and continuance." She goes on to explain water's role: "The nature of the cosmos, of the human, the creaturely, and the supernatural universe is like water. It takes numerous forms; it evaporates and it gathers. Survival and continuance are contingent on its presence. Whether it is in a cup, a jar, or an underground river, it nourishes life" (*Sacred Hoop,* 101). Water properly navigated can bring one safely home. Thus Marie (whose name encodes the sea: *mare*) pulls Nector in over the deepening lake between them at the end of "Flesh and Blood." And Lipsha crosses the water and brings the novel home.

Erdrich reinforces the novel's movement through her narrative style. She playfully and coherently blends Indian and Western technique to produce a work of swirling, singing prose. Many contemporary Indian novelists have crafted their writing to reflect tribal concepts of time (timelessness) and space (multidimensionality). Allen points out, for example, that "achronology is the favored structuring device of American Indian novelists since N. Scott Momaday selected it for organizing *House Made of Dawn*" (*Sacred Hoop,* 147). There are many ways to describe traditional tribal narrative, several of which suit *Love Medicine*. For example, Thomas B. Leckley writes in *The World of Manabozho*:

> Indian folklore is a great collection of anecdotes, episodes, jokes, and fables, and storytellers constantly combined and recombined these elements in different ways. We seldom find a plotted story of the kind we know. Instead, the interest is usually in a single episode; if this is linked to another, the relationship is that of *two beads on one string*, seldom that of two bricks in one building [italics mine].[22]

Or Allen argues in *The Sacred Hoop*:

> Traditional American Indian stories work dynamically among *clusters of loosely interconnected circles*. The focus of action shifts from one character to another as the story unfolds. There is no "point of view" as the term is generally understood, unless the action itself, the story's purpose, can be termed "point of view" [italics mine]. (241–42)

Or:

> The *patchwork quilt* is the best material example I can think of to des-
> cribe the plot and process of a traditional tribal narrative [italics mine].
> (243)

Erdrich, the contemporary Western artist, plays these traditional patterns
into a narrative that doubles back and darts forward, recalling Cree storyteller Jacob Nibènegenesábe's conventional tale opening: "*Usá puyew usu
wapiw*" ("I go backward, look forward").[23] Erdrich begins her novel in 1981,
then shifts to 1934. The rest of the book proceeds fairly chronologically (in
the end circling back to and beyond its beginning), but within tales events
are told and re-told (or pre-told) until the meaning flows in all directions
at once. Thus, in *Love Medicine*, what Mikhail M. Bakhtin called "double-
voiced discourse" becomes double vision; a traditional patchwork becomes
a powerful and sacred star quilt.[24]

Within this fabric, place and naming become very important. These
concepts link in the Cree world, as Howard Norman points out in *Wishing
Bone Cycle*: "To say the name is to begin the story."[25] Names bring alive what
has happened; names affect behavior. In *Love Medicine*, characters' names
place them in their own history and in relation to other characters. Thus
in "The World's Greatest Fisherman"—set in 1981—Marie is "Grandma,"
exclusively. In "Saint Marie" she becomes her 1934 mail-order-Catholic-
soul-Marie self, squaring off against Leopolda. But the reader cannot know
that Grandma is Marie until she encounters Nector on the convent slope
in "Wild Geese." And Albertine, in "A Bridge," sees an Indian-looking soldier who remains anonymous for three pages until he emerges as Henry
Junior, back from Vietnam. In such ways Erdrich tangles the skein of lives
in the novel a little, then shakes it loose, then tangles it again. By the end
the web is smoothed out and traceable: ends reconnect, patterns are relaid.
Achronicity plays an important role here, since, Allen says, it "connects
pain and praise through timely movement, knitting person and surroundings into one" (*Sacred Hoop*, 150).

"We shall not cease from exploration / And the end of all our exploring
/ Will be to arrive where we started / And know the place for the first
time," writes T. S. Eliot in "Four Quartets."[26] We began with an invocation
of critics, literary folk who seem to misread *Love Medicine*, unlike the tribal
people who, Erdrich points out, tend to focus first on its humor (Wong,
214). Perhaps the latter group reacts as do many people in the novel, and
laughs out of place, or in "inappropriate" spots. Erdrich's characters keep
chuckling, especially when—by rights—they shouldn't. But that is pre-

cisely the nature and function of *Love Medicine*'s compassionate humor: it heals, it renews, it integrates, it balances. It *belongs*, in short, where it should not. "Belonging is a basic assumption for traditional Indians," comments Allen, and "narratives . . . that restore the estranged to his or her place within the cultural matrix abound" (*Sacred Hoop*, 127). For Lipsha, "belonging was a matter of deciding to," and *Love Medicine* thus restores an estranged son to his mother and grandmother (255). Finally, Erdrich herself, through the project of this novel, demonstrates a special kinship to one of her own favorite authors: William Faulkner. For it is Faulkner—no stranger to humor—who accepted the 1949 Nobel Prize for Literature by noting that a writer's aim is "to help man endure by lifting his heart."[27]

Notes

1. Gene Lyons, "In Indian Territory," *Newsweek*, 11 February 1985, 70–71 (reprinted in *Contemporary Literary Criticism* 39 [1986]: 132); *Kirkus Reviews*, 15 August 1984, 765–66 (reprinted in *Contemporary Literary Criticism* 39 [1986]: 128); Robert Towers, "Uprooted," *New York Review of Books*, 11 April 1985, 36–37 (reprinted in *Contemporary Literary Criticism* 39 [1986]: 133).

2. Louise Erdrich, *Love Medicine* (1984; reprint, New York: Bantam, 1985), 16. Subsequent references to the novel will be identified by page numbers in parentheses in the text.

3. Mary Douglas, "The Social Control of Cognition: Some Factors in Joke Perception," *Man* 3 (1968): 361–76.

4. Henri Bergson, "Laughter," in *Comedy*, edited by Wylie Sypher (New York: Doubleday, 1956), 187.

5. Johan Huizinga, *Homo Ludens: A Study of the Play Element in Culture*, 2d ed. (Boston: Beacon, 1972), 28. Subsequent references will be identified by page numbers in parentheses in the text.

6. Sigmund Freud, "A Special Type of Choice of Object Made by Men," *Jahrbuch* (1910); reprinted in Benjamin Nelson, ed., *On Creativity and the Unconscious: Papers on the Psychology of Art, Literature, Love, Religion* (New York: Harper, 1958), 166.

7. John (Fire) Lame Deer and Richard Erdoes, *Lame Deer, Seeker of Visions: The Life of a Sioux Medicine Man* (New York: Simon and Schuster, 1972), 225.

8. Paul Radin, "The Wakdjunkaga Cycle and Its Relation to Other North American Indian Trickster Cycles," in *The Trickster: A Study in American Indian Mythology* (New York: Schocken, 1972), 164.

9. Kenneth Lincoln, *Native American Renaissance* (Berkeley: University of California Press, 1983), 122.

10. William Jones and Truman Michelson, eds., *Ojibway Texts* (Leyden: E. J. Bruss, 1917), and Basil Johnson, *Ojibway Heritage* (New York: Columbia University Press, 1976), cited in Alan R. Velie, "Beyond the Novel Chippewa-Style: Gerald Vizenor's Post-Modern Fiction," in *Four American Literary Masters* (Norman: University of Oklahoma Press, 1982), 131.

11. Gerald Vizenor, *The People Named the Chippewa: Narrative Histories* (Minneapolis: University of Minnesota Press, 1984), 3. Subsequent references will be identified by page numbers in parentheses in the text.

12. Keith Basso, *Portraits of "The Whiteman"* (New York: Cambridge University Press, 1979), 3.

13. Vine Deloria, Jr., *Custer Died for Your Sins* (London: Collier-Macmillan Ltd., 1969), 27.

14. Jan George, "Interview with Louise Erdrich," *North Dakota Quarterly* 53, no. 2 (Spring 1985): 246.

15. Louise Erdrich, "Where I Ought to Be: A Writer's Sense of Place," *New York Times Book Review*, 28 July 1985, 25.

16. Paula Gunn Allen, *The Sacred Hoop: Recovering the Feminine in American Indian Traditions* (Boston: Beacon Press, 1986), 135, 138, 190. Subsequent references will be identified by page numbers in parentheses in the text.

17. Northrop Frye, "The Mythos of Spring: Comedy," in *Anatomy of Criticism* (Princeton: Princeton University Press, 1957), 170; Sigmund Freud, "Wit and the Various Forms of the Comic," in *Sigmund Freud: The Basic Writings*, edited by A. A. Brill (New York: Random House, 1938), 802; Julia Kristeva, *Powers of Horror: An Essay in Abjection*, translated by Leon S. Roudiez (New York: Columbia University Press, 1981), 8; Tim Giago, "Nothing Can Top Indian Joke Session," in *Notes from Indian Country* Vol. 1 (Pierre, S. D.: K. Cochran., 1984), 238.

18. *Chippewa Tales*, retold by Wa-be-no O-pee-chee, 2d ed. (Los Angeles: Wetzel Publishing Co., 1930), 38.

19. Gertrude Jobes, ed., *Dictionary of Mythology Folklore and Symbols* (New York: Scarecrow Press, 1962), 1:229.

20. Julia Kristeva, *Desire in Language: A Semiotic Approach to Literature and Art*, translated by Thomas Gora, Alice Jardine, and Leon S. Roudiez, edited by Leon S. Roudiez (New York: Columbia University Press, 1980), 225.

21. Hertha D. Wong, "An Interview with Louise Erdrich and Michael Dorris," *North Dakota Quarterly* 55, no. 1 (Winter 1987): 210. Subsequent references will be identified by page numbers in parentheses in the text.

22. Thomas B. Leckley, *The World of Manabozho* (New York: Vanguard, 1965), 7–8.

23. Howard A. Norman, trans., *The Wishing Bone Cycle: Narrative Poems from the Swampy Cree Indians*, 2d ed. (Santa Barbara: Ross-Erikson, 1982), 135. For a further discussion of "*Usá puyew usu wapiw*," see Lincoln, *Native American Renaissance*, 127.

24. Mikhail M. Bakhtin, *The Dialogic Imagination*, translated by Caryl Emerson and Michael Holquist, edited by Michael Holquist (Austin: University of Texas Press, 1981), 324.

25. Norman, *Wishing Bone Cycle*, 49. Norman here is quoting Samuel Makideme-wabe, a Swampy Cree elder.

26. T. S. Eliot, *The Complete Poems and Plays: 1909–1950* (New York: Harcourt, Brace and World, 1952), 145. These lines are from part 5 of the "Little Gidding" section.

27. William Faulkner, "Address upon Receiving the Nobel Prize for Literature," *New York Herald Tribune Book Review*, 14 January 1951; reprinted in *Essays, Speeches, and Public Lectures by William Faulkner*, edited by James B. Meriweather (New York: Random House, 1965), 120.

Opening the Text

Love Medicine *and the Return of the Native American Woman*

ROBERT SILBERMAN

◆ ◆ ◆

L OUISE ERDRICH'S *Love Medicine* opens with June Kashpaw, middle-aged Chippewa woman, wasting time in the oil boom town of Williston, North Dakota, while waiting for a bus that will take her back to the reservation where she grew up. She allows herself to be picked up by a white man in a bar; after a short, unsatisfying (for her) bit of lovemaking in his pickup, she takes off, cutting across the snowy fields as a storm begins to hit. There is a narrative break and then we learn that she has frozen to death.

This opening immediately establishes a relationship between *Love Medicine* and a well-known group of works by Native American authors: D'Arcy McNickle's *The Surrounded*, N. Scott Momaday's *The House Made of Dawn*, Leslie Marmon Silko's *Ceremony*, James Welch's *Winter in the Blood* and *The Death of Jim Loney*. These works are central texts in Native American literature, bearing a striking family resemblance to one another.

Reduced to bare essentials, they all tell of a young man's troubled homecoming. The opening line of *The Surrounded* sounds the theme: "Archilde Leon had been away from his father's ranch for nearly a year."[1] The book's title proclaims the outcome; in the final line of the text, Leon extends his hands to be shackled. From *The Surrounded* a clear line can be drawn to the later works by Momaday, Silko, and Welch, in effect defining the backbone of contemporary Native American fiction.

Given this closely related body of texts, Native American literature seems made to order for recent developments in literary criticism and critical theory. The writings of McNickle, Momaday, Welch, Silko, and others seem especially amenable to the analytical and interpretive preoccupations of such broad movements as structuralism and deconstructionist criticism. The many shared elements in the works, as well as the equally telling differences, make them a perfect case study for the analysis of combinations, oppositions and inversions beloved in structuralist criticism. Though not engaged in a technical, philosophical debate, Native American writers reveal an obsessive concern with the relation between speech and writing that is worthy of the deconstructionist critics. Finally, this body of literature incorporates among its major social and political concerns a preoccupation with origins, marginality, and otherness that would have delighted Foucault. Notwithstanding the focus in these books on a central individual, the writers address broad historical relations between groups as well as individual psychology, dramatizing, for example, the conflicts between tribal peoples and institutional authorities such as the police, the Bureau of Indian Affairs, and the church. In such a context, questions of language and discourse—Indian language(s) versus English, native forms of expression versus nontribal literary forms such as the novel—are inevitably questions of power.

It is possible to speculate on the reasons that the narratives of McNickle, Momaday, Silko, and Welch take the forms they do and hold such a central place in Native American literature. One could consider McNickle and Momaday in relation to Harold Bloom's theories of influence, or the relation of the works to the broader tradition of the bildungsroman, a common enough form for writers of first novels. One could consider the problem sociologically and historically, with McNickle first and then Momaday, Welch, and Silko marking a distinctive point in assimilation and education, moving in the crosscurrents between oral tradition and the Western literary tradition. Then there are obvious practical reasons: using a young man's rite of passage (or failed rite of passage) provides a central dramatic conflict that makes the individual's dilemmas representative of tensions shared by the larger community.

With such a clearly defined tradition, it is not difficult to see any new Native American novel as a response to the assumptions governing these books, different as they may be in detail. To write a historical novel like James Welch's *Fools Crow* may mean entering or criticizing an alternative tradition such as the historical romance, which like the bildungsroman has its own genealogy, in this context running from James Fenimore

Cooper and Karl May to *Hanta Yo*. Similarly, Gerald Vizenor's decision to write satirical trickster narratives, short stories in length only, is implicitly a comment on the mainstream tradition in Native American writing. That tradition is marked by a relatively conservative brand of literary realism in spite of its unmistakable discomfort with the conventions of realism and its occasional experimentalism and pursuit of a transcendental frame of reference.

The beginning of *Love Medicine* therefore signals a recasting of the tradition represented by the other works even as it partly continues to work within the older conventions and share many of the same concerns: the consequences of an individual's return or attempted return to the reservation, the significance of home and family, the politics of language, and the relation between speaking and writing. *Love Medicine* has its own distinctive style characterized by the use of multiple narrators and a relaxed, informal approach that is, like June Kashpaw herself, good-humored and graceful yet hard-bitten. *Love Medicine* has little of the violence and stark, tough landscapes that characterize the work of McNickle, Momaday, Welch, and Silko; perhaps that can be ascribed to a midwestern, as opposed to a western, sensibility. All the same, if in its opening *Love Medicine* suggests a move away from McNickle, Momaday, Silko, Welch, and company, in the end (perhaps understandably) it moves more centripetally as the similarities with the other authors become increasingly evident. Yet *Love Medicine* remains a striking achievement, in part because of its subtle balance between a willingness to present a new approach marked by a narrative openness and the need to address important if familiar topics and find a satisfactory form of closure.

The narrative at once departs from the earlier novels in several key ways. The central figure is a woman, not a man. The return, the first step, does not lead to the prolonged series of encounters and soul searching that make up the body of the other works and ultimately prove defeating or redeeming; instead, June's first step is her last. The narrative does not develop directly out of the problems caused by a return; it arises out of questions raised by the failed return. Somewhat in the manner of a murder mystery, the death becomes a means of exploring not only the victim's life but the lives of those around her. *Love Medicine* could have been called "Who Killed June Kashpaw?" or rather, "What Killed Her?" since the responsibility and guilt are shared by many individuals embedded in an entire way of life, a complex mesh of biographical and historical factors. The remembrance of the death wells up from time to time, as when June's son King, in the middle of a fight with his wife, suddenly breaks into sobs and screams at his father, "It's awful to be dead. Oh my God, she's so cold."[2] The sadness observed in the young June's eyes by the woman who took her in as a child (68) underlies the entire text. It is the fundamental subtext, even with Erdrich's wonderful comic sense: June's presence, that is, her absence, haunts the book. The oppressive weight of her death is not exorcised until the final page.

With June Kashpaw's death, more lyrical but no less surprising in terms of narrative conventions than the murder of Marion Crane (Janet Leigh) in the shower in *Psycho*, Erdrich immediately decenters the novel; unlike the earlier novels, *Love Medicine* has no sustaining central consciousness or protagonist. Part of the shock arises from the fact that the narrative begins neutrally but then clearly leans toward June's point of view:

> She was a long-legged Chippewa woman, aged hard in every way except how she moved. Probably it was the way she moved, easy as a young girl on slim hard legs, that caught the eye of the man who rapped at her from inside the window of the Rigger Bar. He looked familiar, like a lot of people looked familiar. She had seen so many come and go. . . . She wanted, at least, to see if she actually knew him. (1)

While the descriptions of the man's actions and statements remain objective, the narrative keeps moving toward the woman's point of view: "She couldn't help notice, . . . He could be different, she thought. . . . It was later still that she felt so fragile" (3–4). Though identified as "Andy," the man remains "he," while the narrator refers to the woman familiarly as "June."

Following the embarrassing experience in the pickup, bordering on comedy but too unpleasant for laughs, the first section ends with a dream-like poetic figure: "The snow fell deeper that Easter than it had in forty years, but June walked over it like water and came home" (6). Abruptly, the second section undercuts the redemptive imagery:

> After that false spring, when the storm blew in covering the state, all the snow melted off and it was summer. It was almost hot by the week after Easter, when I found out, in Mama's letter, that June was gone— not only dead but suddenly buried, vanished off the land like that sudden snow. (6–7)

This statement in the first person—the speaker is June's niece, Albertine Johnson—establishes the narrative style for the novel. *Love Medicine* presents a collection of interlocking narratives, each focusing on a different narrator or major character, yet all ultimately related to that original event, the death of June Kashpaw. The characters often tell their own stories, not only explaining their relationship to the dead woman but also spinning out a larger web of relationships that appear as a comment on her death, thereby providing the context in which it can be understood. June Kashpaw is referred to occasionally in these personal narratives, but she is rarely central until the concluding section. Although some characters are deliberately prevented from taking over the narrative voice—for instance, June's unsympathetic son, King, and her sympathetic lover, Gerry Nanapush—there is neither a continuous omniscient narration nor a central character. Instead, the role of narrator moves freely from character to character, and the storyline moves forward and backward in time as well. The opening chapter takes place in 1981, the second in 1934, the fourteenth and final one in 1984. Thus the novel takes on the character of a jigsaw puzzle; different areas are filled in at different times. Spatial and temporal order follows a logic of development apart from simple chronology or the existence of any individual character; for example, the chapter describing June's husband, Gordie, appears past the book's midpoint, though it picks up only a month after June's death.

Michael Wood once remarked that Faulkner was a key figure for many of the Latin American writers of the "Boom" (Vargas Llosa, Donoso, and above all García Márquez) because he demonstrated that novels could be formally experimental works of modern art while not abandoning the traditional concern with social description.[3] Faulkner, after all, wrote family sagas, historical novels portraying communal life from generation to generation. Faulkner is a favorite author of Erdrich's; *Love Medicine* has more than a passing resemblance to *As I Lay Dying, Absalom, Absalom!,* and *The Sound and the Fury.*[4] Whether or not Erdrich was directly influenced by the Latin Americans, and in particular by García Márquez, her work uses some of the same methods and at times a similar tone.

The constant shifting of point of view and the chronological jumps in the narrative make divergent versions of a single event possible, introducing a modernist sense of relativism and discontinuity as well as a good deal of ironic humor.[5] The attempt to hang June as a child is recalled twice, once in Albertine's narrative (19–20) and once in Marie Kashpaw's (67–68); the appearance of Beverly Lamartine at Lulu Nanapush's house is told first by a neutral narrator (75–76) and later by Beverly's rival for Lulu's affections, Nector Kashpaw, who describes Beverly as "a slick, flat-faced Cree salesman out of Minneapolis . . . a made-good, shifty type who would hang Lulu for a dollar" (102). As this bit of invective suggests, the language used in *Love Medicine* is not radical at all. Though not without some poetic

passages, as one would expect from the author of *Jacklight*, the text generally avoids the difficulty characteristic of so much modern literature; the
language used to tell the story is a lively combination of down-to-earth
colloquialism and occasional literary flourishes. Throughout *Love Medicine*,
one of Erdrich's key concerns is narrative agility and speed, as in the works
of García Márquez; confronted by alternative narrative media such as television and movies, these authors resort to an armory of devices that would
make Dickens proud. Like García Márquez, Erdrich uses the artful prolep-
tic tease:

> At the time her [Lulu Lamartine's] hair was still dark and thickly curled.
> Later she would burn it off when her house caught fire, and it would
> never grow back. (83)

> It would not surprise Bev to hear, after many years passed on, that this
> Gerry grew up to be both a natural criminal and a hero whose face ap-
> peared on the six-o'clock news. (84–85)

And she delights in making the story seem more immediate by shifting the
narrative from the past tense into a dramatic present tense. This technique
is used with Nector Kashpaw, who loses his memory, thereby becoming
the perfect embodiment of a conflation of past and present:

> Anyway, once I got to town and stopped by the tribal offices, a drunk
> was out of the question. An emergency was happening.
> And here is where events loop around and tangle again:
> It is July. The sun is a fierce white ball. Two big semis from the Polar
> Bear Refrigerated Trucking Company are pulled up in the yard of
> the agency offices, and what do you think they're loaded with? But-
> ter. That's right. Seventeen tons of surplus butter on the hottest day in
> '52. (95)

Or again, later in the same chapter: "No sooner had I given her up than I
wanted Lulu back. It is a hot night in August. I am sitting in the pool of
lamplight at my kitchen table" (104).

Such devices date back at least to Victorian melodrama, as do some of
the thematic concerns such as the fascination with matters of paternity
and maternity. These are serious matters: the novel concludes when a
sympathetic character, Lipsha Morrissey, discovers the true identity of his
mother (June Kashpaw) and his father (Gerry Nanapush). His meeting
with his father is as important for the narrative as some of the great recognition and reunion scenes in classical literature, such as the recognition of

Odysseus' scar and his reunion with Telemachus in *The Odyssey*. But typically for Erdrich, this climactic scene is played in a low-key comic fashion. It takes place in a kitchen in the Twin Cities, over a card game. The father and son recognize their shared kinship in part because they both learned to cheat at cards from their mother/grandmother, Lulu Lamartine. The comic side of the scene is complemented, however, by each man's intense awareness of the missing mother and lover, June Kashpaw. They are playing with her other son, King, for a car purchased with the insurance money from her death; as the game progresses, Lipsha (the narrator for this section) reviews the life of father, mother, and son before bringing the story full circle:

> I could see how his [Gerry's] mind leapt back making connections, jumping at the intersection points of our lives: his romance with June. The baby given to Grandma Kashpaw. June's son by Gordie. King. Her running me off. Me growing up. And then at last June walking toward home in the Easter snow that, I saw now, had resumed falling softly in this room. (262)

With the family history clear at last, the disruption caused by the death can now be overcome. And so the meeting of father and son leads to a fairytale, Hollywood ending: the son helps the fugitive father escape to freedom across the Canadian border, and the father tells the son of a genetic heart defect, so that Lipsha is freed from the need to either make good on his enlistment in the army or continue his flight from the authorities.

This resolution suggests how Erdrich takes apart and puts back together the traditional narrative. Instead of a man, it is a woman returning home at the beginning. She dies immediately, but the traditional dilemma of the individual—home as freedom versus home as trap—reappears tied to a mystery of identity, which is resolved favorably. The son meets his father, who successfully escapes while the son resolves an identity crisis and returns from his wanderings with a newly found peace of mind. The last word of the novel, significantly, is "home."[6]

Georg Lukács described the novel as the form "like no other," expressing a "transcendental homelessness."[7] In *Love Medicine*, the concern with home informs the entire narrative, as Erdrich rings the changes upon the term, which is by no means always identified with a condition of bliss. Albertine (in some ways a double for her Aunt June) is both ambivalent and matter-of-fact in describing her return to the reservation after her aunt's death: "Just three miles, and I was driving down the rutted dirt road, home" (11). But she immediately finds herself in the middle of a squabble between her mother and her Aunt Aurelia:

> "June was all packed up and ready to come home. . . . She walked out there because . . . what did she have to come home to after all? Nothing!"
>
> "Nothing?" said mama piercingly. "Nothing to come home to?" She gave me [Albertine] a short glance full of meaning. I had, after all, come home, even if husbandless, childless, driving a fall-apart car. (12)

The family get-together sours. Near the end of Albertine's narrative, King and his wife have a massive fight; as they go out leaving the kitchen a shambles, the wife says, "You always get so crazy when you're home. We'll get the baby. We'll go off. We'll go back to the Cities, go home" (39). There's no place like home—but which one?[8]

Clearly, home in *Love Medicine* is an embattled concept, as ambiguous as June Kashpaw's motives in attempting her return. When Lipsha tells his father that at last he's "home free," Gerry Nanapush immediately contradicts him: "'No,' he said, ' . . . I won't ever really have what you'd call a home'" (268). As his son realizes, Gerry is a man on the run. But he is strong and self-confident, unlike Henry Lamartine, Jr., a tragic figure whose return from the Vietnam War makes him an updated version of earlier figures such as Tayo in *Ceremony*. His brother, Lyman Lamartine, says, "When he came home . . . Henry was very different, and I'll say this: the change was no good" (147).

Like *House Made of Dawn* and *Ceremony*, *Love Medicine* seems to fall on the optimistic, ultimately upbeat side of the great divide governing the Native American novels of homecoming.[9] Yet Erdrich's multivoiced, multicharacter narrative method enables her to establish a complicated system of narrative balance. Thus, if two favored figures escape in a kind of romantic fantasy, another perishes; Henry Junior drowns before he can sort out any of the confusion caused by his war experiences. The gentle Lipsha benefits from discovering the identity of his father, regaining his special "touch" in both healing and card playing; but Lyman Lamartine gains nothing from the knowledge that Nector Kashpaw was his father. His mother, Lulu, sees his problem:

> "You know what," he sighed after a while. "I don't really want to know."
>
> Of course, he did know that Kashpaw was his father. What he really

meant was there was nothing to be done about it anymore. I felt the loss. I wanted to hold my son in my lap and let him cry. Even blind, a mother knows when her boy is holding in a painful silence. (233)

Writers like McNickle move in the direction of high tragedy. Their world is oppressive and fatalistic, a throwback to the naturalism of Wharton's *Ethan Frome* or Zola's *La Bête Humaine*. At times the declarative sentences make the prose seem carved from blocks of stone: the narrative provides an immutable record of an implacable fate. Momaday and Silko, in contrast, see ceremony as a means of escaping nature, of leading life and art toward transcendence. With her poet's voice, Erdrich often moves away from the mundane and the matter-of-fact, but she rarely explores exalted realms of the spirit: a vision of the Northern Lights shared by Lipsha and Albertine is perhaps the one notable exception. Indian ritual has no place in *Love Medicine* except in the "touch" of Lipsha, presented satirically when he replaces goose hearts with storebought frozen turkey hearts and watches his "patient" choke to death. Filtered through the survivors' point of view, the ghost returns as a melancholy apparition, not a horrific incubus from the afterlife. (Here is one more similarity with the tone and manner of García Márquez, who favors an equally sad image of the afterlife.) Erdrich seems to find the profane more interesting, if not more desirable, than the sacred; she is a worldly author, and it is difficult not to suspect that she agrees with Lipsha, possibly the most sympathetic character of all, when he says:

Our Gods aren't perfect . . . but at least they come around. They'll do a favor if you ask them right. You don't have to yell. But you do have to know, like I said, how to ask in the right way. That makes problems, because to ask proper was an art that was lost to the Chippewas once the Catholics gained ground. Even now, I have to wonder if Higher Power turned its back, if we got to yell, or if we just don't speak its language. (195)[10]

This is an ambivalent attitude to say the least—one part faith and two parts doubt and disappointment. Lipsha's brief comment about Catholicism is not elaborated upon except as Catholicism is presented in a broadly satirical manner, especially in the character of an intimidating hell-fire and brimstone nun, Sister Leopolda, a figure out of Fellini. (I am thinking in particular of Juliet's childhood experience in the convent in *Juliet of the Spirits*.)

Erdrich, on balance, is essentially a comic writer. Most of the key moments in *Love Medicine* are comic ones, from the fateful encounter between Nector Kashpaw and Marie Lazarre—played out as a love scene complicated by the presence of two dead geese tied to Nector's wrists—to the card game between King, Gerry, and Lipsha. Even a house burning is grotesquely comic, an accident perhaps, but certainly not akin to the mean-spirited Snopes vengeance in Faulkner's "Barn Burning." Erdrich's characters often move into melancholia or wistful reminiscence, as when the high-spirited and assertive Lulu Lamartine (i.e., Libertine), the novel's version of the Wife of Bath, admits that "It's a sad world, though, when you can't get love right even after trying it as many times as I have" (218). With the death of June Kashpaw, Erdrich immediately establishes her awareness of the bleak side of existence; even sweet-natured Lipsha comments that the marked deck was appropriate for "the marked men, which was all of us" (259). Yet the story never lingers on the tragic, returning again and again to a bemused, ironic view of the comic incongruities of parents and children, friends and lovers. In the end, though the love medicine proves fatal to Nector, there is a reconciliation between the rivals Marie Kashpaw and Lulu Lamartine, Nector's wife and his mistress, in the senior citizen's home. All passion spent, Lulu says, "For the first time I saw exactly how another woman felt, and it gave me deep comfort, surprising" (236). The passage ends with a sweet—perhaps too sweet—vision of harmony as Marie puts drops in Lulu's eyes: "She swayed down like a dim mountain, huge and blurred, the way a mother must look to her just born child" (236).

In his famous essay on Leskov, "The Storyteller," Walter Benjamin proclaims that the death of storytelling and its replacement by the novel represented the death of true human communication and wisdom.[11] The villain is the book, which replaces the companionship that exists between teller and listener with the distance between the isolated writer and the equally isolated reader. In most Native American literature, the book is not embraced but accepted as a necessary evil: story and storytelling are the ideals. In "The Storyteller's Escape," Silko writes, "With these stories of ours / we can escape almost anything / with these stories we will survive."[12]

Setting the oral against the written, storytelling against novel writing, indicates a romantic approach to art and life, a literary vision of a fall from a Golden Age to an impersonal present. After all, storytelling might be regarded as a representation of experience with no special status. Nevertheless it is the impression of presentness and of presence, of social intimacy and communion, that matters, and in *Love Medicine* Erdrich subtly shapes the narrative to create a sense of immediacy. The characters themselves almost at once demonstrate the effects of storytelling, for it is storytelling that animates the women in the kitchen after June's death. Their recollection of the youthful hanging episode, a playful yet symbolic anticipation of her fate, brings them all to life, giggling and "laughing out loud in brays and whoops . . . waving their hands helplessly" (21).

The opposition between speech and writing in Native American fiction may not exist in the same conceptual framework as the opposition between speech and writing in the philosophical and theoretical discourse of Derrida and contemporary literary theory. Still, the problem of language, and in particular of finding an appropriate language for writing about Native American experience, remains fundamental in these works. In *Ceremony* Silko frames her narrative with sections that are both poetic and ritualistic. And Momaday frames *House Made of Dawn* with traditional ceremonial introductions and conclusions. These mixed forms straddle Native American and Western forms of expression. There are other signs of the central problems of language and form in the incorporation of episodes involving historical texts, such as the journal in *House Made of Dawn* and the repeated play between characters who speak English and those who speak tribal languages.

In *Love Medicine*, Erdrich takes a different approach to the relation between Native forms and the Western literary tradition. Her work, like the work of Silko and others, seems at times to aspire to the status of "pure" storytelling. This goal would make the literary text appear to be a transcription of a speaker talking in the first-person present tense, addressing a clearly defined listener. Thus, in several of the narratives the speaker addresses a "you." This device can become too insistent, a tic rather than a sign of sincerity, as when Lipsha remarks, "I told you once before" (195), or Lulu Lamartine plays confidante with the reader by saying, "Nobody knows this" (218). Yet the attempt at seeming intimacy does move the text in the direction of informal, colloquial prose. The liveliness of *Love Medicine* has less to do with some formal notion of speech as utterance than its success as dialogue capturing just plain talk—kitchen-table talk, bar talk, angry talk, curious talk, sad talk, teasing talk.

But in a printed text, the return of the literary is inevitable; because all the elements that stylistically mark the pursuit of immediacy are in the end visible as literary devices.[13] Using the first-person present tense as a substitute for third-person past tense omniscient narration, or using colloquial diction and sentence structure as opposed to more elaborate, artificial forms, must be judged within the context of a range of possibilities that govern all "realistic" prose. Erdrich's artfulness is evident, for example, in several beautifully sustained metaphors that appear independently in the narratives of different characters, notably a fishing image connected to Nector Kashpaw's failing memory that first appears in Albertine's narrative and then migrates into Lipsha's (193, 208, 209).

The naturalness of Erdrich's characters is as much a construction as the skill at creating a convincing voice that led Hemingway to see in Twain's *Huckleberry Finn* the start of a genuine American literary tradition—an antiliterary, seemingly informal American style based on colloquial expression.

There are precedents of sorts for much of what Erdrich accomplishes in *Love Medicine* in the Latin Americans, in Faulkner, in Edgar Lee Masters and Thornton Wilder, in the fascination during the past three decades with oral history—from Studs Terkel, to the Vietnam oral histories, to *Black Elk Speaks*—and in the Raymond Carver-Bobbie Ann Mason school of writing, with its seemingly affectless but extremely stylized tragicomic glimpses of lower middle-class life. In each case, literature attempts to free itself of the literary, as if any intervention or mediation by an author were inevitably a falsification, and only a supposed transcription could capture the truth. This literary antinomianism seems distinctly American.

Love Medicine, as its title suggests, is centered in the relationships between lovers and families. Yet because Erdrich moves away from the narrow focus of the earlier novels toward the historical novel and the family saga, she is able to touch upon economic and political matters in an extremely effective way. There are characters who can make money and characters who can't; and since at least one character is engaged in tribal politics, there are some sharp things said about how things get done on the reservation. More pointed are some observations made in passing by the characters in the course of their dramatic monologues, beginning with Albertine Johnson's bitter remark in the aftermath of her aunt's death about "rich, single cowboy-rigger oil trash." To these types, she says, "An Indian woman's nothing but an easy night" (9). Shortly thereafter Albertine notes that "the policy of allotment was a joke" (11). Such asides run through the multiple narrative without ever coming to a head in the action. In *Love Medicine*, the Native Americans speak, and after the appearance of the unfortunate Andy right at the start, the whites are all but invisible, pushed to the margins, except for the caricature of the rich lady who makes Nector Kashpaw famous as a naked warrior in a painting, *The Plunge of the Brave*. There are no political confrontations, perhaps partly because the skepticism is directed inward, as in the case of Lulu Lamartine's battle with the tribal council to keep possession of her house. Even Gerry Nanapush, a colorful, sympathetic, and rebellious desperado leader of the American Indian Movement, is presented by his son, Lipsha, with more than a touch of amusement: "Gerry Nanapush, famous politicking hero, dangerous armed criminal, judo expert, escape artist, charismatic member of the American Indian Movement, and smoker of many pipes of kinnikinnick in the most radical groups. That was . . . Dad" (248). (The passage in which Lipsha addresses the question of his father's guilt in relation to the killing of a federal agent at Pine Ridge [269] is one of the few unconvincing sections in the novel, a too-neat cop-out.)

One of the peculiar aspects of Erdrich's writing, even more evident in *The Beet Queen,* is her presentation of history. In *Love Medicine* individual sections are dated and tied to various before-and-after events in the convoluted sexual/personal relations linking the many characters, but there is little sense of an outside historical framework. With the exception of a few historical references, the episodes in the thirties could as easily take place in the fifties or eighties. This may show that Erdrich is not interested in circumstantial social realism. But *Love Medicine* becomes historical and political through the personal, as when Henry Junior goes to Vietnam and Gerry joins the American Indian Movement.

The sense in *Love Medicine* of being removed from political events is a powerful statement about marginality and disenfranchisement that also suggests Erdrich's preferred concern with the personal and private life of the community. Lulu Lamartine, a tough political commentator, mentions the forced migrations of the Chippewa from the far side of the Great Lakes, but she says only that the story her grandmother used to tell "is too long a story to get into now" (222). She then returns to her own refusal to move from her house. This is a typical Erdrich maneuver; she inserts a broad political and historical point, then channels the narrative back to a seemingly personal issue. The focus in *Love Medicine* on family may reflect an eighties concern with domesticity and "roots" and personal heritage. King's wife, Lynette, "with a quick burst of drunken enthusiasm," says to one of the older Kashpaws, "Tell 'em. . . . They've got to learn their own heritage. When you go it will be gone!" (30) Much later Lipsha refers to his search for his father as his "quest," saying, "I had to get down to the bottom of my heritage" (248).

Erdrich, however, does not present a rose-colored view of an ideal nuclear family in the manner of television series such as *Little House on the Prairie* or the Depression-era drama *The Waltons.* Instead, she offers a completely unsentimental view, both affectionate and angry, of an extremely complicated extended family. And central to that vision of the family is a history that is largely unspoken in *Love Medicine* but that appears at times in personal terms through memory: the memories that exist in the hands of June's husband, leading him to drink when they remind him of the feel of her body (172); the memory that plagues Gerry Nanapush and makes him go see June's son King so that he can be reminded of her through King's features (262). In the final turn to memory and history Erdrich opens up her text, and not only by using multiple narrators, multiple narratives. The move is temporal as well. Storytelling brings everything into the present. But Erdrich hints at a more comprehensive truth that goes back beyond the death of June Kashpaw to a larger source of woe: one that explains why the Chippewa moved west of the Great Lakes to a home on the reservation that drives them into a cycle of departure and return.

By the time Erdrich concludes the extended story of the tragedy of June Kashpaw, the story of the Kashpaws, Lamartines, and Nanapushes, it is clear that she has circumscribed her story temporally, no matter how relatively open it may seem in terms of narrative technique and range of feeling. In a sense all Native American writers are historical writers, their kinship based on the shared assumption that history holds the key to understanding contemporary Native American life. Behind the immediate problems of home, family, and paternity (or maternity) stands the unanswerable past. Max in *The Surrounded* proclaims to Archilde, "We've got to plan something. We won't let it end for you, like you thought. We'll make a new beginning!" But the last spoken lines in the book are those of Parker, the agent, scornfully telling Archilde, "It's too damn bad you people never learn that you can't run away. It's pathetic." What they can't run away from is less a physical location than a historical situation. That accounts for the pain in Jim Loney when he realizes that there is no place where "pasts merged into one and everything was all right and it was like everything was beginning without a past. No lost sons, no mothers searching." He adds, damningly, "There had to be that place, but it was not on this earth." The individual stories of the protagonists in Native American fiction meet in the collective history. They embrace Tayo's awareness in *Ceremony* that "His sickness was only part of something larger" as well as the bitterness at the end of *Fools Crow* when the title character realizes that change, loss, and unhappiness are to be the fate of his people, and that their only consolation will be in stories telling them of "the way it was."[14]

In *Love Medicine* Erdrich is concerned with the experience of the Chippewa in the mid-twentieth century. The story leaves largely untold the parallel story of the whites and the historical background of events. It is not at all surprising that, having concentrated in *The Beet Queen* on the

German side of her heritage and the bleak beauty and twisted emotional universe of the Plains, Erdrich wrote *Tracks,* an historical novel on an older generation, the ancestors of the characters in *Love Medicine*.[15]

Notes

1. D'Arcy McNickle, *The Surrounded* (Albuquerque: University of New Mexico Press, 1964), 1. See also *Winter in the Blood* (New York: Penguin, 1986), in which the main character observes right at the start, "Coming home was not easy anymore" (2).

2. Louise Erdrich, *Love Medicine* (New York: Bantam Books, 1984), 33. Subsequent references to this novel will be identified by page numbers in parentheses in the text.

3. Professor Wood made his remarks as the featured speaker at a meeting in the late 1970s of the Columbus Circle, the organization for graduate students in American Literature at Columbia University.

4. *Love Medicine* recalls the retrospection of *As I Lay Dying*, the idea of the novel as conversation of *Absalom, Absalom!*, and the expressionistic use of point of view in *The Sound and the Fury*. Erdrich expressed her admiration for Faulkner's early writings in an interview with Amy Ward ("The Beet Generation," *University of Minnesota Daily*, 29 October 1986, 18).

5. The only real exception occurs on pages 237–39, when the narrator is Howard Kashpaw (also "King Junior" and "Little King"), whose impressionistic, youthful point of view recalls Joyce's experimentation in adopting the point of view of the young Stephen Daedalus at the beginning of *A Portrait of the Artist as a Young Man* or Faulkner's method in using Benjy Compson as a narrator in *The Sound and the Fury*. But Erdrich's style is not as extreme.

6. The last line, Lipsha's "So there was nothing to do but cross the water, and bring her home" (272) picks up on the final line in the opening section, as June walks over the snow like water. Since the passage contains no clear antecedent for "her," there is a kind of echo of June's presence as well as a play on a colloquial phrase (as in "let 'er rip"). The fusing of antecedents is also used in Henry Junior's narrative, when Albertine merges in his mind with a Vietnamese woman: "She was hemorrhaging" (138). (Albertine seems to be something of a loose strand in the plot. She disappears from the action after her encounter with Henry Junior in Fargo, though she is mentioned in a bit of conversation between Lipsha and Gerry, with Lipsha referring to her as "the one girl I ever trusted" [270]. One of the characteristics of "open" form is a refusal to tie up loose ends and account for all the characters in the manner of the "classical" nineteenth-century novel. But in this case it seems simpler to regard Albertine's absence as a result of Erdrich's method, which brought together short stories as the basis for the novel.)

7. Georg Lukács, *The Theory of the Novel*, trans. by Anna Bostock (Cambridge:

MIT Press, 1971), 41. Lukács is deliberately playing upon a statement by Novalis, "Philosophy is really homesickness" (quoted, p. 29).

8. Erdrich's poem "Family Reunion," in *Jacklight* (New York: Henry Holt, 1984), offers a brief glimpse of a gathering similar to the one that greets Albertine when she returns home following the death of her Aunt June. But it is the first line of the next poem in the volume, "Indian Boarding School: The Runaways," that expresses the essential idea: "Home's the place we head for in our sleep" (11). The line recalls the dialogue between husband and wife in Robert Frost's "The Death of the Hired Hand":

> "Home is the place where, when you have to go there,
> They have to take you in,"
>
> . . . .
>
> "I should have called it
> Something you somehow haven't to deserve."
> > —*The Poetry of Robert Frost* ed. by Edward Connery Lathem
> > (London: Jonathan Cape, 1967), 38.

The relation between Erdrich's poetry and her fiction is a fascinating one (as is the relation between the short stories as individual entities and as sections of *Love Medicine*). *Love Medicine* goes far beyond the poem "A Love Medicine" in *Jacklight*, a good poem marred by the overwrought description of masculine violence ("she steps against the fistwork of a man. / She goes down in wet grass and his boot plants its grin / among the arches of her face" [7]). Erdrich handles male mistreatment in a more complex and subtle fashion with Andy and others in the novel.

As a revision and expansion of the sequence of poems "The Butcher's Wife" in *Jacklight*, *The Beet Queen* (New York: Henry Holt, 1986) seems less than successful. In this case, the poetry goes beyond the novel, especially in the dark, bitter quality of a line like "Something queer happens when the heart is delivered" ("That Pull from the Left," 41-42). I suspect that one reason the book founders is that it is not really about characters and events but about what one character, Karl Adare, describes as "the senseless landscape" (318), that is, the unreal existence induced by living in the kind of place described so prosaically by another character, Wallace Pfef: "I live in the flat, treeless valley where sugar beets grow. It is intemperate here. My view is a flat horizon of grays and browns" (160). In *Love Medicine*, the fields are described as "casual and lonely" (79); in *Jacklight*, Erdrich repeatedly stresses an almost metaphysical aspect of the landscape, as when she has the speaker in "Clouds" note that "The town stretches to fields" (43) and goes on to proclaim:

> We lay our streets over
> the deepest cries of earth
> And wonder why everything comes down to this:

The days pile and pile.
The bones are too few
and too foreign to know.
Mary, you do not belong here at all.
Sometimes I take back in tears this whole town.
Let everything be how it could have been, once:
A land that was empty and perfect as clouds. (44–45)

This lament for "this strange earth / we want to call ours" (45) suggests both the strong response to the landscape and the failure of *The Beet Queen* to present an adequate picture of the relation between character and environment, to capture the emotional tension bred by such surroundings. As a dark satirical portrait of small town life, *Omensetter's Luck* by William Gass seems more successful; as an image of life on the Great Plains—heavenly, hellish, beautifully empty—Terrence Malick's film *Days of Heaven* suggests more convincingly the haunted mood induced by the vast expanses. *The Beet Queen*, with a character like Karl Adare, seems to be caught between the quaintly idiosyncratic ironies of a work like *Ragtime* and the more compelling concern with evil that marks the writings of Flannery O'Connor.

9. *Winter in the Blood* is something of a special case. Alan Velie (*Four American Indian Masters* [Norman: University of Oklahoma Press, 1982], 90–103) discusses the book as a comic novel, using "comic" in a slightly unusual sense, one concerned with notions of character (i.e., with the nonheroic) as well as with a humorous tone. I basically agree with his reading of the novel as a work that uses a sense of irony to play comedy against tragedy with unsettling results. It may be a comedy, but it's not a happy book.

10. In this passage, Lipsha also states that June was "left by a white man to wander off in the snow" (195). This would no doubt be how the incident appeared to June's relatives. Lipsha's statement presents another demonstration of the effect of multiple perspectives, though in this case the reader has been given an apparently privileged, "correct" view. It is also another example of the subtle introduction of essentially political issues and assumptions into a book that appears focused on personal matters.

11. Walter Benjamin, "The Storyteller," in *Illuminations*, trans. by Harry Zohn (New York: Schocken Books), 83–109.

12. Leslie Marmon Silko, *Storyteller* (New York: Seaver Books, 1981), 247.

13. In "Writing and Revolution" (*Writing Degree Zero*, trans. by Annette Lavers and Colin Smith [London: Jonathan Cape, 1967]), Roland Barthes discusses the artificiality and "convention of the real" in the Naturalist aesthetic, which he describes as "loaded with the most spectacular signs of fabrication" and "a literature which has all the striking and intelligible signs of its identity" (73, 74, 76). Native American

writing, in its efforts to attain the condition of speech, has developed a set of what might be called "conventions of the oral," including the use of the present tense and the use of the first person with "you." These are signs of fabrication and therefore of the literary status of the text, especially when occasional statements assigned to a character suggest the consciousness of the hidden narrator. This is most obvious when the author is most literary—usually by introducing the kind of metaphorical language that, as Barthes never fails to point out, constitutes one of the most obvious signs of a literature straining to affirm its identity. (See, for example, "Is There Any Poetic Writing?" in *Writing Degree Zero* [New York: Hill and Wang, 1967] 47, in which Barthes speaks of "the ritual of images.")

For a sharp dissection of the "epidemic" use of the present tense in contemporary fiction, see William Gass, "A Failing Grade for the Present Tense" *New York Times Book Review*, 11 October 1987, 1, 32, 36–38.

14. D'Arcy McNickle, *The Surrounded* (Albuquerque: University of New Mexico Press, 1964) 159, 296–97; James Welch, *The Death of Jim Loney* (New York: Harper and Row, 1979) 175; Leslie Marmon Silko, *Ceremony* (New York: Penguin, 1986) 125; James Welch, *Fools Crow* (New York: Penguin, 1986) 358–60.

15. Erdrich represents not the death of the author but, in her collaborative efforts with her husband, Michael Dorris, the birth of authorial twins. I don't wish to discuss at length the third product of their collaboration, the novel published under his name, *A Yellow Raft in Blue Water* (New York: Henry Holt, 1987); but in the context of the discussion of *Love Medicine*, a few observations are in order. The multiple narratives, moving back in time from youngest to oldest, from the present to a deep secret buried in the past, seems less lively than the comparable overlapping in *Love Medicine*. The duplication of episodes is not entirely compensated for by the insights gained from different perspectives. The use of the first person once again provides immediacy, but at the price of keeping the reader's understanding anchored within a narrowly defined consciousness; the characters' reliance on soap opera as a standard form of reference suggests both an attempt at a realistic portrayal of contemporary working-class life and a lack of sureness in defining a point of view toward the melodramatic plot, which seems part *I Love Lucy* and part *Peyton Place*. As a story of three women, the book continues the Erdrich/Dorris righting of the literary balance the sexes initiated in *Love Medicine* and continued in *The Beet Queen*, but the male characters are once again less interesting than the women. Finally, the book displays a fascination with the idea of storytelling, here regarded not so much as some grand social ritual but as an instrument of survival. For example, Rayona, the youngest of the three narrators, tells an inquisitive priest that her mother is dead and her father is an airplane pilot, neither of which happens to be true. (The most outrageous of all the examples of this kind of story-in-a-pinch-operators in the novels is Sister Leopolda in *Love Medicine*. She saves herself after she has skew-

ered Marie Lazarre by proclaiming the girl's wounds the results of a divine miracle.) Dorris has the last, oldest narrator, Aunt Ida, announce at the beginning of her narration that she will tell the story her own way, then add:

> And though I can speak their English better than they think, better than most of them, I prefer my own language. I use the words that shaped my construction of events as they happened, the words that followed my thought, the words that gave me power. My recollections are not tied to white paper. They have the depth of time. (273)

A powerful statement of the antiliterary position, but a curious one to read on a printed page, in English.

An article in the *New York Times* on 24 July 1988 announced that Erdrich and Dorris had sold the rights to a proposed novel about Christopher Columbus's discovery of America for $1.5 million. Apparently the historical impulse I observed in their work has not yet run its course. See Edwin McDowell, "Outline of Novel about Columbus Brings $1.5 Million" (sec. 1, p. 24, col. 2).

Interviews with Louise Erdrich
and Michael Dorris

◆ ◆ ◆

Louise Erdrich, Michael Dorris, and Laura Coltelli
from *Winged Words: American Indian Writers
Speak* (1990)

Laura Coltelli (LC): What's the source of your storytelling technique?

Dorris: Louise had two stories that were independent stories, "Scales"
and "The Red Convertible." They were published independently and then
there was a contest for the Nelson Algren Award for which they solicited
stories of some five thousand or so words. We got the announcement that
it was due by the fifteenth of January, and this was the first of January, and
we just got back from vacation, and so we started talking about it and out
of that grew "The World's Greatest Fisherman," the opening story of the
novel *Love Medicine*, and we sent it off and thought of all the things that
were wrong with it and what we would revise when it came back, and lo
and behold, it won that contest. There were thousands of entries. We said,
if it's that good maybe we ought to think about expanding this and telling
that same story because there are many stories in that story, from other
points of view. And that expanded to developing the characters of Nector
and Marie and Lulu and on and on. At first it was, I think, a series of stories,
many of which were published independently, and then in the last several

drafts we went back and tied them together. We realized some of the people who had different names were in fact the same character and that they would unite, very much the same way that this book has now turned into four books. . . . It's a saga that takes place over about eighty years, a hundred years, and is an analogy, in a way, of all the processes that people in this part of the country have gone through.

The Turtle Mountain Chippewa people are an interesting group because they came originally from northern Minnesota but are heavily mixed with French and Cree, and so the language that they speak up there is called Michif, which is a combination of all those. And, for instance, Lipsha, the character in *Love Medicine*, is Michif bastardization of *le petit chou*, the French expression of endearment, "my little cabbage," and that's where the name comes from. . . .

LC: So is it a kind of traditional tribal storytelling technique?

Dorris: It's cyclical in that respect and that's why it's disturbing that the last line of the Italian translation does not bring [June] back into it, because basically this is the story of the reverberation of June's life even though she is the one character who does not have her own voice. Bringing her home is finally in fact resolving her life and death in balance.

LC: Can you speak about the point of view in *Love Medicine*?

Dorris: It's what Louise does best, basically. Every one of these stories went through seven, eight drafts, some in third person, some in the voice of a different character, and basically the voices that emerge are the ones that work best. One of my roles in this was to tell Louise that she really did it well. We all think we should be able to do that thing which was hardest for us rather than things which are easiest for us. First-person narrative is easiest for Louise; she does it best. It's not easy, but she does it best. It is a story cycle in the traditional sense. One of the interesting reviews of the book was talking about the fact that nobody in the book is right, that in fact it is community voice, that the point of view is the community voice and the means of exchanging information is gossip, and so consequently there is no narrator; there is no single protagonist, but rather it is the entire community dealing with the upheavals that emerge from the book and now will emerge from four books. [Louise returns from feeding the baby.] Now you can speak for yourself.

LC: In *Love Medicine*, one character, Lipsha, was happy because he hadn't yet acquired a memory, and Grandpa was happy because he was losing his. Memory then is a burden instead of being a source to shape a new identity and as a link between past and present.

Erdrich: That's an interesting tie. I guess for Nector the events of his life and his guilt made his memory a burden for him. It's certainly not a bur-

den for everyone in the book. But for him I think the guilt of his association with his mistress, with Lulu, his rejection of her and burning her
house down, whether he causes it directly or not, made memory something he is not happy to live with. . . .

LC: Humor is one of the most important features of contemporary Native American literature. Is there a difference in the use of humor in the
old Indian stories and in the contemporary ones?

Erdrich: The humor is a little blacker and bleaker now.

Dorris: Louise, have you talked about the ways in which we sort of consciously saw this book differently from much other contemporary fiction
by American Indians? Most of the others, I am sure Laura is aware of, deal
with contact in one way or another—what is the impact of leaving the
reservation, coming back to the reservation—but the outside world very
much imposes on the characters. In some of the drafts of *Love Medicine* that
was the case, the characters went to Washington, or one thing or another,
and basically we made a conscious decision, in the way Louise wrote the
book, to have it all centered in a community in which the outside world is
not very present or very relevant in some respects. This is a world that is
encompassed by that community, and it isn't so much the outside world of
discrimination or wealth or anything like that, but rather this is how a
community deals with itself and with the members of itself.

Erdrich: To go back just for one second, I really think the question about
humor is very important. It's one of the most important parts of American
Indian life and literature, and one thing that always hits us is just that Indian
people really have a great sense of humor and when it's survival humor, you
learn to laugh at things. It's really there, and I think Simon Ortiz is one person who has a lot of funny things happen, but a lot of terrible things as well
in his work. It's just a personal way of responding to the world and to things
that happen to you; it's a different way of looking at the world, very different
from the stereotype, the stoic, unflinching Indian standing, looking at the
sunset. It's really there, the humor, and I really hope that beside the serious
parts in this particular book, people would see the humor. . . .

LC: Could you describe your writing process?

Erdrich: Now we don't know what to do because we don't have a big
table in the living room. Back in New Hampshire, we put the table out,
and we could work with the whole manuscript at the end, when it was
about finished. But Michael will have a draft and show me and we will talk
it over, or I'll have a draft, talk about the whole plan of it, characters out of
it, just talk over every aspect of it.

Dorris: We get to know the characters very well and talk about them and
every situation. If we are in a restaurant we imagine what so-and-so would

order from the menu, and what so-and-so would choose from this catalog, so that we get to know them in a full way, and when they appear on the page, they have that fullness behind them even though it doesn't all get written about.

LC: But who actually writes down the page?

Dorris: Louise. In *Love Medicine*.

Erdrich: Michael writes down on his page, or I write down on my page. I go and work in my room, and in *A Yellow Raft in Blue Water*, Michael goes and works on his computer. . . .

Dorris: And we edit it together. We go over every word and achieve consensus on every word; basically we agree on every word when it's finally finished.

LC: Did it work that way for *Love Medicine* too?

Dorris: Yes.

Louise Erdrich and Joseph Bruchac
From *Survival This Way:*
Interviews with American Indian Poets (1987)

Joseph Bruchac (JB): In the poem "Whooping Cranes," legend-time and modern times come together. . . . There's a sort of cross-fertilization of past and present in legend. . . . In some of Leslie Silko's work you see that mixing of times. Someone may go out in a pickup truck and meet a figure out of myth.

Erdrich: Don't you, when you go on Indian land, feel that there's more possibility, that there is a whole other world besides the one you can see and that you're very close to it?

JB: Very definitely. Crossing the border of a reservation is always entering another world, an older and more complicated world. How do you feel when you go back to Turtle Mountain?

Erdrich: I feel so comfortable. I really do. I even feel that way being in North Dakota. I really like that openness. But there's a kind of feeling at Turtle Mountain—I guess just comfortable is the word to describe it. There are also places there which are very mysterious to me. I don't know why. I feel they must have some significance. Turtle Mountain is an interesting place. It hasn't been continuously inhabited by the Turtle Mountain Band. It was one of those nice grassy, game-rich places that everybody wanted. So it was Sioux, it was Michif, it was Chippewa. There are a soft, rolling group of hills, not very high, little hills—not like these (gestures toward mountains)—and there were parts that my grandfather would

point out. The shapes were called this or that because they resembled a
beaver or whatever kind of animal. He even incorporated the highways
into the shapes because some of them got their tails cut off. [Laughs.] Even
that people can deal with. Not always, though. There are many places that
are certainly of religious significance that can never be restored or re-
placed, so I don't want to make light of it.

JB: As in the Four Corners area.

Erdrich: Yes, I was thinking of Black Mesa. In the case of those hills at
Turtle Mountain, there was that resilience because they were places which
had a name, but not places—such as Black Mesa—much more vital to a
culture and a religion. Catholicism is very important up there at Turtle
Mountain. When you go up there, you go to church! My grandfather has
had a real mixture of old-time and church religion—which is another way
of incorporating. He would do pipe ceremonies for ordinations and things
like that. He just had a grasp on both realities, in both religions.

JB: I see that very much in your work. A lake may have a mythological
being in it which still affects people's lives while the Catholic Church up
on the hill is affecting them in a totally different way. Or you may have
someone worrying about being drafted into the army at the same time he's
trying to figure out how to make up love medicine—in a time when old
ways of doing things have been forgotten. It seems similar, in a way, to
Leslie Silko's *Ceremony*, where there is a need to make up new ceremonies
because the old ones aren't working for the new problems, incorporating
all kinds of things like phone books from different cities.

Erdrich: You may be right. I never thought about the similarity. This
"love medicine" is all through the book, but it backfires on the boy who
tries it out because he's kind of inept. It's funny what happens until it becomes tragic. But, if there is any ceremony which goes across the board and
is practiced by lots and lots of tribal people, it is having a sense of humor
about things and laughing. But that's not really what you're saying.

JB: Maybe—maybe no.

Erdrich: Who knows? [Laughs.] Anyway, I don't deal much with religion
except Catholicism. Although Ojibway traditional religion is flourishing, I
don't feel comfortable discussing it. I guess I have my beefs about Catholicism. Although you never change once you're raised a Catholic—you've
got that. You've got that symbolism, that guilt, you've got the whole
works and you can't really change that. That's easy to talk about because
you have to exorcise it somehow. That's why there's a lot of Catholicism in
both books. . . .

JB: When did you begin writing with Michael?

Erdrich: Once we were married. In '81. We began by just talking about the work, back and forth, reading it. He always—right at first before I got to know him—was the person I would go to with problems. I'd say, "Michael, should I get into teaching, should I quit writing? What should I do?" And he said to me, "Look, there's only one thing to do. Throw yourself into your work. Don't take any more jobs." And I did it. I just tried what he said. [Laughs.] At times I found myself in some unpleasant monetary predicaments. But I've been lucky. I think it is because we started working together. He had ideas for the whole structure of *Love Medicine* that became the book. We worked on it very intensely and closely, and I do the same with his work. We exchange this role of being the . . . there isn't even a word for it. We're collaborators, but we're also individual writers. One person sits down and writes the drafts. I sit down and write it by myself or he does, but there's so much more that bears on the crucial moment of writing. You know it, you've talked the plot over, you've discussed the characters. You've really come to some kind of an understanding that you wouldn't have done alone. I really think neither of us would write what we do unless we were together.

JB: Didn't the genesis of *Love Medicine*, "The World's Greatest Fisherman," come about that way? Michael saw the announcement of the Chicago Prize . . .

Erdrich: Yes. Michael was flat on his back, sick, and he said, "Look, you've got to enter this! Get in there, write it!" And I did, brought it in and out to him, changed it around, together we finished it.

JB: You have such a strong narrative line in all your work and stories seem so important to you, stories told by your characters in the poems, the stories of the poems themselves, and then the structure of story in *Love Medicine*, which is, in fact, many stories linked together. What is story to you?

Erdrich: Everybody in my whole family is a storyteller, whether a liar or a storyteller [laughs]—whatever. When I think what's a story, I can hear somebody in my family, my Dad or my Mom or my Grandma, telling it. There's something particularly strong about a *told story*. You know your listener's right there, you've got to keep him hooked—or her. So, you use all those little lures: "And then . . . ," "So the next day . . . ," etc. There are some very nuts-and-bolts things about storytelling. It also is something you can't really put your finger on. Why do you follow it? I know if there is a story. Then I just can't wait to get back to it and write it. Sometimes there isn't one, and I just don't want to sit down and force it. . . . The story starts to take over if it is good. You begin telling, you get a bunch of situation characters, everything together, but if it's good, you let the story tell itself. You don't control the story.

PART IV

Reading Self/Reading Other

Reading between Worlds

Narrativity in the Fiction of Louise Erdrich

CATHERINE RAINWATER

◆　◆　◆

LOUISE ERDRICH IS A contemporary writer of German American and Chippewa heritage. Like many literary works by Native Americans, her novels, *Love Medicine* (1984), *The Beet Queen* (1986), *Tracks* (1988), and
The Bingo Palace (1994) reflect the ambivalence and tension marking the lives
of people, much like herself, from dual cultural backgrounds. Erdrich's
novels feature Native Americans, mixed-bloods, and other culturally and
socially displaced characters whose marginal status is simultaneously an
advantage and a disadvantage, a source of both power and powerlessness.[1]
In *Love Medicine*, for example, Lipsha Morrissey, born with the shaman's
healing touch, grows up with both Native American and Roman Catholic
religious beliefs. His knowledge of both religions is sometimes an advantage, but at other times he is merely paralyzed between contradictory systems of belief. In *The Beet Queen*, Wallace Pfef, marginalized as a homosexual
in a small midwestern town, plays an ambivalent role as Karl Adare's lover
and as husband-and-father substitute to Karl's wife and daughter. His liminal status is a source of both happiness and grief. In *Tracks*, Erdrich's two
narrators likewise struggle with liminality in their efforts to leave behind
early lives in favor of others they have chosen. Nanapush grows up Christian in a Jesuit school, but later chooses life in the woods and Chippewa
tradition; the other narrator, Pauline, is a mixed-blood raised in the Native

American tradition, but she wishes to be white and eventually becomes a fanatical nun, constantly at war with the "pagans" who "had once been her relatives."[2]

Erdrich's concern with liminality and marginality pervades all levels of her texts. It affects not only characterization but also thematic and structural features. Semiotic analysis reveals Erdrich's preoccupation with marginality beyond the thematic level. Such analysis also discloses various structural features of Erdrich's texts that frustrate narrativity, "the process by which a perceiver actively constructs a story from the fictional data provided by any narrative medium."[3] This frustration amounts to a textually induced or encoded experience of marginality as the foremost component of the reader's response.[4] My study reveals how textual evocation of various conflicting codes, or antithetical strands within associative fields, produces in the reader an experience of marginality.[5] Although no text could ever have completely homogeneous encoding, Erdrich's texts represent extreme cases of code conflict. Frustration of narrativity produces the reader's own liminal experience and thus underscores Erdrich's primary theme.

Conflicting codes in Erdrich's texts fall into two large categories—codes originating within Western-European society and those originating within Native American culture. Conflicting codes involve

- Christianity versus shamanic religion;
- mechanical or industrial time versus ceremonial time;
- the nuclear family versus tribal kinship systems;
- main or privileged characters versus characters of equal status;
- privileged narrative voices as opposed to dialogical or polyphonic narrative development.

Stylistic and rhetorical effects in Erdrich's work often result from these various code conflicts; such effects register most emphatically in the text's symbolic field.[6]

As novels depicting the lives of socially marginal figures, Erdrich's books are rife with conflicting cultural codes to which the reader must respond. Such response involves but is not limited to supplying "encyclopedic," extratextual information, as when, for example, Erdrich's novels require the reader to recognize and assimilate a host of biblical references. More than simple recognition of allusion is required, however. Semiotic studies reveal that such recognition activates not only information but also an interpretive framework in the mind of the reader. In *Love Medicine*, for example, the chapter titles ("The World's Greatest Fisherman," "Saint

Marie," "Flesh and Blood," "Crown of Thorns," and "Crossing the Water") cue the reader to expect the story to unfold within an intertextual framework of references to the Bible and, accordingly, within a Judeo-Christian value system. However, in all three novels, encoded biblical material is juxtaposed with encoded data from the American Indian shamanic tradition. These religions are epistemologically, experientially, and teleologically different. Their simultaneous presence as cultural codes vexes the reader's effort to decide upon an unambiguous, epistemologically consistent interpretive framework. Encoded "undecidability" leads to the marginalization of the reader by the text.

For example, in *Love Medicine*, one of the earliest patterns of Christian references concerns Easter and resurrection. This Christian notion, or code, of death and transfiguration is counterbalanced by Native American notions of immortality. The opening scene depicts the last hours of June Kashpaw's life on Easter weekend. During this time, June goes through a series of "rebirths," and in the last sentences of this scene, June dies: "[T]he pure and naked part of her went on. The snow fell deeper that Easter than it had in forty years, but June walked over it like water and came home."[7] Syntagmatic chains of references to Christianity that describe June's life and death imply for the reader a clear interpretive framework: the reader assumes that June has gone "home" to a Christian heaven, and that the rest of the novel is likely to unfold along the same interpretive path. Chapter 2, which recounts Marie Lazarre's experience as a novice nun, only reinforces such an initial impression.

A nearly identical signifying process characterizes *Tracks*, except that instead of the Christian code, the shamanic code is first activated as an interpretive path. Events narrated by both narrators take on meaning within a framework of American Indian beliefs about life, death, and mystical experiences. Nanapush speaks of the power of storytelling and of how he once resisted the well-intentioned but misguided words of a Catholic priest by keeping "him listening all night. . . . I pushed him under with my words" (7). Pauline narrates the early life story of Fleur Pillager and represents her through a network of references to Chippewa lake beings, magical animals, and Native American social practices.

However, in subsequent chapters of both novels, crosscurrents in the form of antithetical codes traverse the text. In *Love Medicine*, June's "home" might not be a Christian heaven but instead the reservation, where her spirit, according to Native American beliefs, mingles with the living and carries out unfinished business. Competing with the syntagmatic chain of references to Christianity is another chain of references to Native American beliefs about material and spiritual life which, in the American Indian tradition, are not as distinctly separate as they are according to Christianity. While she lives, June inhabits an animistic universe in which machines, landscapes, and other inanimate things are endowed with spirit: a "pressurized hose" is "a live thing," and a car heater is "a pair of jaws, blasting heat" (3, 5). When she dies, her restless spirit does not depart for some separate "heaven," but lingers among the familiar things of the world to trouble at least one character, her husband Gordie, who perhaps goes insane or dies when June comes back to visit him in the shape of a wounded deer.

Likewise, *Tracks* is torn by conflicting codes. Despite her scorn for her Native American upbringing, Pauline (later to become Sister Leopolda) cannot quite escape her old way of construing experience. Part of her notion of evil and the supernatural, for example, derives from a non-Christian frame of reference. Twisted and deformed away from their shamanic matrix, and grafted into a Christian cosmology, such notions mark her sadomasochistic Christianity as marginal and aberrant, even within the conventions of martyrology. For example, according to Chippewa belief, the monster in the lake is a frightening but appeasable entity. When Pauline becomes a nun, she still believes in the lake creature, but she calls him Satan. Pauline's distorted version of the Satanic lake monster is more horrible than either the Christian Satan, who is not appeasable but who cannot victimize the truly innocent, or the Chippewa monster, who can capture the innocent but who is appeasable. Pauline herself knows that her amalgam of religious views is unprecedented. She recounts the sufferings of St. John of the Cross, St. Catherine, St. Cecelia, and St. Blaise and says with pride: "Predictable shapes, these martyrdoms. Mine took a different form" (152).

In the open-ended, or undecidable, question of June Kashpaw's fate, as well as in the warped theology of Pauline, the reader sees cultural, specifically religious codes conflict. June is depicted partially through references to Christian resurrection and partly through references to Native American religious beliefs concerning the place of spirits among their families and tribes. Likewise Pauline/Leopolda's interpretation of experience is dual and irreconcilable, despite her grotesque assimilations. Narrativity usually includes an impulse to resolve such textual tensions through privileging of one code or through synthesis, but Erdrich's texts preclude both options for dealing with these conflicting religious paradigms. Both religious codes allow for the supernatural dimension of existence; however, the ways in which such a dimension is manifest according to each code, as well as the ways in which the individual relates to this dimension and the ultimate meanings and values associated with each code, lead the reader away from synthesis and into a permanent state of irresolution. Consequently, the reader is "marginalized"—left to ponder epistemological dilemmas from the perspective of one at least temporarily situated outside both systems.

Moreover, a hermeneutical impasse confronts the reader as he or she attempts to follow diverse interpretive avenues that refuse to converge at a crossroads. With several avenues of meaning remaining open, the text does not overdetermine one avenue of interpretation and thus endorse one theological view over the other. Indeed, by raising conflicting possibilities, the text displaces the reader from usual positions of theological and epistemological inquiry. In *Love Medicine*, Gordie sees what he sees, whether hallucination, vision, or empirical observation. Likewise Sister Mary Martin (the nun who tries to convince Gordie that "June" is only a dead deer) sees what she sees, according to her perceptual frame of reference. Like several of Erdrich's characters, she is even dimly aware of experience assuming "a pattern, approaching and retreating from the strength of her own design" (183). This statement accurately describes the response of the marginalized reader, who becomes aware of the interpretive "design" the text first invites, then resists.

In *The Beet Queen*, a similar conflict in religious encoding—this time a conflict within Christianity—is especially noticeable in the portrayal of Karl Adare. Karl is likened to both Christ and Satan. The way he is presented depends upon which narrator is speaking at any given time. In a biblical allusion recalling the Song of Solomon, in which the waiting bride repeatedly speaks of Christ as "honey," Karl's lover, Wallace Pfef, responds to the sight of Karl as if "a hive of golden insects [were] buzzing, floating, gathering the honey that filled" him.[8] Karl's equation with Christ is especially emphasized in the passage where Mary sees Karl's face in the snow, but in the same image the nuns, priests, and the whole Catholic community see Christ's face. Within this same matrix of Christian references, Karl appears also as Satanic, as when his brother says to him, "You're the devil" (74). As a seminarian, Karl portrays himself ambiguously as both Christlike and Satanic. In acts of worship he "would burn and burn until by grace [he] was consumed"; however, he also sees himself as "a pure black flame," and his acts of worship are carnal and homosexual (50). Even in the expression "pure black" there is a connotative conflict, for a reader generally does not associate purity with blackness within the usual interpretive field concerning colors. Whether to regard Karl as Christlike or Satanic becomes a dilemma for the reader, who must negotiate not only the ambiguous message but also the many conflicting narrative points of view. Augmenting this difficulty and finally underscoring the textual emphasis on epistemological enigmas is the fact that when Mary sees Karl's face in the snow and the Catholics see Christ's face, Celestine James—a half-blood—sees no face at all.

Karl's character is encoded in yet another way in Erdrich's text, through references to mythology that seem to compete with the code of Christianity for domination of narrativity. Far from resolving questions about his inner nature, however, this chain of references affords the reader only one more kind of "undecidability." Karl calls himself a "poor fool" (46) in his early wanderings, and he is, in fact, depicted through indirect references to the Fool of the Tarot cards, of which his sister, Mary, is an adept reader. In one passage, Karl (like the Fool) is chased by a dog, carries a sprig of white flowers on a branch torn away from a tree, and falls over a precipice. Narcissistically sensual and bisexual, Karl is also like the Fool in his immature, unindividuated consciousness. Later, he is even further linked with the Fool when he stays at the "Ox" Motel (really the Fox Motel, but a letter is missing from the marquee). The Aleph, the first letter of the Hebrew alphabet, is the letter atop the Fool card and is also the sign of an ox.

This syntagmatic chain of references to archetypal myth does not resolve the ambiguity in the portrait of Karl as both Christlike and Satanic. Instead, it constitutes a textual shift into another cultural code that, finally, overdetermines or insists upon ambiguity, for the Fool is one of the most ambiguous and marginal figures in mythology. He is either a wise man or a madman, or both, and he lives always on the fringes of society as an outcast, both feared and revered as one capable of destroying or transforming society. Like Karl, the Fool embodies traits associated with Jesus and traits associated with Satan. Consequently, for the reader in search of resolution of conflict, this textual shift from one cultural code to another provides one more frustration of narrativity.

Erdrich's texts resist the pressure of narrativity not only to privilege one cultural code over another but also to synthesize these antithetical possibilities by responding to false resolutions of conflict at the connotative level (the level at which the reader constructs theme, based on codes); such false resolutions likewise occur in the text's symbolic field. Many of Erdrich's figures of speech ostensibly reconcile contradictory cultural and religious traditions; however, upon close scrutiny, her metaphors and symbols constitute anomalous moments in the text when the reader must pause "between worlds" to consider perceptual frameworks as important structural principles in both textual and nontextual realms.[9]

In *Love Medicine*, one of the most interesting symbols that seems like a bridge between Christian and Native American religious paradigms is the beads, for which one of the chapters is named. The string of Cree prayer beads is June's only possession when the Kashpaws adopt her. When she leaves home, the beads remain with Marie. Raised Catholic and once even becoming a postulant nun, Marie sometimes calls the beads a "rosary," although this word rarely, if ever, refers to prayer beads outside the Roman Catholic tradition. If they are Cree beads, they should speak to the shamanic dimension of Marie (who is a sorcerer and healer), and if they are a rosary, they should speak to her Catholic dimension. However, as a liminal figure, she is not fully Catholic or pagan. Touching the beads makes her almost aware of her liminal status: "I don't pray, but sometimes I do touch the beads. . . . I never look at them, just let my fingers roam to them when no one is in the house. It's a rare time when I do this. I touch them, and every time I do I think of small stones. At the bottom of the lake, rolled aimless by the waves. I think of them polished. To many people it would be a kindness. But I see no kindness in how the waves are grinding them smaller and smaller until they finally disappear" (73).

To think of the Cree beads/rosary as mere stones is to verge on epistemological insight. The beads *are* stones, called "prayer beads" by Crees and "rosary" by Catholics, according to two different religious frames of reference. These frames of reference are yoked but not reconciled through the symbol of the beads. The beads are only one of many symbols in *Love Medicine* that invite the reader to bridge codes that do not interface.

In this same passage, the metonymic substitution of stones for beads shifts the reader out of the symbolic field back into the connotative code, through which the reader arrives at conclusions about characterization and theme based on many patterns of references to stones. Waterworn stones become part of a pattern of references suggesting diminishment of human beings by life. When Nector feels the course of his life change, he feels "Time . . . rushing around [him] like water around a big wet rock. . . . Very quickly [he] would be smoothed away" (94); and Henry Lamartine, Jr.'s face is described as "white and hard. Then it broke, like stones break all of a sudden when water boils up inside them" (152). In the passage concerning the prayer beads, people, beads, and stones are equated through metonymy. This equation of humans and prayer beads with stones effaces the sacral dimension of existence and reduces everything to its merely phenomenal status. In such an associational field, the rosary/prayer beads become not a bridge between religions or a synthetic expression of religious values, but a reminder of the stark and meaningless aspects of existence that religion fails to eradicate. A similar eradication of the sacral dimensions of existence occurs when contact between one soul and another is described as the touch of "angel wings"; "angel wings" is also, however, the name of an alcoholic beverage—the ruin of many a Native American, including June.

Sacramentality is subverted in *The Beet Queen* when Mary sees Karl's face in the snow, the nuns see Christ, and Celestine James sees nothing but an indentation in the snow. The miraculous image is reduced to the merely phenomenal; the sacral dimension is part of the nuns' frame of reference, and Mary's more superstitious reaction likewise results from her own way of seeing. When "Karl" or "Christ" melts in the spring, Mary describes the melting in rather mystical terms, but still, the text has made its point about the problematic nature of interpretation. Overall, Erdrich's novels confront problems of origination of knowledge, and so resist any interpretive urge that is founded on epistemological or theological certainty.

Another major pair of cultural codes that conflict in Erdrich's texts, particularly *Love Medicine*, is codes of time. A reader's temporal paradigms govern many acts of narrativity and are one major component in the construction of meaning. Despite the many experimental procedures of novels written in the modern and contemporary eras, the reader of novels has fairly standard and predictable expectations of time as a part of his/her narrativity. Most readers expect novels to encode "mechanical" (or Western industrial) time, which is linear, incremental, and teleological. That is, time consists of forward-moving, discretely measurable units, some of which are regarded as momentous and purposive and are thus consigned to special status in memory. Moreover, in the novel, these momentous incidents usually build upon each other and in many cases are considered as pivotal in character development and maturity. In *Love Medicine*, however, the text is encoded simultaneously with mechanical and ceremonial time. The reader's response to this double encoding of time schemes is yet another experience of marginality.

By titling the chapters of *Love Medicine* also with dates, Erdrich implies mechanical time. The reader, employing mechanical notions of time, assumes that these dates are of some special significance as a coherent series of privileged, momentous events in ordinary lives. To some extent, the novel also appears to chronicle the history of various characters in a family, according to the conventions of the family saga. Moreover, the opening chapter begins at Easter, a holiday suggesting Christian millennial time: consequently, the mechanical time code reinforces the Christian code in managing narrativity.

These and other structural traits of *Love Medicine* encourage the reader to apply the norms of mechanical time. However, as Paula Gunn Allen observes about Native American novels that attempt to unfold according to chronological time, linearity is often disrupted by many flashbacks, lateral narrational pursuits, flights of free association, and other indications of the failure of chronology to contain the story.[10] Certainly there are many such narrative disruptions in *Love Medicine*, as if events, with their rippling effects backward and forward in time, were uncontainable within the forward-moving constraints of chronological development. Indeed, "narration" cannot be held within the limits of "plot" or "story," which can be chronicled.[11]

The breakdown of chronological time in this novel produces one of the signal frustrations of narrativity. *Love Medicine* defies the reader's effort to locate a conventional plot—a temporal sequence of characters' actions traceable along a "constant curve" with a teleological aim (the notion of plot as consisting of beginning, conflict, rising action, resolution, ending).[12] Erdrich's novels conspicuously lack plot in this traditional sense of the term. One need only ask oneself for a plot summary of *Love Medicine* to substantiate this claim. The novel seems rife with narrators (eight, to be exact), bereft of a focal narrative point of view, and replete with characters whose lives are equally emphasized.

A main feature of narrativity is the urge to plot-summarize, an essential step in constructing a diegesis. According to Robert Scholes, "One of the primary qualities of those texts we understand as fiction is that they generate a diegetic order that has an astonishing independence from its text. To put it simply, once a story is told it can be recreated in a recognizable way by a totally new set of words. . . . [M]emory stores not the words of texts but their concepts, not the signifiers but the signifieds. When we read a narrative text, then, we process it as a diegesis," or as streamlined "story" as opposed to narration, or as a set of ideas (signifieds) as opposed to words (signifiers, text) (112). Western time, from which derives the Western reader's diegetic structural principle, is especially amenable to the plot summary. Erdrich's texts vex the reader's diegetic impulse by encoding ceremonial time together with linear time and by coaxing the reader to abandon fixed notions about what kinds of experience are "important." As Lulu Lamartine says, "All through my life I never did believe in human measurement. Numbers, time, inches, feet. All are just ploys for cutting nature down to size" (*LM*, 221).

Ceremonial time is cyclic rather than linear, accretive rather than incremental, and makes few distinctions between momentous events and daily, ordinary events.[13] When we consider the traits of ceremonial time, and the differences between it and mechanical time, *Love Medicine* suddenly appears much less chaotically constructed. One of the first cues to the ceremonial paradigm is the chronological loop that the text makes, as if to satisfy both mechanical and ceremonial time schemes. *Love Medicine* opens in 1981, loops back through the forties, fifties, sixties, and seventies, returns to 1981, then proceeds to 1984. Through this organization, Erdrich's text suggests that the meanings of events and conditions in the present moment lie piecemeal in the endless round of time.

Likewise, the text implies that cyclic patterns, which describe the seasons of the earth, best disclose the meanings of individual lives. For example, Nector Kashpaw's life is a river: it proceeds from a deep source, wanders the earth, and once even changes course; finally, it returns to a deep source, when Nector retreats behind the "smokescreen" of senility to "fish" for "deep thoughts" in "the middle of Lake Turcot" (*LM*, 208).

Throughout the text, this code of fishing constitutes one major avenue of characterization and also breaks down notions of mechanical and millennial time by challenging the conventional barriers between the spiritual and the material worlds. Jesus and various spiritual beings, including Satan, "fish" for the souls of human beings, while human beings, in turn, "fish" for intuitively sensed connections with a spiritual realm beyond the earth. Contacts between the earthly and the spiritual realms occur not in time, or at some imagined end of time, but when time seems to stop. Thus the text implies through the code of fishing that the meaning of life appears through a cyclic interchange between spiritual and material worlds, not in linearly "measured" events that "cut . . . nature down to size." In *Tracks*, this implication is even more overt. The monster or "lake man" of Matchimanito periodically catches people—especially fishermen, but also anyone who swims in the lake. In this novel the spiritual and material realms are not separate at all. Though conventional Christianity sees a clear distinction between these realms, Pauline as a nun never accepts it; she sees Satan in closets, behind doors, and looking out through human eyes.

The Beet Queen unfolds much more strictly within mechanical time, with only one slight disruption of the chronological progression through the years. The book opens in the 1930s and proceeds through the 1970s; the only fracture in chronology is the placement of 1972 before 1971. However, this chronological unfolding conceals the novel's frequent narrational retreats into the timeless and into mythical dimensions signifying timelessness. Rather than characters who develop according to various life experiences occurring throughout the years—as in the conventional chronological novel—the characters' major stages of development are—

as in *Love Medicine*—marked falls or deliverances from time. For example, *The Beet Queen* is punctuated by mythical flights, as when Mary and Karl's mother, Adelaide, vanishes from their lives by flying away with a stunt pilot named Omar. For Mary, Adelaide is mythologized, frozen into an eternal moment of falling back out of the sky. The only time Mary ever again corresponds with her mother, she sends her a postcard with an "aerial view of Argus," as if to substantiate her vision of her mother still in the sky looking down at her.

Chronology yields to mythical timelessness again in Mary's trance vision and her subsequent formation of a spiritual tie with Celestine's baby, Mary's niece. As Mary "sees" the person the embryo will be, time speeds up and she sees an entire season elapse. Likewise, Mary's prophetic dreams break down the notion of the sequentiality of time and imply a standard of time based on simultaneity rather than linearity.

Tracks pursues a similar line of temporal development. Chronological events—the storyline—contained between 1913 and 1924 exist in tension with narration, which departs (as in *The Beet Queen*) into mythical or ceremonial time. In the Native American tradition of positing few distinctions between "real" and "imaginary" events, *Tracks* interweaves dreamed events with those of the story; consequently, the eleven years supposedly contained by the narrative constantly exceed their boundaries. Indeed, Nanapush declares that whites imposed their ideas of measurement and boundaries on the Native Americans, and he implies that the separation of experience into real and imagined events, and of time into past, present, and future, is part of an alien and oppressive world view that, together with writing, makes communication extremely difficult.

In all three novels, another significant conflict of codes occurs at the hermeneutic level (the level of the text at which the reader is "cued" to apply certain hermeneutic, or generic, principles and thus predict outcomes). The texts to some extent proceed according to the conventions of the Western family saga. *Love Medicine* and *Tracks* also affirm the traits and values of the tribal kinship system, while *The Beet Queen* likewise insists that many alternative kinds of ties, not biological, link people. Taken together the three novels are a Faulknerian portrait of a group of variously related people in or around Argus, North Dakota. The story evokes from the reader a structural principle germane to the code of family novels, but then proceeds to defy many of the expectations generated in the reader.

Love Medicine opens in the 1980s, as Albertine Johnson laments the behavior of her mother and grandmother. The next chapter reverts to the 1930s, as if to begin with the grandmother, Marie, and to trace the development of a nuclear, though matrilineal, family. Values associated with the Western nuclear family are evoked by the text, especially in the arguments that occur concerning the "real" status of Marie Kashpaw's biological children, as opposed to the outcast status of adoptees such as June (actually Marie's niece) and Lipsha (June's son). The idea that biological children are some-how superior or preferred over other children who belong in a nuclear family is a Western-European, not a Native American, concept. On the con-trary, the Native American "family" allows for various ties of kinship—including spiritual kinship and clan membership—joining the individuals living together in one house.[14] This family-saga code encourages the reader to take many of what Eco calls "inferential" walks. That is, once aware of overt features of the novel that suggest it will be a family saga, the reader be-gins to predict various outcomes in accordance with these expectations, in-cluding the assumption that certain Western norms and values apply. How-ever, Erdrich's text also encodes the norms and values of the tribal kinship system. First, it makes the reader work especially hard to trace out and re-tain in memory the direct lines of descent among members of the families in *Love Medicine*. Indeed, some of the relationships are not clarified in the novel at all; Sister Leopolda, for example, appears in both *Love Medicine* and *The Beet Queen*, but we find out her origins only in *Tracks* (the third published novel but chronologically the first). Erdrich's texts variously obscure biological lines of kinship even as they appear to chronicle generations.

Whereas *Love Medicine* denies the significance of biological lineage, *The Beet Queen* emphasizes the arbitrariness of ties between people. Like its com-panion novels, it suggests that people who are biologically related are often much less central in each others' lives than the traditional family saga suggests. This novel concerns breakages in biological lines of kinship. Karl and Mary, abandoned by their mother, are raised separately from each other as well as from their baby brother, who is kidnapped and raised as Jude Miller. Mary grows up with her aunt, who prefers Mary to her own daughter, Sita. Another character with a confusing lineage and pattern of relationships is Celestine James, a half-blood with a number of half-siblings. She becomes Mary's friend and Karl's wife, though Wallace Pfef, also Karl's lover, acts more like a husband to her.

In *Tracks*, some of the mysteries of identity and kinship raised in the other two novels are clarified, but again, this novel does not confirm the importance of such identifications and linkages. To give Lulu a "legitimate" name, Nanapush declares her to be his biological child when she is born. However, he also calls her "granddaughter" and she calls him "uncle." She is really the child of Fleur Pillager and Eli Kashpaw, and not directly kin to

Nanapush at all. However, because Nanapush saved Fleur from death, she is a "daughter," and Lulu is thus a "granddaughter."

Opposite to the ways in which the family saga makes clear lines of relationship and focuses upon the family as insiders while other characters are outsiders, Erdrich's texts deemphasize the importance of biological ties and emphasize the significance of other, particularly spiritual, ties of friendship and love. Such unclear lines of relationship and implied gaps between the phases of individual lives run counter to the norms of the family saga, which suggests continuity and historical coherence; these gaps are more characteristic of ceremonial time—basic to tribal kinship systems—which implies that our experiences quite often change us dramatically from one phase of our lives to another. Dramatic spiritual experiences, for example, often result in naming or name-changes, as well as in realignments of individuals with new groups.[15]

Reinforcing the conflict in Erdrich's texts between nuclear family and tribal kinship codes is her method of characterization. Characters in Erdrich's novels are not "fully developed" or defined in relation to each other according to the conventions of the family saga. Not only are the boundaries between nuclear and peripheral family and patriarchal and matriarchal lineage obscured, but in *Love Medicine* and *The Beet Queen* there are no "main" characters, just as there is no focal narrator among the many narrative voices that speak in these texts. Narrational authority or centrality shifts constantly from one narrating voice to another. These narrating characters exist on the margins of each others' lives, and often their stories do not match, because each person has only various little pieces of the whole "truth." Not even the third-person omniscient narrator (a curious presence in both novels) is a center of authority.

The intertextual relationship of Erdrich's novels only compounds these features. The novels contain many of the same characters but devote different amounts of attention to each. Dot Adare receives much narrative attention and is even herself a narrator in *The Beet Queen*; however, *Love Medicine* traces only a small portion of her adult life. Other characters such as Eli and Pauline are featured in *Love Medicine* and in *Tracks* but are only mentioned in *The Beet Queen*.

Ideas about individuality constitute yet another instance of code conflict in these novels. Modes of characterization in the Anglo-European novel usually presuppose the measurable reality of psychological essence.[16] Indeed, our ideas of individual identity presuppose that the essential being of each person can be identified, analyzed, and mimetically represented in various coherent stages of development from birth to death. Erdrich's texts to some extent suggest such a concept of individuation, but her texts are also traversed by a conflicting code which has to do with American Indian concepts of individuation that are not based on psychological essence or individual psychology. Especially in *Love Medicine*, characters are formed through various syntagmatic series of references to natural elements such as air, earth, fire, and water. In the opening section, June walks on water, figuratively, and in the end, Lipsha travels across the water that now covers his ancestral lands. Nector's life is a river, which sometimes rushes on, sometimes pools and is still, and sometimes takes a fateful change of course. In his life, as in the text in general, the water code becomes one of the avenues of meaning by which the reader constructs character.

Marie's personality is evoked through references to fire. In the second chapter of *Love Medicine*, her sadomasochistic relationship with Sister Leopolda includes the desire to see the nun's heart "roast on a black stick" (45). Marie is burned with scalding water; her visions "blaze," and when she sees the old nun for the last time, she thinks to herself there is not enough left of Leopolda to serve as kindling for a small flame. The changes in Marie's personality as she grows older are implied by changes in the way she "burns" or thinks of burning, not by changes in her owing to momentous events resulting in mature vision or human completeness. By putting "the tears [back] into" Lulu's eyes (helping her feel emotions again), Marie helps her old enemy, who is blind and whose eyes still recall the image of her burning house (235).

In *Tracks*, Fleur Pillager's personality accrues through references to "wolf teeth," to a fishlike creature from Lake Matchimanito, and to cannibalistic or at least feral practices. This building of character out of syntagmatic chains of natural elements comprises one half of yet another code conflict. As these references imply, Native American individuation occurs in close relationship with nature, whereas Western individuation is conceived as a coherent development of a unique psychological essence present from birth but formed and shaped by civilization.

All of these conflicting codes in Erdrich's text produce a state of marginality in the reader, who must at some point in the reading cease to apply the conventional expectations associated with ordinary narrativity. The reader must pause "between worlds" to discover the arbitrary structural principles of both. This primary value—epistemological insight—which Erdrich's text associates with marginality might then be adopted through a revision of narrativity. Stranded between conflicting codes—deprived of "a stable point of identification" within the world evoked by the text—the reader is temporarily disempowered.[17] However, such disempowerment or "alienation" leads to another kind of power. The reader must consider a possibility forcefully posited in all of Erdrich's works (as well as in those of other contemporary Native Americans): the world takes on the shape of the stories we tell. Exposure to radically different stories as ways of structuring the world brings the reader to see what Lipsha Morrissey understands when he says, "You see how instantly the ground can shift you thought was solid. . . . You see how all the everyday things you counted on was just a dream you had been having by which you run your whole life. . . . So I had perspective on it all" (*LM*, 209, 211).

Notes

1. Some of the best-known studies of marginal and liminal states and their sociological effects within oral and traditional societies are those of anthropologists Victor Turner and Arnold Van Gennep. See Turner's *The Forest of Symbols* (Ithaca: Cornell University Press, 1967) and "Variations on a Theme of Liminality," in *Secular Ritual*, edited by Sally F. Moore and Barbara G. Meyerhoof (Assen/Amsterdam: Van Gorcum, 1977), 36–70. See Van Gennep's *Rites of Passage* (London: Routledge and Kegan Paul, 1960).

2. Louise Erdrich, *Tracks* (New York: Henry Holt, 1988), 189. Subsequent references to this novel will be identified by parenthetical page numbers in the text.

3. Robert Scholes, *Semiotics and Interpretation* (New Haven: Yale University Press, 1982), 60. Subsequent references to this book will be identified by parenthetical page numbers in the text.

4. I am ostensibly at odds here with the thesis of Marvin Magalaner, who argues ("Of Cars, Time, and the River," in *American Women Writing Fiction: Memory, Identity, Family, Space*, edited by Mickey Pearlman [Lexington: University Press of Kentucky, 1989]), that Erdrich's texts aim primarily to establish an "equilibrium" in the reader. I disagree that this is their immediate effect, though I would agree that ultimately, in acquainting the reader with the experience of marginalization, Erdrich's texts produce a new kind of equilibrium in the reader, an equilibrium based on a revised narrativity, as I conclude at the end of this essay.

5. Roland Barthes explains that codes comprise "associative fields"—"supratextual organization[s] of notations which impose a certain notion of structure" (*The Semiotic Challenge* [New York: Hill and Wang, 1988], 288).

6. Barthes speaks of the symbolic *field* rather than the symbolic code because the significance of symbols accrues within the text, whereas "codes" have extrinsic origins.

7. Louise Erdrich, *Love Medicine* (New York: Bantam, 1984), 6. Subsequent references to this novel will be identified by parenthetical page numbers in the text.

8. Louise Erdrich, *The Beet Queen* (New York: Bantam, 1986), 213. Subsequent references to this novel will be identified by parenthetical page numbers in the text.

9. "Anomalous moments" is Michael Riffaterre's term to describe the ways in which words in literary contexts function in unusual ways contradictory to their immediate contexts. They "force the reader to become aware of the form of the message he is deciphering." See *Text Production* (New York: Columbia University Press, 1983), chap. 4 on the literary neologism.

10. As Paula Gunn Allen points out, for Native American writers the so-called "traditional" linear novel form is "experimental"; the Anglo-European concept of "experimental" (or modernist and postmodernist) fiction is more "traditional" for the Native American (*The Sacred Hoop: Recovering the Feminine in Native American Traditions* [Boston: Beacon, 1986]). See also Brian Swann and Arnold Krupat, eds., *Recovering the Word: Essays on Native American Literature* (Berkeley: University of California Press, 1987), which contains various essays on aspects of Native American novel development; and Gerald Vizenor, ed., *Narrative Chance: Postmodern Discourse on Native American Literatures* (Albuquerque: University of New Mexico Press, 1989), a collection of essays devoted to the study of the many connections between postmodernism and traditional Native American storytelling.

11. I am relying here on Robert Scholes's conception of the ways in which "events" and "narration," or "story" and "discourse," become separate parts of a text (*Semiotics and Interpretation*, 60, 62).

12. This definition of plot is Umberto Eco's (*The Role of the Reader: Explorations in the Semiotics of Texts* [Bloomington: Indiana University Press, 1979], 132).

13. On ceremonial time, see Allen, *Sacred Hoop*.

14. See Allen, *Sacred Hoop*; Swann and Krupat, *Recovering the Word*; and Hertha D. Wong's "Adoptive Mothers and Thrown-Away Children in the Novels of Louise Erdrich," in *Narrating Mothers: Theorizing Maternal Subjectivities,* edited by Brenda O. Daly and Maureen T. Reddy (Knoxville: University of Tennessee Press, 1991), 174–92.

15. See, for example, Carter Revard's "Traditional Osage Naming Ceremonies: Entering the Circle of Being," in Swann and Krupat, *Recovering the Word*, 446–66, and Hertha D. Wong's discussion of naming practices in *Sending My Heart Back Across the Years: Tradition and Innovation in Native American Autobiography* (New York: Oxford University Press, 1992). Paula Gunn Allen also discusses the significance of naming in Native American culture.

16. Robert Scholes and Michael Riffaterre discuss this notion.

17. "Stable point of identification" comes from Kaja Silverman, *The Subject of Semiotics* (New York: Oxford University Press, 1983), 281.

Reading Louise Erdrich

Love Medicine *as Home Medicine*

GREG SARRIS

✦ ✦ ✦

Y OUR GRANDMOTHER DIDN'T WANT to be Indian," my
Auntie Violet remarked as she put down the photograph of my grandmother I had given her. She leaned forward in her chair, as if for a closer
inspection, one last look at the picture, then sat back with resolve. "Nope,"
she said, "that lady wanted to be white. She didn't want to be Indian. I'm
sorry to tell."

I shuffled through the assorted black-and-white photographs I kept in a
plastic K-Mart shopping bag. They were pictures I had taken from my
grandmother's family album. I handed Auntie Violet another picture,
hopeful that she would change her mind, discern something similar,
something good, Indian. We were all related, after all. We shared the same
history: the invasions by the Spanish and Russians, the Mexicans, and the
Americans. We shared the same blood: my father's great-grandfather Tom
Smith, my grandmother's grandfather, was married at one time to Auntie
Violet's great-grandmother, the Kashaya Pomo matriarch Rosie Jarvis. My
grandmother grew up among her grandmother's people, the Coast Miwok
who lived south of the Russian River in Sonoma and Marin Counties, and
she had lived in San Francisco and Los Angeles. Violet and many of my
other relatives identified as Kashaya Pomo grew up on the Kashaya Reservation in Kashaya Pomo territory north of the Russian River. I wanted des-

perately to know everything I could about my grandmother, whom I had never known. Grandpa Hilario, her husband, didn't know that much about her Indian background, only where she was from. "Take what pictures you want," he said as I looked through her album. "Maybe those ladies up there [at Kashaya] can tell you something."

Violet held the picture close to her face, scrutinizing. She adjusted her glasses, then carefully placed the photograph in the neat line of photos she was making before her on the kitchen table. She reached for her cigarettes. "Nope," she said. "You see, Greg, those Indians down there, those south people, they lost it a long time ago. Those ones around there. Shoot, they don't have no one speaking their language now. They speak more Spanish, Mexican. A few of them, they didn't even want to be Indian. They're mixed, light-skinned."

Violet stopped talking to light her cigarette. She pushed the pack of cigarettes to Auntie Vivien, who sat directly across from me. Violet was at the head of the table. It was late, around one in the morning. We often visited, talked about people and places until sunup. Now I was sharing the pictures and what I learned from my grandfather during my recent visit with him. In the quiet of the room, in those spaces between our words, I heard loud music coming from a neighbor's house. The heavy bass sounded through Auntie Violet's trailer home walls. I looked down at her clean white-and-orange-flowered oilcloth. Up here on the reservation, on top of a mountain in the middle of nowhere, at least forty long, winding miles from Healdsburg, the nearest town, and all this noise.

"Drinking, fighting each other," Vivien said, as if reading my thoughts. Vivien was quiet, to the point.

"No," Violet said, exhaling a cloud of smoke, "a few of them people down there, they would ignore us if they seen us in town. Those Bodega ones, especially. Act too good, act white, them people. Like that guy, what's his name. YOUR cousin, Greg. Now he wants to be Indian. But, oh, his mother. Stuck up. Used to be she see us Indians and laugh at us. And what's she got? Who is she?"

Auntie Violet didn't say all that she could have just then. I knew the stories, the gossip that one group armed themselves with against the other. Indians, I thought to myself. "Indians, you know how we are," my Miwok cousin once said.

I opened the plastic bag, then closed it. What I was sensitive to, what made me uncomfortable, was Auntie Violet's dismissive tone. I knew she loved me; she and Uncle Paul were like parents to me. But wasn't my grandmother a part of me also? Wasn't there some common ground that could be talked about?

"But my grandmother didn't like white people," I protested. "Look, she married a Filipino. In those days a Filipino was considered low as an Indian. And Grandpa Hilario is dark."

"Well, she might not liked whites, but she must not liked herself, too. She didn't want to claim all of what she was. Those people, well, besides they had no Indian upbringing really. No language. I know those people. Laugh at us, but others are laughing at them. To whites they're nothing either."

Violet shifted in her chair, tugged at the ends of her white cotton blouse. "Viv," she said, "remember what's his name's mother, how she act when she seen us downtown that time? I felt like saying . . . I just wouldn't lower myself to THAT level."

Just then a woman screamed from the house across the way. There was a loud crash, a spilling of things, as if a table had been overturned, and the music stopped.

"Oh," Violet sighed, blowing smoke. "How embarrassing. Gives Indians a bad name."

I looked down at the oilcloth and the Tupperware bowls of leftovers from dinner. Beans, fried chicken, salad, a plate of cold tortillas. Auntie Violet's pink poodle salt-and-pepper shakers. I looked at her row of my grandmother's photographs. My grandmother, Evelyn Hilario, looking up to Auntie Violet in at least a half-dozen different ways. All of us, I thought, fighting each other. I reached into the plastic shopping bag for another photograph, one where my grandmother might look more "Indian."

FAMILIES BICKERING. Families arguing amongst themselves, drawing lines, maintaining old boundaries. Who is in. Who is not. Gossip. Jealousy. Drinking. Love. The ties that bind. The very human need to belong, to be worthy and valued. Families. Who is Indian. Who is not. Families bound by history and blood. This is the stuff, the fabric of my Indian community. It is what I found in Louise Erdrich's Chippewa community as I read *Love Medicine.*

In the first chapter of the novel, Albertine Johnson comes home to her reservation after hearing the news of her Aunt June's death. Albertine is one of Erdrich's seven narrators, whose interrelated stories readers follow throughout the novel. The death of June Kashpaw becomes the occasion around which the narrators tell their stories, stories that chronicle in a variety of ways life on and around the North Dakota Chippewa reservation. As Albertine comes home, readers witness with her the general reservation setting and the interpersonal dynamics of her family. When I found Albertine caught in the middle of her mother and aunt's bickering about who was white and who was Indian, I immediately thought of the time I came home and spent the night showing Auntie Violet picture after picture of my grandmother. So much seemed familiar.

> "That white girl," Mama went on, "she's built like a truckdriver. She won't keep King long. Lucky you're slim, Albertine."
>
> "*Jeez*, Zelda!" Aurelia came in from the next room. "Why can't you just leave it be. So she's white. What about the Swede? How do you think Albertine feels hearing you talk like this when her Dad was white?"
>
> "I feel fine," I said. "I never knew him."
>
> I understood what Aurelia meant though—I was light, clearly a breed.
>
> "My girl's an *Indian*," Zelda emphasized. "I raised her an Indian, and that's what she is."
>
> "Never said no different." Aurelia grinned, not the least put out, hitting me with her elbow. "She's lots better looking than most Kashpaws."[1]

The bickering about who and what is or is not Indian is not the only phenomenon about Albertine's Chippewa reservation and family that made me think of home. There is the drinking and associated violence. And the bickering, gossiping, and drinking Albertine introduces readers to in the first chapter continue throughout the novel. The general scene readers walk into with Albertine does not change particularly, even though, as some critics suggest, certain characters seem to triumph over it.[2] Images and sounds, bits and pieces of conversations, people and places from home and from the novel, came together and mixed in my mind. Albertine in a bar, "sitting before [her] third or fourth Jellybean, which is anisette, grain alcohol, a lit match, and a small wet explosion in the brain" (155). My cousin Elna seated in the neon light of an Indian bar on lower Fourth Street in Santa Rosa. Marie Lazarre Kashpaw responding to the gossip about her: "I just laugh, don't let them get a wedge in. Then I turn the tables on them, because they don't know how many goods I have collected in town" (70). My Auntie Marguerita: "Ah, let them hags talk. Who are they? Just women who kept the streets of lower Fourth warm." "My girl's an Indian." "Your grandmother didn't want to be an Indian." Albertine jumping on June's drunken son King and biting a hole in his ear to keep him from drowning his wife in the kitchen sink and the fighting that follows and the cherished fresh-baked pies getting smashed: "Torn open. Black juice bleeding through the crusts" (38). The loud crash, a spilling of things, as if a table had been overturned.

Drinking, fighting each other.

I began asking questions, if at first only to sort things out. Are these two communities, one in northern California and one in North Dakota, really that similar?[3] Are these conditions and scenes the same for all American Indians? Is this situation the common ground, finally, on which over three hundred different nations and cultures meet? Is there more to see and know about this situation than Erdrich has painted? Where does all of this come from, this bickering, this age-old family rivalry and pain?

This last question brought me back to the feuding families in *Love Medicine*: the Kashpaws, the Lazarres, the Lamartines, and the Morrisseys. They reflected in their quarrels and pain my own relatives and the families on the Kashaya reservation feuding with other Kashaya families and with Coast Miwok families from the southern territories.

I thought again of the history of the Kashaya and the Miwok families. The Coast Miwoks in the southern territories suffered cultural and political domination early on. The Spanish missionized the Coast Miwoks and broke apart most of the tribes early in the nineteenth century. The northern Indians, the Kashaya Pomo who were colonized by the Russians, were not affected in the same ways. The Kashaya were virtually enslaved by the Russians, but they were not converted to Christianity, nor were they broken apart as a tribe. The Miwoks learned Spanish and changed their ways earlier and faster than the Kashaya Pomo to the north. They had to. No wonder the Coast Miwok people "don't have no one speaking their language now."[4] No wonder my grandmother wasn't Indian in ways Auntie Violet is. Still, what the Coast Miwok and Kashaya Pomo people have in common, albeit in somewhat different forms and situations, is that history of cultural and political domination by European and Euro-American invaders. Today so much of our pain, whether we are Kashaya or Miwok or both, seems associated with that history, not just in our general material poverty but also in the ways we have internalized the domination. Low self-esteem. A sense of powerlessness. Alienation from both past and present, the Indian world and the white world, and from the ways the two worlds commingle. We often judge ourselves in terms of the dominator's values ("laughing at 'Indians'") or create countervalues with which to judge ourselves ("they act white"; "they're mixed, light-skinned"). We internalize the oppression we have felt and, all too often, become oppressor-like to ourselves.

So one answer, at least, to my question regarding the origins and perpetuation of family bickering and pain at home is internalized oppression. I began seeing signs of internalized oppression as I remembered again people and events at home on the Kashaya Pomo reservation and in the town of Santa Rosa. Our quarrelling, name-calling, self-abuse. And when I looked back at *Love Medicine*, I found the same signs reflected from my community. And couldn't this be the case? Just as Erdrich's Indian community reflected in ways my Indian community, might not my community with its history reflect that of Erdrich's in her novel? After all, the Chippewa Indians, on whose stories Erdrich's fiction is based, suffered European and Euro-American domination also.

But to answer my question about whether the concept of internalized oppression as I see its pertaining to my community can be applied to Erdrich's fictional Chippewa community, I must turn back to my first questions. Are the two respective Indian communities really that similar? Is life on and around the Kashaya Pomo reservation the same as life on and around Erdrich's fictional Chippewa reservation? Are the conditions and scenes I have noted about both my community and Erdrich's in *Love Medicine* the same for all American Indian communities? I think of Auntie Violet arranging photographs of my grandmother and seeing in the photographs what she wanted to see, what she knew to be true, and of how I might be doing the same thing with respect to *Love Medicine*. How might I be perpetuating biases, limiting communication and understanding, rather than undoing biases and opening communication and understanding? My community and that in Erdrich's text do not exist side by side, nor do they necessarily reflect one another in the manner I describe, independently of me. As a reader, and ultimately as the writer of this essay, I position the mirror so that certain reflections occur. I am the reader of both my community and the written text. How am I reading? Am I merely projecting my experience and ideas from my community onto the text? Am I thus framing or closing the text in ways that silence how it might inform me? What about the cross-cultural issues between Kashaya Pomo culture and Chippewa culture? What do I know of Chippewa life? Again, are these two different communities really so similar that I can make generalizations suitable for both?

Current discussion regarding the reading of cross-cultural literatures centers on these same questions. How do we read and make sense of literatures produced by authors who represent in their work and are members of cultures different from our own? If, say, we compare and contrast themes or character motivation, how are we comparing and contrasting? What of our biases as readers? What of the ways we hold the mirror between a canonical text such as *Hamlet* and a text such as Leslie Silko's *Ceremony*? Can we read these different texts in the same ways? In this essay I want to relate how my reading of *Love Medicine* helped me to recognize and think about (and ultimately talk about) what Erdrich's character Albertine Johnson felt as the "wet blanket of sadness coming down over us all" (29). To relate the story of my reading, I must also discuss my own reading, asking how I read or how anyone reads American Indian literatures written by American Indians. Remember, as many of my questions suggest, my being Indian does not necessarily privilege me as a reader of any and all American Indian texts. My discussions and stories, then, while concerned with my reading of *Love Medicine*, contribute to current discussions regarding reading of American Indian literatures in particular and cross-cultural literatures in general.

What makes written literatures cross-cultural depends as much on their content and production as on their being read by a particular reader or community of readers. Many Americans from marginal cultures with specific languages and mores write in a particular variety of English or integrate their culture-specific language with an English that makes their written works accessible in some measure to a large English-speaking readership. These writers mediate not only different languages and narrative forms, but, in the process, the cultural experiences they are representing, which become the content of their work. Their work represents a dialogue between themselves and different cultural norms and forms and also, within their text, between, say, characters or points of view. This cross-cultural interaction represented by the texts is extended to readers, many of whom are unfamiliar with the writers' particular cultural experiences and who must, in turn, mediate between what they encounter in the texts and what they know from their specific cultural experiences. As David Bleich observes regarding literature in general, the texts are both *representations* of interaction and the *occasion for* interaction.[5] Of course, this general truth can become more pronounced and obvious in situations where literatures that represent cross-cultural experiences in their content and production are read by readers unfamiliar with the experiences.[6] And here the questions surface regarding how readers respond to what they encounter in texts. In their practices of reading and interpretation, do they reflect on their making sense of the texts? Do they account for their interaction with what constitutes the content and making of the written texts? In their practices of reading, are they limiting or opening intercultural communication and understanding, undoing biases or maintaining and creating them anew?

Scholars who study American Indian oral literatures have become increasingly aware of the fact that the *oral* texts they *read* have been shaped and altered not only by those people (for the most part non-Indian) who have collected, translated, and transcribed them but also by the Indians who have told them to these people. Arnold Krupat defines narrated Indian autobiographies, in which a recorder-editor records and transcribes what was given orally by the Indian subject, as *original bicultural compositions*.[7] His definition holds for many, perhaps most, of the American Indian oral texts—songs, stories, prayers—read and studied. Scholars such as Dennis Tedlock and Barre Toelken account for and question their encounters with both the Indian speakers from whom they collect texts and the texts themselves, which they transcribe and attempt to understand.[8] At its best their work provides a record of the various dialogues they have with the Indians and the Indians' texts. Readers have an account of how these scholars collected the Indian material and how their transcriptions and analysis continue the life of the material in given cross-cultural ways.

Such is rarely the case for Indian literatures written in English by Indians, or for what I am calling in this essay American Indian written literatures.[9] Most critics neither question nor account for the ways they make sense of what they encounter as readers of these written literatures. Some critics do consider the ways certain Indian writers mediate, or make use of, their respective cultural backgrounds or specific themes considered to be generally "Indian." But these critics do not seriously consider or reflect upon how they are making sense of and putting together the writers' cultural backgrounds and the writers' texts. They attempt to account for the interaction represented in the texts, but not for their own interaction. They might, for example, attempt in their various approaches to locate and account for an "Indian" presence or "Indian" themes in a text, but they do not consider how they discovered or created what they define as Indian. Citing Michael Glowinski's observation about so much contemporary literary criticism, Bleich notes that critics provide "a *history* of the literature, while rejecting [their] own historicity" (402). The result is that they do not see how their practices of reading and interpretation are limiting or opening intercultural communication and understanding. They don't see themselves and their work as an integral and continuing part of the cross-cultural exchange. Their practices are characterized by one-sided communication: they inform the texts, but the texts do not inform them and their critical agendas, or at least not in ways they make apparent.

Lester A. Standiford, in his essay "Worlds Made of Dawn: Characteristic Image and Incident in Native American Imaginative Literature," notes that "it is important that we seek a greater understanding of [Native American imaginative written] literature" and that to gain a greater understanding we must not enforce "old assumptions on those new aspects of a literature that draws from sources outside the Anglo-American heritage." Standiford's strategy for approaching and, subsequently, for helping other readers gain a greater understanding of these cross-cultural texts is to use a generalization gleaned from his studies about Indians and their literatures to find and hence account for that in the texts which is "Indian." Standiford writes:

> I will be speaking of contemporary Indian American poetry and fiction according to this archetypal concept of the poet as shaman who "speaks for wild animals, the spirits of plants, the spirits of mountains, of watersheds" (Snyder, p. 3). If you must have a worldly function of the poet, base it on this example from Snyder's remarks: "The elaborate, yearly, cyclical production of grand ritual dramas in the societies of Pueblo Indians . . . can be seen as a process by which the whole society consults the non-human powers and allows some individuals to step totally out of their human roles to put on the mask, costume, and mind of Bison, Bear, Squash, Corn, or Pleiades; to re-enter the human circle in that form and by song, mime, and dance, convey a greeting from that other realm. Thus a speech on the floor of congress from a whale. . . ." (p. 3). Poetry that speaks with the voice of the whale resounds with the true power of Indian American imaginative literature.[10]

Standiford typically moves thus from a generalization about Indians to a citation from an Indian or authoritative non-Indian to support and make legitimate his use of generalization to identify and understand things Indian in the text(s). He then further generalizes or restates the previous generalization, eventually returning to the written Indian text(s). See the pattern again within the following paragraph:

> Here [in Durango Mendoza's short story "Summer Water and Shirley"] the key to understanding is the Native American concept of the great and inherent power of the *word*. Because the boy [in Mendoza's story] can force his will out through his thoughts and into words, he succeeds in his task. This sense of the power of the word derives from the thousands of years of the Native American oral literary tradition. From its

labyrinthine and tenuous history the word arrives in the present with inestimable force. As Scott Momaday points out in his essay "The Man Made of Words," the oral form exists always just one generation from extinction and is all the more precious on that account. And this sense of care engendered for the songs and stories and their words naturally leads to an appreciation of the power of the word itself. (183)

Using a similar strategy, Paula Gunn Allen, renowned Laguna Pueblo/ Sioux literary critic and poet, summarizes (interprets) what she saw in Cache Creek Pomo Dreamer and basket weaver Mabel McKay and in Kashaya Pomo Dreamer and prophet Essie Parrish and then makes generalizations based on what she saw to further develop and support what she calls a "tribal-feminist" or "feminist-tribal" approach to Indian women's written literatures. Allen says that "the teachings of [Mabel McKay and Essie Parrish] provide clear information about the ancient ritual power of Indian women." She summarizes what she heard Mrs. McKay say during a basket-weaving demonstration as follows:

> Mrs. McCabe [sic] spoke about the meaning of having a tradition, about how a woman becomes a basketmaker among her people—a process that is guided entirely by a spirit-teacher when the woman is of the proper age. It is not transmitted to her through human agency. For Mrs. McCabe, having a tradition means having a spirit-teacher or guide. That is the only way she used the term "tradition" and the only context in which she understood it. Pomo baskets hold psychic power, spirit power; so a basketweaver weaves a basket for a person at the direction of her spirit guide.[11]

Allen then summarizes what she heard from Mrs. Parrish on a "field trip with [Allen's] students to the Kashia Pomo reservation" (203)[12] and what she heard and saw in the documentary films on Mrs. Parrish and Kashaya religious activities:

> In one of [the films], *Dream Dances of the Kashia Pomo,* [Essie Parrish] and others dance and display the dance costumes that are made under her direction, appliqued with certain dream-charged designs that hold the power she brings from the spirit world. She tells about the role of the Dreamer, who is the mother of the people not because she gives physical birth (though Essie Parrish has done that) but because she gives them life through the power of dreaming—that is, she en-livens them. Actually, the power of giving physical birth is a consequence of the power of giving nonmaterial or, you might say, "astral" birth. . . .

The Dreamer, then, is the center of psychic/spiritual unity of the people. . . . In another film, *Pomo Shaman*, Mrs. Parrish demonstrates a healing ritual, in which she uses water and water power, captured and focused through her motions, words, and use of material water, to heal a patient. She demonstrates the means of healing, and in the short narrative segments, she repeats in English some of the ritual. It is about creation and creating and signifies the basic understanding the tribal people generally have about how sickness comes about and how its effects can be assuaged, relieved, and perhaps even removed. (204-6)

Allen relates other observations she has about Indian women and shamanism from a few other tribes (e.g., Kiowa) and proclaims finally:

One of the primary functions of the shaman is her effect on tribal understandings of "women's roles," which in large part are traditional in Mrs. McCabe's [sic] sense of the word. It is the shaman's connection to the spirit world that Indian women writers reflect most strongly in our poetry and fiction. (208)

It seems that in Allen's strategy to develop and support a tribal-feminist or feminist-tribal approach to American Indian women's written literatures—an approach that can both locate an Indian (woman) presence in the texts and critique patriarchal tendencies to suppress Indian women's power and subjectivity—she replicates in practice what she sets out to criticize. Allen does not question how she reads each of the Pomo women's words and performances she translates and discusses in her scholarship. She does not examine the women's particular histories and cultures to inform her ideas regarding what she saw and heard. She says these women provide "clear information about the ancient ritual power of Indian women," but in actuality the Dreaming and other related "ancient" or "traditional" activities associated with Mabel McKay and Essie Parrish that Allen cites to substantiate her claims are tied to the nineteenth-century Bole Maru (Dream Dance) cult, a revivalistic movement. Though many, if not most, of the more recent Dreamers have been women, the first Bole Maru Dreamer, Richard Taylor, and many of the earlier Dreamers were men. The Kashaya have had four Dreamers in this order: Jack Humbolt, Big José, Annie Jarvis, Essie Parrish. My grandmother's grandfather, Tom Smith, who was half Coast Miwok and half Kashaya Pomo, was one of the most influential Dreamers and doctors throughout the Coast Miwok and southern Pomo territories. How does what Essie Parrish demonstrates in her healing show "the basic understanding the tribal peoples generally have about how sickness comes about"? Which tribal peoples? Where? When? Neither Mabel McKay nor Essie Parrish is allowed to talk back to or inform Allen's conclusions about them. Neither woman has an individual voice represented in the text. Allen provides no direct quotations. Like Standiford, Allen has shaped what she heard and saw to inform the Indian presence in the texts she reads.

How then can Allen's readers take seriously any account she might give of the interaction represented in Indian women's written literatures or of her interaction with the Indian women's texts she reads? While Allen opens important and necessary discussions about American Indian women and their written literatures that make a significant contribution to American Indian and feminist scholarship, she, perhaps inadvertently, closes discussions with those women and the texts she sets out to illumine.[13]

William Gleason, in his essay "'Her Laugh an Ace': The Function of Humor in Louise Erdrich's *Love Medicine*," works to avoid the tendency to generalize across tribal cultures and histories that is associated with the work of Standiford and Allen. Gleason looks at the ways the trickster, which Gleason refers to as a "pan-Indian character," is presented and functions in Chippewa stories and legends. But then Gleason takes what he has gleaned from his studies of trickster in Chippewa culture and lore and, without reflecting on how he understood what he studied or on how he uses it in *his* reading of *Love Medicine*, he frames what he finds in the novel.[14] He says of Erdrich's character Gerry Nanapush:

> Gerry *is* Trickster, literally. Alan R. Velie records that "the Chippewa Trickster is called Wenebojo, Manabozho, or Nanabush, depending on how authors recorded the Anishinabe word." This Trickster (as is true for most tribes) is able to alter his shape as he wishes. . . . The first time we meet the adult Gerry he performs a miraculous escape: though spotted by Officer Lovchik in the confines of a "cramped and littered bar . . . Gerry was over the backside of the booth and out the door before Lovchik got close enough to make a positive identification." (61)

Later, in another scene from the novel, Gleason finds that:

> By . . . teaming with Lipsha to defeat King in a quick card game ("five-card punk," Gerry says), Gerry unwittingly re-enacts a classic Chippewa Trickster story. For, according to legend, Manabozho/Nanabush journeys until he meets his principal enemy, "the great gambler," whom he defeats, saving his own life and the spirit of the woodland tribes from "the land of darkness." (63)

Here the strategy and the end result are the same as in Standiford and Allen: nail down the Indian in order to nail down the text. The Indian is fixed, readable in certain ways, so that when we find him or her in a written text we have a way to fix and understand the Indian, and hence the text.

I am not suggesting that whatever these critics—Standiford, Allen, Gleason—might be saying is necessarily untrue, but that whatever truth they advance about Indians or Indian written literatures is contingent upon their purposes and biases as readers and their particular relationship with the worlds of what they read or otherwise learn about Indians and with the worlds of the written texts they study. And here I am not suggesting that critical activity is impossible and that critics and other readers cannot inform the Indian worldviews and Indian written texts they encounter. What I am suggesting is that the various Indian worldviews (and whatever else comprises the Indian written texts), as well as the texts themselves, also can inform the critics and their critical enterprises, and that genuine critical activity—where both the critics' histories and assumptions as well as those of the texts are challenged and opened—cannot occur unless critics can both inform and be informed by that which they encounter. At some level or at some point in the encounter and interaction between critic and text, there is a dialogue of sorts, even if it is merely the critic responding (dialoguing) by saying, "This is what you are saying to me and I won't hear anything else," that is, responding in a way that prohibits the text from talking back to and informing the critic about what the text said. But the critics I have cited, and most other literary critics for that matter, do not record their dialogue or even the nature of the dialogue they may have had with what they are reading. Instead, they report the outcome, what *they* thought and concluded.

Of course, by looking at the essays of Standiford, Allen, and Gleason, much of what characterizes their work as critics becomes apparent. As I have noted, these critics tend to generalize, to "circumscribe and totalise" the Others' cultures and worldviews in order to "circumscribe and totalise" the Others' written texts. Each uses, most plainly in their encounters with the Indians' cultures and worldviews, what Johannes Fabian has called the "ethnographic present tense." As David Murray observes:

> The effect of this is to create a textual space, in which a culture is shown operating, which is not the same historically bound present as the one in which the reader and the writer live, a product of grammar (the present tense) rather than history (the present). Accompanying this ethnographic present tense is a generalising of individual utterances, so

that they illustrate an argument, or fulfill a pattern, rather than function in the context of any dialogue.[15]

When Standiford, quoting Snyder, describes "this archetypical concept of the poet as shaman 'who speaks for . . .' " or when he states that "this sense of the power of the word derives from the thousands of years of the Native American oral literary tradition," he is creating this space Murray describes. Note how Allen describes the work and art of Mabel McKay and Essie Parrish, and how she proclaims "one of the primary functions of the shaman is her effect on tribal understandings of 'women's roles,' which in large part are traditional in Mrs. McCabe's [sic] sense of the word." Gleason quotes Velie: "'The Chippewa Trickster is called. . . . This Trickster (as is true for most tribes) is able to. . . .'" Again, these critics overlook their own historicity; they remove themselves from the present of the occasions of their interaction with whatever they encounter and create in their reports a world from which they attempt to separate themselves and purport to understand and describe plain as day. The communication is one-sided and represented textually so that it stays that way. What would happen if Standiford were to question an Indian shaman or storyteller from a particular tribe? How might the content of the Indian's responses and the Indian's language and history inform Standiford's "archetypical concept of the poet as shaman"? How might the Indian's responses, language, and history illuminate the gaps in Standiford's conclusions, his generalizations about Indians? In what ways is the Indian more or less than the poet/shaman who communes with nature? And wouldn't answers to these questions, or at least a consideration of these questions, afford Standiford the opportunity to see himself present as a biased thinker tending to shape in certain ways what he hears or reads? Wouldn't he then have the opportunity to see and question how his critical activity opens or closes intercultural communication or how it maintains and creates biases about American Indians? If Mabel McKay and Essie Parrish could talk back to Allen, if Allen could know more of their personal lives and particular cultures and histories, wouldn't she have, or have the opportunity to have, a broader understanding of two women as well as of herself and her critical practices? Might she not see herself as present, as an Indian woman silencing in certain ways those women she wishes to defend and give voice to? How might other elements of Chippewa culture, and the ways Erdrich might understand them, inform both an understanding of the Chippewa trickster and the character of Gerry Nanapush? Couldn't these other elements inform William Gleason and his approach?

At this point, one might ask why readers of American Indian written literatures seem to be generally less reflexive in their work than contemporary readers of American Indian oral literatures such as Tedlock and Toelken. Perhaps because the former are written in English and intended for a reading audience, readers feel that they have the texts carte blanche, that the cross-cultural elements that comprise these texts are somehow transparent (Murray, 117), or can be made so, because the writers have provided the readers a medium (English) for looking at them.[16] Perhaps those who study oral literatures—folklorists, anthropologists—are more aware of the current discussions in their respective disciplines regarding translation, representation, and interpretation of the Others and their works of art and literature. Perhaps readers of written literatures cannot escape the tenets of New Criticism and text positivism. I am not sure. But given what constitutes Indian oral literatures and Indian written literatures—songs, stories, as-told-to autobiographies—readers must consider the worlds of both the Indian speaker and the recorder-editor who has mediated the speaker's spoken words for the reader. With Indian written literatures, the Indian writer is both Indian speaker and cross-cultural mediator, and readers must consider the Indian writer's specific culture and experience and how the writer has mediated that culture and experience for the reader. In both situations—with oral literatures and with written literatures—readers must interact with the worlds of the texts, which are cross-cultural, comprised of many elements foreign to the worlds of the readers.

The task is to read American Indian written literatures in a way that establishes a dialogue between readers and the texts that works to explore their respective worlds and to expose the intermingling of the multiple voices within and between readers and what they read. The objective here is not to have complete knowledge of the text or the self as reader, not to obtain or tell the complete story of one or the other or both, but to establish and report as clearly as possible that dialogue where the particular reader or groups of readers inform and are informed by the text(s). The report, or written criticism, then, would be a kind of story, a representation of a dialogue that is extended to critics and other readers, who in turn inform and are informed by the report. Thus in the best circumstances reading and criticism of American Indian written literatures become occasions for a continuous opening of culturally diverse worlds in contact with one another.

Of course any report, or any piece of criticism, represents a dialogue of sorts that the critic has had with the text he or she has read, even if the dialogue is presented as mere conclusions, and that report is extended to critics and other readers who will dialogue with it in turn. But at each step of the way—reading, criticism, response to criticism—the critics as readers, as I suggested above, remove themselves from the encounter, from the present of the occasion of their interaction with what they encounter, so that by the time they write their reports they may not see or think about how they have interacted and are interacting, how their response may be, for example, "This is what you are saying to me and I won't hear anything else." The Other, the text or whatever else has been encountered, is that which can remind the critics of their presence, of their own differences and culture-specific boundaries. If readers don't hear the texts, if they don't notice and explore those instances where the texts do not make sense to them, where the texts might question, qualify, and subvert the readers' agendas, the readers systematically forsake the opportunity not only to gain a broader understanding of themselves, of their own historicity, but also of the text. Criticism that reveals the questions and problems of reading, evoked by the experience of reading itself, can help illuminate for the critic and for others what has made for cross-cultural understanding or misunderstanding.

More often than not it is something strange and unfamiliar that can make us aware of our boundaries. For many non-Indian readers of American Indian written literatures, it may be that elements of a particular Indian culture represented in the text stop them and ask them to think and rethink how they read and make sense of the Others. The same perhaps could be said for Indians reading other Indians' written literatures.

In my own case, as I continued to read and think about *Love Medicine*, I found myself coming back to the concept of internalized oppression. Erdrich's fictional Chippewa characters manifested the symptoms of this disease just as plainly as many people I knew and was thinking about from home. Marie Lazarre Kashpaw, Albertine Johnson's grandmother and one of the most notable characters in the novel, continually wants acceptance in terms of others' definitions. She believes others' ideas about her and sees no value in who or what she has been, where she comes from, her heritage. Nector Kashpaw, in looking back at his first encounter with Marie, who would become his wife, says of her: "Marie Lazarre is the youngest daughter of a family of horse-thieving drunks. . . . She is just a skinny white girl from a family so low you cannot even think they are in the same class as Kashpaws" (58-59). To a large extent Marie accepts this view of herself. She says early in the novel that "the only Lazarre I had any use for was Lucille [Marie's sister]" (65). And when she overcomes the fear of losing her husband, Nector Kashpaw, to Lulu Lamartine, she says, "I could leave off my fear of ever being a Lazarre" (128).

Marie not only internalizes others' ideas about her, but attempts to beat those others on their own terms in order to gain self-worth in their eyes. As a young girl Marie was determined to go "up there [to the convent] to pray as good as they [the black robe women] could" (40). She saw the convent "on top of the highest hill. . . . Gleaming white. So white the sun glanced off in dazzling display to set forms whirling behind your eyelids. The face of God you could hardly look at" (41). Of course she realizes in retrospect that she was under an illusion, and, in a hilarious and ironic manner, she does beat the nuns at their own game, getting them to worship her, "gain[ing] the altar of a saint" (53). As a young married woman, Marie reveals her plan: "I decided I was going to make [Nector] into something big on this reservation. I didn't know what, not yet; I only knew when he got there they would not whisper 'dirty Lazarre' when I walked down from church. They would wish they were the woman I was. Marie Kashpaw" (66). Marie succeeds: Nector becomes tribal chairman. Then Marie goes to visit Sister Leopolda at the convent, not to see Leopolda but, as Marie says, "to let her see me. . . . For by now I was solid class. Nector was tribal chairman. My children were well behaved, and they were educated too. . . . I pulled out the good wool dress I would wear up the hill. . . . It was a good dress, manufactured, of a classic material. It was the kind of solid dress no Lazarre ever wore" (113). Marie battles with Leopolda and sees, finally, the limits of her endeavors to win Leopolda's approval. Marie learns something about love and forgiveness, which she shows when Nector comes home from Lulu Lamartine. Yet as much as learning this lesson may constitute a personal triumph for Marie, it does not seem to help her come to terms with herself as a Lazarre, with the self-hatred associated with her background, which appears to influence so much of her behavior.

Marie says, "I don't have that much Indian blood" (40), which, incidentally, is one reason she felt she could "pray as good as [the nuns] could" (40). Indeed, Marie is light-skinned, a mixed blood so fair that Nector in his first encounter with her calls her a "skinny white girl" (40) as an insult. At the time, face to face with another Indian, Marie would have taken Nector's comment as an insult, but Marie knows that among her Indian people white physical attributes are valued. She says: "I could have had any damn man on the reservation at that time. I looked good. And I looked white" (45). She knows how to insult Nector by hissing at him, "Lemme go, you damn Indian. . . . You stink to hell" (59). These characters at times both judge themselves and others in terms of the oppressor's values (e.g., white physical attributes), which they have internalized, and hate the oppressor and any sign (e.g., "skinny white girl") of the oppressor in their own ranks. Racism and hatred are at once directed outward and inward. These characters can't win for losing. Again, in the scene cited at the start of this essay, in which Albertine Johnson is caught in the middle of her mother and aunt's bickering, her mother implies that King's wife and white people in general are undesirable. Her Aunt Aurelia says that Albertine is "lots better looking than most Kashpaws," implying that because Albertine is a mixed blood, "light, clearly a breed," she is better looking and more attractive than the full-blood Kashpaw side of the family.

These characters' gossip and verbal abuse of others simultaneously work to belittle the other and to elevate the self. They take inventories of others' looks (e.g., light or dark skin) and maintain arsenals of information that can be used against others at any time. Marie Lazarre Kashpaw, responding to the gossip about her, says: "I just laugh, don't let them get a wedge in. Then I turn the tables on them, because they don't know how many goods I have collected in town." Of course, when it's wrong to be Indian and wrong to be white, when these people can judge one another in terms of the oppressors' values and in terms of their own countervalues, they don't have to look far to find faults in themselves and others. When Albertine Johnson thinks of her family and life on and around the reservation, she thinks of the phrase "Patient Abuse," a title from her nursing textbook. She says: "There are two ways you could think of that title. One was obvious to a nursing student, and the other was obvious to a Kashpaw" (7).

As I also noted earlier, this patient abuse can be physical as well as verbal. Albertine has been home only a few hours when she finds June's son King, who is drunk, beating up his white wife and attempting to drown her in the kitchen sink. King constantly tells stories about his duty in Vietnam; he bills himself as a war hero in an attempt to remedy his low self-esteem, to garner for himself attention and significance (again on others' terms). As his wife points out, the truth is that King "never got off the West Coast" (239). It seems that when his storytelling does not gain for him the attention he needs from others, or when it is questioned, he resorts to violence to feel power and self-worth. Feeling both guilty about his often-times violent past with June and hopeless about his life in general, Gordie Kashpaw drinks himself into oblivion: "Everything worked against him. He could not remember when this had started to happen. Probably from the first always and ever afterward, things had worked against him. . . . He saw clearly that the setup of life was rigged and he was trapped" (179). While driving drunk, Gordie hits a deer and then, assuming it is dead, that he has killed it, he puts it in his back seat. The deer, still alive, raises its head, and Gordie clobbers it with a tire iron and believes he has killed June. In his drunken stupor he has acted out his self-fulfilling prophecy: he has killed June, he is guilty, nothing works out right for him, and he deserves to be punished. He finds his way to the convent, and outside a nun's window he says, "I come to take confession. I need to confess it. . . . Bless me father for I have sinned" (184).

Internalized oppression cuts a wide swath. The oppression that occurred during the colonial period has been internalized by the oppressed in ways that allow the oppressed in postcolonial periods to become agents of their own oppression and destruction. Ironically and inadvertently we work to complete what the oppressor began. At times certain characters sense the depth and breadth of this internalized oppression as a deep, unconscious fear. Albertine says of King: "He's scared underneath" (35). Lipsha Morrissey, King's half-brother and June's other son, asks what King is afraid of, but Albertine can only say she "really didn't know" (36). Albertine can't spell out what causes King's fear or, for that matter, that "wet blanket of sadness coming down over us all." She does not have a way to talk about it. Lipsha wonders "if Higher Power turned its back, if we got to yell, or if we just don't speak its language. . . . How else could I explain what all I had seen in my short life—King smashing his fist in things, Gordie drinking himself down to the Bismarck hospitals, or Aunt June left by a white man to wander off in the snow. How else to explain" (195). Indeed, the sadness is vast, ubiquitous. Isn't its trajectory the history of Chippewa and white interrelations?

Doubtless internalized oppression is not the only way to think about the sadness, and certainly there is much more to this novel than its sadness. William Gleason sees in the novel that "love, assisted by humor, triumphs over pain" (51). And James McKenzie suggests that June's son Lipsha "completes [the journey home June had begun] some three years and thirteen chapters later in the novel's final scene" (58). McKenzie continues:

> Having discovered and embraced his identity and delivered his newly found father—Gerry Nanapush, the embodiment of Chippewa life—to safety in Canada, [Lipsha] heads home to the reservation. Crossing the same river Henry Junior has drowned in (Lipsha calls it the "boundary river" (p. 27), which could only be the Red River, separating North Dakota and Minnesota), he stops to stretch and, looking at the water, remembers the traditional Chippewa custom of offering tobacco to the water. This leads him to thoughts of June, "sunken cars" (p. 271)—

clearly a reference to Henry Junior—and the ancient ocean that once covered the Dakotas "and solved all our problems" (p. 272). The thought of drowning all Chippewa problems appeals to him briefly: "It was easy still to imagine us beneath them vast unreasonable waves" (p. 272), but he quickly dispels this image of tribal suicide and chooses a more reasonable course. He hops in the car and heads back to the center of his tribal culture, the reservation. Lipsha's concluding words ring a change on the sentence describing his mother's death: "So there was nothing to do but cross the water and bring her home" (p. 272). (58–59)

This final scene and the novel's ending in general make me consider again the ways I am thinking about the novel and its sadness. Lipsha happens to be in the right place at the right time. Three-hundred-pound Gerry Nanapush, recently escaped from prison, shows up at King's apartment where Lipsha is visiting. Lipsha helps Gerry escape to Canada, and en route to the border Lipsha's relation to Gerry is made loud and clear when Gerry says to Lipsha: "You're a Nanapush man. . . . We all have this odd thing with our hearts" (271). Of course Lipsha and readers have learned Gerry is Lipsha's father a little earlier, when Lipsha tells how Lulu Lamartine told him the truth. And as McKenzie notes, Lipsha and Gerry each (like Lulu Lamartine, Gerry's mother and Lipsha's grandmother) "partakes in godlike qualities" (60). Lipsha has "the touch" (190), the power to soothe pains with his fingers, and Gerry, as Gleason notes, is able to "perform . . . miraculous escape[s]." Once when he was pursued by the local police, "his [three-hundred-pound] body lifted like a hot-air balloon filling suddenly" (169). Magically he stuffs himself into the trunk of the car he and Lipsha won from King and stays hidden there until Lipsha has driven a safe distance from the law. When Gerry and Lipsha get to the border, where Lipsha will drop Gerry off, "they [hold] each other's arms, tight and manly" (271). Lipsha then turns around and, as McKenzie noted, crosses the water that his uncle, Henry Junior, drowned in. Lipsha heads back to his reservation, to his home. Lipsha says: "The sun flared. . . . The morning was clear. A good road led on. So there was nothing to do but cross the water and bring her home" (272).

I have trouble with all this.

Can I take this ending as a triumph for Lipsha, given the ways and extent to which I see internalized oppression in Erdrich's fictional Chippewa community, in Lipsha's "home"? Has Lipsha or any of the other characters come to terms with the "blanket of sadness" in a way that they can get a handle on it, talk about it, recognize its scope? My agenda and personal experience as a reader surface again, along with all my questions about reading. I come back to myself as mirror holder, as an interlocutor with the world of *Love Medicine*.

I go home again.

Like Lipsha, I traveled far to find my father, and I too headed for home.

I had to go to southern California, over four hundred miles from my family's native homeland in northern California, where I was born and raised.

I worked from a tip my mother's younger brother, my uncle, had given me. I listened to gossip, took notes, followed leads, and found my father in a Laguna Beach high school yearbook. A dark-skinned man in a row of blondes. And I saw myself in that face. Without a doubt. Darker than me. But me nonetheless.

I interviewed several people who went to school with him and my mother. It was my mother's friends who verified what I suspected. Emilio Hilario was my father. They also told me that he had died, that I had missed him by about five years.

I had to find out from others what he couldn't tell me. But now I had names, telephone numbers, addresses. I found a half-brother and uncle in town. My grandfather still lived in the old house "out in the canyon" where he had moved his wife and children nearly fifty years ago when he took a job as a kitchen worker in Victor Hugo's, a glamorous waterfront restaurant.

Going to the old house was something. After all these years to find a place that was home, where my own father had grown up, where he had a mother and father, a brother and sister, where he sat at a kitchen table, where he took off his shoes at night and dreamed. Years of wondering leveled now by the sight of a small, ordinary house set back a ways from the road. I turned in the driveway, past the metal mailbox that said HILARIO.

I was amazed by Grandpa, how small he was as he held me in his arms. A small, dark Filipino with quick black eyes holding his six-foot-two, blue-eyed grandson. But I lost track of him. I forgot his first words, "the oldest son of my oldest son," and I forgot even that it was Grandpa who clutched my wrist and was leading me through the house. I was lost in the photographs. Photographs everywhere. High school graduation. Baby pictures. Family reunions. Weddings. Mostly black-and-white, except for the newer ones on top of the color TV. They lined the door frames, covered entire walls and the end tables on either side of the sofa. In Grandpa's bedroom there were several photos of my father and uncle in uniforms—football, navy, army. One of them caught my attention, a head shot of my father in his sailor's uniform. He was smiling, handsome, his white grin almost boyish. He wrote on the picture:

Dear Mom and Dad,
    Had fun seeing you last week.
Love,
Your Son
        Emilio   May 15, 1951

He also saw my mother that week. Nine months later, February 12, 1952, he would have his first son.

Grandpa and I settled at the kitchen table. I took in other things: the faded beige kitchen walls, the odor of his pipe, the black dog at his side, his thick accent. I watched as he boiled water in an old pot, the kind that is tall with a spout and lid. "Your Grandma, she used this," he said and poured water in a cup for instant coffee. "She used this to boil her water. Only thing she drank Hobo coffee, just boil the water and run it over the coffee in a strainer." He set the pot on the stove then picked up a small stained strainer from the stove top. "This is it," he said. "She sat right there in that chair next to the stove. She smoke and drink Hobo coffee. Here's her ashtray." He held the small ceramic bowl in his hand then placed it neatly on the stove top with the strainer. He told me she died thirteen years ago. Obviously Grandpa had not changed a thing in the house.

"What happened to my father, Grandpa?"

I had heard my father died of a heart attack. But I wanted to hear it from Grandpa. Had he been sick a long time? Did he suffer?

Grandpa was at the stove watching me. I caught his eyes. He turned around and lit his pipe. Then all at once he put it down in a tin ashtray next to Grandma's ashtray on the stove top.

"Finish your coffee. Then we go to the cemetery," Grandpa said.

We got on the 405 freeway, then went east through the city of Orange. We stopped at a supermarket and bought flowers, mixed bouquets, the kind you see road vendors selling. I could see now that Grandpa lived by routine. He had probably been coming to the same market, one of dozens we had passed, for thirteen years.

"Something with his heart," Grandpa said. "All screwed up."

I was startled, caught off guard when he spoke. He had been quiet, and now the rolling green cemetery lawns were in view. It took me a minute to realize he was talking about my father.

"Yeah," he said. "Smoke too much. Fix his heart bad. Same thing with your grandmother. She smoke too much cigarettes. Get cancer. I tell 'em not to. Well. . . ."

My grandmother and father are buried next to each other. The graves are close to the road. They are under a small cypress tree that marks the place for me. Grandpa performs a kind of ritual there. He leans over, and with his index finger on the raised letters of the metal grave plaque, he talks to the dead. That day, as always, he went to my grandmother first. He said: "Mom, here is your grandson. You didn't get to know him because. . . ." He didn't finish the sentence. He turned to my father and said: "Son, you can rest now. . . . Your boy is home."

EMILIO HILARIO   EVELYN HILARIO

In Laguna Beach I talked to more people who knew my father—friends, ex-wives, relatives. They told me he was charming, charismatic. He loved his family. He was a fine athlete at one time, a boxer who knocked down Floyd Patterson. But a few people told me that there was another side to him. The drinking and violence. He broke his first wife's jaw. In a drunken brawl he mistook a friend for an enemy and threw the friend out a second-story window. He talked badly about white people. All three of his wives were white. He was alcoholic, overweight, down on his luck when he died of a massive heart attack at fifty-two.

Growing up in Laguna Beach was not easy for any of the Hilario children. My Auntie Rita Hilario-Carter tells me that when she was in fourth grade her teacher told her to clean up another girl's urine. "She told me to do it because when I grew up I was going to be a maid," Auntie Rita said. "I was the only brown child in the class." Although the town exalted my father as an athlete, he was discouraged from dating the white daughters of the townspeople.

My father's cousin told me that near the end of his life he would call her sometimes late at night. She said he would be drunk and fighting with his last wife. "How should I kill this white bitch?" he'd holler over the phone. "Strangle her? Drown her?" My father's last wife told me that my father talked about a son he had somewhere in the world. "I want him to feel welcome if he ever finds his way home," he told her. "I want him to know us."

I thought of my mother and how she died shortly after I was born so that the truth never got back to Laguna Beach about what happened to her or me. Rumors. Gossip. No one had the full story. Auntie Rita said: "I always wondered what happened to Bunny. No one talked about it. It was hush-hush around our house. Of course I was only about twelve at the time. Bunny was so nice. I thought it was such a big deal that this older white girl would come and take me for ice cream. Hah, little did I know what else was going on!" Ironically, I was born in Santa Rosa, where my mother's mother took my mother to have me, four hundred miles from Laguna Beach, on the same land my father's mother left decades before. And I would be taken in by my father's mother's people. Where was home? Santa Rosa? Laguna Beach? The Kashaya Reservation?

Before I left Laguna Beach, I went back to Grandpa's house. I wanted to visit and say goodbye.

He was waiting for me. He had coffee ready. Two old photo albums, one on top of the other, were on the kitchen table. On a faded green cover I saw in an elaborate scroll the words "Family Album." Grandpa sat next to me and opened the top album. He started talking about the assorted black-and-white photos. "This is your grandmother when I met her. . . . Oh, that's her sister, Juanita. . . . That's your great-grandma, the old Indian from up there, Old [Tom] Smith's daughter. . . ." It was truly a miracle. Pieces of a puzzle fell together. With names, I now knew how I was connected to everyone I knew. I could trace my genealogy. Auntie Violet was actually my grandmother's cousin. I had dated a girl from the reservation who was my second cousin, my father's first cousin. Grandpa told me that he met Grandma in East Los Angeles. She had come from northern California to stay with her sister.

"Did she speak Indian, Grandpa? Did she tell any of the old-time stories?"

"Take what pictures you want," he said. "Maybe those ladies up there [at Kashaya] can tell you something."

We went through the second album, and then Grandpa found a plastic K-Mart shopping bag for me to put the photos in. I felt shy. I didn't want to take too many, leaving gaps all over Grandma's pages. I took my time and picked out a little over a dozen. Then I stood up and looked around one last time before I had to go.

The house wasn't the same as when I first walked in. It was familiar now, and not necessarily because I had been in the place before and knew its layout. It was the photos. The smiling faces. The uniforms. Party dresses. Sportcoats and ties. I kept thinking of what I had heard from the people I'd talked to during the last few days. Grandpa caught me standing in the middle of the living room. He handed me the plastic bag of pictures.

"It's too bad," he said. "I tell your father not to smoke. Your Grandma, too. It done 'em in. Too much smoking. . . . Heart, you know. Cancer . . . I tell 'em not to."

"Yeah," I said and hugged him.

I HAD DRIVEN NEARLY five hundred miles by the time I reached Auntie Violet's place. Nine hours north from Laguna Beach on Highway 101 and then the long climb from Healdsburg to the reservation on top of the mountain. Still, I was wide awake, excited.

I told Auntie Violet and Auntie Vivien everything I'd learned. Uncle Paul, Violet's husband, sat and listened for a long time too. I sounded like Auntie Violet. I rattled off names, went up and down family trees. I knew names. I knew my relations. I was telling Auntie Violet things she didn't know. I knew what happened to Rienette "Nettie" Smith, my great-grandmother, and her three children, Juanita, Albert, and Evelyn.

"Grandma Rosie knew that old lady. She knew them people," Auntie Violet said.

I could tell in Auntie's voice that she was holding back something. I saw it in her eyes, as if she was watching for something behind her or underneath the table that might pop out anytime. She was anxious to see the pictures, and it wasn't until she had four or five of them in front of her that she let out what she was holding back, that my grandmother didn't want to be Indian. Her people were stuck-up, not good Indians. Related, yes. But so what? Auntie knew.

Auntie kept the photographs in front of her all night. Now and then she glanced at them, even after we finished talking about my trip and my grandmother. She reminded me how lucky I was to have been raised around Aunt Mabel and close to people on the reservation. "You learned from a great Indian," she said, referring to Mabel McKay. I was lucky. I was lucky to know Mabel and I learned a lot from her, things I would not have known otherwise. I wanted to tell Auntie that I agreed with her, that I was lucky. And I wanted to thank her and Uncle Paul for all they had done for me, all the love they had shown. But I was tired. I hardly remember getting up from the table and going to bed.

I woke early, before anyone else, and made my way to the kitchen. You could still smell food, the heavy odor of homecooking, but now it was cool, damp. And the kitchen was dark, the curtains pulled over the windows and across the sliding glass doors. I went to open the curtain next to the kitchen table when I caught sight of Auntie's row of my grandmother's pictures. They seemed so still. Everything else had been cleared away—the leftovers in Tupperware bowls, Auntie's pink poodle salt-and-pepper shakers. I started for the photographs. I say I started, but I didn't actually move, except to stand up straight and look around the room. Photos everywhere. Auntie's case of babies' pictures. Pictures of her Mom and Dad, Auntie Essie and Uncle Sid. In one picture Auntie Essie is standing in front of the roundhouse in her beaded buckskin ceremonial dress. And there is a picture of Auntie Violet with Robert Kennedy.

I heard birds outside. I thought of what Auntie said about my grandmother. Again I had the urge to pick up the photos left on the table. But I couldn't move. I felt as if my slightest gesture would wake the entire household.

Home, I thought. Home again.

I COULD BE JEALOUS of Lipsha. He got to meet his father, see him face to face. They "held each other's arms, tight and manly." Of course, miracles happened for both of us. The miracle of finding our fathers. The miracle of being lucky enough to be raised and cared for by our own people, even when we didn't know about our blood relation to those people, and then the miracle of finding out. The miracle of always having been home in some way or other. But none of those miracles changes the nature of home for Lipsha or for me. There is still the drinking and violence, gossip and bickering. Indians fighting each other. Is finding our fathers and knowing our families love us as much as they can medicine enough? Lipsha observes: "The sun flared. . . . The morning was clear. A good road led on. So there was nothing to do but cross the water and bring her home." If in the novel we were to see Lipsha make it home, as I did, what would he find?

As I noted earlier, certain of Erdrich's characters sense the depth and breadth of the problems around them. Certain characters have their moments, their insights that help them come to terms with the pain. At the funeral of Grandpa (Nector) Kashpaw, Lipsha felt his "vision shifted" (211). He says:

> I began to see things different, more clear. The family kneeling down turned to rocks in a field. It struck me how strong and reliable grief was, and death. Until the end of time, death would be our rock.
>
> So I had perspective on it all, for death gives you that. All the Kashpaw children had done various things to me in their lives—shared their

folks with me, loaned me cash, beat me up in secret—and I decided, because of death, then and there I'd call it quits. If I ever saw King again, I'd shake his hand. Forgiving somebody else made the whole thing easier to bear. (211)

Lulu Lamartine reflects on her long affair with Nector Kashpaw, Marie Lazarre Kashpaw's husband, and says:

We took our pleasure without asking or thinking further than a touch. We were so deeply sunk in the land of our greed it took the court action of the tribe and a house on fire to pull us out.

   Hearing [Marie's] voice I tried imagining what Marie must have thought. He came each week in the middle of the night. She must have known he wasn't out taking walks to see the beauty of the dark heaven. (231)

Later Lulu confesses: "For the first time I saw exactly how another woman felt, and it gave me deep comfort, surprising" (236). Here Lulu is able to empathize with another human being, to see the limits and consequences of her needs and wants. The same thing happens for Marie Lazarre Kashpaw, who attends to Lulu with the kindness of a mother in the Senior Citizens' home. As Lipsha reports, "[Marie] and Lulu was thick as thieves now" (241).

These characters' insights, their moments of understanding and forgiveness, are a balm for the soul, certainly love medicine. And the fact that they are telling their stories, leading us through their pain to some resolution about it, means that they are talking, that they do in fact have a way of talking about the pain. But do their insights and stories touch upon a large cause of so much of their pain? Does their love medicine treat the symptoms of a disease without getting at the cause?

Again, the disease I am talking about, internalized oppression, cuts a wide swath. So much is unconscious, passed down through generations, family to family. So much is unrecognizable. Is Marie Lazarre Kashpaw simply an insecure woman driven to garner for herself self-worth? Isn't her insecurity, her denial of her origins, rooted in a history of which she is a part? Is King merely another male with low self-esteem who must beat his wife to feel significant and powerful? Is Gordie just another drunk, down on his luck? As I said earlier, to me much of the pain these characters experience and inflict upon one another is tied to colonialism, and ironically and inadvertently they work to complete what the colonizer began. Gabriele Schwab observes: "Only when the colonized's own native culture has been relegated to the political unconscious and become internalized as the Other, only then is the process of colonization successfully completed. As Fanon shows, the success of any cultural liberation would depend upon reaching these unconscious domains."[17] If Erdrich's characters' insights and stories, if their forgiveness and empathy, can put them in touch with that which is unconscious and historical, then the cause of the disease can be treated. I'm not sure this happens. Lipsha says, "I had perspective on it all." What is "it"? If "Forgiving somebody else made the whole thing easier to bear," did forgiving expose what "the whole thing" is? Can Lipsha now name what King is afraid of? Can Lulu's empathy for another woman open the door to their shared history? Does it?

Of course, readers of *Love Medicine* sense the larger historical picture. As Peter Matthiessen writes on the jacket cover of the first edition of *Love Medicine*, Erdrich "convey[s] unflinchingly the funkiness, humor, and great unspoken sadness of the Indian reservations, and a people exiled to a no-man's land between two worlds." Robert Silberman notes that "[Erdrich's] concentration on personal, family matters may be intentional, but the sense of being removed from political events is a powerful statement about marginality and disenfranchisement while also suggesting a preferred concern with the personal and private life of the community."[18] And given the larger historical picture and the nature of these characters' lives, there is no doubt the insights and stories of Lipsha and Lulu are triumphant. But, again, are their triumphs great enough to touch that which is a large source of their pain, at least as I see it?

And here I must come back to questions raised earlier. I must come back to where I started, for the pain and the triumphs of Louise Erdrich's fictional Chippewa community may not be as I see them or have read them. Again, is Erdrich's Chippewa community really that similar to what I know of and read into my own Indian community? Am I merely arranging photos just as Auntie Violet did? What about the specific circumstances of Chippewa colonial history that may affect both the nature of Chippewa oppression and of Chippewa triumph over that oppression? How has Erdrich as a writer understood that history? How might I understand it?

These are just some of the questions that I should pursue regarding internalized oppression and *Love Medicine*, although I do not have space here to fully explore them. Then again, my purpose was not to come up with definite answers. Rather, I hoped to raise questions, to expose my interaction with Erdrich's novel, and to extend my story of that interaction to other readers. Other readers with other stories can explore what I have said and what I have left unanswered. They can continue what I have just barely started. A testimony of the novel's power and strength is that it shocked me into thinking about my own community, and by looking back and forth at the community in the book and the one I know as Home, I found a way, however tentative, to think and talk about the pain in both places. The book raised questions for me about my own community, and it touched my own pain and the history of that pain. Reading *Love Medicine* became Home Medicine.

In closing, I want to tell one last story, because I cannot stop thinking about it. It has lived with me through the writing of this essay. I want Auntie Violet and Louise Erdrich and others to have the chance to see it. So I need to tell it.

It is about Crawling Woman. She was a Coast Miwok woman who was born in the old village that was called Nicasias, near the present town of Nicasio in Marin County. Crawling Woman is not a real name. It is how she is remembered. Even her great-great-granddaughter, Juanita Carrio, the noted Miwok elder and matriarch who told me the story, could not remember a real name for Crawling Woman. She was one of my grandmother's ancestors too, though I'm not sure of the blood connection.

Anyway, she got that name because at the end of her life she became childlike, an imbecile, Juanita said. She did not know anybody or anything. She didn't talk. She only made babylike sounds and cried. And she crawled. She crawled everywhere, out the front door, up the road, into the fields. People said she was at least a hundred and ten years old by that time. She was a grown woman when the first Spanish missionaries invaded her home. She was a grandmother by the time General Vallejo's Mexican soldiers established a fort in Petaluma, and when California became a state in 1850, she was already a very old woman.

She never talked about her past. She was quiet and she worked hard. Kept her nose to the grindstone, Juanita said. She washed clothes for the Americans and she sold fish she caught herself. This was when she was over eighty years old. But people did know some stories about her. Once she ran away from the mission in San Rafael. She heard horses come up and she hid in a dry creekbed. She was on her stomach, face down, flat out and stiff as a board. It wasn't until she was home, back in Nicasias, and had opened her eyes that she realized the men who picked her up and loaded her onto the wagon bed were Indians.

No one can remember how she lost her mind, whether gradually with age or suddenly, say from a stroke. She became a nuisance. She had to be watched all the time. She would get out of the house and go great distances. She could crawl as fast as a person walked, even at her great age.

She would hide and then resist coming home when she was found. Juanita's mother used to babysit the old woman. She was just a young girl at the time, and to get the old woman to behave she would put on an old soldier's jacket they kept in the closet. Crawling Woman would see the brass buttons on the coat and let out a loud shriek and crawl as fast as she could back to the house.

That coat was the only thing she recognized, Juanita said.

Notes

1. Louise Erdrich, *Love Medicine* (New York: Bantam Books, 1984), 23. Subsequent references to the novel will be identified by parenthetical page numbers in the text.

2. See James McKenzie, "Lipsha's Good Road Home: The Revival of Chippewa Culture in *Love Medicine*," *American Indian Culture and Research Journal* 10.3 (1986): 53–63; William Gleason, "'Her Laugh an Ace': The Function of Humor in Louise Erdrich's *Love Medicine*," *American Indian Culture and Research Journal* 11.3 (1987): 51–73. Subsequent references to these essays will be identified by parenthetical page numbers in the text.

3. For purposes of clarification and simplicity, I am referring to both the Coast Miwok community and the Kashaya Pomo community as my one Indian community. Coast Miwok and Kashaya Pomo people share a long history of trade, intermarriage, and cultural exchange.

4. Mrs. Juanita Carrio, a Coast Miwok elder who passed away in 1991, did possess a large Coast Miwok (Nicasias dialect) vocabulary, but she did not consider herself a fluent speaker. No one living knows as much of any Coast Miwok language as Mrs. Carrio did. People may know a few words or phrases. Sarah Smith Ballard (1881–1978), a Bodega Miwok, was the last fluent speaker of a Coast Miwok language. Her Bodega Miwok dictionary was published by the University of California Press in 1970.

5. David Bleich, "Intersubjective Reading," *New Literary History* 27, no. 3 (1986), 418. Subsequent references to this essay will be identified by parenthetical page numbers in the text.

6. This general truth can become more pronounced and obvious also when readers are familiar with the culture or cultural experiences being represented and have difficulty with the representation or the ways in which the writer has presented the cultural experiences. Some contemporary Kiowa readers, for example, might have trouble with N. Scott Momaday's prose and narrative format in *The Way to Rainy Mountain*. How would certain Chippewa readers see their experiences as represented in Erdrich's rich, figurative, largely standard English?

7. Arnold Krupat, *For Those Who Come After: A Study of Native American Autobiography* (Berkeley: University of California Press, 1985), 31.

8. Toelken lists Tacheeni Scott, an Indian speaker and collaborator, as coauthor of *their* work together on certain texts.

9. Certainly non-Indian fiction writers, most notably James Fenimore Cooper, have written about Indians in their fiction. For purposes of clarity here I would refer to their work about Indians as non-Indian literature about Indians. Without a doubt, their work is cross-cultural; after all, they mediate and represent what they find in people from cultures different from their own—American Indians.

10. Lester A. Standiford, "Worlds Made of Dawn: Characteristic Image and Incident in Native American Imaginative Literature," in *Three American Literatures: Essays in Chicano, Native American, and Asian-American Literature for Teachers of American Literature,* edited by Houston A. Baker, Jr. (New York: MLA, 1982), 169, 170, 171. Subsequent references to this essay will be identified by parenthetical page numbers in the text. Standiford in this instance cites Gary Snyder, a romantic non-Indian poet who generalizes about Indians to support his ideas about ecology and so forth. Here, then, Standiford is basing his generalization about Indians on another's generalizations about Indians. How might individual Indian voices from a particular tribe talk back to or inform these generalizations across tribal cultures and histories? How might the generalizations be qualified in the context of a specific culture and history?

11. Paula Gunn Allen, *The Sacred Hoop: Recovering the Feminine in American Indian Traditions* (Boston: Beacon Press, 1986), 222, 204. Subsequent references to this book will be identified by parenthetical page numbers in the text.

12. "Kashia" is a variant spelling of Kashaya. "Kashia" is used in many of the ethnographies and older government records.

13. At various times in her work, Allen sets out to show how people from various communities read the same Indian text differently. In her essay "Kochinnenako in Academe: Three Approaches to Interpreting a Keres Indian Tale" (in *The Sacred Hoop,* 222–44), Allen presents "A Keres Interpretation" (232) and "A Feminist-Tribal Interpretation" (237). Yet each point of view or perspective appears a generalization created by Allen. She writes, for example: "A Keres is of course aware that balance and harmony are two primary assumptions of Keres society and will not approach the narrative wondering whether the handsome Miochin will win the hand of the unhappy wife and triumph over the enemy, thereby heroically saving the people from disaster" (234). Is this the case for *all* Keres individuals? Another example: "A feminist who is conscious of tribal thought and practice will know that the real story of Sh-ah-cock and Miochin underscores the central role that woman plays in the orderly life of the people" (239). And, again, I ask: A feminist who is aware of *which* tribal thought? What tribe? What feminist? In creating and presenting

multiple points of view, how might Allen, as creator/writer of these points of view, have diminished the complexity and power of those points of view? Who is Allen as mediator and presenter of the different points of view?

14. Earlier in his essay Gleason refers to scholars such as Freud in his discussion of the function of humor in general. Can Freud's model of the function of humor be applied to all American Indian cultures? To Chippewa culture? If so, how and under what particular circumstances? How is Gleason reading both Freud and the Chippewa Indian culture to make sense of what he encounters in *Love Medicine?* In this essay I have not discussed critical approaches that are comparative—where critics examine, say, written literatures by different Indian writers in relation to one another or to Western canonical works (e.g., *The Odyssey, Absalom, Absalom!*). Clearly, and perhaps even more obviously, the questions and concerns I have raised throughout this essay would apply to comparative approaches.

15. David Murray, *Forked Tongues: Speech, Writing and Representation in North American Indian Texts* (Bloomington: Indiana University Press, 1991), 117, 141. Subsequent references to this book will be identified by parenthetical page numbers in the text.

16. As Murray points out, "the ideal of transparency here is also an ideal of totality—a totality of understanding, in which we can seal off the work of art, and see it whole, or we can circumscribe and totalise the other culture in which it operates" (117). He suggests that even while Tedlock is reflexive and dialogical in his work, Tedlock works with, or toward, an ideal of totality, of obtaining a full and complete knowledge of the other.

17. Gabriele Schwab, "Reader-Response and the Aesthetic Experience of Otherness," *Stanford Literature Review* (Spring 1986), 130.

18. Robert Silberman, "Opening the Text: *Love Medicine* and the Return of the Native American Woman," in *Narrative Chance: Postmodern Discourse on Native American Indian Literatures,* edited by Gerald Vizenor (Albuquerque: University of New Mexico Press, 1989), 114.

Vision and Revision in Louise Erdrich's *Love Medicine*

ALLAN CHAVKIN

◆   ◆   ◆

Love Medicine made Louise Erdrich famous almost overnight. This novel prompted an unusual amount of critical attention, won the National Book Critics Circle Award, and has since become a work frequently anthologized and taught in colleges and universities. Yet in 1993 Erdrich republished the novel after revising it, adding four new chapters and a new section that become the second part of "The Beads," and resequencing the chapters; the title page of the book was changed from *Love Medicine: A Novel* to *Love Medicine: New and Expanded Version*. Although occasionally writers have revised and "corrected" published books, there have been very few instances in which a major modern novel has been so substantially revised and expanded as *Love Medicine* was.

If *Love Medicine* is a collection of stories, as Gene Lyons in a review in *Newsweek* insists, the importance of Erdrich's publishing a new edition of her book would be less problematical than if it were a novel.[1] Adding a few more stories to a collection would not result in the kinds of critical problems that occur when adding new parts to a novel; on the other hand, if *Love Medicine* is an integral work, the addition of the new chapters should influence one's reading of the entire book. Hertha Wong, who sees *Love Medicine* as a short-story cycle, challenged Erdrich and Michael Dorris, her collaborator on *Love Medicine,* to defend their claim that it was a novel.

"It's a novel in that it all moves toward a resolution," Erdrich responded, and Dorris quickly added, "It has a large vision that no one of the stories approaches."[2] After Erdrich stated that she was not worried about the issue, Dorris then elaborated upon why they regarded the book as a novel:

> If it had been a collection of short stories, it would have been very different. . . . We went through the entire manuscript. We wove in all the changes and resolutions and threads to tie them [the stories] all together. By the time readers get halfway through the book, it should be clear to them that this is not an unrelated, or even a related, set of short stories, but parts of a larger scheme. (Wong, "An Interview," 47)

In an interview with Malcolm Jones, Erdrich stated that while she knew she would have been able to write the plot as a traditional novel, she decided to use an experimental but legitimate novelistic form of interrelated stories because it was "something I have always loved reading."[3]

If *Love Medicine* is a novel and not a collection of stories, then the existence of two versions of the work becomes much more problematical and raises some perplexing questions. Which version reveals Erdrich's "real intentions"? Which version of *Love Medicine* is "definitive"? Which version is the better work of art? Why did Erdrich decide to substantially change a novel that was so highly regarded by both the critics and the public? What constitutes *Love Medicine,* a work with a complicated textual history that includes the publication of parts of the book, sometimes in different form, in periodicals before incorporation in the novel? Is a work that exists in multiple versions, such as *Love Medicine,* "a single version of the work or all the versions taken together?—and if it is all the versions taken together, is the work constituted by the process of its revisions, one after another, or by all the versions considered as existing simultaneously, as they might in a variorum edition giving a complete account of the successive readings?"[4]

Love Medicine *and Textual Pluralism*

The usual assumption of scholars who have published criticism on *Love Medicine* is that while the two versions of the novel are not substantially different, the 1993 *Love Medicine* must be the more authoritative because it is the latest version of the text. This assumption of the textual stability of *Love Medicine* is a commonplace belief founded upon one of the basic premises of twentieth-century criticism and editing—the idea that there can be only one "definitive" or "correct" or "best" text, which is the latest one the author has approved. Since the 1960s this assumption has been challenged by James Thorpe, Hans Zeller, Jerome McGann, Donald Reiman, Peter Shillingsburg, James McLaverty, and most recently by Jack Stillinger. Stillinger has explored the problem of multiple versions with greater thoroughness and sophistication than any other contemporary theorist, especially in his *Coleridge and Textual Instability,* and I will summarize his ideas on multiple versions that are relevant to the problem of the two versions of *Love Medicine.*

Stillinger rejects the traditional notion that the latest text must be the best; he also refutes a more recent theory that the earliest text is the best because it reveals the author's first and therefore real intentions. Instead of textual stability and the notion of a single best text, he argues for "textual instability" or "textual pluralism"—the idea that there is no one version of the text that is "correct," "most authoritative," or "best."

> These theories are also related to ideas about authorial intention. The latest-text theory is based on the notion that the latest is best because it is the best representative of the author's intention; the earliest-text theory is based on the notion that the earliest text (rather than the latest) is where the author's "real" intention resides; and the newest theory, which I shall here call textual pluralism, is based on the idea that each version of a work embodies a separate authorial intention that is not necessarily the same as the authorial intention in any other version of the same work. (119)

Stillinger argues that for obsessive revisers like Wordsworth and Coleridge (and I would add Erdrich as another good example) the theory of textual pluralism, which allows for the uniqueness of aesthetic character and authorial intention of each version, is a much more sensible way to see their work than the other approaches that neglect the work's "extended textual history" (121). In addition to being true to a work's textual history, Stillinger's notion that "a work is constituted by all known versions of the work" and not one single most authoritative version, has the advantage of enhancing the "richness" and "complexity" of the author's writing (132, 140).

Stillinger also suggests that obsessive revisers like Wordsworth and Coleridge become readers and interpreters of their own writing and deliberately add "their intentions in the process of revision" (107), and thus their poems can be profitably examined by critics who are trying to ascertain the author's ideas (or "ideology") embodied in the work. Prompted by his realization that the two most difficult of Coleridge's seven major poems have "relatively little revision" in them, Stillinger presents this tentative gener-

alization: "the more revision in a Coleridge poem, the greater the likeli-
hood of receiving determinate (authorial) meanings—and, conversely, the
less revision, the greater the indeterminacy in situations where the lines
come 'by chance or magic . . . as it were, something given'" (246). If
Stillinger is correct, then an analysis of the revisions in *Love Medicine* reveals
Erdrich's ideas that are embodied in the novel since it has been so extensively revised. In short, by regarding *Love Medicine* as constituting both versions of the novel, instead of merely selecting the early or late version,
readers can comprehend the textual history of the book and have a better
chance of understanding it in all its complexity and richness.

Athough the paperback cover of the 1993 book proclaims that "this is a
publishing event equivalent to the presentation of a new and definitive
text," it is probably best to conclude that neither *Love Medicine* is "definitive,"
and that each should be regarded as unique. Sounding like a deconstructor
of her own work, Erdrich rejects the idea of a single "best text" when she was
asked if the expanded 1993 *Love Medicine* was intended to replace the original
1984 *Love Medicine*: "I have no great plan for the reader here—some may
prefer the first version without the additions, others the next. I don't think
of the books as definitive, finished, or correct, and leave them for the reader
to experience."[5] In fact, Erdrich seems to share with some contemporary
critics and theorists influenced by deconstructionism, such as Jack Stillinger, the belief in the legitimacy of multiple versions of the text and has
remarked: "There is no reason to think of publication as a final process. I
think of it as a temporary storage" (Chavkin and Chavkin, 232).

The Politics of the New Love Medicine

While the 1984 book attracted enormous attention, the 1993 edition did
not. Reviewers and critics, with few exceptions, ignored the publication of
the 1993 edition.[6] Critics have continued to select for their study either the
original *Love Medicine* or more often the expanded version of the novel, with
little or no explanation for their choice.[7] The assumption seems to be that
the two versions are not substantially different and the additions to the
novel do not change one's interpretation of the work.

In the few cases where critics provide any explanation for the purpose
of the new and expanded version, they suggested that the main reason for
it is to "help make clearer and more coherent connections to the planned
tetralogy."[8] It is likely that the source for this explanation is the author
herself. Marion Wood, Erdrich's editor at Henry Holt, reports: "New things

were taking shape that she [Erdrich] felt needed a beginning [in the first novel]."⁹ Perhaps because some interviewers were puzzled or even unsympathetic to the idea of revising such a successful and admired novel, Erdrich seems to downplay the difference between the two versions. While admitting to Elizabeth Devereaux that she would not be pleased if a novelist changed a book that was important to her, she claims that after the original publication of *Love Medicine* she discovered more stories that appeared to belong to it and therefore the additions to the expanded *Love Medicine* seemed the natural step (30). "I feel this is an ongoing work, not some discrete untouchable piece of writing," Erdrich informed David Streitfeld.¹⁰ But she also qualifies that statement in her conversation with Streitfeld: "When I went back to *Love Medicine,* I didn't tamper with what is there. If I did that, I'd feel funny" (15).

Actually Erdrich did revise parts of her novel, and in any case, the addition of four new chapters and the new section of "The Beads" influences one's reading of the entire book. And while she does include material that provides bridges and links to her other novels that comprise her vast Chippewa epic, the revisions and additions to the expanded *Love Medicine* are much more elaborate than her comments would suggest. Although one might be tempted to conclude after examining the numerous and varied changes and additions in the 1993 *Love Medicine* that the revision is extraordinarily complex and that no argument can explain the source of the new edition, actually a careful exploration of the changes reveals the premise behind the 1993 version—the need for a *Love Medicine* that more effectively than the 1984 book conveys its political ideology. Erdrich has emphasized that "any human story is a political story" and that writers do not have to express political opinions openly in fiction to convey their politics; actually, she suggests, such overt expression is often counterproductive, for the subtler and more artistic work can change more minds than the preaching of didactic protest novels. With these assumptions in mind, Erdrich created the 1984 *Love Medicine.* Art must come first, and the politics would be implicit in the art.

But for those whose first concern is more for political intent rather than art, Erdrich's subtle writing lacks force and commitment. In an essay-review of *The Beet Queen,* Leslie Silko harshly attacked Erdrich's fiction, which she believed lacked political commitment, and even suggested that Erdrich was ambivalent about her Native American origins.¹¹ According to Erdrich, as a result of careless reading, Silko criticized the characters in *The Beet Queen* because she incorrectly assumed they were Chippewa when in fact they were whites and thus "they must have seemed shockingly assimilated" (Chavkin and Chavkin, 237). Even more sympathetic reviewers than Silko, however, have grossly misinterpreted Erdrich's work, and they may have caused her to wonder if perhaps the 1984 *Love Medicine* might be too open to misreading, especially by those inclined to view the characters as the usual negative stereotypes of Indians.

Although Erdrich has stressed that people should be politically committed in their personal life but not in their art, for to do so makes the art "polemic and boring" (Chavkin and Chavkin, 241), apparently she decided at some point after the initial publication of *Love Medicine* that it did not adequately express her political ideology, and she needed to revise the novel to make it more political without becoming polemical. It is worth noting that in interviews Erdrich and Dorris stated that they deliberately set out to compose a novel that would not be as political in its subject matter as other Native American fiction. Instead, Dorris stressed, their focus would be on a reservation community, "not on the conflict between Indians and non-Indians," in order to remind readers "that in the daily lives of contemporary Indian people, the important thing is relationships, and family and history, as it is in everybody's life, and not these sort of larger political questions, although they do impinge" (Jones, 7).

Like the 1984 *Love Medicine,* the expanded version is not overtly political; it avoids didacticism and expresses its politics subtly. Nevertheless, the 1993 *Love Medicine* embodies a powerful political vision that is absent in the original novel. This new vision includes four interdependent objectives: (1) to argue for the importance of preserving American Indian culture and resisting complete assimilation into the dominant white culture; (2) to undermine the popular stereotypes of American Indians; (3) to promulgate a feminism that is in accord with traditional American Indian culture, underscoring the crucial role of motherhood and independent women who are activists for Indian rights; and (4) to present a more affirmative vision than the one in the 1984 *Love Medicine,* which for some readers reinforced the notion that the situation of American Indians today is hopeless, and to suggest that there are possible political solutions to the dire problems confronting American Indians.

. . .

Conclusion

It would be a mistake to conclude that the 1984 *Love Medicine* is completely apolitical. In the first version of the novel one does recognize Indian issues, including sovereignty, assimilation, Indian activism, substance abuse, problems of the Indian Vietnam War veteran, clan rivalries, ambivalence over Indian identity, reservation politics, and cultural alienation. These issues are developed and presented more directly in the expanded 1993 version as a result of Erdrich's greater immersion in Chippewa and Turtle Mountain culture and history. While one of her motivations in republishing *Love Medicine* is to connect it better to the other novels comprising her vast Chippewa epic, she also revised and expanded the book in order to express her new political commitment.

It is likely that Erdrich concluded after the publication of the 1984 *Love Medicine* that the novel was too pessimistic. It vividly presented the dire problems of the contemporary Indian—poverty, dysfunctional families, sexual promiscuity, abused and abandoned children, alcoholism, and cultural estrangement—but it did not present practical solutions to these problems, or indicate even in a more general way that solutions were possible. Nor did it clearly indicate the origin of these problems. The 1984 *Love Medicine* is largely ahistorical compared to the 1993 *Love Medicine.* History and current events do not much impinge upon the 1984 *Love Medicine* characters, who seemed isolated from mainstream America, and by and large, with the exception of Gerry Nanapush, they have little knowledge of or interest in politics. All of this changes in the more affirmative 1993 edition of the novel, where the "Indianness" of the book and especially of the need to return to one's heritage are underscored.[12] A number of the characters reconnect with their heritage, and even at times speak in "the old language," some of which Erdrich includes in the expanded edition. A number of the major characters now are politicized, including some women who become activists, and the characters who might have been seen as negative stereotypes of Indians in the 1984 *Love Medicine* are presented more sympathetically. Perhaps an apt symbol of how much the book is changed is the figure of Lyman. In the 1984 *Love Medicine* he is an insouciant, apolitical minor character, but in the 1993 version even this typical entrepreneur-hustler preoccupied with making money speaks like a radical Indian activist.

In short, then, it should be clear that the two versions of the novel present different visions because of different authorial intentions. Neither version can be considered "definitive," for each is unique, embodying Erdrich's "real intentions" at the time she composed that version of the novel. Jack Stillinger sardonically observes, "In theory, everybody can be right in such matters, and the one who is rightest will be the one who musters the best rhetoric" (140). More significant than questions about which edition is the better work of art are historical considerations of Erdrich's process of writing. If future critics of *Love Medicine* are to understand this complex work properly, they must see the value of employing the theory of "textual pluralism" and recognize the need to focus upon the whole textual process and read the different versions of the novel in relation to one another and the author's developing intentions.

Notes

1. Gene Lyons, "In Indian Territory," review of *Love Medicine: A Novel* by Louise Erdrich, *Newsweek* 11 February 1985: 70–71.

2. Hertha D. Wong, "An Interview with Louise Erdrich and Michael Dorris," in *Conversations with Louise Erdrich and Michael Dorris,* edited by Allan Chavkin and Nancy Feyl Chavkin (Jackson: University Press of Mississippi, 1994), 47. Subsequent references to this interview will be identified by page numbers in parentheses in the text.

3. Malcolm Jones, "Life, Art Are One for Prize Novelist," in *Conversations with Louise Erdrich and Michael Dorris,* 4. Subsequent references to this interview will be identified by page numbers in parentheses in the text.

4. Jack Stillinger, *Coleridge and Textual Instability: The Multiple Versions of the Major Poems* (New York: Oxford University Press, 1994), v. Subsequent references to this book will be identified by page numbers in parentheses in the text.

5. Nancy Feyl Chavkin and Allan Chavkin, "An Interview with Louise Erdrich," in *Conversations with Louise Erdrich and Michael Dorris,* 247. Subsequent references to this interview will be identified by page numbers in parentheses in the text.

6. Notable exceptions to the failure to review the expanded *Love Medicine* are Rubinstein, Stretifeld, Bomberry, and Bennett. Bennett is the only reviewer to discuss insightfully some of the differences between the two versions. (Roberta Rubinstein, "Louise Erdrich Revisits the Complex World of the Chippewa," Review of *Love Medicine: New and Expanded Version,* by Louise Erdrich, *Chicago Tribune* 14 November 1993: sec. 14:3, 11; Victoria Bomberry, Review of *Love Medicine: New and Expanded Version,* by Louise Erdrich, *Wicazo Sa Review* 101 [1994]: 76–78; Sarah Bennett, Review of *Love Medicine: New and Expanded Version,* by Louise Erdrich, in *Studies in American Indian Literatures* 7.1 [Spring 1995]: 112–18.) Only two critics analyze in detail some aspects of the expanded *Love Medicine.* Focusing upon "The Island," Elizabeth Mermann-Jozwiak, " 'His Grandfather Ate His Own Wife': Louise Erdrich's *Love Medicine* as a Contemporary Windigo Narrative," *North Dakota Quarterly* 64.4 (1997): 44–54, explains Lulu's powers by arguing that her encounter with Moses Pillager transforms her into a kind of windigo, the cannibalistic demon of Chippewa myth. In *Writing Tricksters: Mythic Gambols in American Ethnic Literature* (Berkeley: University of California

Press, 1997), 100–103, Jeanne Rosier Smith focuses upon how some of the additions in the expanded version enhance the trickster aspects of the novel.

7. While in "Life Into Death, Death Into Life: Hunting as Metaphor and Motive in *Love Medicine* (*The Chippewa Landscape of Louise Erdrich* edited by Allan Chavkin, Tuscaloosa: University of Alabama Press, 1999), Robert F. Gish states that he uses the 1984 *Love Medicine* because he considers it to be superior to the expanded edition, John Purdy uses the 1993 book despite his belief that it is "a less engaging read" than the original version. (John Purdy, "Crossing the Waters to a *Love Medicine* [Louise Erdrich]," in *Teaching American Ethnic Literatures: Nineteen Essays,* edited by John Maitino and David R. Peck [Albuquerque: University of New Mexico Press, 1996], 83). Usually, though, scholars and critics do not provide any explanation for their choices of editions.

8. Hertha D. Wong, "Louise Erdrich's *Love Medicine*: Narrative Communities and the Short Story Sequence," in *Modern American Short Story Sequences: Composite Fictions and Fictive Communities,* edited by J. Gerald Kennedy (Cambridge: Cambridge University Press, 1995), 181.

9. Elizabeth Devereaux, "*Love Medicine* Redux: New and Improved, but Why?" *Publishers Weekly* 23 November 1992: 30.

10. David Streitfeld, "Love and Its Risks," Review of *Love Medicine*: New and Expanded Version by Louise Erdrich, *Washington Post* 13 February 1994: sec/WBK: 15. Subsequent references to this review will be identified by page numbers in parentheses in the text.

11. Louis Owens defends Erdrich, observing that Silko herself does not assume the role she would have Erdrich embrace. (Louis Owens, "Erdrich and Dorris's Mixedbloods and Multiple Narratives," in *Other Destinies: Understanding the American Indian Novel* [Norman: University of Oklahoma Press, 1992], 192–224; Leslie Silko, "Here's an Odd Artifact for the Fairy-Tale Shelf." Review of *The Beet Queen,* by Louise Erdrich. *Impact/Albuquerque Journal* [8 October 1986]: 10.)

12. But at least one critic found the new and expanded *Love Medicine* still politically wanting. Bomberry concludes that the novel portrays "Indians, especially the Indian woman, in a negative light," and "What *Love Medicine* gives us is a snapshot of hopelessness and despair" (Bomberry 77–78).

Rose Nights, Summer Storms,
Lists of Spiders and Literary Mothers

LOUISE ERDRICH

◆　◆　◆

ONCE AGAIN MY roses are blooming outside the window, a tough
rugosa called Therese Bugnet. Their full, glowing, pink heads droop
directly outside the screen, heavy with last night's rain—their fragrance a
clear, unspeakable luscious berry, sweet as thunder. The churr of wood
frogs is still loud in the night. Clouds darken in the north. Storms hammer down from Quebec. The sky crackles, a cellophane sheath crumpled
suddenly overhead. Gnats, bloodsucking, hairline loving, bite raw welts
into our napes. On the outermost petal of the farthest blossom, I spy
something black, large, and velvet. A huge spider made of plush. It is an
opulent thing, its legs thick and curved, its eyes blue glowing spots. There's
a screen between the two of us. Still, I am startled when it jumps. It moves
with such mechanical and purposeful energy. Blossom to blossom, stuff-
ing aphids into its jaws with thick limbs, mandibles clashing, it hunts.

When mating, these blue-eyed jumping spiders hold hands in the classic stance of either bashful lovers or wrestlers lethally balanced. If the male
is not deeply vigilant and ready to leap backward as soon as he has suc-
ceeded in delicately thrusting the packet of his sperm into—what shall I
call it—his lady's love chamber, she will grasp him closer, killingly, loving
him to death, making a meal of him with her sudden sexually quickened
appetite. To her, devouring her mate is a bit like smoking a cigarette after

sex. That is why the male so tenderly clings to her hands, her tough pincers—he is trying both to make love to her and to survive her.

The example of the spider's courtship, like that of the praying mantis who cannibalizes her mate, fascinates because it seems so improbable in its contrast to our human arrangements in which men are physically the stronger and in most cases still dominate the world despite our hopeful advances, our power feminism.

Women writers live rose nights and summer storms, but like the blue-eyed jumping spider opposite our gender, must often hold their mates and families at arm's length or be devoured. We are wolf spiders, carrying our babies on our backs, and we move slowly but with more accuracy. We learn how to conserve our energy, buy time, bargain for the hours we need.

Every female writer starts out with a list of other female writers in her head. Mine includes, quite pointedly, a mother list. I collect these women in my heart and often shuffle through the little I know of their experiences to find the toughness of spirit to deal with mine.

Jane Austen—no children, no marriage. Mary Wollstonecraft—died in childbirth. Charlotte Brontë—died of *hyperemesis gravidarum*, a debilitating and uncontrollable morning sickness. Anne Brontë and Emily Brontë—no children or marriage. George Eliot, a.k.a. Mary Ann Evans—banned from society for an illicit liaison with a married man. No children. George Sand, Harriet Beecher Stowe, Elizabeth Gaskell—children. Emily Dickinson—no children, no marriage. Virginia Woolf—no children. Willa Cather, Jean Rhys, Djuna Barnes, Isak Dinesen—none. Kay Boyle and Meridel LeSueur—many children and political lives. Sigrid Undset, children, and Anna Akhmatova. Zora Neale Hurston, Dorothy Parker, Lillian Hellman. None. None. None. Grace Paley, Tillie Olsen—children. Toni Morrison—children. Anne Sexton. Adrienne Rich—children. Anne Tyler, Erica Jong, Alice Walker, Alice Munro, and Alice Hoffman. Children. Joan Didion. Mary Gordon. Rosellen Brown, Robb Forman Dew, and Josephine Humphreys and Mona Simpson. Children. Isabel Allende, Jayne Anne Phillips, Linda Hogan, Sharon Olds, Louise Glück, Jane Smiley, and many, many others.

Reliable birth control is one of the best things that's happened to contemporary literature—that can be seen from the list above. Surely, slowly, women have worked for rights and worked for respect and worked for emotional self-sufficiency and worked for their own work. Still it is only now that mothers in any number have written literature. I beg a friend to send me Jane Smiley's thoughts on the subject—"Can Mothers Think?" In this piece, she speculates on writing and motherhood, upon what we do write, what we will write, how it will be different.

A mother's vision would encompass survival, she says, *would encompass the cleaning up of messes.*

A mother's vision includes tough nurturance, survival love, a demanding state of grace. It is a vision slowly forming from the body of work created by women. I imagine a wide and encompassing room filled with women lost in concentration. They are absorbed in the creation of an emotional tapestry, an intellectual quilt. Here a powerful blossom forms, there a rushing city, a river so real it flows, a slow root, a leaf. And, too, pieces that do not seem to fit into the scheme at all incorporate themselves in startling ways.

There is labor itself—birth as original a masterpiece as death. There is the delicate overlapping flower of another human personality forming before your eyes, and you blessed and frightened to be part of it. There is the strange double vision, the you and not you of a genetic half replicated in the physical body of another—your eyebrows appear, your mother's heart line, your father's crooked little finger. There is the tedious responsibility of domesticity that alternates with a hysterical sense of destined fate—the bigness and the smallness.

Writing as a mother shortly after bearing, while nurturing, an infant, one's heart is easily pierced. To look full face at evil seems impossible, and it is difficult at first to write convincingly of the mean, the murderous, the cruelty that shadows mercy and pleasure and ardor. But as one matures into a fuller grasp of the meaning of parenthood, to understand the worst becomes a crucial means of protecting the innocent. A mother's tendency to rescue fuels a writer's careful anger.

The close reexperiencing of childhood's passions and miseries, the identification with powerlessness, the apprehension of the uses of power, flow inevitably from a close relationship with a son or daughter. Perhaps most shaking, the instinct to protect becomes overwhelming. A writer's sympathies, like forced blooms, enlarge in the hothouse of an infant's need. The ability to look at social reality with an unflinching mother's eye, while at the same time guarding a helpless life, gives the best of women's work a savage coherence.

Rather than submit her child to slavery, Toni Morrison's Sethe kills her daughter, an act of ruthless mercy. The contradiction, purity, gravity of mother love pulls us all to earth. "Too thick," says a character of Sethe's mother love, "too thick."

Sigrid Undset's extraordinary Kristin Lavransdatter, a woman whose life is shaped by powerful acts of love, commits sins unthinkable for her time and yet manages to protect her children.

"Milk brain," a friend calls these maternal deep affections that prime the intellect. Milk wisdom. Milk visions.

I exist, I simply breathe, I do nothing but live.

One day as I am holding baby and feeding her, I realize that this is exactly the state of mind and heart that so many male writers from Thomas Mann to James Joyce describe with yearning—the mystery of an epiphany, the sense of oceanic oneness, the great *yes*, the wholeness. There is also the sense of a self merged and at least temporarily erased—it is deathlike. I close my eyes and see Frost's too peaceful snowy woods, but realize that this is also the most alive place I know—Blake's gratified desire. These are the dark places in the big two-hearted river, where Hemingway's Nick Adams won't cast his line, the easeful death of the self of Keats's nightingale. Perhaps we owe some of our most moving literature to men who didn't understand that they wanted to be women nursing babies.

Chronology of Events in *Love Medicine*

PETER G. BEIDLER AND GAY BARTON

◆　◆　◆

THE ORDER OF EVENTS in *Love Medicine* at first seems confusing. Although Erdrich often gives dates along with the titles to the various stories, and though after the first one, these stories are presented in chronological order, many of them include references to earlier incidents whose dates are unspecified. Thus, in the following summary we have re-arranged the novel's most important events and presented them in chronological order. The dates are taken either from the chapter heads or from internal evidence. Where we have guessed at a date we include a par-enthetical indicator (?) of the uncertainty. Dates that are uncertain in *Love Medicine* but are revealed in another novel (without contradicting *Love Medicine*) are supplied in square brackets—[1919]. Readers may also be con-fused by the fact that in the expanded (1993) edition of *Love Medicine* Erdrich has not only added new material but changed some of the old. In the first edition, for example, Eli and Nector are twins, while in the expanded edi-tion Eli is said to be Rushes Bear's "youngest son" (*LM*, 101). That fact is in turn contradicted by information in *Tracks*, where Nector, born about 1908, is said to be the "younger brother" (*Tr*, 39) of Eli, who is born around 1898. There is no question that Erdrich intended the revised and expanded 1993 edition of *Love Medicine* to be definitive, and our guide accordingly uses this version as its standard text. To indicate where large blocks of new material are added in the expanded 1993 edition, we put those events in italics.

Chronology of Events in *Love Medicine*:

1898–1908(?)	Nector and Eli Kashpaw are born to the original Kashpaw and Margaret (Rushes Bear).
[1919]	Young Lulu Nanapush finds the body of a dead man in the woods.
c. 1920	Marie Lazarre is born.
[1924]	*Lulu returns from an off-reservation boarding school as a result of letters written by Nanapush.*
1934	Marie goes to stay at the convent, where Sister Leopolda scalds her back and stabs her in the hand. On her way down the hill not long afterwards, Marie is accosted by Nector Kashpaw.
1934–1935	Marie and Nector marry. Lulu goes to Moses Pillager's island, where she becomes pregnant. Before the baby is born, Lulu leaves Moses and returns to town. Marie and Nector's first child, Gordie, is born.
1935–1936	Lulu's first son by Moses Pillager is born (we do not know his first name, but his last is Nanapush).
1936–1940(?)	Son and daughter born to Marie and Nector. (Both die of a fever sometime before 1948.)
c.1939	June Morrissey is born to Lucille Lazarre and Morrissey I.
1941	Zelda Kashpaw is born to Marie and Nector.
c.1945	Gerry Nanapush is born to Lulu and Moses.
1948	Lucille Lazarre dies, leaving her daughter June, age nine, to survive on tree sap. Lucille's mother and Morrissey I bring June to Marie to raise. Gordie and Aurelia Kashpaw try to hang June. June goes to live with Eli. *Rushes Bear moves in with Marie and helps her give birth to her last child, a son (Eugene).*
1950	Henry Lamartine is killed by a train. His brother Beverly comes to the funeral and makes love to Henry's widow, Lulu, in a shed after the wake. A boy named Henry Lamartine Junior is born to Lulu nine months later.
1952	Lulu and Nector begin an affair.

c.1953   Lyman Lamartine is born to Lulu and Nector

195_(?)   *Gordie and June honeymoon at Johnson's motel.*

1957   The Lulu-Nector affair ends, and Lulu marries Beverly, who has come to take Henry Junior home with him. Lulu discovers that Beverly is already married and sends him back to the Twin Cities to get a divorce. Marie takes Zelda to visit Sister Leopolda. Nector burns Lulu's house, and Lulu is made bald as she rescues their son, Lyman, from the fire.

c.1958   Albertine Johnson is born to Zelda and Swede Johnson.

196_(?)   King Kashpaw is born to June and Gordie.

c.1963   Bonita is born to Lulu and a Mexican man.

1965 (?)   Gerry kicks a cowboy in the groin and starts the first of many jail terms.

c.1965   Lipsha Morrissey is born to Gerry and June, then taken to Marie and Nector to be raised.

1969(?)   Henry Junior and Lyman buy a red convertible

1970   Henry Junior goes to Vietnam.

1973   Henry Junior returns from Vietnam. He and Albertine chance to meet in Fargo, where Albertine loses her virginity to him.

1974   Henry Junior drowns himself in the Red River, watched by Lyman, who is unable to save him. *Lyman goes on a one-year drinking binge before starting to work for the Bureau of Indian Affairs and becoming involved in tribal politics and business.*

1979–1980(?)   King Howard Kashpaw Junior is born to Lynette and King Kashpaw.

1980   Shawn Nanapush is born to Gerry and Dot (Adare) Nanapush. Gerry kills (?) a trooper.

1981   June is picked up in Williston by a mud engineer who says his name is Andy. June tries to walk home, but freezes to death. King buys a new car with the insurance money. The Kashpaw family assembles at the old Kashpaw place. Gordie gets drunk, hits a deer with his car, and believes that he has killed June.

1982   Lulu, Marie, and Nector all live at the Senior Citizens. Nector chokes to death on a raw turkey heart brought by Lipsha as love medicine. Marie moves back into the Kashpaw house for a time. *Gordie comes home drunk, drinks Lysol, and apparently dies.* Marie helps Lulu after Lulu's eye surgery.

1983   *Lyman's tomahawk factory venture ends in an interfamily brawl. Lyman makes plans for a bingo hall on the reservation.*

1984   Lipsha learns from Lulu that Gerry and June are his parents and that Lulu is his grandmother. Lipsha visits his half brother, King, in Minneapolis, wins King's insurance-money car in a poker game, helps Gerry escape to Canada in the car, and then brings "her" home.

Selected Bibliography

Primary Texts

Novels

Erdrich, Louise. *The Antelope Wife*. New York: HarperFlamingo, 1998.

————. *The Beet Queen*. New York: Holt, 1986.

————. *The Bingo Palace*. New York: HarperCollins, 1994.

————. *Love Medicine*. New York: Holt, 1984, 1993.

————. *Tales of Burning Love*. New York: HarperCollins, 1996.

————. *Tracks*. New York: Holt, 1988.

Erdrich, Louise, and Michael Dorris. *The Crown of Columbus*. New York: HarperCollins, 1991.

Poetry

Erdrich, Louise. *Baptism of Desire: Poems*. New York: Harper, 1989.

————. *Jacklight: Poems*. New York: Holt, Rinehart, and Winston, 1984.

Autobiography

Erdrich, Louise. *The Blue Jay's Dance: A Birth Year*. New York: HarperCollins, 1995.

Route 2. with Michael Dorris. Northridge, Calif.: Lord John Press, 1991.

Textbook

Erdrich, Louise. *Imagination.* New York: Charles Merrill, 1980.

Children's Book

Grandmother's Pigeon. New York: Hyperion Books for Children, 1996.

Essay

Erdrich, Louise. "Where I Ought to Be: A Writer's Sense of Place." *New York Times Book Review,* 28 July 1985, 1, 23–24.

Criticism of *Love Medicine*

Aldridge, John W. *Talents and Technicians: Literary Chic and the New Assembly-Line Fiction.* New York: Charles Scribner's Sons, 1992.

Bak, Hans. "Toward a Native American 'Realism': The Amphibious Fiction of Louise Erdrich." In *Neo-Realism in Contemporary American Fiction,* edited by Kristiaan Versluys, 145–70. Amsterdam: Rodopi, 1992.

Barnett, Marianne. "Dreamstuff: Louise Erdrich's *Love Medicine." North Dakota Quarterly* 56.1 (1988): 82–93.

Barry, Nora, and Mary Prescott. "The Triumph of the Brave: *Love Medicine*'s Holistic Vision." *Critique: Studies in Contemporary Fiction* 30 (1988): 123–38.

Beidler, Peter G., and Gay Barton, eds. *A Reader's Guide to the Novels of Louise Erdrich: Geography, Genealogy, Chronology, and Dictionary of Characters.* Columbia: University of Missouri Press, 1999.

Bowers, Sharon Manybeads. "Louise Erdrich as Nanapush." In *New Perspectives on Women and Comedy,* edited by Regina Barreca, 135–41. Philadelphia: Gordon and Breach, 1992.

Brady, Laura A. "Collaboration as Conversation: Literary Cases." *Essays in Literature* 19.2 (1992): 306–11.

Brewington, Lillian, Normie Bullard, and Robert W. Reising, comps. "Writing in Love: An Annotated Bibliography of Critical Responses to the Poetry and Novels of Louise Erdrich and Michael Dorris." *American Indian Culture and Research Journal* 10.4 (1986): 81–86.

Castillo, Susan Perez. "The Construction of Gender and Ethnicity in the Texts of Leslie Silko and Louise Erdrich." *Yearbook of English Studies* 24 (1994): 228–36.

———. "Postmodernism, Native American Literature, and the Real: The Silko-Erdrich Controversy." *Massachusetts Review* 32 (1991): 285–94. Published as Chapter

10 of *Notes from the Periphery: Marginality in North American Literature and Culture.* New York: Peter Lang, 1995.

Catt, Catherine M. "Ancient Myth in Modern America: The Trickster in the Fiction of Louise Erdrich." *Platte Valley Review* 19 (1991): 71–81.

Chavkin, Allan, ed. *The Chippewa Landscape of Louise Erdrich.* Tuscaloosa: The University of Alabama Press, 1999.

Chavkin, Allan, and Nancy Feyl Chavkin, eds. *Conversations with Louise Erdrich and Michael Dorris.* Jackson: University Press of Mississippi, 1994.

Flavin, Louise. "Louise Erdrich's *Love Medicine*: Loving over Time and Distance." *Critique: Studies in Contemporary Fiction* 31.1 (Fall 1989): 55–64.

Holt, Debra. "Transformation and Continuance: Native American Tradition in the Novels of Louise Erdrich." In *Entering the Nineties: The North American Experience,* edited by Thomas E. Schirer, 149–61. Sault Ste. Marie, MI: Lake Superior State University Press, 1991.

Kolmar, Wendy K. "'Dialectics of Connectedness': Supernatural Elements in Novels by Bambara, Cisneros, Grahn, and Erdrich." In *Haunting the House of Fiction: Feminist Perspectives on Ghost Stories by American Women,* edited by Lynette Carpenter and Wendy K. Kolmar, 236–49. Knoxville: University of Tennessee Press, 1991.

Lee, Robert A. "Ethnic Renaissance: Rudolfo Anaya, Louise Erdrich, and Maxine Hong Kingston." In *The New American Writing: Essays on American Literature since 1970,* edited by Graham Clarke, 139–64. New York: St. Martin's, 1990.

Lincoln, Kenneth. "'Bring Her Home': Louise Erdrich." In *Indi'n Humor: Bicultural Play in Native America,* 205–53. New York: Oxford University Press, 1993.

McKenzie, James. "Lipsha's Good Road Home: The Revival of Chippewa Culture in *Love Medicine.*" *American Indian Culture and Research Journal* 10.3 (1986): 53–63.

Matchie, Thomas. "*Love Medicine*: A Female Moby-Dick." *Midwest Quarterly* 30 (1989): 478–91.

Medeiros, Paulo. "Cannibalism and Starvation: The Parameters of Eating Disorders in Literature." In *Disorderly Eaters: Texts in Self-Empowerment,* edited by Lillian R. Furst and Peter W. Graham, 11–27. University Park: Pennsylvania State University Press, 1992.

Mitchell, David. "A Bridge to the Past: Cultural Hegemony and the Native American Past in Louise Erdrich's *Love Medicine.*" In *Entering the Nineties: The North American Experience,* edited by Thomas E. Schirer, 162–70. Sault Ste. Marie, MI.: Lake Superior State University Press, 1991.

Owens, Louis. *Other Destinies: Understanding the American Indian Novel.* Norman: University of Oklahoma Press, 1992.

———. *Mixedblood Messages: Literature, Film, Family, Place.* Norman: University of Oklahoma Press, 1998.

Rainwater, Catherine. *Dreams of Fiery Stars: The Transformations of Native American Fiction.* Philadelphia: University of Pennsylvania Press, 1999.

Rayson, Ann. "Shifting Identity in the Work of Louise Erdrich and Michael Dorris." *Studies in American Indian Literatures* 3.4 (1991): 27–36.

Schneider, Lissa. "Love Medicine: A Metaphor for Forgiveness." *Studies in American Indian Literatures* 4.1 (1992): 1–13.

Ruppert, James. *Mediation in Contemporary Native American Fiction.* Norman: University of Oklahoma Press, 1995.

Schultz, Lydia A. "Fragments and Ojibwe Stories: Narrative Strategies in Louise Erdrich's *Love Medicine.*" *College Literature* 18 (1991): 80–95.

Schweninger, Lee. "A Skin of Lakeweed: An Ecofeminist Approach to Erdrich and Silko." In *Multicultural Literatures through Feminist/Poststructuralist Lenses,* edited by Barbara Frey Waxman. Knoxville: University of Tennessee Press, 1994.

Smith, Jeanne. "Transpersonal Selfhood: The Boundaries of Identity in Louise Erdrich's *Love Medicine.*" *Studies in American Indian Literatures* 3.4 (1991): 13–26.

Stripes, James D. "The Problem(s) of (Anishinaabe) History in the Fiction of Louise Erdrich: Voices and Contexts." *Wicazo Sa Review* 7.2 (1991): 26–33.

Studies in American Indian Literatures 9.1 (Winter 1985). Special issue on Louise Erdrich.

Towery, Margie. "Continuity and Connection: Characters in Louise Erdrich's Fiction." *American Indian Culture and Research Journal* 16.4 (1992): 99–123.

Van Dyke, Annette. "Questions of the Spirit: Bloodlines in Louise Erdrich's Chippewa Landscape." *Studies in American Indian Literatures* 4.1 (1992): 15–27.

Wong, Hertha D. "Adoptive Mothers and Thrown-Away Children in the Novels of Louise Erdrich." In *Narrating Mothers: Theorizing Maternal Subjectivities,* edited by Brenda O. Daly and Maureen T. Reddy, 174–92. Knoxville: University of Tennessee Press, 1991.